CHARIS IN THE WORLD OF WONDERS

MARLY YOUMANS

Charis in the World of Wonders

IGNATIUS PRESS   SAN FRANCISCO

The author gratefully acknowledges the American Antiquarian Society
in Worcester, Massachusetts, for use of the library
and a sojourn in the Regent Street Fellows Residence.

Cover art and design by Clive Hicks-Jenkins

© 2020 by Ignatius Press, San Francisco
All rights reserved
ISBN 978-1-62164-304-3 (PB)
ISBN 978-1-64229-111-7 (eBook)
Library of Congress Control Number 2019952974
Printed in Canada ∞

For R. H. W. Dillard and Susan Hankla

As runs the Glass,
Man's life doth pass.

— *The New-England Primer*, 1690

CONTENTS

I

Sup Sorrow

May 1690, near Falmouth

I have heard tell that truth loves the light and is most lovely when most naked; and yet I have dreaded sunrising for half my life, and misliked the sounds of birds waking and the look of naked skin when rose and gold were lighting up the quarrels in the window. And in meetinghouses, I have listened as the ministers raged against the wilderness, the lair of Satan, and though I know more of both the beauty of the trees and the burning-flax flare of hell-fire than any of them are likely to know, I do not deny the power of the gloom lodged in groves or the mystery that flashes behind the leaves, eager to devour us, eager to transform us. For this is the world of wonders, an enchanted place of dreams, portents, and prodigies.

My mother woke me in the dark; I felt the absence of my brothers and father from the room as something empty and cold before I heard the black-powder bang of distant pistols and the blasts of musket-fire. Mother's hands smelled of smoke, and I knew she must have been loading muskets while John, Joseph, and Isaac fired from the house with my father and Blue Jonas, our indentured man who had come to us only the month before, and the others—my uncles and aunts and older boy cousins, together with Onesimus, my uncle Thomas' African, who my father said should have been named Philippou or *friend-of-horses* because he had such a rare gift with them, although I always thought that he was fond of horses because a rider feels so free on horseback. Mary lay curled beside me in the trundle, warm and breathing dampness against my shoulder. A mosquito hummed by my ear, hunting blood. Faint pink flushes washed over the room.

Mother was murmuring at me, pulling me to my feet and thrusting a gown over my petticoats and shift. She bade me sit and tugged on my woolen stockings and shoes. When I stood, she tied a blanket into a sling around my back. I reeled a little, still waking into the fear and the trembling of that morning. White smoke drifted into the room, smelling of brimstone.

"Climb down the wych elm," she said to me, tucking my hair into a coif. The tree was no wych elm, but we liked to call it so because we didn't know the name, and there had been a wych elm sent from the north of England planted outside my mother's hall across the sea. Not that she had ever seen the tree, for her father, a younger brother with small inheritance and one of the godly, had sailed to this country in 1630 on the *Arbella*, before the distemper of civil wars broke out in England. The men had cleared the trees from near the house, all save this one mighty bole.

"Climb down," I repeated.

"And run like herringbone stitch, back and forth to the woods, and so flee to the hiding place. The house is clear on that side now, at least for this moment. We will find you. Stay for us, Charis. We will come."

I clung to her arms, but she pushed me away and tugged Mary from under the coverlet and set her feet on the floorboards. She collapsed, still asleep.

"Can you carry Mary pickpack? I can lash her to you."

I nodded, the tears seeping into my eyes and stopping up my voice, as tears can do, though a voice and eyes are so altogether different.

"Charis, go with my love. Do not tarry. Fare thee well," she said, binding Mary to my back with a long piece of linen.

"Mother—"

"Make haste," she said, yet held me close, and I cannot ever forget the scent of her with the brimstone and fragrance of rosewater mixed, and how I shivered in her arms.

She soothed me as if I were a little child like Mary and not a young woman, and kissed me as she led me through the hall and opened the shutters to the window that looked out onto the wych elm. I had clambered down its branches many times, and now I suspect that my parents must have ignored our mischief and let us climb harum-scarum in preparation for a day like this one, with the Indians in chaotic number around the house and the fear in us that we would all be knocked on the head and split open by the tomahawks of savages who loved us not, nor our ways.

"Hearken," she said, as I crawled out the window onto the branch that nearly touched the house. "Be resolved, and divine Providence go with you, my sweet Charis."

"Mother," I called, reaching back toward her, shifting on the thick branch that Onesimus had trimmed to make room for the wall.

When I swung over the sill, everything changed for me. We are meant to go in and out of doors in civilized style, but my mother bade me climb into woodsy wildness and a darkness flushed with crimson light and torches where godly men and women are not meant to go.

Though sent, I abandoned my own to whatever martyrdom might come, and to whatever defense or escape might be attempted.

All would have been different if we had stayed settled in Boston. In the town, my father was well respected. Our dwelling-house was secure among many others, and Sewalls and Mathers and Winthrops were offered fine talk and drams of black cherry brandy or glasses of Canary in our parlor.

The May air washed over me, cool and tinged with smoke. I almost over-toppled from the weight on my back. Bark tore at my arms; Mary's fingers dug into my skin.

My mother's voice was calling, though softly. What words did she say? *Laus Deo? Love?*

Branch by branch I lowered myself awkwardly through the tree, birds waking in their nests and Mary complaining as I scraped her through twigs, and I saying *hush, hush, hush* all the way. Like an ill-hung pendulum, the weight of her swung me from side to side, and I feared each grasp of a branch would not hold. The ground met the leather of my shoes with a slap. Standing in the gloom under the tree with my palms smarting and Mary shifting on my back, I looked about me. Smoke wafted from the far side of the house. I could glimpse torches in fields where the corn stubs had been plowed into earth. Abruptly a great fountain of birds jetted forth from some remains of last season's stalks, crying against the flames and the hubble bubble of strange men. Shouts and shots from the front of the house sounded far away, though an arrow wound with burning flax from the barn slew past me and woke me further to our danger.

All at once I darted away, following my mother's advice to move like a thread of silk skittering in quick herringbone stitches across a field of linen. I dove into a patch of last year's corn, still standing, and out again; the rattling noise frightened me worse than the open where surely I was more likely to be pursued. The burden of Mary slung me one way, then another. Ahead, the black, irregular line of trees was quiet and still as if waiting.

From the time I was old enough to spy on gossip in Boston, I knew to keep clear of wilderness. The realm where the bad lord Satan ruled, the forest was savage, boiling with wild men and women who spat leaves from their mouths and somersaulted around a stew pot that danced with the bones and flesh-gobbets of children. In the trees, animals not known to the English lurked, great green or tawny cats who would pounce from a branch. Didn't the ancients set two bears, mother and son, among the constellations? Ursa Major and Minor seemed to shadow forth some truth because bears burned for us and lumbered forward to give a hug, all scimitar claws and curved teeth. Our Boston weaver, Goodman Turell, claimed that unicorns and basilisks played deep in the forest, though my father laughed and said that basilisks were naught but snakes, and that no cockerel would ever hunch on the egg of a serpent to hatch a basilisk. Why, the basilisk, if it existed, would devour the cockerel when it pipped!

Now the forest would be either my refuge or my grave. If descried by the Indians, we would be knocked on the head and killed, or perhaps we would be marched on trek to the French in Canada and then ransomed, traded away for good English coin if we did not die of trials on the journey. Any weakness, and we would be murdered at once. I knew the stories. I remembered a once-captive woman in Boston whose little sucking babe had been jerked from her arms, its head dashed open with a mallet. Indians had no love for us, though they could be unexpectedly kind. Sometimes they made a child of ours their own, so that she grew up with strange gods and stamped in mad jigs in the firelight, forgetting her mother and father and all our lamplit knowledge handed down through generations. (Once a traveling trader told us of curious monsters and alien powers that lived in rocks and whirlpools and trees by a bend in a river, but whether he truly knew the myths and histories of the tribes or only fooled us with wild tales, I do not know.) The French, I feared, might be even quicker death-dealers than the savages, and I was glad of Father's insistence that we learn something of the language of our enemy.

I set Mary down, my back already aching, and headed for a hillock, now lit by the gold of sunrise. From there, I could find the hiding place. The fall before, my brother Joseph had knotted a string dyed with berries between trees, and our secret was thirty man-steps west from the end of the string. More than once we had practiced meeting in the woods, though in truth no one ever believes that such hard times will come to them. The godly talk of brave fortitude, but all of us are taken unawares by such change, I find, and are ever and always unready.

"Why?" Mary resisted my hand and looked up at me.

"What *why*? I don't know." In truth, I was roiled in my mind and unwilling to explain any *why* of hers.

"I want Mother," she said, her voice quavering in the still-cool morning air. She spun away from me as if she meant to traipse back to the house.

I dived for her hand. "You would be clubbed senseless crossing to the door."

"I would not," she retorted.

I grasped hold of her rope-plait, tumbled down from her coif, and gave it a tug. "As soon as they have driven away the Indians, Mother and the others will meet us in the hiding place. We have to find it. Then she will come."

A scream broke the sky into pieces. I glanced up to see an eagle, floating magically on a current of air. *Perhaps*, I thought, *the birds are fleeing the torches, shouts, and gunfire.*

"I don't like it here," Mary said, blinking up at me.

"The forest is the storehouse of nature," I said, though I had no wish for trees and hills and the fine meanders of streams. But I had heard some preacher call it so, back in Boston, before we traveled to the land near Falmouth. Perhaps he was quoting some Greek thinker, brave as he lectured to students among olive trees swept by a wind from the sea that might at any moment waft sails from barbarian kingdoms. Thousands of years later, I would have to find the courage to dare the wilds for Mary. Inside, I felt none so stout, my thoughts brooding on the nest of souls back at our small settlement.

How strange to fear that God had turned his face from our families and allowed the wilderness to snatch at us! And yet our pastors in Boston had assured us that suchlike trials made us united with the obedience and sufferings of Christ, and that all our secret pains and future hardships were known to God before the worlds were made. Some words are easy enough in Sabbath meeting, hard when a body is cast houseless upon the world.

"I want John and Joseph and Isaac," Mary said. Her voice sounded forlorn to my ear, and I bent to embrace her. "I want my cousin Tom."

"Tom is helping, or perhaps he is already at the hiding place. We have to go on, or we won't be where Mother knows to find us," I said. "Shall I carry you?"

I knelt down and let Mary clamber onto my back, binding her again with the linen cloth. The hem of my gown sagged, heavy with dew. The blanket sling Mother had tied around me earlier was now damp against my side. Mary settled against me, adding her heat so that I felt oddly warm and chilled at once.

Bearing the solid weight of Mary's seven years, I stumbled getting to my feet, and walked off in a hunched-over trudge.

One way to reach the hiding place hugged the farthermost cleared lands of the farm. I would have been glad for ribbons of corn to make a low rustling and keep us company, even when I wandered just out of sight of the fields of flax and grain beyond the house and the big garden of beans, marrows, and pumpkins. But the farm was still nearly bare in May, the fields nigh-silent except for the patter of my shoes. Only occasionally did I catch the news of shots, a faint peppering.

But at a low rise beyond the far fields, I hoped to scan the landscape and see across to our very doorstep.

My footsteps quickened as I thought of the twenty-seven left behind inside the fortified house, my brothers, my parents, my aunts and uncles, their sons, and others who were as known and essential as family. The path to the hill was roundabout, and yet not so far from the farm that we could be assured of safety there. But a glimpse of the house walls would comfort me. Father always said that I was eaglet-eyed. I had a keen wish for news of the assault, and the light was now gold morning in the leaves. Birds were waking, singing us on our way.

Catching a flicker of movement in the trees, I stiffened, pausing close to a trunk, my heart jumping and racing back and forth like a rabbit that spies the cat creeping forward, one paw in the air. And I saw a truth of the wilderness that I never wished to be revealed, though the sight is encamped in my mind as something strange and even beautiful. It seemed a piece of moving silk, drawn through the boles like floss needled in and out of linen warp and woof. I pressed one hand against the flittering of my heart. Mary shifted on my back and muttered two or three words I could not make out.

The vision grew more distinct, came nearer, a fast-running stream of shadow that wove through trees. Birds shot from the brush, trilling and shrieking toward the light. What the gloom might be, I remained unsure until the current of dusk poured closer, flowing some twelve footsteps away from me: the darkness resolved into doglike shapes, and one of them swung his head and stared at me with pale eyes. No doubt she and her kind were fleeing the noise of muskets.

The gaze went on and on. She seemed to plumb the deeps of me and to know me as God knows us, reading past the cage of bones, the garb of flesh. She might have stabbed me to the spot, so unable to move and hardly to breathe was I. Her face with those luminous eyes staked itself to my memory.

All my life I had been warned of wolves, and now I had been observed and inspected by one. A line from Jeremiah burned through my mind and went out like a flame: *Wherefore a lion out of the forest shall slay them, and a wolf of the wilderness shall destroy them: a leopard shall watch over their cities: everyone that goeth out thence, shall be torn in pieces....*

To be touched by perilous sights and yet live is a rare fate. But it was mine that day. The wolves poured away, vanishing as if they had never been, and left me drenched in perspiration. Hadn't I been warned that wolves were the hounds of Satan, ravening through the hinterlands? Hadn't they been so troublesome in many towns that large bounties were offered for every pelt of a wolf? And yet something nearly human had glowed in their eyes, and something lovely moved in their appearing and disappearing as if by some conjurer's trick with a silk scarf—a feigned magic I had never seen but had heard about and imagined—made me stare after them, almost with regret at their passing.

I knew not what to think, save that my fear for our safety was a returning stitch, catching again and again at the material of the day, the thread of that sewing twisted together with a fibril of imploring. My mother, my father, all my kin: inwardly they went along with me like that shadow flock of wolves, and their faces likewise veered to look at me with beautiful, unreadable eyes.

God forbid that they fade away and melt into the forest like the wolves! Such was my prayer.

Birds catapulted past us, caroling to the leaves and sky above. I remembered how Father said that the birds were the glory of the woodlands, that he knew neither so many nor so sweet as in the depths of the forest. When I looked to the east, I saw the rising bonfire of the sun and seemed to glimpse shapes like tumbling leopards, playing joyfully in flames.

My face was wet. But I had no time for infant tears, so blotted my eyes on my sleeve and plodded on, my back sore from pickpack Mary. The undergrowth of briars and shrubs hampered my feet as

I neared the slope, my first destination. By some trick of the wind or the shape of the land, I could hear shouts again, just little nicks at the air.

At the hill, I wandered around the base before deciding on a path between stones, with what I hoped would be sufficient handholds. Though lowish, the way was rugged. I thought to let Mary down to climb, only to find that she had fallen asleep and left me alone in the wild.

"As you will."

Perhaps talking to one's own self is a variety of madness, but it was a madness I found to be of some small comfort. Perhaps the human syllables suggested that there would be again a purpose in talk, or that the family would sit again in the cool of the evening after laboring in the fields, my mother and I stitching at a garment for one of the fast-growing boys and listening to Father read by candlelight—or holding still from work as he led us into prayer, the crooked arms of moon-clutching trees and the claws of wild men and animals barred from the door.

My feet crushed the thorns and nameless spring plants as I stitched my way upward, bent forward so that my sister would not slither and fall.

Near the top, I let Mary slide to the ground. She curled up on a patch of soft spring growth as peacefully as if it were a trundle bed. Her hair was pasted to her damp cheek in curls, her child's cap dangling by a lace. The linen cloth that had secured her to my back now made a covering to keep off the midges and flies, though by the red welts on her arms and neck, I knew that she had been bitten on the march through the brush. In the woods near Falmouth live humped black insects that swoop and do not sting but nip the flesh with such celerity that the victim never knows until too late.

"No thorns in Eden," I said aloud. *Nor pricking flies. Nor the dead skins of animals on our feet.*

I dropped the sling with its contents onto an outcropping of stone and realized that the blanket was my mother's best, a thin-woven wool with a brushed nap, dyed indigo with a stripe of chamomile yellow near each end. The news startled me, made me more apprehensive than before. Why had she sent me off with such a choice covering, the fine thread spun and dyed with her own hands and given over to Weaver Turell's handiwork on the loom?

The one most suitable to tie around a body, I told myself. *Others were surely too thick and coarse.*

Uncomfortable in the open air where I might be spied from below, I sought the trees and ranged along the brink, slapping away insects and searching for a view of the house. After scrambling over rocks, I found a safe peep-hole through branches. The prospect revealed most of the front and the clearing before the house where stubs and stalks of last year's corn halted and, in summer, rows of wortes ran up to the very foundations.

"Mother," I whispered.

Clouds of smoke drifted in the yard. Several tiny bodies lay flopped before the door, but whether they were our men or theirs—likely the Mi'kmaq or Maliseet of the Wabanaki people, or perhaps the French—I could not tell for the obscurity and distance.

I climbed onto a branch to secure a better look, just as a man with a torch loped from the barn and across the wortes-plot.

"No, no, no—"

He was struck before reaching the stone at the doorsill. In the field, the barn with a store of our hard-won flax and a portion of last year's harvest was ablaze. The fallen brand smoked against the earth and died.

"Fire the house with our own burning tow, would you?" I gripped the trunk and peered outward.

The wind shifted, and again I could detect the popping of guns and the cries, tiny bits of noise that chipped at the air. Streamers of smoke rose from the upper windows and gun slits where muskets were firing. Evidently we still held the house.

One of the little figures vaulted through an open window and disappeared. Instantly, the body was hurled back out. When three others met at mid-front and began thundering at the paneling with clubs, the door swung open to a blast of fire. Though several toppled to the ground, the third Indian managed to drag a woman into view. Two men of our family sprang from the hall where she must have been loading muskets but were too late to stop the fellow from dashing her to the ground with a blow of an axe. The murderer plunged after her, downed by fire from an upper window. One of our men was hit and let go his musket, but another grasped for the weapon and towed his companion back inside.

Mary woke and shrieked so violently that I leaped from the tree, landing with a thud and staggering into a run. But when I reached her, she was only fighting with the linen cloth around her face, and I pulled it roughly away.

"What ails you, Mary? Are you hurt? Hush, be quiet this instant, or Indians will come and crack open your head with tomahawks. Like a bird egg smacked by a mallet. And then you will have something to wail over!"

She stared at me, abruptly silent, and we both broke into tears, she for the fright she took from me, me from my own words.

One of our men was hurt, and one of my aunts surely dead—my Aunt Mercy or Aunt Hannah, my Aunt Sarah or Aunt Rebecca. I could not contemplate that little doll flopped on the dirt as possibly my own mother. She had been on the second floor when I left and she would surely still be above stairs. So I told myself. Because some possibilities cannot be borne. To see my mother clubbed over the head ... I prayed for the dead woman, whoever she was, and for all my blood kin and for Onesimus and Blue Jonas.

Yet heat and anger sparkled in me like a burning line of gunpowder. I felt myself a mine of munitions set to explode. Hate and uncanny darkness roiled my mind, and I learned that a part of me could wish to maim or destroy all that threatened my kin.

To calm myself, I kept my arms around Mary, and whispered, "Lord of all things in heaven and earth, let those we love shadow themselves and hide from raveners who would devour them."

I recalled my father saying that the Wabanaki tribes had their own customs and fashions of doing, which were not our ways but made a kind of sense to them, and that the English who had fared over the ocean now crowded and hemmed in many of the Indians. And many Wampanoags had died in some great, mysterious plague just before the English settled in this country. Our ministers called this the hand of God preparing our way, though Father, who was always of a singular cast of mind, said that God did not wish pestilence on any but that they find the fullness of life in Christ. All the same, I had scruples and could not find a chamber in my heart to pray for the French or the Indians, knowing many ruthless acts that had been visited upon our own people, merciless disembowelings, torturous slicing away of body parts of captives, and the battering open of heads as if a brain were only a walnut meat to be shaken from its shell. I could not pray, any more than others could sit listening to talk of ingenious torture and captivity without sickening.

But I *meant* to. For aren't we to pray for our enemies? It is hard when they are not like us and wish to murder everything we have ever loved and admired.

"Is this our hiding place?"

"What?"

"Our hiding place," Mary repeated.

"No," I said, "but there's no hurry. I wonder if we're not safer here, away from the woods. I expect no bears or leopards would ever lope this way."

"Not any such beasts as leopards."

"There are," I said, "and green dragon-lizards and phoenixes and horned sea-unicorns and many another fantastic-seeming creature. The mind of nature is a very opal, packed with strangeness and as changeable as the color in the jewel."

"An opal," she said, though I doubt now that she knew the word.

I wanted to go back and survey the house and fields but knew that Mary should not behold such brutality as I had seen. She was young yet, although seven is age enough for many abhorrent things to be known.

"Such harsh, uneven ways," I said.

"Charis—" Mary grasped at me as I rose. But I slipped away and shook the motes of earth from my gown, having concluded that I should search further and so be mistress of our nesting-ground.

But in exploring the rest of the hilltop (for I had reflected that we might well linger here, where I could observe, from time to time, the ferocities of our enemies and assess how the defenses held at the house), I discovered the remains of a charcoal fire and some knapped flakes of stone. Raking my fingers through ash and remnants of sticks, I found no warmth. Still, I knew that the Indians often retraced steps and used the same paths on their excursions. The ones who built the fire might intend a return to the same site.

Mary called to me. "What is it?"

"Hush," I said, afraid even to tell my alarm.

When I peered over the edge of the drop, the scene looked quiet. Perhaps we could repair to the house soon; perhaps we could watch and wait without the savages finding our refuge. Or perhaps we would be trapped on the hill, unable to escape. No, it would not do to stay. Feeling considerable reluctance, I took up the blanket sling and grasped Mary's hand.

"We'll steal through the forest and find the hiding place now," I told her.

"I'm hungry," she said.

I'm worried, I thought, *warm with worry*.

"And weary and dirty, too," I said. "But it's not far from here. And we will break fast with what Mother packed. Or I will dig us something to eat when we get there. The cache has carrots and parsnips and turnips. Maybe a basket of Indian corn to grind for meal, though we can't make a fire. And there's a stream nearby. We can wash, and we can drink as much as we like."

While striving to soothe, I began to feel impatient to be away.

Mary was so stiff and unwieldy that I had to half hoist and half drag her down the hill. Before we were halfway to the foot, I was soaked with perspiration from the unpleasant combination of my fear of what I had seen and the effort of managing Mary. Her resistance added fuel to the bonfire of my feelings, and I struggled to remain calm. She wore the rebellious aspect that I recognized from when she had to work at her sampler, and I did not have Mother's knack of forcing her will with kindness and firmness. I knelt and bid her climb onto my back, but she did so most unwillingly.

"Mary, go aright and help me more," I said, "as you would our mother."

"No," she said.

"You make this journeying harder than it is," I told her.

"No," she said again.

"Do not be so choleric!"

At that, she thrashed to and fro until I feared we might fall down the slope. I snatched at her fingers. "Mary, please—"

Wrenching her hand from my damp grip, Mary thrust at me and tumbled backward. Though I whirled about and grasped at her skirts, I was not quick enough to keep her from spilling onto the ground. She looked at me, all defiance vanished, and tears welled in her eyes, though she was so quiet that it took me some moments to realize that my little sister had gashed her head on a jagged outcropping of stone.

Not until I glimpsed with a new access of fear the blood pooling and sopping the earth did I understand. The cut bled smartly, the blood clotting in the hair at the base of the skull, so that I could not tell how dire the blow was and simply set to work on bandaging it with our length of linen. What else could be done? I was lucky to have the cloth. Tears blurred my own sight, and I longed for our mother more than ever before.

While Mary's initial silence and the sight of the injury made me anxious, her sobs afterward made me cringe and fancy that she would call down arrows on our heads.

"They will clip and carve us, they will prick us with arrows," I hissed at her. "They do not care how much they hurt us. So stop that roar or you will have a worse stroke soon!"

She cried jerkily but more softly and at last looked at me with what I could have borne better if it had been choler or reproach. The shock, it seemed, had quieted her distress. Her countenance showed only emptiness, innocent of thought or feeling.

"Come." I hauled my sister to her feet. "Can you walk? You must. It is time to flee away."

She trailed me obediently, hanging on to my dress and leaving damp handprints on the green fabric. I fear that I may have thought almost as much about the harm to my gown as my anger or what was worse, the harm to Mary. My mother had spun thread and over-dyed woad blue with goldenrod. Afterward, she carried the yarn to our skillful Boston weaver, and we sailed away with a great bolt of green cloth for waistcoats and gowns.

If only we had stayed there in company with Goodman Turell and the bakers and brewers and builders, all of whom made life easier and fairer in aspect! My father was not like most who were drawn to the Fort Loyall and Falmouth area, those who felt a laxity in their fellows and wished to renew the original stringency of thought that sent our people across the sea to build a shining New Jerusalem. Oh, he was a devout, a covenanted man, but more than that he owned the pluck and heart of an explorer and was undaunted by the wilderness that made so many others quake and cling to the seashore like oysters. If only he had been a little more retiring, more circumspect in his desires . . .

My mind rambled through the tangled brush of such useless thoughts, now and again returning to the image of the woman— one of ours!—clouted on the head at our doorsill. But my feet knew the ways that Mother had made us practice until we were weary of obeying, and before long I discovered the red string half-hidden in some running cedar.

Mary stopped when I did, swaying in place, a bunch of my gown in her fist. "Hurts," she said.

With renewed apprehension, I saw that the linen strip I had wound about her head was almost black with blood. Fresh blood still seeped from the wound and had stained to redness the coif dangling by its strings. Midges wove a moving halo around her face.

"See if you can find the scarlet vein in the earth," I said, thinking to distract and make a kind of game of finding the hiding place.

She let go of my skirts and looked about her. "I see it! The same as my gown." She caught up the yarn and showed how, though faded from rain and sun, it matched the cloth. Crumbs of dried leaves were caught in the fibers and sifted onto her bodice.

"One of the Farriers—do you remember them, from Boston, or were you too little?—told me about seeing a man in London who played on a thread like that but pulled taut in the air. He danced and skipped and made little pirouettes." I brushed the jots of leaves from her gown as I spoke.

She pushed back the sweaty curls stuck to her cheek and looked up at me, forgetting her pain, forgetting where we were at the thought of such novelty. "Is that magic?"

"No, it was his artfulness. He probably tripped and plummeted a thousand times before he could make such pretty motions on a string. Magic is not about practice, not about working hard to learn and master knowledge."

"What is it, then?"

"Power, I expect."

Kneeling, I took the yarn from her fingers and wove it back through the running cedar and teaberry leaves—those and some other plants whose names I did not know.

"Supernatural power," I added. "Like the bundles Onesimus told me about when we lived in Boston. A tithingman chanced upon a sack of cloth beside a stream. Inside, someone had packed up a magpie treasure of nails and bent pins, a broken quarrel and pieces of bottles, shell buttons, bits of mica, and lumps of chalk. And Onesimus said that back in Africa, bundles like that one breathed forth magic."

"Why?"

"He never explained. But they meant sweet fortune or healing or days without hazard."

Mary's response, a comical little face of discontent, made me laugh. One remarkable thing that I learned that day was how impossible it is in the midst of alarms and worry and even pain—my poor sister!—to be despairing and melancholy in every instant.

"*Faire la moue*," I said, more to amuse myself than Mary, who was young yet and cared less for words and learning.

She ignored me, intent on her own thoughts.

"If I had magic," Mary said, "I would make a land with always kind savages. No aches. And fly there with you and Mother and Father and the boys. And all our family." She nodded, looked down at the thread, and began to step along it, putting a hand out to steady herself as she passed saplings and shrubs.

"String-walker," she said softly. "I am a string-walker."

I followed along, watching her feet move through the greenery, searching out the glimpse of color. Though pretty certain that my uncle Thomas in particular would have scolded me for dropping nonsense into Mary's head, I did not reprove her. Who would not wish for an earthly country of peace, and even hope that such magics could be white and fair?

"Sewing land," she said.

"Yes, like a twist of silk that appears and disappears."

The blanket was unpleasantly hot against my back and side. I wondered whether I should pause and see what Mother had put inside. We were hungry and thirsty, and perhaps she had packed bread or dried meat. But even the sound of the sticks breaking under our feet daunted me; I would not pause.

"My head. It hurts."

Mary kept on padding on the wisps of red that showed among the leaves, and I kept following after, all the time puzzling over what Mother would say if she could see us now. If she still lived! I did not think she would like talk of magical powers.

"You know, Mary, that magic and spells are blasphemous. If you could conjure a land with no enemies and flit there, you would become the Devil's own child. Because human beings cannot make something out of nothing, and we cannot fly."

"I could fly," she insisted. "I would ride pickpack. On an angel with six wings."

"Heavenly beings are not the same as magic. It is their nature to do what we cannot."

Was magic always evil? I was not so sure where magic left off and right religion began, nor where the proper healing of women learned in herbs left off and charms and spells began. Had not Goody Cotton, back in Boston, boiled her nephew's urine in a witch bottle with nails and pins to discover who had bewitched him? And in England, cunning folk were said to be useful healers. But Mother told us more than once never to rely on palmistry or "the turning of the sieve" or "book-and-key" to delve into mysteries, as others she knew in Boston had done to answer questions.

Old as I was and with some accumulated wisdom in the ways of the world, I wished Mary's angel would come and alight like the most impossible string-walker on our red yarn and offer us a pickpack ride. We would sail over the treetops and see where the eagles nest. We would find out if the butterflies, insects, and birds stitch in and out of the canopy the way little fish leap in and out of the shallows of the sea, or if above the trees the air is still and quiet.

"Perhaps your archangel would have friends to rescue us all, and we could swoop about the trees and soar away to a better land." But I remembered how the greeting of an angel begins with *Fear not*.

"See, Charis, here is the end," Mary said. She swayed and reached to steady herself against a tree.

"What are you saying?" Her words startled me; how silly that was!

She squatted in the greenery and last year's brown leaves. When she looked up at me, I saw with a prick of dismay that streaks of tears had washed clean a path down each cheek.

"The tail of the string. See?"

"Ah, I thought you intended something else." I could have laughed, my assurance returning as quickly as it had flown. "And now we go thirty footsteps to the west. Footsteps the size of Father's feet. So maybe forty of my footsteps or thereabouts."

Mary put her hand on my arm. "That way," she said, and pointed. Even a little girl in the wilds must know how to mark the sun's position and be a kind of compass.

"Good," I told Mary. "You have a sound sense of direction."

Setting my feet carefully, right heel to left toe, left heel to right toe, I walked slowly westward. A needless thing to be so painstaking, I suppose, when the passage was only a count of footsteps, and none of them so very large!

Mary romped ahead as if she had taken no hurt at all, and soon shouted that she had found the spot. And yet when she wheeled toward me, I was frightened by the whiteness of her face, bled clean of color. I longed for my mother, who would have known what to do, and how much concern the injury warranted.

"Hush," I said, but broke from my fussy steps and hastened after her. Yes, the bower place was there. Three years before, my brothers and cousins had transplanted bushes in the rain, and now what had been low scrub appeared as a thicket, tall and leafy, around our root cache. I had often wished that Mary and I were not the only girl cousins in the family, but I did not envy the boys on that day, for it was a hard afternoon of digging and watering, and they were eager for porridge and beer when they trooped home again.

We would be secure and sheltered. The massed walls of stem and young spring leaf around the cache were not stone or brick or board, but no one could spy us out, once we were tucked inside. Or so was my hope that day. The thought that such packed boscage might appear as a spectacle in our woods crossed my mind and made me feel less easy. Were there other such stands, each shrub fertilized with a dried fish and spiring up so lushly? No. Still, who would suspect that English settlers would make a garden of wild bushes in the midst of a forest?

A green crack: Mary broke a branch, squeezing inward, and I begged her to creep and dawdle, treading more carefully.

"We don't want to gift the Indians with a single token that people were here. They are quick to mark hints and clues in the woods. We want to be secret. We want to be shielded."

I tore away the remainder of the branch and plucked up a few leaves that had drifted to the ground. "Slow, slow."

The twigs lashed at her face, but Mary bent and wormed inward, vanishing from my sight. I had more trouble than she, the branches so limber and closely spaced that they bowed under me and sprang back with sounds of snapping, so that I feared leaving legible signposts to any Indian roving that way. But I burst through, tumbling onto the cache. It had not been touched by us since the plentiful harvest in the prior fall, and new green now masked the surface. Mary already lay at full length on the frail plants, arms out, staring up at the trees and sky.

"Charis—"

"Shhh," I said, holding up a finger. "Just a whisper from now on."

Tears glazed her eyes, but she nodded. "I will. Like a game. I hoped Tom would be here. When will Mother and Father and the others come?"

"Like a game, yes. I cannot tell when they will be here. But let's see what is in the blanket. Otherwise we will have to burrow in the cache like woodchucks and gnaw on raw, dirty roots."

"We can make a bed." Mary patted the cloth. "I could sleep now. Thirsty, and my head—"

"Food will help. Look, here's ashcakes. The purple kind made of acorn meal and dried blueberries. And here's a skin bag—maybe Aunt Mercy's mincemeat? You like venison and chokecherries, so that's good."

"I'm not hungry."

"Not hungry? How can that be?" I reached for something else to entice her. "Maybe a bottle of beer?" The clay bottle had a wax stopper that I broke with a stick. I sniffed the contents, drank, and passed it to Mary.

"Aunt Hannah's blackberry cordial," I told her.

She made a face but drank thirstily anyway.

"We can scoop water from the stream when the bottle is empty. It's not far."

Ashcake might never have been so welcome as it was to me, but the bag turned out to hold strips of venison, which proved tough. Have you seen beavers chisel and chop at a tree with their front teeth, intent on damming a brook, making a pond, and fashioning themselves a tidy new lodge? That is precisely how I gnawed the venison—just so determined.

If bound for some hunting feast or country banquet out-of-doors, as in family stories about England our mother would sometimes tell, I would have judged that the manner in which she had handled the packing was comical. Clearly she was in a dire hurry. She had snatched up my old sampler to wrap the bread. I inspected the long cloth with its row after row of neat patterns. The stitches had not always been so tidy, but Mother made me work and re-work the bands until they were as nigh-perfect as my fingers could make.

In truth, the sampler was a folly in the wilderness, as strange as sons poring over Greek and Latin with my father. Mary rested her hand on the linen, where each band showed off mastery of different stitches: rococo, rice, tent, stem, split, chain.... Her fingers plucked at the bands of stars, flowers, miniature trees, acorns, and love knots, all worked in silks. "Colors," she whispered.

I moved my finger across the stitched landscape, naming the dyes one by one to please her: *indigo blue, madder rose, Kendal green, russet,* and *chamomile yellow.*

The hues were well enough, but what need did we settlers have for fancy stitches or fine couching? Here in our bower, the sampler was even more out of place, as unaccountable and downright peculiar as one of Ezekiel's chrysolite wheels within wheels, rimmed with eyes. But that it pleased my sister, despite her pain, was perhaps enough. She rested her hand on mine as I slid a finger over my name, the date, the verse by Mistress Bradstreet at the foot. Softly I read the words to Mary:

> *My hungry soul He filled with good,*
> *He in His bottle put my tears,*
> *My smarting wounds washed in His blood,*
> *And banished thence my doubts and fears.*

Why had Mother sent me off into the woods with a sampler?

"We should have washed. And you must eat something," I said.

My sister bit down, yanking at a strip of venison, and set it aside.

"Sleepy," she said. "My head beats."

She looked bruised under the eyes, and I wondered what more I should do for her. How serious was a head that pounded? Worry stayed with me, sometimes rising until I had to press it down, fearful that I might frighten Mary. Sleep might mend her. But surely she should have food. When she closed her eyes, I could not bear it and tapped her gently on the face until she opened them again.

"Let's go through the rest and spread out the blanket," I proposed. "Maybe there's more to eat."

Mary was pleased to find a doll in the blanket sling, and let me place it in her arms. The little figure was unfinished, made of linen and a few scraps with hair from combings, mine and Mary's and even our mother, who already had threads of silver and white in her gold. A needle was tucked into the face, connected by a thread to a silk eyebrow, still unfinished. Though the doll lacked eyes and nose and mouth, Mary had no trouble loving it and whispering a secret into invisible ears.

The blanket held scissors, a sharp knife, a coif embroidered with the outlines of tiny white leaves, my gown dyed with elderberries, spare woolen stockings for both of us, a shift for Mary, and a paper sack of sugared almonds that Mother must have been saving for some special occasion.

"Oh!" Tears came into Mary's eyes again as she sucked on an almond.

The unexpected delicacy made us both sad.

"You'll see Mother by morning," I promised.

"And Tom and Father and my brothers?"

"Yes, and the others, too."

Mary slept without eating more, once vomiting unexpectedly, and I had some trouble waking her later on when I wished her to take more nourishment. For perhaps half an hour in the late afternoon, I managed to keep her from sleep, though she ate nothing. Her face matched the little doll for pallor, and she would only let me lift her into a half-seated position. Both of us drank a good deal of the cordial, with the result that we were drowsy. We curled on the blanket, watched as the occasional bird crossed the sky, and talked in a whisper of the day, of our hopes that Mother and Father and the others would come to us soon.

"This is our green room, and that is our blue sky ceiling, and we are snug inside," I said, though worry stayed ever with me, and the memory of my sister's hand slipping from mine kept recurring to me like an ill dream.

"Our green room, our blue," Mary said sleepily. Tears shone in her eyes. I knew she dreaded the coming dark—as I did—in the forest. Our people have always feared such places, for only God is safe in a wild realm where the Devil stamps and roars, tormenting and tempting all of moral kind luckless enough to lose the way.

"My head," she whispered. She wept a little but seemed too weary even for that effort.

The sun seemed careworn, too, blinking through the trees, and before the sunset began to dye the world to rose madder, we were both drenched in sleep, I curled around Mary, and Mary curled around the faceless doll.

Once the war-noise of a mosquito woke me in the night, my mouth parched, my dress dank, and Mary's face close to my own. The colorful sun-dreams of day's end must have been long chased away by the dark. My sister's breath was labored and harsh, and I thought she must still be in misery, even in sleep. I rolled over and stared up at the stars, and though I could smell a faint odor of smoke in the air, they were unobscured by fire or clouds, and my eyes were dazzled.

"Lord Christ," I whispered, the fright slamming into me that my mother and father and all my family were slain, nevermore in this life to walk the earth. The stars shone on, careless of me, and never gave a sign of comfort or greeting, though once I had told Mary that they were the travel-fires of angels, where they toasted fine Boston bread, as tender and good as bride cakes.

My brother Joseph had reproved me for saying it, and now I thought that he and John and Isaac and all my kin could scold me ten times a day for the rest of my life, and yet I would still be full of joy that they were mine and I theirs, with no mischance come upon us.

Mary sighed, trembling, and turned away from me on the blanket.

I stared into the dark and bright of the sky, unable to consider the next day and what I must do. Once I glimpsed the flick of a falling star that lashed me with portent-fears. My head, dense and afflicted with pangs, longed for sleep. Surely we had taken far too much of the cordial. At last, the ground and the shrubs seemed to change place with the sky and stars, so that I pitched headfirst into a sleep that grew brighter and brighter until I vanished into light.

I knew nothing but the depths of sleep until drops of dew rolled from leaves and splashed onto my face the next morning. The world was blurred through that cold water. Shivering lightly, I rubbed away the dew and saw the green stand of shrubs and the tint of dawn chinking their stems.

Like a great stroke of light that slams across the horizon, the whole memory of the day before flashed into my mind.

I sat up, pressing one hand against the runaway beat of my heart.

Mary was still asleep, her aspect mysterious and closed. A dried spill of vomit caked one cheek.

Only when I attempted to wake her did I realize that something new was the matter. She made no answer and did not open her eyes and slap at me, as she often did when I roused her.

Kneeling, I noticed that one ear and a portion of the linen cap close by were soaked with clear fluid. A strange purpling like a bruise had bloomed behind the ear and ran down her neck, though I was certain the color had not been there on the day before.

I shook her, called her name without fearing alien warriors, lurking and spying in the brush. "Mary, Mary, Mary—wake!"

I clutched her to me, rocked her in my arms, moaned to the green walls and the blue sky.

How strange to be like someone in a parable! And this is how it seemed: once there was a maiden who rose to find that her sister could not be wakened. And no one could ever rouse her again, never again, never. And why it happened or what it meant, the girl never knew, though someone knew. But God did not tell her, though something seemed to quiver in the leaves and utter meanings that she could not understand. To that young woman, it appeared terrible to be alone with the dead, and tragic that out there, Indians and settlers roamed the world when now her sister would not stir and walk with her. It was dreadful, impossible that a cur dog would chase a squirrel on some Massachusetts village green, or that some scraggy cat would pounce on a bit of leaf teased by the wind, and yet this child would not rise, would not speak, would not breathe. How could so much of the world shine and so many drink at the air with pleasure when Mary lay so still?

It is our common human blight, and yet for me nothing in that awakening was common.

Could the blow to her head have been so much worse than it seemed? It had alarmed me, but I had not thought that it could destroy her life. And yet now I must believe that she was dead. Dear God! I had not loved and minded her well enough, and so had allowed rugged stone to strike against her tender skull.

"Mary."

What ailed me that I worked for such a long time at combing her hair with my fingers and tucking the curls into her child's coif, scrubbing at her cheek and ear with leaves, and straightening her limbs and arranging her so that she looked comfortable? For she would no longer need to be made content on the earth. But we mortals cannot help striving to do some good to another when it is far too late, with those we love stricken dead, and so I could not help smoothing Mary's dress and dropping tears onto her face as I toyed with her hair. I plucked up the doll and held it against me for comfort, though I was far too old for such plaything-love. The little creature had suffered along with Mary, and now a single drop of blood stained the linen face. There would never be call to finish embroidering the features.

And all that time with Mary and the doll made of scraps and hair, I did not brood on the house or my mother and father and the boys, or my aunts and uncles and cousins. I did not remember them or Onesimus and Blue Jonas but thought of myself, alone, and of Mary, who would never again have to be afraid of what lurks and schemes in the forest. I nearly envied her peacefulness. Now she was truly a Bible–lily of the field who would neither spin nor grow weary.

I prayed that God would have mercy on her now and on the Day of Judgment, and that even if some spoke against her, the divine energies of making and re-making would remember her still. A conviction, golden and blessed, of her essential goodness and harmlessness came over me and felt intense and sweet so that I forgot everything and seemed to float, transparent, in a stream of light that flowed around and through me.

But every gleamy instant on a mountaintop must be followed by a return to the shadows of the valley, where someone in anguish or lost in madness is always howling.

My head throbbed; I wanted water but sipped more of the cordial, which did not please me as a morning drink. For some minutes I lay down in a stupor beside my sister on the low, crushed plants that smelled of springtime and mint, until at last I began again to come to my senses and cry a little and sit up.

"Mary," I said, and then was silent, thinking how King Death had come while I slept and led away my sister. *And was I half a murderer for not saving her?* That loss would haunt me, I felt certain.

But the sun had swung further into the sky than I liked. I wanted to leave. Our green shelter had been partially riven by our passage and was no more an unbroken secret, and I could not bide longer for those who might never come. I needed to *know*. Hastily I drank the remaining cordial (now detestable to me), ate frugally of the ashcake, and packed the remains of bread and venison, wrapping them in the sampler as my mother had done. The scissors and knife I swaddled in the spare coif, for they were all I had to serve as weapons. If I must, I would wield them as best I could. I smoothed the clothes with my hand and made a lodging for them as well. Mary would not need the shift and spare stockings, and who knows what need I would have before the day was out? They might somehow prove useful, though far too small to be worn by me. How could I know what might be important? Much might have been damaged in the attack. Bandages might be needed.

I put one of the sugared nuts in my mouth and stowed the rest. I shut my eyes, sucking on the sweet paradise of the almond. My tears were for Mary, who had flown beyond all earthly pleasures. It was not what I had meant when longing for her angel and a better world. And I had promised she would see all our kin this morning!

I bent to hoist the blanket sling. The bundle made an unwieldy burden, but I would not have to bear the weight of my sister—only the heavy thought that I might have cared for her better and saved her from dashing against the rocks.

I tied the blanket about me, shoulder to hip, and knelt to bid Mary my farewell.

"They will come," I promised what remained of her; "Father and Blue Jonas and Onesimus will come back and fetch you and take you home properly. Someone will be here." But I thought of the ancient injunction, *Let the dead bury the dead*, and was afraid.

The tears *would* rise from their fount at such words, but I wiped them away, sure that I had no space for mourning.

My flighty mind, so often thinking of the curious and even silly when I should be serious and reverent, darted straight to a memory of Boston, and how after some indulging in beer and funeral cakes, Weaver Turell lost his footing in the rain and tumbled into his mother's grave. I was young enough to forget, but I had older brothers who occasionally reminded one another and laughed heartily at the memory.

"You would be blessed if you lived so long and usefully and died in such a state of grace as old Goody Turell," our mother told Joseph when she caught him telling the tale.

"Yes, I know ... but it *is* comical."

"Joseph, you saucebox," she said, and then smiled, though later in the day she bade him to think on his own spiritual estate.

The memory brought up more tears that made the green room soften and wave. My mother had always been unfailingly kind (if there were moments otherwise, I have a pardonable memory and have forgotten them), and unlike many I have known in Massachusetts who were ever disquieted and uneasy about the destiny of their souls, she put her confidence in Christ's mercy and bid us do the same.

The weight adjusted, I picked up the clay bottle that I meant to fill with water. Out of weariness, I had not searched for the stream before, but when I woke in the night, I heard a liquid, silvery song and knew it played and rambled close by.

I kissed my sister on the forehead and bade her body farewell, and clambered back through the branches of our green room.

The stream was my first stop. The day was still, and so I easily followed the sound of water. I clambered onto the wet stones to scoop from where it whirled fastest and freshest. Thirst had been plaguing me, and I drank until I could not swallow another mouthful, and afterward filled the bottle once more, plugging it with a wad of moss, all the while remembering Mary and how she would never thirst.

I was not sure whether safety meant rounding the fields and going as yesterday, or whether it might be better simply to plunge across without concern for the roundabout way. The morning before, I was intent on not being pursued to the hiding place. A direct course might have aroused attention and led the Mi'kmaq or their French leaders to us.

Now I felt anxious and stirred up about my family. I did not let myself examine my thoughts and situation too closely because I knew there would be nothing of comfort in them. No one had come to the hiding place, not the day before and not in the morning after the attack. I determined to head in a straighter path for the house, keeping to the shadows as best I could. This slender plan meant that I would be completing a sort of jagged circle that looped from the house to the hiding place and back again.

My feet were sore, and I stopped often to drink from the bottle. But I never let myself pause for long. All my eagerness was to embrace my mother and father and brothers and whole family, to find out any dead or injured, and to do what I could to assist. I wanted to confess my carelessness, my angers, my sorrow. I wanted my mother's arms and my mother's forgiveness and comfort. And we would bring Mary home. She and I being the only girl-children among the cousins, her loss would be especially grievous to all.

"I am so sorry for not saving her, not protecting her," I said aloud. The image of Mary, all deathly white in the green oval of the room, held place in my mind as I moved through the woods.

I sobbed now and then, partly because I was bruised from the rough, quick-paced walk on the day before, partly because of Mary and my own loneliness without her, and partly because of the dread that went along with me. When I wept, the tears seemed not proper mourning but jerked from my eyes with each footstep.

On the shore sometimes I remember seeing waves that were larger than the others, that seemed to hang in the air for instants before curling over and collapsing into foam. The fear in me was like one of those waves that seemed outside of time and holding still in the midst of change.

Only once did my fear break into a shout: it was no surprise, for do we not all prove mortal and as one in folly and dearth of mastery over our passions?

Intending to pass through a nigh-leafless but close-set thicket of high-bush huckleberries so that I might crouch in more secrecy and arrange my bundle, I stumbled and nearly fell, crying out in startlement so that my heart, grown so accustomed to shakings, set off running. But I stopped, staring down at the man who had tumbled down in the berry shrubs, leaving a broken, awkwardly-pruned gap.

Quivering, I bent and touched a finger to his arm. I placed my hand where I knew the blood in his throat should pulse but could feel nothing. I could not tell whether he or I ran hot or cold, my body felt so strange, betraying me with flush and chill like a fever. Fearing that I would slip and sprawl and kick in a swoon, as my brother John had done when gripped by an ague, I nerved myself to thrust at the man. He flopped heavily onto his back, glaring up at the sky as if a gaze could strike it like an arrow and bring down the heavens. At that, I felt he had passed far from us, for the dead are more unwieldy and clumsy in their movements than the living who must carry, strip, and wash them.

"Mother," I whispered, wishing for any familiar form to appear and call my name.

What was I to do? The world, I thought, was proving a charnel house where many might need burying. But that would not be my work—this day mine was to live and return to my family. For without kindred we are prey to the world's bears and panthers, wild or human.

The household might yet be under siege. Perhaps how to return to my own was still a puzzle-knot that only time could untangle.

As my heart eased in its drumming, I considered the dead man closely, concluding that I must search and see if there was anything I ought to take from him. I did not want to walk back to the green room where Mary's body lay waiting. But what if I had to sleep out-of-doors another night or two? Of a surety, he had left his possessions behind on earth and would have no more need of them.

"Mi'kmaq. You are most probably a Mi'kmaq sort of Indian," I whispered. Really, I knew little enough about the various tribes, but guessed from his clothes and from the accounts of travelers I had heard when visiting Fort Loyall. The French were luring the northern Mi'kmaq and Maliseet peoples of the Wabanaki to move against the English. All week, my uncles and father had been arguing about the right time to leave for the Falmouth fort. Well, we had judged that hour wrong. No one knows the instant of strange appearings, whether for good or ill.

Over the shoulders was draped something like a cloak, silky and smooth to my touch. I supposed it might have been the skin of a seal or perhaps some pale creature of the forest deeps, a unicorn or a leopard without spots. I was surprised that he had bothered with such a garment, yet it could be cold in May, and the skin would make a good bed for a traveler in the wilds. *I could sleep in its shelter*, I thought, and lifted the edge, which proved the skin to be heavy and thick. The Mi'kmaq (if so he was) wore sleeves attached to a kind of rough jacket, painted with red and yellow ochre and lashed front and back at the center with leather strings. Uneasily I wondered if I should undress him; I might find those garments useful on a chilly May night. Below the jacket were long deerskin breeches and a loose piece of hide tied to a kind of girdle. I drew back my hand. Those I did not want to touch.

Growing braver and untying several pouches, I shook the contents onto the ground. Inside one was a little quill-ornamented birchbark box containing a stitching awl, a long strip of leather, and sewing needles of bone and copper. I sniffed at another, packed with smoked smelt and shattered pieces of what I suspected to be dried herring.

"The life is more than meat, and the body is more than raiment," I murmured.

Perhaps I was already, in some sad corner of my mind, planning on what to do if I proved entirely solitary in the world because I also determined to take his jacket and moccasins and some of the gear he carried—the pouches, the box with awl and needles.

Gingerly, I tugged at his sleeves. His eyes seemed to look into mine and then slide past; I sat back on my heels.

Though intending to regard him with disgust as monstrous and condemned, I was surprised to find that his face appeared open and shorn of any anger. He was not repulsive in features—a straight nose, dark eyes and brows, and an impossibly sheer-falling spill of hair that I went so far as to handle. The gleaming strands felt alive in my fingers, and I dropped them hastily. Oil with a smear of red ochre made his skin shine. I wondered if he had been loping a long way from the lands to the north.

When pulling at the sleeves, I noticed that his hands and nails were grimy with gunpowder, and concluded that he may have owned but lost a musket and been left with only bow and arrows. The points were not knapped stone but iron—the treacherous trade gifts of the French. I was careful not to brush against the tips because I had heard a minister at Falmouth say that the forest was a storehouse for devilry, a pantry stocked with Indian poisons and a pharmacopoeia of maledictions. They might be tainted, and even a careless scratch could mean that poison could go sparking and sizzling through my veins.

Why did he care to travel so far just to attack a few settlers? Ransom monies to be had? The wiles of the French?

Mother always said that my main lapse in understanding was an inability to perceive the ill and warped in others, that I was only too likely to think well of all the world. Such an error could be my undoing, she warned me. Prudence and good judgment depended on an accuracy and clarity of sight. Lack of discernment would be as a moth hidden in my cape.

True, I could hardly detect the murderer inside the youth—it seemed to me that he was half a boy and half a man. My brothers had been toiling as men for a long time now, but at times they seemed boys, often playful and laughing when not at their labors. Perhaps it is entirely a mistake to believe that evil intents show like ochre on the skin or in the face.

Up in his home, far north, he probably fished and hunted for seal and perhaps even the mysterious whales that rose out of the sea with jeweled fountains crowning their heads and then slammed out of sight, down into the region of the Leviathan and the monstrous, pearly octopus. Perhaps he felt how wondrous and strange the world is when he floated on the sea. He might have speared the very seal—for I had decided that the silvery pelt must belong to a seal—whose skin became the robe over his shoulders, or thrown a net after smelt, or stabbed larger fish from a birchbark canoe. Those arrows in the cleverly dyed and woven quiver must properly be meant for elk and bears in the woods near the coast, and not for us; it was those whore-master rogues, the French, who had turned the Indians against us, or so Joseph once said, and earned a reproof for talking so loosely.

Jesuits wandered in the wilderness, converting the savages to their secret ways and their rituals that were said to be akin to magic, with their censing, indulgences, and silver and gold mice that were like tiny idols to ward off the plague—as is said of the precious mice of the Philistines in the First Book of Samuel—blessed on French altars and paraded through towns. I had heard tell of silver, gold, and porcelain hands and eyeballs left on Romish altars in thanksgiving after recovery from an illness. How I shivered, a heap of false body parts rising up in fancy! Somehow I could not blame the Mi'kmaq for yielding to the persuasion of the cunning-tongued, especially now that he was dead and so young that I could hardly fathom his being like one of those who knocked my aunt—*which* aunt?—over the head. Blood stained one cheek and was clotted in the dull-shining hair.

How did you die?

He had been shot not long before he collapsed among the huckle-berries. Where the halves of his jacket met in the back, the ties hung down, and a pistol wound about the bigness of a coin was visible in the gap. When I shoved him onto his side and pulled the two pieces of the garment away, I found another great wound near the shoulder blade that made me wonder at his power, to suffer such injury and yet muster the strength to stagger on until he dropped in the huckleberries.

Yet soon I began once more to feel something like a horror of him, dwelling on how he might have killed someone of my own family in devilish hate or by terrible mischance, permitted by Providence. The darkness I had felt earlier crept over me. Here I sat so close beside him, and yet he would be forever swaddled in mystery, without a name or my having any sense of him save that he had come south in order to do evil with the French and with others of his kind. Not even his tribe was altogether sure to me: though I guessed him to be Mi'kmaq, one of the Wabanaki, even that was not certain. How little I could know of what had happened, until I found my kin! Shudders jolted me until I could not say whether I shook from May warmth or from May cold.

Time being such a strange fabric, slow or quick-spun, woven tight and small or loose and open, I was uncertain how long I had knelt in the thicket. A thread of longing for my own people pulled taut in me, and I hurriedly arranged my bundle. Grave-stuff the contents seemed to me, like relics from the old pagan barrows of England carelessly broken open by a plough.

I moved more quickly now, despite the weight of the unfamiliar sealskin pressing against my shoulders. It smelled of the young man's far-off village, an odor of fish mixed with smoke from last winter's fires and something less nameable, intimate, and almost fragrant. Perhaps it was the scent of his oiled skin. So the things of this world tell us a tale, though whether true or feigned, we never know.

My feet worked mechanically over the ground as my mind shuttled from the figure of the dead Indian to my family. Was he married? Did such people wed at all? Did he have a mother to grieve his disappearance? Who of my aunts had fallen by the door? Were survivors coming for me and Mary even now?

Too much thinking gave way to little thinking, and several times I found myself wandering out of my way. Then I searched the treetops for a clue and checked the direction to the settlement by the hazard of a guess.

But I was no newcomer to the place and its landmarks.

Once I dropped to my knees, stunned by a rush of fear. How long I held still, I cannot stay. At last, taking hold of a branch, I pulled myself onto my feet. Though weary, I set off again, determined not to rest again until I reached our cluster of houses.

That was a failed plan. My belly hurt, heavy with water from the stream. Before long I felt weak and insubstantial and stopped to eat the remainder of the ashcake and a piece of the Indian boy's fish, strongly flavored and rich with oil. Afterward, I slumped down under the shade of trees. I imagined drifting into a drowse that would refresh and help me to go on but somehow could not sleep. I made myself rise and stumble away.

But my steps quickened when I came close enough to see a spiral of smoke that must be floating up from the chimbley. A skirmish meant that many hungry people to feed. And surely the distance was now not so very far. I trotted clumsily, eager to be with my family, but the soreness of my feet had nigh-lamed me and soon made me go on more slowly.

Where the edge of the forest curved around the field directly opposite the house stood a tall tree that my uncle Thomas said is called *tamarack* in the Algonquian tongue, and from there could be gained a full view of the clearing. I aimed toward that tree, keeping its top always before me, my thoughts stirring from their torpor.

Some sensations feel almost creaturely—good ones can be like a child curling up by a fire or like a kind, wish-granting stranger met at a crossroads, but ill ones are cannibal witches, creeping heavily beside us, coaxing us into the forest. And what are these wish-granting wayfarers and woods-witches, these beings no proper stay-at-home Englishwoman knows? Goody Waters of Boston knew and told me their stories. More than a century ago, her ancestors fled to Frankfurt during the bloody queenship of Mary, and one of them heard and passed down the crooked German stories of the place. I often dreamed of them, imagining a long ago when wishes could still come true, though I was scolded for such wastes of my time.

Now my mind felt as if some unseen companion was close at hand, one who meant no good to me. Any stranger nearby must have been flinty-hearted and bitter. Any creature at my heels must have been demoniac. My thoughts were shaded. Hellish daydreams crept into my head, visions of crawling monsters, slithering upside down in the crevices of the underworld or sneaking into the light of sun in order to sting and scratch and whisper curses and threats into our ears.

The story of Mistress Rowlandson in the time of King Philip's War came to me, and how the scene of her capture held "the lively resemblance of hell," and how her small daughter died in her arms during the night, departing from her like a lamb in the midst of wolves. *Wolves.* And yet my father always declared that every human being showed forth the image of God, however marred. The remembrance comforted me and yet could not stop the sense that something shadowy scampered after me.

Lord, have mercy. Lord, have mercy. The words jostled through my head.

I dashed the last stretch of ground to the tamarack, the blanket sling thumping against my hip. I lowered it, the heavy sealskin sliding from my soaked back at the same moment. Ducking under the lower branches, I dropped to my knees to survey the house and the yard before it.

The great trunk of chimbley still stood. Smoke curled up from within the stone base of what had been my house. I saw something, yet nothing that was a house or family.

"Mother," I shouted to the air, and the air did not answer.

I rested my head against the trunk of the tamarack and wept.

A wave that was my own fear crashed down and drowned me in teardrops and in a tide of uselessness and helplessness to change what had been done.

Who can say how long such hours go on? They seem to drop into eternity. I cried, I thumped down and howled on my knees for what had departed, and did so without a care for who or what would hear me, and it did not come to me until later that perhaps some of my family lived, that perhaps some of them had escaped to Fort Loyall without me, or that others might have been taken by the Indians and could be ransomed by the money gifts of charitable souls in Boston.

Creeping nearer, I discovered that the ground near to the stone foundation of what had been the house felt warm through the leather soles of my shoes, so I slipped the moccasins over them. Here and there beams still smoldered and sent up fresh trails of smoke. Half-collapsed into the cellar, the rubble that remained was plainly much too hot to explore, though I took a stick and stirred about near foundered timbers, unsure what I saw. Was that rounded shape a skull or a burned pot, that form a blackened post or a body, that slender bar a bone or some charred spindle, the remains of my uncle Thomas' carpentry?

The bodies of the warriors were missing as well. I supposed them to have been borne away to be buried, seated in pits with bows and beads. For when the English pilgrimed to Cape Cod some seventy years before, they dug up several Indian graves in uncouth curiosity and found the tenants seated, heads bent to knees.

I wanted none of this. I wanted nothing that was in my mind. Only this: I wanted to know that those who were mine had been saved, and that I could find them in this life. The shade of grief enveloped me. The lithe, leopard ferocity of the wilderness grinned at me from the trees. Though the sun's eye bore down, my skin felt chilled, and I trudged around the foundations in a darkness invisible to eyes. I myself was the wild cat-of-the-woods, uselessly chasing my own tail as I circled the base of stones, though not in play. Dragging the blanket sling and sealskin, I made every inch of the circuit. I was fierce—or there was something fierce in me, tearing me—and would have leaped on sorrow and ripped it to pieces if we mortals could destroy what stirs us up and makes us mad with desolation.

The face of the Mi'kmaq came into my thoughts, and the threads of his hair that still seemed to hold a sparkle of life; I hated him and was helpless to do otherwise. Sobs choked me, stole my breath. Soon I could hardly tell whether I hated him for what he and others had done or whether, indeed, I hated him for showing me that I, too, seethed with rage. In me turned something murderous—a shadow from the wing of a dark bird.

Fury might have set me alight to burn until the ash of me blew away in the wind. Because all I ever learned of the civil wars of England and the struggles of the ancients told me that hatred destroys and that anger means chaos.

Even the outbuildings were razed, burned to the very earth, leaving only scorch marks and blackened shafts of wood.

I alone was left to the company of a thousand thousand trees and the trampled fields and the smoke going up to the heavens like a bad offering.

They have all gone into the world of light.

Light! Yet I could not bear to think of my mother and father with the boys and Mary and the rest in the regions of death that seem such an unknown—a darkness—to the living.

In my extremity, I wanted to die and be with them. I did not wish to press on and needle a way through the pathless places that lay at every compass point around me. What I wanted was to cease earthly awareness, to fly wholly from the horror that bent my back and tripped me so that I was knocked to my knees again and grasped at the weeds as though I drowned on dry land and reached for any help, even the little roots and leaves of plants.

My mind with all thought was overthrown for a time, shoved away from me by wildness and grief. I was not myself, or not as I was before. My spirit seemed to drift out of my body and float upward toward the burning disk of sun. I looked down with pity upon myself, at the fingers gripping the stems of grasses, at the bent shape of my form with the blanket and the silvery skin cast aside, at the unkempt hair spilling down my back.

I heard a voice that sounded like Father's calling out, *I will not fail thee, neither forsake thee*, and my spirit sank back into the body below.

I knew the verse and the words that came after: *So that we may boldly say, The Lord is mine helper, neither will I fear what man can do unto me.* Even now, I believe that without those words, my soul would have spiraled up toward the sun and jumped through that bright door and been glad to go from the world and not return, burned clean of sin and ill memory. In Boston, I had heard of many wonders of the invisible world, stories of the newly dead in England appearing on the day of their great change to a long-separated brother or sister in our own colony of Massachusetts Bay. Remarkables were ever occurring. Nothing was accident. The smallest act mattered. So our ministers taught, and so I had learned. The world was crammed with signs and messages, if only we had the wit and discernment to see, mark, and read. Wisdom revealed a voice murmuring in the leaves, cursive in the running streams, and sermons compacted in the bright veins of stones. God or Satan could speak out of the mouths of infants. Saving providences stood shining around us as beacons and messages. Yet the ink-black, gleaming magics of the Devil's wrath were also a script written into the world.

Now I did not know whether the voice I heard was my father's, though he read to us morning and night and would have sent me a word of comfort if he could, sailing across the river between death and this life, reminding me that a child of God can never be alone, though she can forget. We are always forgetting. It is our nature to forget and fall away. Possibly it was the voice of a passing angel, comforting me with my father's tones and weeping for the world that goes on murdering Abel still, and sorry to see me in such a plight.

Sitting up, I gasped at the air, tasting smoke and flowers.

What am I to do? My little commonwealth—everyone who ever loved me and wished my safety—is gone.

The reply came to me as if I were still divided in twain—it seemed to come from a distance, as if my spirit were not quite married again to the body.

You must get up on your legs. You must walk to Fort Loyall. It is not so far. You can walk there on your own feet, and be there by evening, or in morning.

I obeyed myself. I stood.

I shouldered the blanket sling, letting it slide down into place and knotting the cloth tighter at my hip.

In that manner, setting one foot in front of another, I bowed to my fate and left that place where everything I had ever loved was murdered or stolen away from me. I hardly flinched when I passed by the other sites in our little settlement, the dwelling-houses all burned to the foundation stones, scorched and blackened. They had been empty for several days, the inhabitants fled to Fort Loyall. Another day or two and we would have done likewise. But we had waited too long and thought too highly of our fortified house. And now our name and place had been obliterated.

To meditate long on even the most abominable and detestable events is impossible. Weariness takes us and strips away thought and puts us into a sleep to shield us from what has occurred. I had not been departed from the house site but half an hour when I started from a sort of walking daze, alerted by a low ruttling in the forest.

Alarm passed through me like a flaming arrow and was utterly quenched. I had left much of my caution behind at the house and needed to be reminded that the world was perilous, and that a Frenchman or Indian might be hidden behind any stand of leaves. Too much affliction is like a potion that, for a time, makes the heart slow to scare, unable to throb in fright.

Sometimes I believe that if a Mi'kmaq had appeared, eager to club me over the head, I would have knelt and let him do his bloody work without resistance or any attempt to appease his wrath. I might even have thought such yielding to be an act of prudence and good judgment. Like Abraham's son Isaac in the land of Moriah, I was ready to bear the fardels to my own burning. Death was an occasional visitor to our street back in Boston, but I had not seen his face for several years; not even a stillborn child or an uncle's slip from the roof had come to us near Falmouth. Now, suddenly, we were terribly familiar with each other.

After letting the blanket and sealskin slip to the ground, I held still and listened, but it was several minutes before the sound came again. It was close and appeared to be the noise of an animal. I did not suspect some New World dragon or leopard-panther of the woods, but more likely the blowing and snorting of deer. I moved slowly between the trees, wondering if I was right, wondering if Providence was with me today, Christ on the mercy seat pitying my poor estate and grieved at the cruelty of men that will go ever on until God whispers *finis* to the world and makes the new heaven and earth.

Why did I feel the need to know? My decision not to flee seems peculiar and without wisdom.

I flitted back and forth between the trees, now hearing the noise at one place, now at another, and frequently glanced back to make sure I didn't lose sight of where I had been. But at last I came to the edge of a stream where a tree, the great work of centuries, had burst toward the forest floor, leveling many large but lesser trunks. Here the sky shone brightly through a gap in the forest. I ducked beneath the boles that lay one astride the other like mad, mighty bridges running from one nowhere to another nowhere, and looked about me.

"Hortus!"

How strangely a human voice clangs on our ears in the deep forest when no one seems near! And yet the word was only my own, eagerly ringing out.

Our Lincolnshire black—so my father called the gelding because he was a sturdy horse with the white stockings of the old breed, though he might not have been English at all—was standing in a deep pool below the lacy white frills where a stream tumbled over ledges, and never did I find water with its fine meanders and laughing over stones to be as beautiful as at that moment. He lifted his head and surveyed me and knew me.

I smiled for the pleasure of gazing at him and for the hour that turned more golden than before, the beams of sun growing intense and gilding Hortus with its rays.

"Hortus. Hortus, come to me," I called softly.

He dipped his head to the water and drank before moving down the stream, his head rocking. I reveled in the sight of something saved from the mayhem of the day past. His legs splashed in the water. I could see right through the current to the pebbles underneath, and the jocund sunlight struck sparks from the water. As if in a mirror-glass, I glimpsed another world of gay-colored agates and purest clarity and playful stars.

Bending low, I crept under a trunk and scrambled over a wedge of stone to gain the brink.

"Hortus, Hortus." I found myself again in tears and reached for his neck. The anvil of his head nudged against me, and he blew air shudderingly from his nostrils.

"I must have sensed that you were something good for me and not some wild beast," I told him.

His lips mumbled at the stream. When he caressed me with the side of his head, I reached for the unfamiliar reins.

"Who put this on you?"

The simple bridle was not leather but a fine basket weave of some unfamiliar sort, the brow- and nose-bands dyed with red ochre.

"And where did you toss the horseman?"

I swept a hand over his side, noticing a streak of yellow earth on his haunches.

"Hortus, what an adventure you must have had," I said. "Did someone ride you bareback into the woods? And where is he?"

I whirled and stared behind me. The gloom of the trees beyond the glade did not answer, and Hortus kept the secret of his brief captivity among the warriors. Turning back, I seized the reins and bent his head to mine.

"Wait here for me. Stay. Stay."

He snorted at me as I stepped slantwise, keeping my eyes on him. I climbed from the stream, hauling myself up by a root, and hurried to where I had dropped the sling and sealskin. Once or twice I felt affrighted that my way had vanished, but I looked over my shoulder at the spot too often to be truly lost.

"Hortus!" The sound of his name was all that connected us, once he was no longer in sight.

One worry often gives way to the next; having a fear that he would be gone on my return, I grasped my few worldly possessions in my arms and did not stop to arrange them.

"Hortus, Hortus—"

In the clearing where the higgledy-piggledy trees were jackstraws for giants' play, Hortus lifted his head and glanced at me, asking, I guessed, why I called his name so often. I set down my burden on a log and went to him.

"My flower, my black-shining sun, my sweet garden of silk," I said to him, and petted his nose. "Let us gallop away. We can find out some paradise with a wall around it, one where no arrows and spears can pierce the air, and where the orchard trees are ever in lusty fruit and bloom, and the springs jet forth as crystal fountains."

Hortus must have agreed with me because he nodded his head and blew air in gusts from his nostrils. And though he was but a beast, I could not bring myself to tell him how our family had melted away, and that my father, mother, and brothers might never ride him again.

Nor would any of my kin mount his back. And no Onesimus or Blue Jonas would ride to the fort. Mary's face rose up before me, her eyes closed. To say the words of those raw losses: I could not. An unexpected tear launched from my face and plummeted into the stream.

Once, long ago in Boston, I had asked Mother if we would meet a centaur in the forest. She laughed at me but then shrugged and said, "Who may say? Perhaps. Would you be afeared to see such a marvel?"

"No, I would be glad, so glad!"

"Are centaurs not wild?"

"But not Chiron. He was wise and a master of medicines."

Now, years later, I knew the alphabet and many words in Greek and had translated a few lines about Apollo and the Daphnean tree, as well as a passage concerning the views of Democritus on the nature of atoms, air atoms being light and whirling, fire atoms sharp and light, interlocking iron atoms hard, and water atoms sliding-slick. My father said that I might be the only girl in the colony who knew any jots and smatterings of the ancient languages, for he set me to learning with my brothers, though never could I study before I had finished my house chores and stitched for an hour.

What was the use of acquiring a minim of Greek and a little more Latin when we were so far from England and culture? And yet study had proved sweet to me and, indeed, to all my brothers, though they could be marvelous complainers at times.

"Hortus."

I led him from where he had lingered, cooling his legs in the stream, over to the jumble of downed trees. Holding up the sealskin, I let him smell the unfamiliar scent. He backed away, snorting, but after some sweet talk let me drape it over his back.

"I might have left the hide, Hortus, but now I am full glad that I did not," I told him. "That was a blessing."

After climbing onto a slanted trunk, I tied the blanket about me and reached for the horse. The skin would make a slippery saddle. I did not wish to slide off and strike the ground or trees and suffer injury, no one around to help.

"Come here," I coaxed Hortus, tugging at the reins. "Come closer to me. Show me your smooth ride. Show me your country-gait."

Not until he was pressed against the tree did I mount and straddle his back, warm and wide and lofty in the air. Now I regretted not stripping the Mi'kmaq of his sturdy leg coverings, for I had no care to be a lady of the wilderness. First tucking up my gown until my draggled-down stockings and bare legs showed, I tapped him with my heels and drew his head to the left with the reins.

"The land past Round Marsh, between the Casco River and Back Cove. Fort Loyall," I told him. "That's where we need to be. You've been to Falmouth before, more often than I have. If only I could prevail on you to tell me the easiest way to travel there. But we will find the stockade together."

And that was how Hortus and I, Charis, left the woodsy wild regions west of Fort Loyall and ventured east in search of succor and haven. It would have been fine if rest and safety proved all my story. I should have had the brave tale of a wander through dainty hillocks and goodly groves, with a firm confidence in what I would discover at the stockade, and without my heart changed to iron in my breast. But the way to Fort Loyall was for me a passage through memories. When my ride went well enough, I could not help poring over what I would wish to forget, the scorched foundation stones, the smoking shapes in the cellarage, all family vanished, and Mary dead, her body waiting for someone to come with a mattock and spade. When I grew alarmed, I could not help picturing the Mi'kmaq and the arrows in his fine-woven quiver. He had not come to our settlement alone.

Despite Hortus being an easy ride, sure-footed, a bit stiff-backed but easy in his gait, I am afraid that we mistook the direction for a time and circled about uselessly, for the sky was exchanging its colors not long after we passed Round Marsh, north of the ferry at Brimhall's Point, and wove our way through the forest along Back Cove, southwest of Sandy Point. Staying close to the sound of the sea, I missed the windmill and the Half Moon garrison, resolving to progress southeast, leave Hortus in trees, and aim for the cluster of streets along the Casco River.

"Soon you will hide, Hortus," I told him. "And I will just see if all is well ordered. I will come back for you, and then there will be something savory to eat for us both, and straw for you and a bed for me."

Although I had no reason to mislike the help I might find at the fort, I seemed to have lost faith in men and their assistance. The smell of wood smoke alternately alarmed and reassured me. Where there was smoke, kettles and spits meant supper. Yet where there was smoke, there might be greater fires. I found myself questioning every possible step, every thought that drifted into mind. Had I not been taught that though God knew and destined all before the globe and stars were hatched, yet the depravity of man cut him off from the divine? It could not be wise to trust in those I did not know well, or in strangers.

"But who is not a stranger? Only you, Hortus," I told him.

Hortus moved steadily beneath me, and there was nothing alien or monstrous or satanic about him. His flesh and hide wrapped a spirit that neither fretted about his salvation nor clung to remorse. His low nickering and occasional snort was conversation enough for me. I was glad to have his strength to join with mine.

I leaned forward to pat the horse's neck. "We must take care, my lovely Hortus. And you must be noiseless, or someone may pirate you away from me."

I was grateful that horses tend to be fairly quiet animals. My thoughts flashed here and there, swerving from the burned house to the fort ahead to, absurdly, the thought of riding a giant cockerel, for just such a strangeness happened in one of Goody Waters' German tales. Startled, the bird might have betrayed me with a shrill note or tried to crow the sun up and over the dark edge of the world! Hortus gave his head a toss, as if to bring me back to him and shake away fancies. The mortal mind shelters strange whims, flittering and never controlled, flying where they will.

We traveled in dusk and near-silence for a time, following the irregular shape of Back Cove, shielded by forest land, until at last I moved eastward toward Falmouth, concluding that the settlement on the bay was quite close. In falling twilight, I recognized a cairn of heaped stones erected near Queen Street. Another would mark the start of a rutted path that wound some thirty feet to the top of the bluff; there stood the stockade with its black-mouthed cannon cocked toward land and sea. At the fort, I hoped to discover some of our neighbors and perhaps family. How glad I would be to see their faces!

"Already so inky," I whispered. "Cimmerian seas."

A shiver ran through Hortus, rippling his hide. I pressed the palm of my hand against his neck.

"You are the garden of the sea where water-chimeras under the surface stir the waves." I wondered if the ocean had mermaids for gardeners and, if so, what sort of flowers grew in their deep, walled gardens.

"My mind is a whirligig of strange fancies," I said to Hortus. "How can I dream anything but the dead?" I was reminded of Sabbath morning and afternoon sermons, and how thoughts wanted to wander.

"We must cling to the task," I said, though I did not feel valiant.

A dense clump of trees seemed a likely place to leave Hortus and my few belongings. Determined to see what I could find out by my wits and nerve before committing myself to the unknown, I slid down from the horse, falling most of the way and landing hard on my knees. I felt for Hortus' legs, steadied myself, and rose, my bones aching.

"Shhh," I said, placing my hand on his muzzle.

He showed his teeth and seemed to be laughing. I slapped him lightly.

"Are you making mock of me?"

Leaving my few possessions close by, I kept only the knife and scissors, which I thought to fasten at my waist but ended up carrying in my hands. I took measure of the landmarks. A dead tree with a broken top reared above other trees. I would count my paces to the stockade wall and often glance over my shoulder, setting the changing aspect of the place in my mind.

Because I could not risk losing Hortus. And yet every step away from him meant hazard. Not braving the dark was also hazard. *I should have left him closer to Back Cove. I should return to him, hide him. I should creep like a mouse to Captain Davis' house. Unless I could be confused and too far southwest ... but then I would reach Captain Tyne's door, or even the Ingersoll garrison. No. I could not be so far.*

When I paused, Hortus whinnied softly, and I called for him to hush.

My people have long believed that the night is frightful and no friend to human beings, who belong inside houses, away from outlandish noises and demon-dangers, but now I was half-glad to be hidden in its cloak. The lamp-bringer in the sky was firing the wicks of stars so that at each moment, new fire bloomed forth. On the ground, the dark ruled, and I was surprised by how little in the way of lights appeared—just one that seemed as if it burned in a high tower. Surely that lamp meant Fort Loyall.

Two hundred sixty-one, two hundred sixty-two, two hundred sixty-three ...

After so many steps, I peered back, but the broken-topped tree had grown invisible in the darkness. The gloom was pitchier than I deemed right for a settlement with fort, and now a long, winding sheet of cloud smothered up the moon and a portion of the stars. The memory came to me of the prior year's protests made by my father and others to Major Church and the General Court, that Falmouth remained in danger from Boston's stingy, hesitating policy toward frontier settlers. What if all our strongholds were in peril? I held still and listened hard but could hear only the noise of the bay waters sloshing against the shingle and the drowsy note of a bird on its nest. My knees ached from the fall, and already I was sore from riding. But that did not matter.

No, I heard nothing untoward.

The air smelled sickroom-peculiar with an unpleasant mixture of smoke and filth. The stench reminded me of Father's dislike for "bad airs" in the towns. Looking again for the gleam in the tower, I realized that what I had taken for a lamp in a window was only a low star.

This mistake frightened me, and for a moment I believed that I was not near Falmouth at all. I dropped onto my knees, and crossed my arms over my chest, doubly caging the heart that wanted to leap the bars of my ribs and bolt away. The cold points of scissors and knife pressed against me.

No, no, no, this is the place. It must be. It is. And I cannot lose Hortus in the dark.

The whole world transforms to a labyrinth after dusk, I told myself, a mad stitchery of twists and turns and no helpful thread to guide the way. And so I stood and listened to the night and then went on. All was gloom where I expected lamps and welcome, as if the order of the place had been turned back past Genesis to chaos and unmaking.

A half-burned building that I guessed to be near the juncture where Fore Street met Broad startled me. That was no more than a natural unnatural thing, for candle fires and ruins commonly mar the world. But surely, not every place would be destroyed. I wandered farther in the darkness, my hands outstretched for fear of my head striking a wall or pillar.

A breeze from the ocean tossed away the heavy odor of smoke, and I felt—not better, exactly, but more courageous. My reaching hands met an adzed log wall, not in ruins but plumb-straight and strong. Perhaps it was Goodman Seacomb's ordinary? Was that where I was? But I saw no signboard. Once Richard Seacomb had been fined fifty shillings for selling liquor to the Indians; my brother John told me, and said it was a rogue's trick to do so. My pulse slowed. I could have sobbed in relief to find a solid, made thing hidden in the night.

I felt my way forward to the entry and leaned against upright boards, feeling worn solidity against my hands and forehead.

But I would not knock or call or fling back the door, as I feared who might answer my greeting.

Instead, I would find the fort and take refuge. And after that, I would fetch Hortus. The captain would send soldiers to go with me and guard my passage.

The thought encouraged me. I pressed forward, passing another house and moving toward the sound of water—that would be the Casco River, washing against Broad Cove, across from Stanford's Point and Purpoduck.

Floundering over a deep cleft in the road, I slipped to my knees, losing hold of the scissors and groping until I found them splayed on packed earth.

And there! Close by, the cairn of stones piled by men who had cleared the land. The path upward to the cannons. The law declared that a fort meant a captain, a sergeant, a gunner, and ten privates. That was the rule of such places. And the presence of soldiers promised safety.

Yet I recalled my Uncle William saying that our captain, Sylvanus Davis, often complained of a perilous shortness of men.

Lifting my hem with both hands, I darted up the slope but soon found the way too crooked to navigate quickly. Perhaps the night made it seem so. Perhaps I had not found the right marker and the main path.

The stink of the place mixed with the smell of brine from the sea. Nausea made me squat, drag up my skirts, and breathe through the cloth. But to pause might mean danger. I pushed off from the earth and stood, swaying a little. On spitting the sour taste from my mouth, I felt stronger.

Two dogs darted past me, one dragging something in its mouth and the other one growling and snatching at whatever the first bore.

"Oh," I cried out.

Where are the lights of Fort Loyall?

In memory, pitch-dark and loneliness make up that walk. The sea rang in my ears, slamming against the stones below. Nothing for which I searched appeared, not even when I gained the very crest of the rocky bluff.

The palisade and the defensive towers were gone.

No part of the fort stood out against the stars. The refuge that we knew as Fort Loyall did not exist any longer. Emptiness yawned in its place. At once the need to find my way back to Hortus pressed on me. My breath came quick and shallow. Fumes of charcoal and something worse befouled the air. Stepping away, I stumbled over some scorched spars that must have been part of the stockade and landed heavily on my hip. The dropped scissors struck my knee—patting the dirt, I felt for scissors and knife and clutched them hard.

The wind changed, and an evil fetor wrapped me round. A moon-white mouser dashed at me and rubbed against my skirts. I shuddered at the ill omen: I had seen boys stone a white cat in Boston, the poor thing hissing and yowling and trying to slither away. Such creatures came as emissaries from the Evil One, or so people said. My father mocked such superstitions, but now I feared them and sprang up, not wanting one blue and one gold eye to bewitch me, as was rumored of white cats. Even with so little light, I could see that its glare flashed eye-shine into the darkness.

All I could think was to flee from that gleam; the panic made me lose my bearings and veer away wildly. A cloud slipped across the stars. Though I have never lost myself in a stone maze, I know that in a branching maze of wilderness, there can seem no exit. Race from one horror and you find out another, perhaps more fearful than the Minotaur imprisoned by Daedalus in his labyrinth.

A hill loomed above me.

Terrible vileness poured in waves from its sides. The sound of dripping came from somewhere close. By the faint light of stars, I could discern that the mound loomed wide, high, and irregular in form. I touched the surface and jerked back my hand, for its nature was fearfully perplexing to me.

I glimpsed a flash of candlelight and heard a man laugh and say in a jeering tone, "Vous avez justement ce que vous méritez." His companion answered in a low, angry voice, but I could not catch his words for the odd accent.

So one was French. French and ...

"Diantre," the first man said.

I listened hard and strained to see. The spit and crackle of a bonfire, just out of sight, might mean more soldiers. I caught names. *Baron de Castine. Sieur de Portneuf. Madocawando.* Nothing more. Little noises, a smear of moonlight on something lifted up: it seemed that one man halted to drink from a bottle and pass it to the other.

Wabanaki? Some Indian ally of the French.

Instinctively I pressed closer to the hill.

The first appeared to be a soldier, for the light revealed a metal breastplate. As he spun around, laughing at what seemed nothing more than the joke of his own drunkenness, the lantern he carried shone directly on my hiding place. Its shaky beams illuminated the flank of the slope.

The mound that protected me was monstrous, human, with hands and profiles and hair, spines and naked buttocks and breasts. Hellish spoil, the scene showed forth faces staring in what was surely agony, some decorated with the drill-marks of musket or pistol or fouled with gouts of blood from where hatchets had crashed to the bone. Raw, bloody caps showed where their enemies had yanked hair and scalp from the skull. Some of the bodies were dressed or partially so, but many had been sacked, stripped, men and women alike, by someone who craved a soldier's coat or a woman's gown. From what I could guess by the quavering light of the lantern, several hundred English soldiers and settlers were the murdered earth making up that ridge of flesh. Maybe my own neighbors, the faces and voices I knew well and had hoped to see, lay stilled among the others. A white flag flapped from the crest. What mockery to plant a banner pole in the rotting clay of the murdered!

As I pulled away from the bodies, dead fingers tapped against my shoulder. A thin sluice of vomit splattered on the ground before me, my gorge rising to spew so quickly that I had no warning.

The two men abruptly ceased talking, and the French soldier, the one with the lantern, snatched it high in the air.

Trembling, I pressed close to the dead once again.

The soldier took a step forward. My heart tried to skip away as I closed my eyes and leaned against naked flesh, pretending to be a corpse, though I was one who could dread the approach of swirling and brightening light seen through her eyelids. My hands tightened on the scissors and knife.

I wanted to shriek but did not. I was being a dead girl. I could not call or move, could not break stillness. My limbs were heavy ballast, and the sea-sound of blood surged at my ears. A foul ooze moistened my back. Smatterings from tales about the outrages of the French jostled together with images of ingenious Indian torture. My breath mingled with the reek of Falmouth corpses. But something in me was wild for life, my heart beating strongly and all of me like a taut bowstring. Unable to bear sightlessness, my eyes flashed open and witnessed the Frenchman striding forward, lantern dangling from his fist. He was two rods from me, one rod, ten feet, six feet—I quivered, sweating, the desire to flee washing me with heat.

The white cat flickered by me, arrowing toward him.

"Palsanguienne!" He jerked the lantern upward, the light dazzling my eyes so that it took me instants to realize that he was staring me in the face, his mouth agape.

The mouser tangled with the man's feet just as I jolted out of hiding with a howl that must have been composed of fear, sorrow, and rage. I hurtled at him with arms extended like a ghost from some ancient barrow of the dead, a shocking wraith who would knife him and gouge out his eyes with blades and spirit him into the wet core of that headland of flesh.

He let loose a great flaring scream and toppled over backward. The wick of his candle was at once extinguished. While he flailed about and cursed, I thrust off, springing at the dark in the direction of the path. The lantern clattered as if kicked, and two sets of footsteps thudded behind me, perhaps following, perhaps pounding another way, the fright sending Mercury-wings to their heels. Who knows? Too panicked to be able to make a proper judgment, I only fled the faster when a pistol fired.

At the risk of tumbling from the bluff into the waves or braining myself on the bole of a tree, I flung myself into the nothingness of night. All my fears of foe-men and dark and the sneaking witch-ways of white mousers—but she had saved me!—bundled together and shoved me forward. Rocks and uneven ground slapped at the soles of my feet. The moldered, vile-tasting air sawed in and out of my mouth.

A stitch in my side stalled my feet before I could do myself any great harm. I leaned over, panting, sobbing and gasping, the spittle drooling from my lips. Slowly I grew calmer and knelt on the ground, letting go of the knife and scissors. My fingers dug into the earth and eventually relaxed when I heard no further noise of men. Behind me, a pillar of fire surged up, and I knew that soon nothing would remain of the place called Casco or Falmouth.

Gunpowder and whiskey tossed on the bonfire, surely . . .

I rested in a blank state, emptied of fright and the will to stir, my gaze resting on the blaze that mounted, taking arms against the sky, as calmly as if I watched hearth-fire flare and snap. My thoughts drifted to the days that had sunk into the abyss of the unreachable past, when I lived in my father and mother's house with Mary and our young men, and with all my kin close by. The women might be gathered to sew by the fire in the evening—my mother, Aunt Rebecca, Aunt Mercy, Aunt Sarah, and Aunt Hannah, who looked like a child, her nose dusted with cinnamon freckles, though she was big with child herself. But by this hour, I would have been asleep in the trundle with Mary, the breathing of my family all around, the whole fortress of a house alive with breath of aunts and uncles and children. We slept well after our labors; we would have worked all day and been glad to laugh at one another in the silly moments that would never come again, and to listen to my father read from Scripture or pray aloud, his voice rising and falling, as regular as the waves of a peaceful sea.

Thy hand strews blessings. Thy power turns aside evil.

I could almost hear the words.

But not quite.

The very atoms of me wanted to spring apart over the Atlantic, there to slip as dew into some phosphorescent patch of ocean and be lost. How tired I was! My sore legs and back made me long to stop. Just to stop. I could have curled there in the damp May grasses and slept, breathing in the scent of smoke. But the rising flick, flick, flick of fear is a goad, and so instead I walked, counting my footsteps once more, moving steadily down the rutted path. Once I spun around in a frenzy, fearing that I could not find the broken tree, but the moon glided out from behind a cloud, and by that illumination and by starlight I went forward, away from fire and the villainous works of men, and at last put my arms around the strong, towered neck of Hortus, wept, and then left that place forever.

2

Wilderings

Late May 1690, Massachusetts Bay Colony

Because of Indian attack or ill judgment in the original siting, a house is occasionally dismantled and much of it taken away in fragments. First, the crown glass, fragile quarrels, or sheet glass panes are carefully removed and taken up and packed in sawdust or rags, and next the shutters and doors carried away, and any clapped-on boards pried up and the squared nails removed to use again. For many hours, the sense of a place for the life of family lingers, but bit by bit the house loses all sense and meaning until it is only a bedlam collection of unwanted or too-heavy remains, and perhaps only a tumble of logs or a massive central chimbley or a stepping stone before the absent door.

So it seemed with me when I flew from Falmouth. *I was dismantled. I was a house without walls where the mad winds play.*

What was left to me but the three-personed God and Hortus? Faith that the divine was always near comforted me; and yet, the fresh thought that God did not order and arrange every detail of our lives was both solace and terror. I had stepped outside the pale of my childhood's teachings into a world that was a fallen realm, invaded by evil. Any unexpected event could happen without notice, without time to call for mercy. I pondered the thief on the cross, so brazen and yet innocent in his request, and how Christ promised him the outrageous boon of paradise. And were not all my family more deserving of such a reward than a thief? I prayed for them. I prayed for myself. I prayed for any captives who were stumbling through the wilderness, feeding themselves on roots and hogweed and rotten acorns, lashed on by those who did not love them.

Hedge up my path lest I wander into camps of the wild men and the French who would ruinate me. Keep my lips far from tainted streams; direct my feet that I be not entangled in Satan's covert snares, nor stumble before the arrows of his followers. Spike the artillery of hell and the flintlocks of Frenchmen; defend me from tomahawks, from ill circumstance, and from myself. Restore my soul to peace, remember Mary and Mother and Father and John and Joseph and Isaac and all my family and lead them to a paradise of rest, and if any are now hostage, keep them safe within the circle of your almighty power. Save me from the tribes of forest and seashore, from the fathomless evil that Frenchmen do, and from the ills of my own nature that barnacle and fast-hold me. Let me think on Christ's mercy, and how lovely are his footsteps on the mountains and on the tops of waves.

My hope was to go south, perhaps to Salmon Falls, Kittery, Portsmouth, or Exeter as perhaps the nearest places, though they were merely names to me, and I did not know the way to any. Perhaps some no longer existed. Boston allured me as my former home, but it was farther, beyond Salem and Lynn, with probably more water to cross than I could manage. *Portsmouth* meant a town on the coast, perhaps on a tidal river. Any watercourses I might have to ford remained a mystery to me, and I wished that I had heeded my father more when he talked of the newer towns of the colony. Newbury and Rowley were somewhere farther south, perhaps below the Merrimack. Haverhill, if the place still existed, stood above the river—I could follow the coast and the Merrimack.

Surely it would be impossible to become entirely lost, hugging the Atlantic, and perhaps I would discover some smaller settlement clamped to the edge of the sea like a mussel to its rock. I would dare; I still had the dried fish to eat, an Indian jacket and a blanket against the cold, and a horse, though riding him had made me bruised and tender. Though it was too soon for mulberries or raspberries, I hoped there might be a handful of ripe strawberries in the meadows. About that, I was disappointed. Though doubting the current usefulness of spare clothes, stitching awl and needles, sampler, and doll, I determined to preserve what I had. For I owned nothing more. The scissors and knife would serve well, surely, and were my only harvesting tools and weapons. I did not have water for my clay bottle and needed to find some that did not taste of brine.

My journey southward resembled in small the sea-voyage accounts heard from those who sailed for three months on the ocean to the New World, an endlessness with one day much like another, interrupted by peculiar prodigies like Christly fish that could skip and fly on waves or whales breaching the surface, spraying a crown of diamonds and glory from their blowholes, or by sudden storms that slammed the ship to one side, then the other. On especially fair nights, the travelers might be permitted to come on deck to view the star meadows and bright-edged wisps and cloaks of cloud moving over the moon. Though the largest and most risky distance any of them had passed before, the voyage seemed to dissolve in the memory of travelers like a shaving of Barbados sugar dropped in a cup. For those brave far-farers, the undertaking might as well have been a single wondrously long day.

So was my journeying, each day mirroring the one prior, only with more or less water, more or fewer alarms, more coast or else more forest.

As soon as I left Falmouth and forged on, I lost all sense of where I was, as if wandering through a forest where no thing owned a name—for on home ground, all was known and named, the tufted place in the corn field where the plough never reached, the little hillock crowned with firs, the spinney of birches hung with curls of paper, the boulder that glittered with tiny isinglass windows that must be where infinitely small beings lived. A thousand landmarks stood all around us there, but the wilderness has no landmarks for the stranger. Perhaps it was but an untamed fancy, but at times I wondered if I had lost my name there, for I too was not known to any tree or stone or patch of earth. But I would speak to Hortus and know that the world still had names.

"Hortus, Hortus, do you know your name?"

Hortus would always give me a sign that he knew, swinging his head toward me or nickering or blowing a long, fluttering breath from his nostrils.

If Hortus was still Hortus, surely Charis was still Charis.

"My name is Charis," I told him, "and we will find our way to a town and learn all the names and—"

And what? No names can summon the dead. No names can stop this sense of reeling, tripping into an abyss where all that should be is . . . just not.

I stayed wildered in my mind, a weathercock at the mercy of changeable gusts, my thoughts rushing to Mary, unburied, to my family and whether any of them still lived, to the ox and cow that must have been driven away and perhaps killed. My fears flashed to the mountain of flesh in Falmouth and the lives snuffed out, and sped on to the Mi'kmaq and the French who would murder me if they could. That first night, I rode by sparse moonlight, pointing Hortus' head southward and letting him tread the sand or forest floor at his own pace, often lying against him and clinging to his neck out of weariness. For a horse is a great, feral-fragrant, seldom-sleeping beast, but a Charis must find sleep.

The journey to what became my final goal might have occupied only four days if I had been entirely fearless, owned such a precious rarity as a map, traveled by day, and had no rivers to ford. But I was not so courageous, however determined I was to do what I feared to do. My brothers had talked of the torments visited on settlers by the savage men of the woods, and sometimes repeated rumors of the cruelties of the French in urging them on. And the mound of murdered settlers loomed in my thoughts and cast a shadow. Had they held out and been killed, every last man, woman, and child? Or had they surrendered and been slaughtered despite a white flag and negotiation of terms? If that, what abomination!

From my hiding places, I watched a pouring, winged river of pigeons blot out the blue and clouds. Once an enormous gray heron, black-crowned and spectral, flapped from the tree where I had taken shelter, startling Hortus so that he shied and squealed and needed much coaxing before he would grow calm. (I slept not far from him, though I was wary, afraid that he would step on me.) Gulls screamed out unrest; they stabbed at my dreams. I regretted paying so little attention to the names of hawks and songbirds and sea fowl. Gathered like threads, their myriad lines of flight made only a nameless tangle in memory; yet is it strange that I felt an ache at the beauty of winged creatures, and a sense of being somehow mysteriously more than I was in earlier times? For loveliness mingles uncannily with grief and desolation.

Often I sought the sea's edge and let Hortus plod on damp sand or earth. The ocean breeze tossed away the insects that sought to mine my flesh when I rode through the forest, for I could not sprout a whipping, fluttering spill of horsehair to fan them away. Moonlight made the whitecaps gleam and threw a moving smear of pallor on sand studded with shells and rocks that the waves had bowled to shore. How strong and muscled the ocean is, that it can dredge up heavy stones and pitch them along the beach for sport and pleasure! And I, sore and chafed, was not like the sea, all rhythmic force and endurance.

As the dusk settled and we ventured out from the trees where Hortus had been hobbled with strips torn and knotted from Mary's shift, it often seemed to me that he and I wandered in what the ancient Romans named a *locus amoenus*, a pleasant place. Here were the desired grasses and trees and water. And the wild world was often more lovely than I had been told. Yet this was no delightful Edenpark, these no enchanting grounds with pools and water dripping over stones. If a garden, this land must be a treacherous one, ever close to roaring shoals. It was a boundlessness that looked at and measured me.

Only once did I encounter others face-to-face in the forest.

We had sallied forth at twilight, and Hortus was ambling along a dim trail in the woods when we came on Indians in single file, the foremost wearing a headdress with a horn extending from it as if he were some man-unicorn and, perhaps because he was leader, holding a staff. A long row of others padded behind him.

A flash of startlement cut through me. Though Hortus stopped, rocking his head and showing the whites of his eyes when he twisted his neck to look at me, and though I held still, my pulse set off like a pheasant in a burst of scuttle and flight.

Absurdly, awkwardly, as though I had come on some dear friend in the civil streets of Boston, I cried out, "How now? What cheer?"

The man-unicorn roared, "How now? What cheer?" and the others laughed and took up the shout, echoing, "What cheer, what cheer, what cheer," until the blue dusk of the woods rang with noise.

The shadow figures vanished at a crook in the path, although I could still make out the occasional "How now?" or "What cheer?" and a rumble of what might have been laughter.

Trembling, I lay against Hortus and let myself sob once but no more.

"Pater," I whispered, wishing hard that I could be a little child, safe on a bench by the chimbley, and near to my strong father.

Why did I not master my dread and dare to ask them the way to a town? How strange it was! They might have wrested the horse from me but did not. They might have brained me with a tomahawk, tugged scalp from bone, and catapulted my soul into death. Laughter, though, could not injure or kill me.

Sometimes when I made my hiding place at dawn, near a stream with mist rising off the surface and the spring flowers chilly under trees, the ancients' vision of the underworld drifted into my mind— phantoms wandering the meadows of asphodel, unable to collect together the wisps of thought and speak without first drinking blood. That the biting insects sought my life made it seem even more so.

The water near the coast often proved briny and no good for replenishing my bottle. Thirst for fresh water began to shape my journey, for Hortus needed water even more than I did. I had no idea how many creeks and wider floods lay between me and any possible destination. Nor did I wish to leave the shore. But frequently I moved inland on the hunt for sweet water, and in that way I managed to miss, as it later proved, a few settlements entirely. Nor did I ever discover a ferry to help me across any watercourse, though I was grateful for deadfalls when they bridged a stream and often crossed alone, leaving Hortus to pick out a separate way. Once I came upon the abandoned foundation of a few houses and a log road to nowhere, packed and made smooth but deep in fallen twigs, needles, and leaves. More often I stumbled on the abandoned fields and tattered remains of Indian villages with bones and long-haired skulls left unburied, the residue of the pestilence that had swept along the coast not long before our colony was born, carrying off Wampanoag, Abenaki, and other tribes whose names I did not know. Yet I found no haven of an English house, no settlement of any kind. The world is so very large, and a horse and a maiden are tiny.

When I woke at sunset, insects buzzed near my head or crawled near my eyes. Once I found a pearly dodman climbing my hose, leaving a silvery track of his own slime.

"Measure me for a shroud, would you?" I flicked him away into the scrub and wiped my stocking with leaves.

Deer roamed the woods, appearing and disappearing with ghost-like ease that I envied. Once I saw a scattering of gigantic creatures like deer, some of them standing in a rushing creek, others moving ponderously into the forest. In a sunlit meadow I glimpsed the patriarch of the herd, his head crowned with new spring antlers.

Searching for a nest for the day, I smelled the rank, heavy scent of bear and heard a crashing noise nearby but only once spied bears in the open. They were eating a late supper of grubs or shoots, maybe, and did not pay heed to us, though Hortus minded them, bolting into the cover of trees while I hung onto his mane.

"Go easy," I shouted at him, "easy!" but a horse can never take bears for granted.

Another time at twilight, a bobcat bounced with a rocking motion across the ground in front of us, as quick and weightless-looking as a moving shadow. Hortus stopped, planting his legs against such magics, but the beast vanished into the air.

Far more frightening images visited me in sleep. I dreamed of a giant hand with long, curved nails that pinched the flame from wicks of soft, melting candles and dropped them into a high, slovenly mound. Mary stirred in our green bower, reaching for me and calling to me reproachfully, "Charis, Charis, why did you leave me with the dodmen and angleworms? Help me up!" I would jerk and start from sleep, my pulse flittering, tears on my face. Sometimes I dreamed that I was back in our house near Falmouth or else in Boston, hunting for Mother, and that a clock was striking somewhere in a distant room. As I followed the sound through a maze of dark chambers, it grew louder until I realized that tomahawks knocked against the door. Waking, I would seek for Hortus and lay my hands on his back, taking comfort from the mighty bridge of his spine and his steadiness of breath.

Hast thou given the horse strength? Hast thou clothed his neck with thunder?

It is much to be a mortal woman and alive, walking though the realm where ground and heaven meet. But it is much also to be a horse, "swifter than the leopards" and "more fierce than the wolves in the evening."

Without Hortus, I must have died in the wilderness, for it was he who ferried me over wide waters, and even across a terrible fast-running river like none I had seen before—one I could not ford in the night. I found a crossing place where the channel narrowed, and a ledge of stone extended into the water. That day I stayed awake, hunkered beside the flow, watching for the tide to turn and drain the salt sea back to where it belonged. And though I observed the billows rising and ebbing for a long time and tested the irregular, stony bottom in the shallows with a stave, I was not ready for cross-currents that ripped us sideways down the bed of the river when the ground beneath hooves dropped away. Hortus sank low, screamed his anger once, and lurched upward, swimming strongly against the muscular shove of water. Once, twice he leaped up like a locust with a loud noise and wings of water whirling from his sides. Never had the seal-skin felt so slippery and uncertain a seat. I forgot every other trouble. I forgot the raw burning of my limbs. I forgot loss and family. I forgot the sight of the dead heaped like firewood. The skirts of my gown dragged, and I knew that if I tumbled in, my layers of cloth would weigh me down like petticoats of stone. I seized hold of Hortus' neck and mane, lying close against him.

And I called aloud to God and horse alike. "Christ, have mercy! Hortus, swim, swim hard for land, fleet as a leopard!"

At the farther shore, Hortus shouldered from the waves and stood shuddering with his legs quivering in the rock-bottomed shallows. I could not unclench my hands and slumped against him, shaken by memory of the river and by the horse's trembling. Slowly his legs quieted. He moved onto the edge of land and stood with head cocked as if listening to the tap-tap-tap of water dripping from his body onto stone. When I slid from his side, I collapsed onto the rocks, lying with my arms out and skirts spread in the sun. A glouse of heat did me good, and I did not stir for a long time, though the sow-pigs crawled from the cracks in the stone and came trundling to investigate the drenching I had given their houses.

"Little old-sows," I whispered.

All that I possessed was soaked, and what was left of the Mi'kmaq's shards of fish had been eaten by the waves, along with the moccasins and birchbark box. The last of the sugared almonds were food for the fishes. Hortus nosed me, mumbling at my arms, and I laughed for the first time since the burning of our house, surprised to find myself pleased to be alive. Satisfied, he walked off and began lipping at some weeds growing among boulders.

Unexpectedly, tears coursed down my face.

Warm and damp, drifting in and out of a drowse, I was gathered into a dream or something more. A smolder of light on the spring sky divided, flickered, and sparked; it seemed to me that three figures danced on a tightrope, tossing a blue and green ball between them. They wove and leaped on the line so that I could not tell one from another. What I knew was that they were full of joy, and the glory of it filled me up, as if I were a little holy house that could be bright within, and maybe even float up and meet them in the air. I stared, held by their playfulness. Only slowly did they vanish into the brightening sun, taking their joy and frolic and love for one another away from me. Though I watched the sky, they had passed through some secret door and were not to be seen again.

A bishybarnybee lit on my hand, as if to bring me some color and cheer. I admired her nine spots on a coat like blood.

"Go you on—fly away and fetch me better luck," I told her, but she only crawled from finger to finger, tickling my skin.

So I sang a verse to her in a weak, rickety manner, for that was all I could do.

Ladybird, ladybird, fly away home,
Samuel lies under the grindlestone.

Your house is on fire, your children will burn,
And Hannah goes hiding beneath the churn.

Ladybird, ladybird, mind the bishopman,
Your Liz is a-creeping in the porridge pan.

Bloody Bones Bonner is on your doorsill
To snatch and to catch and to burn little Will.

That was not much of a nursery song but the best I could manage. The creature perched on my fingernail, twiddling her front legs. Her red martyr-wings and the secret bronze ones beneath flashed, and she was away.

"Good fortune to me," I murmured, reaching up to pat Hortus, who had come to see why I lay so still and now leaned down his head to blow warm breath on my cheek.

"You are the godly, neighing wonder-horse in Job that swallowed the ground as he galloped in fierceness and rage," I told him. "And that power has saved us both."

Soaked and chilled, I fell asleep on the stones and dreamed that I sailed in a ship with Hortus, who stood tall by the mast, his mane ruffled by the breeze. When I woke, I picked violet leaves and flowers to eat and was content. Wearied by the waves, Hortus drowsed, his lids shuttered and lips drooping.

Weeks later, poring over a map, I found that we must have slipped downward between the settlement at Salmon Falls and Portsmouth in the hunt for fresh water. And perhaps we forded the Piscataqua far inland, a hard-enough labor even at slack tide, before passing west of what they call the Great Bay in a land of many streams and smaller rivers. So Hortus and I wandered southward, wading the spring growth and the waters, until we came to the Merrimack and a road over wet ground built of logs, adzed flat and held secure by wedges, leading into a hard-packed cart path that wound on through wilderness.

3

Haven

June 1690, Haverhill

I dare say that my wayward peregrinations could have gone on for more days, but when I came upon a rough-ribbed road at dawn, and met laborers uprooting stumps and preparing new ground for planting, my journey found its end. The youngest of them led Hortus by the bridle—after a few balky moments when my horse laid back his ears and showed the whites of his eyes—to a fine dwelling-house nearby, stealing looks at me with some wonderment. I was quite the wild-woman spectacle with my filthy and torn garments, Indian-style seat, and scratched and mosquito-bitten arms, and neither bonnet or hat but only a wreck of braid tumbled from the coif that dangled down my back. He seemed no more than fifteen, boasting a mighty thatch of straw-colored hair, a great flaming push on his neck, and such a look of innocence about the eyes that I suspected he might be daft.

People at the house were not slow to come and greet me, being as curious as the boy who showed the way. He bowed to them, mumbling, "Your Honors," at the ground in a bashful manner when one of them spoke. A fine-looking couple of middling age were trailed by a young woman bearing a child around a year old or thereabouts in her arms and an older woman dressed in an undyed linen gown and neck kerchief, who I took to be a servant.

The master, geared for labor in leather breeches and Kendal green waistcoat (Major Saltonstall, as I soon learned he was called), strode forward and lifted me from Hortus, calling out, "Lud, see to the horse." He carried me into a parlor and set me down in front of a big central chimbley, where there was a pleasant summer fire burning. The walls were white with clam-shell lime, and the bare floors had been scoured and sprinkled with fine sand. And that short passage was a fine thing, as it seemed I was a babe in arms again and had forgotten how to walk, now that I no longer needed to rely on my feet. They quivered like the legs of Hortus after he swam the Piscataqua.

"How now, what has happened to you—what is your name, child, and where have you come from?"

My eyes glazed over with tears as I named my father and mother and told him how I had come on Hortus from near to Falmouth.

73

"I once met your father—a staunch friend, I believe, of Mr. Samuel Sewall."

Mistress Saltonstall brought me a glass of hippocras as a restorative, and when she saw that my hands shook, she knelt beside the settle and helped me, tipping the glass.

"Better," she said, and pressed her hand to my cheek.

The color and flavor of wine, the taste of ginger and nutmeg and clove, the shine of glass: they touched me, made me want to weep for the beauty of made, human things. I heard the speech around me like the echoing ring of struck crystal, the questions humming on the air. To my ears, my own voice seemed equally chiming and otherworldly.

It sounded high, a little cracked in tone, the voice of someone who had gone beside me and knew my losses and trials but who was not quite me.

"Sir, the Indians raided us in the morning. My mother bade me climb down the tree at the rear of the house with my sister Mary and go to our meeting place and bide until—but they never came to get us, and when I went back—"

"And now perhaps you fear being the mistress of your family, all that is left. Do not trouble yourself with overmuch of talk," Major Saltonstall said. "You will have to tell us everything that you remember, later, so that I can write Governor Bradstreet and some others, to inform them of your story and to see what can be done."

My fingers trembled, and I pressed my hands together on my breast.

"At Falmouth," I began, guessing that I should tell the worst.

"Casco Bay," the major said. "I was there once with sixty soldiers. A most precarious settlement."

Mistress Saltonstall held the glass for me again. I rested my hand on hers as I drank, my head tilted up so that the tears wet my temples and wandered back into my knotted hair.

I shut my eyes, remembering the lantern swinging in the Falmouth dark.

"Children and women and men. Butchered," I said. "Hundreds of them, a midden of flesh, a mountain. The fort destroyed."

In the silence that followed, the others stared at me.

"Oh," the young woman cried out suddenly, "monstrous!"

"Murderous acts fomented by New France," Major Saltonstall said, resting a hand on her arm. "The French are so small in number compared to our people that they incite the tribes to devilish crimes against us."

"God, have mercy! So dreadful," she said.

"Indeed, I wondered," Major Saltonstall said, "to see that Major Church was returned with his troops to Boston from Falmouth after the struggle with the French and Indians last year. It seemed meet and right to me that he stay to protect the English awhile longer. And this the event sadly proves."

"Nabby," Mistress Saltonstall said to the woman in the doorway, not taking her eyes from mine, "make haste and bring me a bowl of bread and milk. And what of your sister," she added, though it did not sound like a question.

"I left her in the forest. In our hiding place. She fell from my back and struck her head when we were fleeing. And later died in the night." I recalled the glaze that soaked her hair, and the inexplicable bruising behind her ear and on her throat.

"So I am at fault, I fear."

"You endured the perils of flight, and that is often when mischance occurs. Though our every act matters, we cannot foretell what comes to us," Major Saltonstall said.

"I should have cared for her better," I said softly.

"Do not reproach yourself," he said. "It is a hard thing for any of us to navigate a wilderness without paths. Many have come to grief there."

"Be of good comfort and know that you are safe now," Mistress Saltonstall added.

She had lifted my right hand, inspecting the weals left by insects, lashes from twigs, and black crescent moons under my jagged fingernails. Now she turned to regard her husband. "The poor young woman is weary and should sleep soon, though I would like to have the grime of the journey scrubbed away," she said, "and we must take good care that she be not chilled. She must be kept warm."

"Yes," he said. "Such labors I leave to you, madam; I shall write letters to the governor and General Court. Though I do not find it much avail if soldiers visit once mischief is done to us. Still, so many burials demand our attention."

One of the men from the fields appeared with my few chattels in his arms and said that my horse had been watered and was being rubbed down. After bidding him to lay the bundle on the floor,

Major Saltonstall excused himself, and the two left the parlor. I must have been worried about my goods because I felt glad to see that they had not been cast aside, filthy from travel as they were. Nabby came in with a bowl of milk and bread sweetened with dried blueberries, which I ate with as much pleasure and thanksgiving as if it had been marchpane and a rich bride cake stuffed with almonds and citron and currants, Mistress Saltonstall feeding me with a spoon as if I were a baby.

"Eliza, will you ask Nabby to bring the kettle of water on the kitchen fire to the westerly bedchamber, with a piece of lye soap for the young mistress' hair? Have her put more on to heat. And could you bring a shift from my chest, with some of the linen scrubbing strips as well? I do not see how we can avoid the hazard of bathing."

The young woman, who I suspected must be her daughter, nodded and disappeared from the chamber, taking the sleeping child with her.

Though I felt stronger, they still treated me as if I were as helpless as the babe in arms. Upstairs, the mother and daughter washed the sand and soil from my hair with their own hands and brought me water scented with mint for soaking the rest of me, Nabby fetching a little more warm water before the whole process was ended, for despite my dunkings in streams, I was powerfully dirty and stank of horse and fish.

Dressed in clean linen and tucked into the bed with covers to my chin, women's voices murmuring around me as they wiped the floor near the washing bowl, I felt wholly warm and safe, drifting with the tide of sleep. And for weariness, I slept all that day and the ensuing night and only woke to the smell of wood smoke and the sound of voices when the sun searched me out the following morning.

The Saltonstalls were there, peeping in at the door when I opened my eyes. I looked around at the white walls and the sun flooding in.

"Is this Haverhill?"

Mistress Saltonstall laughed in surprise and came forward.

"Yes, the very same," the major said from the doorway, "bought almost a half-century ago from Passaconnaway, Chief of the Pennacooks and great sachem of all the Merrimack Valley tribes. We are a little ways east of the village."

"Good," I said. "I am glad and grateful to be here."

"And we to have you here," Mistress Saltonstall said, smiling down at me.

Perhaps it is strange that I slept so well that night, for certainly I had somehow lost my ability to sleep soundly and be renewed on the day that my family was torn from me. In later nights, I was so troubled with evening dreams that Mistress Saltonstall took to bidding me to go to bed early. It seems she would sit up in my bedchamber, and often held my hand if I wept in my sleep, or else stroked my forehead until I wandered past nightmares and into an easy slumber. She had me placed alone in case of some contagion, but I was not ill, despite my days and nights exposed to the wilderness and dark. At least, I was not *unwell* in any common sense of that word. It was strange to have no bed-mates. Even once I proved healthy, I still lay alone in my bed, for I proved no quiet slumberer. In the early morning, while still dark, Elizabeth Saltonstall or sometimes the husband and wife together would come to my bedchamber again and sit vigil, for in those hours I was restless and disturbed in my sleep.

Certain images came back to me, and others cropped up fresh, as if I had some secret window for news into past events. And while many of the godly have put great credit in dreams as telling us something we did not know, and which might be whispered to us through word or image in the night, Major Saltonstall advised me that a mind roiled by the sights of such a massacre and wild adventure was a mind untethered, and that I should pay no heed to my dreaming hours once awake, with the vision dissolved into motes. Looking back, I think this assurance a proof of considerable wisdom in him, though it went against what I had often been told about the matter of dreams.

Many times I awoke with a terrible cry trembling in my throat, only to find the pair of them seated with a candle burning in between. Startled from their own low conversation, the couple sometimes looked as affrighted as if a bold, murderous fiend had just appeared at the door. Mistress Saltonstall would rise and wipe my forehead with a damp cloth, soothing me the way a mother soothes a little child with words that flowed over me like water. What kindness it was in her to see me first through the evening's rough shoals until I sank deeper and could sleep without disturbance, and later to come to my bedchamber in the early morning dark and see me safely to the shores of wakefulness.

Since Eliza had a child to tend, she was often up in the night. The black ribbons on her arm told me why Eliza Dennison was home again, a mother returned to be a daughter, with her own griefs to master. Though only now and again at the house, Nabby was afraid of my outcries, which she described in comical fashion as "a whoop in her stroop." While Mistress Saltonstall did sometimes wish to hire other women servants to assist in the kitchen in times of need, little help was available in such a raw frontier town.

Most often I dreamed of Mary. Sometimes it was only a voice. "Charis, Charis—"

The name murmured in the dark of sleep would start me from the depths and set me to dreaming.

Sometimes I was back in our room of leaves with Mary leaning toward me with her hand outstretched. I felt an intense horror that she would touch me. Because she was neither living nor dead but in some tomland in between, I could not bear to look at her and yet could not swerve away, as is sometimes the manner in a dream. Her flesh was changed to be like death, but spirit still animated her limbs and face. When her hand brushed against my shoulder, I would cry out to be saved, and someone always came. I shall never forget that mercy.

Whenever I woke, it seemed as if the elements around me changed and my body plunged abruptly into cold, so that I shivered under the bed-coverings. I do not know; perhaps it was from seeing such strange images. Perhaps it was simply that I often floated close to the door of death in sleep and found it hard to return to the regions of the living.

Once I dreamed of my brother Joseph, bending to half-hide the red thread on the forest floor. I was so glad to see his face, the blue, blue eyes under the thicket of hair, the straight nose, and the little scar shaped like a sickle on his cheekbone.

"How do you fare, sister? Come on," he said to me. "You're late—everyone else has gone home."

He moved so quickly through the trees that I could not keep up, though I cried out to him. "Joseph, Joseph, wait for me! I don't know the way."

I could hear him laughing and calling to me, but he would not bide. I followed the red thread deeper into the woods, and at last saw that it was no longer yarn but a free-flowing vein of blood, winding around the leaves and bubbling into the distance.

"Brother! Joseph!" I listened but there was nothing, and I woke to see Elizabeth Saltonstall's face, bending over mine.

"Charis," she said, "Charis," calling me by my first name in a high, sweet tone.

"I can be more," I whispered, "be stronger."

"What do you mean? What are you saying?"

"I do not know," I said, and fell asleep again. And if she had not told me of our words later, I would never have known them.

At times I dreamed of the Mi'kmaq, and in those dreams he stirred and raised himself and was turning toward me. Fright flashed along my spine; I opened my mouth to shriek. But I never saw his face, always waking before I could glimpse his expression—strange that I felt so curious to know how he would look on me, whether with anger or sorrow or scorn.

Other times I roved through our house near Falmouth, everything tidy and a fire burning on the hearth. My voice echoed like the sound of a clapper striking bell-metal.

"Mother, Father—Isaac, John, Joseph! Onesimus! Blue Jonas!" I called for Mary and her playmate, cousin Tom. I reeled off the names of aunts and uncles and cousins, the long list of those who had sheltered in the house on that last day, but no one answered. Once I heard the sharp noise of boot heels on steps, but no one was there when I ran to the stairs. I hurried from hall to parlor to bedchambers, calling, and when I woke mumbling their names, I found that tears had drenched my face and pillow.

Mistress Saltonstall showed compassion to me, more than my wayward sleep behavior deserved, I fear. On my third morning in the place, I slept late after restless dreams and rose to find my mother's blanket stretched out and drying in the sunshine. She spent a deal of time mending the snags in the cloth with her own hands, and I can still picture her with the indigo blue draped over her lap, working with a little hook to even out the surface until it was restored to much of its former appearance. Likewise, she caused my sampler to be cleaned and set across a paneled chest that stood at the foot of the bed. Mary's unfinished doll and the scissors and knife were placed close beside, so that I could always see a few remains of the past.

In the day, life became practical, and I could laugh with the women as we sewed or took turnabout to dandle and play with Eliza's boy, fourteen months old and merry and in the thick of whatever went on around him. *Eliza.* She was friendly to me, as I could expect from meeting such kindness in her mother. Eliza was my elder and by rights should have been Mistress Dennison to me, but she bade me treat her as a sister. I liked best that she told me stories about Governor Dudley's family and Mistress Anne Dudley Bradstreet, the poet, for her late husband's grandmother was Mistress Bradstreet's sister. We women often sat together, sewing companionably. Mistress Saltonstall was determined that I should have garments suited to my station in life, though I had been cast out of my place and felt uncertain where and what it should be, now that my father and mother and all the signs of worldly rank were lost.

My green gown was nearly past mending, but Nabby repaired it as best she could, cutting away the tattered, stained hem and adding a brick-red band around the foot of the skirt and a matching band that covered a rip in the bodice. Until then, I wore my violet gown and the coif with white leaves, for I had nothing else.

Mistress Saltonstall set us to work cutting down gowns, shifts, and petticoats that had belonged to a young woman who had no longer any use for them, having been felled by typhus some years before while on a journey westward. Evidently she possessed letters of safe conduct signed by the governor and a magistrate but little more in the way of an introduction—she must have been a bold, enterprising person to set off journeying with strangers. No one lives lone among the godly, so she would have been placed with a family. But she never reached her far destination of Westfield. Having no known will and no living relations in the New World, she left no worldly goods to anyone, and the clothes remained in the place where the unfortunate traveler had died.

"You could see that she was a lively sort of young woman, even as she fell into sickness," Mistress Saltonstall told me. "She came to us by accident, out of need, when I was still a young woman. The constable brought her to our doorstep because she had newly arrived and had yet to notify and be confirmed by the courts. She did not mean to stay long. But she was unwell and never left, poor thing. I can still see her flushed face as she rattled off the oath of fidelity. My husband paid a bond to admit her to the town, for it was evident she could not yet go on to Westfield."

"A coppet young lady," Nabby said.

"Coppet," I repeated.

"Oh, she was a saucy one, full of humor and good spirits. But soon she was taken down. And though I nursed her as if she were my own sister, she sickened so fast that she seemed almost to run toward the burying ground."

The waistcoats of the dead traveler went to a Haverhill tailor for renovation. Soon I was the possessor of a silk gown of dull blue, a close-fitting gold-yellow jacket to accompany a sadd-colored wool skirt of *feuillemorte*, along with an indigo skirt and light-colored jacket of pale muted rose, a color that would never have been useful to me near Falmouth, and a wealth of hose (both knitted and sewn cloth), wool petticoats, chemises, and coifs. I even owned a white Flemish lace whisk with velvet knots (old-fashioned but lovely) to wear with my new blue gown, as well as cambric falling bands. For out-of-doors, there were a few simple bonnets to wear over a coif and a felt hat for colder weather. When Eliza presented me with the poor deceased young woman's cloak, a camlet of grain scarlet on one side and russet camlet on the other, along with a black silk hood, I felt as fine as some prosperous English tradesman's wife who sits by the shop door to vaunt her duds and so lure in the customers.

"You have made me as rich to the eye as I was poor."

It seemed that I should never be done thanking Mistress Saltonstall.

"The sumptuary laws are not what they were, with their rulings against fallals—ruffs and wide, slashed sleeves and immodest hair," she said. "I feel sure she would have been taken to court for the silk hood and the blue gown with gold threads in the warp, our towns-people having a strong spirit of interference. But the garments will probably pass now, though I would take care not to flaunt them."

"You are too generous to me," I said. "You are like the linden tree that grows out of the mother's grave in the German story and speaks through a bird and the blowing leaves, and tosses down dresses like the moon and stars and sun."

"I don't know that tale," she said.

"Goody Waters told it to me, back in Boston. Her mother's people escaped to Germany and lived as exiles there for many years. And I suppose one of them had a love for the stranger fancies of the Germans and handed them downward. So Goody Waters learned curious stories from her grandmother, and she passed them to me. I never heard the like of them anywhere."

"Her mother's family must have had many adventures," Mistress Saltonstall said. "The godly have been well traveled, then and later. I do not envy our people who sailed to Ireland or the Rhineland or the West Indies. But perhaps they would not envy us either. What happened in the story?"

"The girl's mother died, and the father married a cruel widow-woman with two daughters no better than she. But a white bird and the linden tree on her mother's grave helped her. She wore a dress that glowed like the moon, and a prince fell in love in raptures over her just as soon as he saw her. Then she wore a gown that glittered like stars. And next, a gown yellow and shining like the sun. And she marries the prince. There was more to it, but I cannot conjure it now."

"Well, you have your three sets of duds, at least," Mistress Salton-stall said, "though there is a great dearth of princes in New England."

I thanked her again.

"You will do," she said. "There are some shoes to try, and you must plait a summer hat. And aprons must be sewn, but you will pass muster."

Mistress Saltonstall gave me a copy of Mr. Herbert's *The Temple* as well, when she learned that I loved poetry and would treasure it, and a little memorandum book with poems by Mistress Bradstreet copied out in gall ink.

When I protested at their generosity, the Saltonstalls told me that a collection was being taken up in town, and that I would have coins of my own, but that they were glad to restore me to my rightful rank in the world. In truth, that feat was an impossible one to perform, and yet they were concerned that I still be welcome among others of the same background as my family.

Major Saltonstall ordered a small paneled coffer to be made for me, and eventually my old and new worldly wealth was placed inside. He was considerate of me in another manner, writing letters to friends in Boston and on the General Court with news of the massacre in Falmouth, as well as information as precise as I could give about the location of our house and the little green room. Word came that Major Church, who had defended the fort the year before, would be sent to bury the dead and examine the inland site where our houses stood. To send a description was the best Major Saltonstall and I could do for Mary, although perhaps I would never know if she was buried aright.

The major also wrote to find out if any of my kin still lived, per-haps taken for ransom to Quebec, but no news came to give me encouragement. The list of known names—Clark, Baker, Morrill, Ross, Brackett, Denis, Alexander, Swarton, Cary, Yorke, Souter—never held mine.

"Do not give over hope," Major Saltonstall told me. "Letters are slow, and queries must be investigated. All such inquiries take more time than we would like."

In the day, I was able to visit Hortus, pace the grounds in sunny weather, and work in company with the women of the house. Little John Dennison staggered about, leaving damp handprints on my skirts and making us laugh with his few words. Peeping into a Hebrew text, I found myself longing for fresh exploration. I discovered grammars in the family library and made a review of my Latin studies and wrote down what I could remember of a Greek poem my father had taught me. I pored over a commonplace book made by some Saltonstall ancestor, its pages decorated with vivid drawings in colored ink and crowded with poems and passages.

When I was alone, the faces of my kin came to me and made the tears prick at my eyes. What else could I do but pray that some lived, or that I would meet them again under the trees of paradise? They seemed to grow hazy in features, so that I could not call them to memory as cleanly as before. I made some little sketches of all my family, with notes on the color of hair and eyes and features. My thought was that someday I could have them painted as miniatures and keep them with me in that way. But I was a poor-enough limner.

I sank so easily into the routines of the place, spending my days sewing for myself or for Eliza's little one, playing with the child or trying to teach him a new word, setting the board for meals, joining the family for readings and prayers at morning and evening, or for lighter moments—telling riddles or reciting psalms and poems as we worked. Almost, it seemed a betrayal of my sufferings. At times, I felt a sudden need to be solitary and think on what had happened, to fling all my grief upward in a single, silent word: to resolve my mind in favor of goodness and in favor of life before I returned to the others.

Always, the hall and parlor were hubs of activity. Often the dining board overflowed with people come to help with planting or visitors arrived to consult Major Saltonstall about militia business and important town or colony matters.

"How did we ever do without you?" Mistress Saltonstall was ever thoughtful, always bent on making me feel that I had a role in the family. She asked me to teach embroidery stitches to a sent-out child who had come to learn knitting and sewing and improve her manners among strangers. Sending out was not much practiced in my own family once we moved from Boston, and I pitied Damaris Hathorne when she arrived in tears with her stern-looking father and a box of clothes.

Damaris looked on me with some astonishment after Eliza told her my story, and said that she repented of weeping, for she would join her mother again in less than a year, but I could never do so.

"It cannot be the same, but she has a new place here," Mistress Saltonstall told her.

When he was twelve, my brother Isaac lived with Dr. John Clarke because of weakness following a bloody flux, and there he learned a good deal about medicine that was helpful to us. But otherwise, we had not been put out, and I was glad of that, especially now. We had been together as much as was possible.

At Haverhill, I was always aware of the need to make myself useful so that I would not be a burden on the Saltonstalls. They were important people in the town and colony. Mistress Saltonstall was a Ward, daughter of the Haverhill minister and granddaughter of Mr. Nathaniel Ward, who wrote the colony's code of laws in the *Body of Liberties*, and that fierce, thunderous book, *The Simple Cobbler of Aggawam in America*. The major descended from nobility and held various magistratical authorities and was even a member of the Court of Assistants for the colony. He led the Northern Essex militias of musketeers and pikemen. Between local courts and the General Court and being clerk of the writs, he was ever worrying over business high and low—sometimes on his doorstep, as when the wastrel Swan boys busied themselves with roguery, twisting off the tails of cattle, stabbing a neighbor's horse with a half-pike, or ripping up rows of young fruit trees.

The kindness the Saltonstalls showed me was always in my thoughts. For what was I now but an orphan of good birth but no inheritance save a horse and some land that men would now fear to settle?

Thus, not being sent-out but homeless, I was conscious of my uneasy position in the world. Occasionally a sense of my own worthlessness would come over me. If a woman had no place, she floated in chaos: I was unmoored, a little boat that drifted on endless seas.

I also was troubled by the sense of some hardness of spirit in hours when I forgot my grief and loss. This trial I kept to myself, just as—at other times—I kept my sorrow locked in the stronghold of my heart, my silence fortified and upheld by my childhood's long schooling in patience and the bending of my will.

A couplet would slyly creep into my mind: *To find if woman owns a soul / Requires a lens and puissant thole.* Then I would be glad that I was one of the godly, who were literate and admitted that those of the female sex possessed a soul. And I knew that as the women of the house worked together—often one read from the Bible, the poems of Anne Bradstreet, or some homemade family florilegium—they showed me in all their kindness how soul-deep their sympathies ran.

I set myself to making perfumes when I saw that the family had none in hand, and busied myself with juniper, balsam, steeped gum dragon, clove water, and musk. My relief from memory and my pleasure lay all in talk or else in being occupied and so dwelling less on what had happened. When I pounded the ingredients into a submissive, sweet-smelling paste, I was also defeating something in me that wanted to revolt and cry out. As I rolled the paste into beads and pressed them between pairs of fresh-picked rose leaves, I became calm and almost content. I heaped them, baked to dryness, in baskets at each Dutch-tiled hearth, ready to be tossed onto a fire.

My old life and my kin kept traveling steadily into the past as the spring gave place to summer, the old landscapes and features blurring until I feared to lose them entirely. I pored over my drawings and made more notes on faces—John's flush along the throat and cheekbones when shamed, Isaac's whorl of cowlicks, Joseph's freckled nose, my mother's long, narrow brows like the wings of swifts—to bring them back to mind, but it was like trying to catch silt in a sieve. Still, I sketched our house near Falmouth, and everything I could conjure of our fine place in Boston.

At the end of high summer, when the goldenrod and asters bloom, a new chance came my way. Though content where I remained, I recalled daily that I had lost every means of succor and abided in the charity of others, however glad they were to provide for and keep me. Because of them, I now had a store of clothes and some coins from the town collection. And I had the golden, godly reputation of my mother and father that would be a key to unlock new friendships,

I hoped, and might find me a settled place if I returned to Boston or journeyed elsewhere.

A few lines in a letter from Pastor Dane of Andover to the major, which he read aloud by the fire, made me ponder a change.

"Goody Rachel Holt is desirous of obtaining a fine-work seamstress for some three months, should you know any persons able and willing to spend so much time with her. She will board the woman and pay handsomely—in coin, mind—and has the cloth and needful wares in hand. I believe it is to equip her daughters with goods and clothes in preparation for married life. The Holts are a numerous family here, but Goody Holt is a widow unrelated by blood to other so-named families in this place; I do not know exactly what sort of taskmaster she might be but expect a strict one."

Major Saltonstall continued on to the end of the letter, but I could not listen. Was this a call for me to travel elsewhere? I would not be ashamed to work for another, though selling the labor of my hands was something that never would have occurred to me if my life had not altered.

The next day, as we were sitting on a bench in the sunshine, I broached the idea of laboring for this Goody Holt.

"Surely you should stay here," Mistress Saltonstall urged me. "Your mother would be grieved to think that you were in such a post. You are no servant to labor for wages."

"But I would like to be useful, and have no other way of putting together coins for my future."

"We know nothing of this woman," Mistress Saltonstall said.

"I don't like you to go," Damaris said.

"Nor I," Eliza Dennison added.

I knelt down and hugged John, who babbled at me and left a smear of damp on my gown, a token of his affection.

"It's not so very different from a daughter being sent out to another family to learn," I said, looking up. "That happens often enough. And she does not pay by corn measure, as most do."

Mistress Saltonstall laid aside her sewing and continued.

"Someday you will marry, Charis," she said. "And we can help you to find someone of your own background who will suit you in education and manners."

My gaze rested on John, who kept on clutching at my skirts. I wondered. Before we moved north, my younger uncles had married.

Aunt Mercy's father had given extensive lands and a house as a wedding gift, all of which was sold before we moved. My aunts brought good dowries to their husbands. Perhaps any gold and silver had melted with our house. Perhaps the French were making free with those spoils.

"But I have nothing to bring to a marriage."

"We can be a help. All will be well." Mistress Saltonstall laid a hand on my arm and leaned forward, looking into my eyes. "And you have your own fine self to bring, Charis."

"Yes. I thank you." I sat down again, lugging John onto my lap. His warmth soothed me, and the sweet smell of his scalp through the silky hair. Indeed, I was content with the Saltonstalls.

Yet I kept on considering whether such work might not be gain for me, and in the end I persuaded them to let me go to Goody Holt for three months. Major Saltonstall knew a man in Andover who could stable Hortus and rent him out to some of those—most—who had no horse, and so I might also be making a few pence there as well, over and above the cost of his board and a proper saddle. At the end of the period, Hortus and I would return to the Saltonstalls' seat, and they would consider further what was to be done with me.

4

The Frampled Household

Andover, early September 1690

From where I stood in the entry, my back to the door, I could hear Goody Holt. I listened closely, thinking that I could still fly to the stables for Hortus and ride back to the Saltonstalls. Though I did not know where my travel companions had gone, I could depend on myself. Didn't I know how to brave the forest? And there were several ferries and a cleared road from Andover to Haverhill.

"I am not well satisfied, Mehitabel," she was saying. "Indeed, I am not. You went out in this slatternly way, and when you met him, you simply scuttled off like an unruly child. You did a disservice to me in doing so—"

Here she must have been interrupted by the woman who had answered the door, a cowed-looking servant in wash-faded blue gown and a much-mended coif, though when she smiled, her face found its way to warmth. She had not spoken in answer to my words except to acknowledge my thanks and "Good health to you."

"Sammodithee," she said, and left to announce my arrival.

Now I heard Goody Holt complain at high pitch how someone had left unfinished the polishing of silver candlesticks and a two-handled bowl. She must have invested much pride in them, for she mentioned their value, the name of the maker, Jeremiah Summer, and the precise date when she had purchased them in Boston.

I mastered the impulse to drag my coffer out the door and bolt to the stables, and only stood a little taller in my new leather shoes, a parting gift from Eliza and Damaris.

When my mistress opened the hall-chamber door and came forward, I again felt frightened and found myself drawing a hand over my heart. How strange to be alarmed in the safety of rooms with English people! But all I knew of Goody Holt was that she owned this house, that she had been married to a prosperous tanner, and that she was speaking in a manner I did not admire.

Her face was severely marked by years, with great parentheses on either side of her mouth and wrinkling under the eyes. I did not reckon her to be more than forty-seven or thereabouts. Under the coif, threads of white blazed through her otherwise dark hair.

She strode through the front room and paused in the doorway to look down at me. To my surprise, she gave me not the least courtesy of a greeting.

"You have no look of a servant, child." She frowned.

"No, I am not a servant," I said with all the firmness and gravity that I could muster. "Nor am I a child any longer."

I handed her my sampler and the letter from Major Saltonstall. She read it, her lips pursed.

"I am sorry for your losses," Goody Holt said at last, though she did not sound at all regretful. "But this is a strange way of finding a seamstress. And a servant who comes from a fine family and knows languages is nonsensical. Like sending cavaliers in feathered hats to muck out a public stables."

As if somewhat pleased with her own cleverness, she nodded and brought my sampler closer to her eyes. I was emboldened to explain.

"Goody Holt, I simply wished to part from my friends awhile in order to earn something rightfully my own, now that my family's wealth is—"

She raised her chin, and my voice faltered.

"Please address me as *Mistress* Holt," she pronounced slowly.

I was silent, startled by her manner.

Do not be angry, I told myself. *Anger is a runaway horse, and I will tame and rein in and ride that shadowy beast. I will be strong, for surely I am a young woman with some abilities, some knowledge, and some memories of those worthy to be called by the title of* Mistress.

She looked me over, starting with the coif and running her eyes over the camlet cloak that hung loosely at my back, for the day was not so cold that I needed wrapping. Her eyes studied my waistcoat, the hat and bonnet in my hand, and the *feuillemorte* gown. At last they found the way to my feet.

"I do not care for philly mort," she said.

Pinching a corner of my sampler between thumb and forefinger, she extended it toward me.

"You are a deal too fine for a seamstress," she said. "If you have something more suitable to your current station, I should prefer that you wear that."

Perhaps I should not have been surprised, but I was. A flush— hated ink of roses, ink of wine—tingled on my face.

"I do not believe," I said, "that I have changed station in life. My ancestral kin are still who and what they were. My education is still what my father gave me in remembrance that Lazarus' sister was found worthy to study at the feet of Jesus! For are we not acceptable as actors in the great drama of salvation? If you have no wish for my abilities with the needle, I can return to Haverhill."

And I will be more, I thought, remembering the words murmured to Mistress Saltonstall when I swam up from sleep.

I should like to say that my voice did not tremble with a note of anger by the close of that speech, but I fear that it did.

Goody Holt was still holding the sampler as if it were a length of befouled linen. I took it.

The tanner's widow daunted my assurance, not entirely but enough that I stepped back, pressing against the door. But I remembered what I had done, riding alone through the wilderness and crossing stream and river; I stepped forward again.

"That word *drama* smells of the theatre." Goody Holt smiled; the change in expression did not soften the look of the harsh lines carved beside her mouth.

"It was not meant so," I said, and thought privately that Goody Holt's world would contain little in the way of revels of any sort. There would likely be no riddles and no poems here. She ignored my reply.

"I will recompense you by the week," she said. "This letter says that you are uneasy in your slumbers and cry out. I will have your bed carried up to the garret so that you are separated from me and my daughters. We cannot have our sleep jarred and jangled. There is a hearth. You should be warm enough."

Not knowing what to say, I gave a little half-curtsey. She was my elder and, at least for now, had the upper place.

She did not return my politeness but stood frowning, her eyes on the letter.

Finally she turned away, calling for someone named John, and vanished into the gloom at the rear of the hall. In only a few minutes, a narrow bedstead, a woolen mattress sewn up in a canvas tick, tow sheets, and a rollipoke of chaff for a pillow were bundled up the stairs and installed in the garret. I followed the sound, taking with me my sack with Mother's blanket and some of my goods. Goody Holt—*Mistress* Holt—was standing over the rope bed and mattress, supervising John and the woman who had answered the door as they tugged at the sheeting and coverlet. The bedclothes were poor and coarse enough, so I was glad that I had brought a better covering of my own.

She spoke, her back to me. "We have already had our meal, but Bess may find you some scrapes and leavings."

Some scrapes and leavings. I did not have presence of mind to respond, but Bess gave me a little smile that said she knew how I felt. She was prettier than I had thought before, with more of a spark of warmth. No doubt life with Goodwife Holt could make anyone look subdued and wan, I reflected.

"Pray pardon me." Her whisper as she passed close by told me she was more mannerly than her mistress.

"After that, I will show you where you may carry out your sewing duties. You will find plenty of linen and silks and wools from England." Goody Holt gave me a nod and ordered the other two out of the chamber.

I say *chamber*, but it was no chamber. The bed was set close to a chimbley hole without mantel, the floor wanted sweeping, and above me were rafters, thatch, and a few bright winks of late afternoon sky.

In a few minutes, John was back with my coffer, which he set down carefully and gave an admiring pat. His blue eyes took in the scene of me on the edge of the bed, the crude hearth, and the bag. John seemed cheerful, perhaps in spite of the dour face of his mistress. He was not a handsome-featured man but strong and well made, and he still owned all his hair, though I guessed him to be past forty.

"Good luck to you in this house, Mistress," he said to me, giving me a smile. "We are glad to meet you, yet sorry you are stowed in such a place. I would not like to see a daughter of mine in such straits, and I can see with my own eyes that you are used to better."

He looked more keen or at least happier than poor Bess, and I thought that he might be able to advise me.

"It's just for three months," I said. "My family—they are all killed by Indians in the northern wilderness—and I thought it would be right to earn a wage and not be so dependent."

"I am sorry to hear that piece of news," he said, tilting his head and looking at me with what I thought was pity. I felt glad to see his sympathy because it meant that he might be a help to me.

"Is she a good mistress?" I whispered, though there was no need—who would have bothered to climb those narrow, crooked steps to spy on me?

Still, he went over to the door and glanced down the stairs, and came back to me, crouching on his heels.

"She will pay you well enough, for that is part of her view of herself as a great lady. And do not mind her manner, which is often crabbed and choleric. 'Tis just her disorderly humors, and she cannot help her way, I have come to see." He shook his head slowly. "The mistress is not the most godly of women, but she has her virtues."

"And you are content here?"

John shrugged.

"The old man supplied my passage, but he is dead, and I have yet 337 days and some hours to go until my indenture is up. People say that Goody Holt insisted that she, too, must have a servant, and so it was that I met Bess on board the ship to Boston. We will be her first and last servants, I imagine. I jog along with her well enough, and on the day when we are done, Bess and I shall marry. We have talked to a few of the selectmen about the old tann-house, or else a parcel of land east of the meetinghouse where we may live and have a shop and workrooms, please God."

"You have a trade?"

"I learned the tanning trade from Goodman Holt, who learned from his father, who had been a tanner in England before he sailed to Massachusetts Bay and was given land of his own. Goodman Holt was not a strutting man, and not too proud to get his hands dirty in the work. Most think it a filthy job, I suppose, but he never minded. And he was never called *Mr.* Holt, and she was always *Goody* Holt. Now she wants to forget the trade and the tann-house and purchase herself more dignities. She sold the tann-house and land when her husband had not been dead a month. There's naught but hay there now."

He put one knee down to the floor to steady himself.

"She seems so high-handed and angry," I said in a low voice, and immediately regretted the words.

"My Bess says that Goody Rachel Holt has forgotten that she abides in the New World, where such things as titles matter less than in the Old. Not that there aren't well-born families and some who are but tradesmen and even a few unfortunates who need help, but there are mighty few fancy lords and ladies here. No offense to you, mistress, for I can see that you come from good stock and are not accustomed to bedding down in a garret."

"Yes," I said, "but how much can being from a well-regarded family matter in a wilderness? It didn't keep my kin from destruction."

He nodded. "We are far from England, where I went to a bit of school and learned to bow to my betters. Many a family in Andover sups with its day-laborers—for who are they but neighbors, to be helped out in turn?—but not the lady madam of this house. Keep up her dignity, and she will be composed enough."

Keep up her dignity. I wondered if that meant losing my own. I reflected that the Saltonstalls were fine people, and yet they often depended on bartering corn for work and the hiring of the occasional laborer like Lud or Nabby, although they held lands in Ipswich and Chebacco that were stewarded by others. And whenever militia men were quartered at the house, Mistress Saltonstall cooked their meals herself.

"Her business in this portion of her life is to marry off her daughters. She has not said so, but I have eyes. She is anxious that they be wed, and tied to something better than a tanner. That is, if she can manage it. Mehitabel Holt is the younger, and can be as shy as a fawn around strangers. The eldest Holt daughter, the one who resembles her mother, is called Lizzie."

Mehitabel Holt. Lizzie Holt. Would they be friendly to me? Did it signify?

"And what should Bess and I call you?"

"What? Oh, I hardly know who I am now." *A servant? The child of a fine family? No one?*

"I expect you are a young woman who has prospects and a future," John said.

"My name is Charis."

I gave my first name only, as if but a poor servant, and I suspect now that I gave it so in bitterness of heart. But he proved more gracious than I was at that moment.

"Oh, that's a beauty name, mistress," John said, "a sweet name. Your father and mother gave you something there."

A voice called for John. He jumped up, bowed to me, and was away.

But he turned back, leaning into the room.

"Mistress Charis, I will fetch you wood for a fire, and a floor-cloth and something to sit on, whatever she will let me have. Some rushlights and a holder. But Bess will broom down the cobwebs and sweep and wet the boards against the spar-dust."

Hearing a shout, he withdrew abruptly with a hasty "by your leave" before I could thank him and clattered down the stairs once more, leaving me in the lonely domain of the garret.

Soon afterward, Goodman Foster paid me a formal visit in the hall-chamber downstairs, for it was his job as constable to report newcomers to the magistrate. He was not a grave-looking man, but his brass-tipped staff, the sign of his office, had somehow a funereal air and made me feel subdued and weary. He asked me a few questions and told me to repeat the pledge required of all new inhabitants.

The words I had to say were almost the same that I had recited before Goodman Sterling, the constable of Haverhill, while still keeping to my bed, for Mistress Saltonstall declared that I was not strong enough to rise and journey into town. Now Goodman Foster offered me a book, pointing to a place and asking me to read the words.

"I acknowledge myself subject to the laws of this jurisdiction of Andover in Essex during my residence under this government, and do here swear by the great name of the everliving God, and engage myself to be true ... "

I paused here, wondering what it meant—had I not been true before, that I needed to pledge so again?

Goodman Foster lifted an eyebrow but said only, "Go you on."

"And faithful to the same, and not to plot or continue or conceal anything that is to the hurt or detriment thereof."

"You read well," he said.

"My mother taught me," I said, not so much to inform him of what he would already assume, but to tell myself that she had been, that she had cared for me to learn and read.

He had me sign a page in his record book and wrote his name below: *pledge witnessed Ephraim Foster Constable of Andover*. Evidently the Saltonstalls had secured my entry into Haverhill by the payment of a bond meant "to secure the town from charge," and this promise had now been transferred by letter to Dudley Bradstreet, Magistrate of Andover. I had not realized their kindness in this matter and now had yet another reason to feel gratitude to them. This further evidence of my dependence unsettled me and made me long to return to such friends.

That night I slept more uneasily than ever, in the bottom of the night going to sit by the coals after being wakened by a noise like the firing of a musket. Such dreams or warnings had happened before; my head knew that no shot had been fired when I woke, my heart springing in my chest as if to pelt away, back to Haverhill. I could not sleep, astir over whether I should leave or remain. The dust, swept by Bess, seemed to have left its delicate sigil on the air. My throat was raw from breathing in the particles that had floated up from the broom. Eventually the upset in my mind grew quieter, and I sat thoughtlessly by the fire a long time before stumbling back to bed and wrapping myself in my mother's blanket. I dropped to sleep remembering that her fingers had spun every thread. That seemed a way of touching and greeting her, and as if she were near.

In the morning I began my work, ruling over a small kingdom with goods and table and the unexpected luxury of a backstool with a feather cushion—though to Goodwife Holt I remained of no account.

It was well for her that the colony's sumptuary laws against luxury had softened, for I found waiting for me glossy lustring silks, ribbed grosgrain ribbons, taffeta ribbons, cotton calico, fine linen cambric, gauzy tiffany for hoods, cloth with satin-woven stripes, and pink and cream fabrics of mixed linen and silk.

The stitcher in me took an intense pleasure in exploring such fabrics. I peered inside thick packages with fulled wool for cloaks that could be left unhemmed without fear of raveling. I discovered lengths made from spiral yarn, the wool and silk twisted together into one thread, the cloth more subtle than wool, more substantial than silk. Most surprisingly, skeins of silver and gold—the fragile metals wrapped around cores of silk yarn—lay among a jumble of thread, some spooled, some lying in loose hanks. I handled them in considerable wonderment.

How can she afford such lavishness?

Here was treasure, far more than I had expected to find and certainly more rich than any tanner's wife could expect to own. Surely Goody Holt was daring the ministers to condemn her for dressing her daughters above their station with such brave metals and silks.

"I want butted seams on wool, no plain ones," came a voice.

Turning, I found one of the subjects for my needle. She resembled her mother, her dark hair spilling from a coif that did little to soften the appearance of a long face, a more juvenile version of the crescent marks around her mother's mouth, and skin that must have been assaulted by smallpox in some long-ago hour, for it was sadly pock-fretten.

She was, I dare say, a pitiable sight, and it was not much of a prologue to our acquaintance.

Still, I rose and nodded to her.

"Good morrow. You are, I suppose, the daughter called Lizzie Holt, the elder sister?"

This attempt did not remind Lizzie of her manners. Her face seemed to harden a little like a west-country flommery cooling and setting up in a bowl. Perhaps I had offended by calling her *elder*. I guessed her to be twenty-five or a bit more.

"You may call me *Mistress*," she said.

I smiled in surprise at this juncture, which was a little wrong of me and clearly a misstep, though she had no rights to the title—less than her own mother. Among us, *Mistress* and *Mister* were uncommon for those without birth and a better than ordinary education. My visitor showed her choler by flushing to the roots of her hair. She stamped her foot like a willful child. Unfortunately, the heel of one of her waxed leather mules came off when she did, so that she was forced to bend and rescue the errant heel and stand, one foot on tiptoe, glaring at me.

Ignoring what made me want to smile, I glanced away at the heaps of materials, my lips curling up in spite of my good efforts.

"What exquisite cloth your mother has ordered," I said. "I will be happy to make you a gown or whatever you like."

She did not respond but turned and left the doorway with heel in hand and an odd, hitching gait as she moved away.

Tempted to flare into laughter, I pressed a hand over my mouth. I did not want an enemy in this house. Surely my stay would not last a week if I could make no one here endure me save the servants.

Startled, I realized that someone was watching me, for an eye and bit of hair and coif was visible near the door jamb.

The eye stared at me and withdrew.

I gazed at the empty air. What strange thing would happen next?

The eye and bit of coif and hair reappeared, and the rest of the body followed. Where Lizzie Holt was tall, this one was short and shaped like a pudding tied up in linen cloth and boiled, with her cheeks speckled by pushes like bits of pink beef marrow and her eyes dented in, as if two dried plums had been forced into pastry. But unlike Lizzie, this young woman beamed at me. She had a beautiful smile, all sun and cherub's bow, that seemed to wake up her whole face and make it attractive.

"Pay no matter of mind to Lizzie Holt," she said. "She is all dolor and doom and thunderclouds because Mother and Father had her sent out to Boston to learn manners and stitchery when she was sixteen, and instead she learned about the pox. And she has never, never gotten over it. Losing her looks, I mean. She managed not to die and to get over the pox ten years back. They sent her home when she was well but before she could acquire any better manners among strangers. Possibly the strangers could not bear the ones she had already."

I surveyed her, not quite smiling because I was not sure whether she was joking or serious. Surely that was a singular, strange way to speak of a sister, and a little alarming.

"I am Mehitabel Holt," she said. "And nobody minds me at all. My mother hates that I take after my father's mother, so she mostly ignores me. Except to plot against my choices, that is. And to scold me and Lizzie. She is determined to marry us off."

This candor amused me, and I thought that in Mehitabel Holt I might just find a friend, or at least someone who was not eager to condemn me.

"And you, what are you determined to do?"

"Mother says we were evidently predestinated by the Lord to be just the sort of irksome, provoking persons who would be trials to her constitution and give her fits," Mehitabel said. "Me, I want to stay in Andover and have nothing much happen to me. Too much happens to people in this life. I want to be jolly—'tis very hard to be jolly in this house—and have seven children who have good health and good spirits. And a merry husband, too," she added. "Preferably someone who will think I am wondrous fair and will let me rule the kitchen without arguing with me, and who will be lively in bed but kind."

I laughed out loud at this closure. "Well, that is a great deal to want, but I hope you find your sweet-tempered husband and your seven healthy children and your innocent and peaceable life where no bad things come to pass."

Mehitabel fussed with her apron, twisting it in her hands. "Mother also says I am too careless about my words. I did not mean to offend. She told me what happened to your family, and I am very sorry. We have family in Newbury, and I would hate to think that they were murdered and gone."

I had not intended to refer to my own situation, but Mehitabel assumed that I did. She plunked herself down on the floorboards and hugged her knees. "Most of them, anyway," she added softly.

As if unconnected to me, my hands found a grosgrain ribbon and pulled it back and forth through my fingers. "Oh, I am not—I am not at all offended. I was not contemplating such things. In the late evening when I have no work to do, my mind runs on them, and at night I dream of the dead. But in the day it is otherwise."

Mehitabel looked at me uneasily. "Why do you suppose such events are allowed to happen? They are so ghastly."

I crossed my arms, suddenly cool beside the slightly raised window, and leaned forward. "The French plot against us. They draw the tribes to them, give them old matchlocks and pleasing toys, make them promises, and talk against us. We give them alien sicknesses. And we possess many of the Indian hunting grounds now. I expect they cannot love us, even when we pay them fairly—but that I do not think we do. Or so my father said, and I have come to believe he was right."

Mehitabel gave a little twitch of the shoulders. "All too late now, isn't it? We cannot go back. We can only go forward. And they are savage in their ways."

"The world is what it is, and we are each what we are," I said. "And we English are so numerous here already." Again I remembered the young Wabanaki man in the huckleberry bushes, a Mi'kmaq intent on murder, yet who like us had a family and some place where he belonged.

"But God let the Indians kill your people," Mehitabel said. She looked up at me with an expression I had come to recognize, her sympathy blended with fear.

"I do not think so. He is with us always, in all times and all places, but I do not believe my family was destined to be killed. The colony government chose not to defend Falmouth properly. More, human hearts are willful and wayward and can be as angry as fire. The tribes are moved by passion and unrest, just as sometimes we are."

My words surprised me. I had voiced my secret thinking to someone barely met, who had plunged into my life without so much as a how-do-you-fare. And I remembered the bright figures I had seen in the sky, the shapes that in my daydreams seemed a joyous glimpse of a three-personed God who did not will our harm. I fancied them as spilling over with gaiety and love as they frisked around a mercy seat of cloud. I imagined that they sorrowed for me as they danced, though they knew some secret that I could not know and so rejoiced.

"You sound ancient," Mehitabel said, "but you are years younger than I am." Elbow on knee, hand on chin, she contemplated me, and there was neither appraisal nor condemnation in that gaze.

"I grew older in a wink," I said, putting down the ribbon. "Death and I have been companions ever since. He seeks me in my dreams. He courts me with his black designs. But I am glad to see the faces of those I loved. They come to me also, and I know them and call them by name. The nights are awful and yet a strange comfort."

Mehitabel stared at me. Tears collected in her eyes, and a droplet dashed down her cheek.

Life is trial; is the path of suffering; is the measure and test of us. So I concluded, meditating on the glistening rivulet of that tear.

I clapped my hands together. "They are gone where I cannot find them or follow, but you are here, and I am here, and life is to be journeyed through to the end. Someday beyond my days, I hope to see them again, face-to-face. So why not be as merry as you wish, when we may have leave to do so?"

At that, she gave me another smile and, after putting one steadying hand to the floor, sprang to her feet so lightly that she might have been a birdlet. It made me smile in turn, and I thought that perhaps we had each found a friend.

"You could call me Bel."

"Bel," I said, "a pretty nick off your name. And I like it better than Hetty or Tabby, which I have also heard as shorter names for Mehitabel. I will call you so, and thank you for the favor."

The summer days were gone, and there was not so much strength of light for sewing as might have been desired. Goodwife Holt was constantly put upon by her desire to continue the work of stitchery on one hand, and the need to purchase better candles on the other. Being dissatisfied with the light from her store of tallow candles, she laid in several bundles of beeswax candles, though she complained mightily and with vigor on a daily basis, as if she thought I might squander the light if I did not continuously recall her dislike and fear of waste. But she had spent too much coin on imported cloth to risk losing her investment.

In the end, she decided that I must do the main part of my labor in the day, with tallow candles as needed and meals brought to my room by Bess or John, but that in the evening I could use the precious beeswax candles in order to prepare the work for the morrow.

That included the fitting of garments onto my two subjects, a process that was, not surprisingly, perilous when it came to Lizzie Holt, who was as likely to become hornet-angry as to be pleased, and amusing with Bel, who treated the matter of her mother's desire to hunt down a fine marriage and the making of new clothes for the purpose of luring a husband into an open game bag as a kind of continuing pleasantry and jest. As she said, with a droll look my way, "Goody Holt and I have very different views of what constitutes an agreeable husband." Bel was a help to me, sitting close by to trim the candle wick, and often putting seams in the garments, though I am afraid that I took entirely too much amusement in her verbal thrusts against her mother. And while I knew her words were not proper, I found a certain satisfaction in them.

I was glad not to endure the stinking of tallow candles as I stitched in the evening hours, and the work was not unpleasant. My only consistent break was on the Sabbath when we walked to the meetinghouse for services and so spent much of the day separated from signs of toil, hunching in the cold to listen to the young pastor who preached so much of Satan, hell-fire, and sin, or else the elder one, who sometimes rambled but never failed to dwell on the beauty of Christ's love and mercy. I liked him the better for it, as I had had enough of flames and hell right here on earth and wanted to receive and give mercy as best I could. When I spoke to the young minister between services, after a long diatribe on the subject of "woman, a desirable calamity"—his exposition made livelier by much gaping, whispering, and laughing, a volley of walnuts from the galleries, and the accidental stabbing of a small child by a careless whittler—he already knew something of my story and appeared to judge that my kin had deserved their fate, for had they not been disposed as the divine mind wished? And had I not spent far too much solitary time in the wilderness, Satan's dancing ground? "For when a woman thinks alone, she needs must think evil," he said, and cautioned me to bow to Goody Holt's guidance.

"Sir, I did not choose either to be or to think alone," I told him, and he admitted that it was so.

But the elder man took my hand and held it a long time and told me that I would be glad to see lost faces again in paradise, and that when the worlds were dissolved at the end of time and re-made, we would be full of joy and together forever. The old one made the tears rise up against me and betray my feelings, but the young pastor made me burn with coals of his own heaping.

Goodwife Holt—yes, I called her *Mistress* when I could not avoid speaking her name, but I shall not here, for she did not merit the title—resigned herself with many grumbles to having me installed near her, though she again objected to the quality of my clothes. Earlier she had indicated that I must find my place with Bess, as the seating committee had failed to mandate where I must be. But when one of Pastor Dane's daughters invited me to sit in the pew for the minister's family, Goodwife Holt interrupted to order that I be seated with Bel and Lizzie. I already knew her well enough to feel that she meant no kindness by it; she could not endure for me to appear so much higher than her own family.

At meeting, I encountered a great many people who had already learned my name but whose names I could not remember, and once a face swam up in the gloom that seemed familiar to me; he looked straight at me, his brow a little contracted as though pondering whether he knew me or not. It was a handsome face, straight-nosed and light-eyed, with well-shaped brows that seemed inclined to join in the middle, but though the image hung in my mind for some minutes, I could not conclude where or whether I had seen his features before and at last concluded that I must have seen, when a child in Boston, many faces now scattered to newer towns.

"Sss!" When Lizzie hissed at me, I was recalled to myself—to where I sat, staring like a goose.

Bel gave me a crooked smile as I flushed and looked away.

I gathered my cloak around me and focused again on the hot brimstone of the young pastor, but his words did not please me. Moving restlessly in my seat, I closed my eyes and remembered the flight from Falmouth, and how I rode high in the air on the back of Hortus. I was as free as any Wampanoag boy roving the wilderness. And the wilds and darkness under trees had been alarming at first but sheltered me on my way. I had found neither dragon nor Satan in the shadows, only the sometimes ill company of my thoughts. Birds I had found, and eels, fish, deer ... My back tired in the hours of meetinghouse sitting, and I often wished to tramp about the little town, mucky as it often was, and perhaps stretch my legs and skip about a nearby field when no one was watching.

And so on the Sabbath I visited Hortus (if he was to be found in the barn and not away on a journey), combing and petting and

talking to him for an hour. *My Hortus*. He heard my complaints of
Goody Holt with the best creaturely composure, even when, as
often happened, I had nothing sweet to tell. He even endured the
vast Roman waterworks of my tears for everyone I had loved and
lost that came on me unexpectedly in my first week, so violent
and harsh and convulsive that it was like a storm blown in from the
north. And perhaps it was just that, a sea of tears bearing the wreck
of wishes, gusting in from the ocean-scoured cliffs at Falmouth.
I am sure Hortus wondered why we did not wander away into
the forest and leave these muddy streets and dreary dun-colored or
silvery-gray houses.

By the second week, I felt confident that I could manage my
months in Andover. I had Bel Holt for company, though she could
be melancholic at times and was weary of her mother's ambitions and
plots. I often talked with Bess when she brought me a meal, for the
mistress did not want my company at the table. Nor could she bear
for me to honor Bess and John with my presence. How different
from life with the Saltonstalls, who seemed much less concerned with
rank and station when it came to feeding the hungry! I found the
contrast curious. When Bess or John came to my garret with aired
linens or an armload of wood, we would chatter in friendly style. But
I never grew to care for either Goodwife Holt or the elder daughter,
feeling them to be sour, dolorous women who disliked me and were
so lacking in courtesy as to be unashamed to show their scorn.

The sewing was good for me. Often I was alone, the room abso-
lutely silent save for the sound of floss whispering through the weave
of cloth. To me, it was the murmuring of grief, the small low cry
that seemed to needle straight through my soul—that tangled net of
glistening, stirring filaments.

I took to waxing the thread with beeswax from a candle, and the
sound of the thread changed, became firmer. If the house was busy,
the voices of the Holts and Bess and John diminished as I moved with
the rhythms of stitchery, a steady and forward gliding that seemed
itself a kind of meditation pulling my thoughts into peacefulness.
The deadliness of always doing, the thought of the impermanence
of everything I could make and achieve, came to me like an anxious
piece of news and fell away again—my mind like a peaceful meetinghouse after the people have come and gone and nothing is left
of the mortal frenzy of uncertainty about salvation, prayers beating
against the windows, hurry, and business. And though I stitched my

way through gowns and shifts, coifs and bonnets and petticoats, yet I sometimes felt an emptiness of thought that seemed sacred and sweet.

In certain hours, I felt more alive than before, and that surprised me because I was more lonely than in Haverhill. But the sewing room was my refuge, my sanctum, my place to front the dark and light facts of my life. Like the outlandish dwarf who could spin straw into gold in one of Goody Waters' German tales, I was spinning my worthless angers and moments of bitterness into a stronger and more precious thread. The chill September sunshine was pale in the open window, and only a few insects droned a song in the air.

The third week began, and I was nearly a quarter of the way through my time in Andover and nearer the date of return to the Saltonstalls, whose welcome and goodness to me seemed more rare as each day passed. Even though the barn was not close to the Holt house, I made sure to keep visiting Hortus, who gave me the balm of love out of his great animal heart. I aspired to his strength and calm, and thought him more than any horse in all the colony or perhaps the world. He was my treasure, and I was disappointed whenever he was absent.

Goodwife Holt often attempted to treat me as a sort of catch-all servant and wished me to tote her basket when she went to buy a cone of sugar or jug of molasses, or to fetch home some of the greenish glass that had arrived in a load of goods from Boston. I only half minded because it was pleasant to escape from the house more often than the one midday walk allotted to me, and surely I was younger and more vigorous than she. Goodwife Holt always insisted that her daughters accompany her, and that I lag behind them with the basket like some poor drudge. But I did not please her by my passed-on finery. More, it was an annoyance and grief to her that I was often waylaid by the town elders and others who had seen or met me at the meetinghouse. They wanted to wish me well, for everyone in town seemed to know my orphan state. Many knew the reputation of my family, and a few had met some now-lost aunt or uncle of mine and wished to share a recollection. People sympathized with my situation and often whispered a message of comfort, often with a glance first at the mistress who ruled my days.

One day Goody Holt asked me to attend her to the goldsmith's shop, and she ordered her daughters to put on fresh attire.

"What do you do to yourself, Mehitabel?" Her voice was severe. "You have slopped milk onto your bodice and not cleaned it. Put on the dark crimson gown and tie the sleeves with yellow ribbons, and in haste!"

Bel widened her eyes as she passed me, and I bent my head to hide a smile. Goody Holt had chosen that fine, delicate fabric, but Bel declared that she looked like a quaking custard in the gown. And though my own workmanship, I admitted that the dress did not flatter her shape, though the color went well with her chestnut hair.

"And you, Lizzie, fetch your tiffany hood. Hard features need some delicacy around them."

Lizzie Holt frowned, more than ever resembling her mother. She was dressed in an indigo gown. I wanted to put her in pale colors, lighten up her clouds and thunderbolts of scorn a little. Lizzie would have looked better in what I was wearing—the handed-down rose jacket—but I was not allowed to choose what looked best on the daughters.

Bess held the door for us, smiling at me as I skimmed over the threshold, the market basket on my arm. I expect she was glad to be alone with John, the two of them hurrying through their labors and talking over their future together and perhaps stealing a forbidden embrace in the shadowy house.

Our shoes clattered and scuffed along boards until we came to a dropping-off point. There it was work to tiptoe through the half-hardened mud, accompanied by many exclamations of disgust from Goodwife Holt.

Mehitabel winked at me and whispered, "You will be surprised when you find who—"

"What?" I had been wondering if there would be a fire for the smithing of metals, and if I could warm myself when the others were busy displaying their finery to the goldsmith. "What are you saying?"

"The one at meeting who—"

"I do not have a relish for the senseless babbling of young women," Goody Holt interrupted.

At the goldsmith's house, she ordered me to tarry while the three of them stepped inside. She gripped a large silver spoon in her hand like a bad scepter, the bowl malshapen. I stood with the basket in the cool breeze, looking across the way at bare houses and a field of beggary edged with goldenrod and asters. Then I turned and examined the goldsmith's shop, admiring a window with glazed panes. He had arranged shelves against the glass, and on each were pieces of wrought silver. Even through the thick glass, I could make out a spoon, a wine cup, a spout cup, one lidded and one unlidded porringer, beakers, tongs, a pepper box, a sugar box, and a tiny octagonal teapot. The shapes seemed bold and strong, with bands and molded rims and gadrooning for decoration. I wondered if he found few buyers for gold work in the New World, and if he had been apprenticed in Boston, and whether he could make much of a living in the wilds of Massachusetts. Surely every family that could afford such artistry would buy fine plates, in part as investment and in part to pass down to their children. But it was likely that the people in such a wilderness would only buy the occasional article of silver.

A slender metal sign hung by the door: *Iothan Herrick, Smith in Silver and Gold. All manner of Silver Work Vessels, as pepper boxes, flagons, cavale cups, beakers, mugs, canns, tankards, &c. Chafing dishes and such larger pieces upon request. Harnesses, hilts for swords, buckles, buttons, and all other kind of GOLDSMITH work. Engraving. Creation. Repair. Exact copies. Special Commissions.* A hallmark of a small box with the initials *I* and *H* was stamped at each end. I admired the grace and flourishes of the lettering, evidence of past study with a master.

How lovely it must be, I considered, to smooth raw metal into objects of usefulness and beauty.

My vigil was longer than promised. I was feeling quite numb and had begun shifting from foot to foot long before the shop bell tinkled its welcome notes.

Glancing to the door, I recognized the face that had twice or thrice looked into mine at the meetinghouse and supposed those pleasant features must belong to the goldsmith. He had one arm flung forward as he ushered the women from the shop and onto the bricks set like an island in mud.

He appeared to be answering a question from Goody Holt.

"As the whitest silver is the fairest and best," he was saying, "the gold of the deepest yellow is most queenly and royal, and the more the gold inclines to a red or pale yellow, the less perfect it is, though some have a liking for those tints."

Goodwife Holt elbowed her eldest daughter.

"We are obliged to you, Mr. Herrick," Lizzie Holt burst forth. Her tiffany hood askew, she looked overheated and scarlet-faced.

Bel glanced at me, her mouth turned up at one corner.

Her mother slapped at her hand by way of a reminder.

"Yes, thank you kindly for your service," Bel said, mumbling not so much to the smith as to the ruts in the road.

"I will send my daughters with a servant to retrieve the spoon in a few days," Goodwife Holt said. She nodded to confirm her words.

But she lost much of her dignity when a teasing wind caught up her big-brimmed wool hat and bowled it across the ground.

"Catch it, catch it," she shrieked, and clutched at her coif and bonnet.

The daughters set off after the runaway hat, Mehitabel laughing as she skipped away.

The goldsmith glimpsed me standing by the window and looked startled. Again, he seemed to know me, and this time he slipped past Goodwife Holt and came close to me. With only a short bow, the goldsmith began speaking. "Pray excuse my boldness and hasty lack of introduction, madam, but I knew your brother Joseph well—we were at college together for a year when we were both fourteen. Indeed, I remember seeing you there with your father. And I have something of Joseph's that should by rights be yours."

"Oh," I said, suddenly bereft of all words.

My eyes met his, so pale a gray that it seemed to my fancy almost silver and that he was bound to be a metals smith by nature. And his hair was a rich yellow, the color of straw spun into gold in the German story. A slim, neat figure in his deer-colored breeches and stockings, linen shirt, and gridolin waistcoat: the needleworker in me approved. I thought him pleasing in the way of one of his own creations, with good lines, shapeliness, and light like the glinting sun. He might have been a royal in disguise, tumbled from some fantastic Goody Waters tale.

"Joseph," I said, and it was strange to me to say his name aloud, though many nights I lay in bed counting over the family names.

To me, the high, sharp cheekbones made the goldsmith seem older than Joseph had looked—though Joseph had stopped growing older for me on the day he disappeared. By this time, I had almost given up on the idea that any of my family had been taken for ransom. One stubborn thread of hope still held.

The tears came into my eyes, though I had promised myself never to cry when near the Holts.

"You look very like him, you know," the goldsmith added, catching up my hand as if he meant to comfort me. Like a stream of sparkles, his touch shot through me.

A pulse flittered at my neck, and my breath quickened.

"Do I?"

"Yes," he said, and stared into my face as if he could conjure Joseph's features from mine.

"A possession of my brother's," I said, suddenly longing to have a memento of my family, something to say that they had been more than a long, complicated dream that had dissolved upon waking.

He bent forward and whispered near my ear before releasing my hand. Even after, the fingers still tingled from lying against his. For was that not forward of him, and too yielding of me?

"Pray you, pardon my temerity. But do come without *them* if you can."

The others surrounded us, a blur of dark crimson, russet, and indigo, and he was busy thanking them for their custom and promising to do the work with swiftness, though his eyes flew to mine, as quick as birds that swerve and light and are gone. Goodwife Holt pushed me, so that I stepped back and stumbled and dropped the basket. She jabbed a glance at me and turned, moving between me and the goldsmith and pulling the girls close.

"She is nothing," I heard Lizzie Holt say.

Bel wrenched her arm from her mother's grasp and came to me, seizing my hand.

The goldsmith watched all without comment, though his mouth was no longer smiling.

After he returned to the shop, I glimpsed him by the window. He seemed to bow, his face and form made rippled by the glass.

"Here to me, Bel," Goody Holt commanded.

She must have wholly forgotten the remainder of her errands, for I carried the basket to the house, trailing the others. In the sewing room, Bel told me that her mother had insisted that they charm the goldsmith, who was a town officer as well as a craftsman and small importer.

"He went to college for a year with my brother Joseph." I sat with a gown on my lap, the work untouched. *Joseph, Joseph. My dear brother. What could the goldsmith have to give me?* It would not be easy or, indeed, entirely proper to venture alone, but I did not fear him. The shock of his touch lingered, a memory to my fingers.

"They say Jotham Herrick only became an apprentice to Mr. Dummer in Boston after his father died," Bel said. "I have heard tell that he did not need to be put to apprenticeship as a mechanic but chose out of his own deep desire to work in gold and silver. At least, that is what Goodwife Rebecca Osgood told our mother, and she ferrets out the news about all the men of marriage age. Mother is set on him for Lizzie, though a goldsmith is not quite as high as she likes. But since he is a college-trained town selectman who might have been a minister and is considered to be promising, that makes up for some lack in her mind."

It made me sad to think of the silver-and-gold man with Lizzie Holt, so flint-faced and demanding.

"Mayhap she will not have her way," I said.

"Mother does often manage to get her desires, but Mr. Herrick likes you better than Lizzie. He observed you quite closely," Bel said. "And he has looked at you often in meeting."

"I—I do not know." But I remembered the silver in the window and his pale eyes and golden hair, and how there was some secret between us. *Joseph.*

"I do," she said. "And I think that another way—a way where my mother does not have all matters as she wishes—is good."

"Bel Holt, I have no family to smooth the path and encourage courting, no place to meet with someone, and no fortune to bring to a marriage. Unless a man be bold, honorable but impetuous, and also sacrificial, there can be no Charis-courting. And how many men are all those things?"

"Few, I suppose, though it is a mighty shame."

"Perhaps *you* want to get your own way," I proposed, my mind resolutely turning from the face of Jotham Herrick and the feel of the slender, capable fingers pressed next to mine.

I gazed at Bel, wondering if she had the strength to defy her mother in such an undertaking. Most of our people have wished for happy marriages, for love, and joy in bed. That is a kind of innocence in them, to believe in true love between man and woman, a reflection of the union between the divine Christ and his bride, the Church. And in this they seemed curious to the nobility in England, who jockeyed for position and advantage in marriage like Newmarket riders racing for some royal purse.

"Is there someone you fancy?"

Bel, who usually seemed self-possessed and unflappable when we were alone, blushed. "I like one of the Dane men. And he likes me, too. He's round like me," she said. "He says we will trundle on finely together."

"That is comical but sweet," I said.

"Not many of us *are* round," Bel said. "And so we ought to go together. Apples in a barrel of beans."

"But your mother—"

"She does not care for him, even though he is a Dane. She wants a good name but more than that; he is not high enough for her regard. She wants someone with a rank in the militia, or who holds an important town office. Something like that. She has fantasies of our being married to men on the General Council or to ministers. My mother would rather marry us to some princox or mean-spirited old man, so long as he had gold and a Mister or captaincy before his name." Bel wound a sky-blue ribbon around her finger, staring but not seeming to see what was before her. "But we are the daughters of a tanner, so why should she be displeased? I shall sue her, you know, if she does not give me her consent. The courts say what she does is forbidden—to refuse permission for no sound reason—and Richard Dane is as good as we are. His family name is better. Pah!"

Goodwife Holt and Lizzie appeared at the narrow door, each jostling the other but neither wishing to give place. At last the elder woman hunched the daughter aside, thrusting with her elbow.

After straightening her coif, knocked askew in the struggle, she spoke. "How proceeds the sewing?"

"Well. Quite well. I thank you." I lifted the needle and pricked the air to show her that I had not forgotten the business I was about.

"I have determined that I do not care for the zaffer-blue bodice and skirt," Lizzie said. "You may make it over for sister Bel. Or for that matter, Bess." She frowned at me.

But if she thought to strike sparks from me over my handiwork, she was wrong.

"Bess could well use a new gown," I said, "or I could redo the waist for your sister." I was careful not to call my friend Bel in front of her mother, fearing that she would forbid any intimacy between us.

"No, indeed, no, certainly not Bess," Goodwife Holt said with considerable sharpness. "You must keep the garment, Lizzie. That is sure. A gown of watered paragon is no rag."

"It does not suit me!" Lizzie shook out her skirts as if ridding herself of an annoyance and flounced away. Her heels clack-clack-clacked on the stairs. When the sound had died away completely, Goodwife Holt spoke up again. She had been fingering a piece of camlet and no doubt meditating on what she would say next.

"In future days, Charis, I would prefer if you would not be so very pushing in nature. Do not thrust yourself forward when we are with townspeople."

"She did not put herself forward, Mother," Bel said. "She did not."

"Do not contend with me," began Goodwife Holt, but her daughter pressed on.

"And the family was much approved in the colony. She is no servant to be shooed and scolded."

"They were well enough," Goodwife Holt said grudgingly.

"Among the first families of the colony, you mean," Bel told her. "Such standing is known even in Andover. You make us look ill-natured to declare otherwise."

"Mehitabel Holt," I said in a low voice. "Please do not defend me."

"However fine a family she had, what does she have now? A bit of made-over finery wrong for her station, a coffer, and a Norfolk County deed to some savage-held lands that no one will be fool-hardy enough to settle again." Goodwife Holt made a brute noise to emphasize her disapproval, a sound stranded between a grunt and a jeer. "And who would marry such a poor creature as that? She has little now and will no doubt have less as time passes."

I made no response, staring at the pool of silk in my lap and wishing for her to be gone.

"That changes naught of who she is," Bel insisted.

"Mehitabel, please," I whispered.

Perhaps Goody Holt might have refrained from speaking if she had been aware that her words would make me muse more often of the goldsmith and wonder whether I had only dreamed a thread of liking between us. He had not seemed to regard me as "a poor creature."

The next day Mistress Holt barred me from my midday walk with a feeble but firmly voiced excuse, but on the day following I crept out without telling anyone. The women of the family were entertaining the young pastor in the parlor. Evidently he was reading to them from Cotton Mather's *Memorable Providences, Relating to Witchcraft and Possession*, as he had promised when invited to partake of tea. I paused and heard him reading a passage about the Devil attempting to lure a boy in the colony, "telling him many stories of Dr. Faustus, and other witches, how bravely they have lived, and how he should live deliciously, and have ease, comfort, and money; and sometimes threatening to tear him in pieces if he would not."

And I slipped out the door.

The minister's words lingered in my mind as I paused to listen before the house, so that I wondered if I could be like the boy, sliding into sin through the desire to "live deliciously." But no voice called me back, and I shook off the thought. I had seen the work of Satan up close and knew something about the stamp of his presence. Still, the risk was high; I might be whipped for wanton dalliance if accused of visiting a man. And what else was I doing—was I, indeed, wanton? A memory of the face of the goldsmith and the spark of his touch had returned to me more than once when I was alone in the sewing room.

I kept my head down in passing the front windows.

As I walked away, I felt a twinge of sympathy: Bess was stirring a wooden tub of laundry outside the wash-house. She stopped to wipe her nose with the hem of her apron and did not see me. Behind her, the ever-escaping speckled pig rooted in a mess of corn stalks.

I hurried on, as quickly as if I had joined Mercury's wings to my heels. Soon I reached the shop and glanced in the front window at the silver. The night before, it had rained, and I leaped a little wavering stream to gain the square of bricks set before the door. There I paused to look about me. All was the same, save for the borderline of the rivulet and a loud ringing noise that came from the side yard where a boy was hammering an ingot to flatten the silver.

I curtseyed when a finely dressed gentleman came out of the shop, his gaze bent on a handful of gold buttons. Some visitor from Salem, perhaps, one who could afford and merit cloth of deep black and a touch of lace. He hardly glanced at me but prayed my pardon and went on, the treasure now locked in his fist.

Once inside, I leaned against the door, the bell tinkling. Mr. Herrick must have passed into the back room, for the curtain was still stirring.

"I shall return posthaste—"

The sound of his voice startled me, even though I had come expressly to talk with him. Suddenly weak-limbed, for I had eaten nothing since a dish of tea with milk in the early morning, I longed to sit. Most of all, I wondered what he had to give me. What had my brother left with his school friend? The noise of the mallet from outside died away into silence and began again, beating faster than before.

The goldsmith ducked under the curtain and saw me and was still. "Ah," he said.

"Mr. Herrick," I said, and stopped there, not knowing what greeting suited the moment.

"I am right heartily glad—you found a way," he said. "I was afraid Goodwife Holt would not let you quit the house."

"Yes," I said, "but I have the favor of a daily walk."

"I am glad," he said, though he looked solemn. "She has the renown among gossips of being the dragon of Andover. However it is, I have found her fair in her dealings with me."

I smiled at this description but made no reply. John had once explained to me that Goody Holt resembled a porcupine, a curmudgeonly, waddling beast that was said to shoot its quills—barbed and magical—at anyone who strayed too near.

"Do you mind that we are alone? Not many come to the shop."

"No," I said.

He drew back the cloth and beckoned to me. The back room shone dully with metal—chargers and cups and some pewter plates—but we met beside the curtain in the shadows. His hair gleamed in the darkness.

"The first time I sighted you across the room, I recognized you," he said. "I knew who you were, even though when I had seen you last, you were still small. I knew it in my bones. I knew it the way a touchstone knows the gold. And knew that I wanted to meet you."

I didn't speak but turned my head away from him.

"Forgive me for being rash and headlong, over-hasty," he added.

The silver called to me, seemed to announce that here was one who was caught by beauty and who aspired to make marvels. The pulse at my neck quickened, whether it was from his words or from the strangeness of being alone with a man in the shadowy and silvery chamber.

When I met his gaze again, the goldsmith went on. "You don't recollect me, but I feel as if I understand you—I felt so when I glimpsed you at the meetinghouse. I don't know why that could be, except that I saw you and sensed that I would come to know you."

"To be understood is sweet, and something I thought lost forever," I said. "But how could that happen?"

"A kind of light shone around you. To me you were like a dove glimmering in the midst of crows. I know the royal nature of gold, and at that instant I felt alchemically changed by grace, and that all of me was malleable and perfect like gold. It sounds like bedlam madness to me now, but I—I loved you and wanted to be with you always. Does that sound like madness?"

"Perhaps," I said. "No. I do not know."

I remembered my words to Bel, saying that a young woman with no fortunes and no family and no place to meet and court was not likely to wed. *Unless a man be bold, honorable but impetuous* ...

His fingertips found mine, and our hands laced together. Where we touched, I seemed more alive than I had been since leaving our house near Falmouth. My pulse flickered like a bird's.

"You are milk and flame and gold," he said. "Your white skin, the changing reds of your hair in the different lights of the sun. I dreamed about us last night; I think about you all day long."

The fire of a blush rose in my face, so that I was glad of the curtain's shadow. My skin was ever a betrayer of my feelings, as bold as a white cloth stained to red with the dye called *kermes berries*. That he desired my company was pleasing; I did not ask myself how much I wished him to say, or how well I wished him to make use of this time that might not come again. To be alone with a man was a rarity, and even more so to be alone with Mr. Herrick the goldsmith— Goodwife Holt would make sure of that.

But now we were together, and I could feel the blood moving in his hand and the slight roughness of the skin, callused from working the metal. The scent of him was pleasant, a musky mixture of sweat with ambergris.

"Pardon my forwardness, that I have dreamed of you, and that even now I may be profaning your maiden privacy with my touch."

We stood silent, but when he made as if to release my hand, I spoke. "I would not be called too quickly won," I said. "And should be more strange and distant. But in traveling through the wilderness, I may have lost all rules of courtesy and sense of how to behave."

"You don't yet fathom me," he said. "And such sudden loves may seem too rash."

"Yes," I said.

"And unadvised," he added.

"Yes."

"And dream-like and frail, not likely to endure," he said.

"Yes," I said.

"But would you marry me," he said, but not as if it was a question— more like words in a trance. And all the time the vein at my wrist flittered and said that I was already his.

But fear of my own wild impulse was in me also. I might have been skimming along Falmouth cliff, about to jump into the waves below.

"Yes," I said, "yes."

"Forever and ever," he said, as if this life could go on without change.

"If your bent toward me is as bright and pure and sterling as your own hammered silver. Or more—like the miracles of gold that the Wise Men from the East carried."

"It is," he said. "Like the star that stood over the babe and his mother. Like the night fields when there are no clouds, and the stars are spilled."

"Yet how can I be sure when I know so little of you?"

"You must sense it already, surely. We are both so solitary. We have fallen out of the world, all our people dead. And our former places know us no more. But I love you, and I will love you more when I learn your ways. Will you marry me," he said, again not as a question but dreamily.

"Yes," I said again, "yes." My feet, so long careful, now seemed to skip from secure ground. And this time I added, "I will."

His face was close to mine. I could feel something sparking and lighting between us, as when a bolt of brightness is turning in the atmosphere, enlivening the motes of air, and abruptly I feared that the moment would flash away as quickly as lightning, leaving nothing but shock and a smell of sulphur, a devilish perfume.

"Call me Jotham," he whispered.

"Jotham," I said, feeling the power, the intimacy that sleeps inside a name and wakes when a woman is given the right to say a man's Christian name. And I gave him the right to my forename in turn.

"Charis," he said, "the marvelous red-and-white grace of Charis."

His lips discovered mine in the dark. My pulse flicked faster and faster and sent out stars like struck flint. Our veins turned to white flame that ran from one to the other. For how does a woman feel when she is first touched by desire? I was a tree of liquid silver that budded with white flowers and erupted in white leaves inside his embrace. We were more—orchards of gold-fire and flower. For a long time, I leaned against him, caught and burning yet unconsumed.

Some moments stand like landmarks on a journey, as when Jacob crossed the river and wrestled until he won a new name and a blessing. And though he was lamed, all things seemed new; the morning leaped from the horizon, and there was the gold of light.

Afterward, when the boy who hammered at silver ceased his pounding and we returned to the shop, I looked around and saw the world had altered. The flintlock above the hearth floated close to the wall. The silver by the window seemed buoyant on the shelves, as if the bowls and teapots were planets that might lift and whirl around my sun. For I felt glowing, radiant in the gloom. A little branch of red coral burned among the silver, along with a tiny dish of moon-bright pearls and a chunk of lapis lazuli, its deep blue like something quarried from the depths of the sea.

That we had no one to watch and keep us from mischief and ruin was no matter to me. Were we not both innocent of guile? Even the thought of the whip with its embedded smarts of bone or metal had not kept me from the goldsmith's shop. I had fled from both normal life and massacre long before that day. Hortus had borne me into a new realm where I saw more strangely than others of my kind. And I knew in my marrow that Mr. Herrick—*Jotham*—would never harm me.

He passed out of the shop, and I could hear him talking to the boy. I began to dread that I had been away from the house too long. But he came back inside and dashed upstairs, and returned with something cradled in his arms.

"Here," he said, "take this. I want you to keep it. About the time your family sailed from Boston, Joseph brought me a book and asked me to add silver to strengthen and protect the corners. He knew that I was still an apprentice and intended to retrieve the book at some future date when I was my own master. But he never came to get it, though I had a letter from him about a proposed return a year back. And when you came here and I learned from the town talk that he and all your family were lost, I added the engraving to the front and a latch."

The volume was heavy in my hands, bound in leather with wide silver corners, each decorated with a medallion. A broad silver band wrapped the book, with a central oval containing a portrait engraving of my brother. And it was like enough to make me catch my breath.

"You must go," he said, "and see me again only with someone to accompany you, or else there will be the evil of meddling whispers and perhaps worse. I will meet with Mr. Dane, who has been like a grandfather to me. He will declare the banns for us if I ask him."

Abruptly, I was afraid not of the lash but of how I hardly knew Jotham. Mr. Herrick. What if the encounter just past was but a dream, too glistening-sweet to be substantial? But I said nothing and only gripped the book more tightly.

"See, the book is blank inside, and the band has a lock and key," he said. "I made it secure so that you could write down all that has happened to you without fear of others reading your words. Someday your children and grandchildren will want to know the story of your courage. They will want to hear how you escaped your troubles and fled through the forest to safety. Or perhaps you will want to write it so that you know what and who you were when you went to the wilderness, and how you were changed afterward. To put your days in order."

He offered me the key on a chain.

I bent my head and let him slip it around my neck and was startled when his hand brushed against my skin.

"All will be well," he murmured, a little sadly.

"I trust so," I said, though was not sure. *Children and grandchildren.* Through him, would I have and be important to a household again? Would I belong to family? Would I give my own offspring the names of those I loved and missed? Was there anything earthly of more consequence to me in the New or Old Worlds? I did not think so.

"Major Saltonstall should know of this; I will write to him if that seems good—I know him through the militia and town business. He thinks well of me, I believe. At any event, I shall ask his blessing on us. For we must have consent from a magistrate since you have no parents to speak for you."

"Oh," I said. "Why?"

"It is the law that 'no orphan not disposed in marriage' by parents may marry except by consent of all the town selectmen, or else more easily by a member of the General Court—and Major Saltonstall may serve us there."

Another worry had come to me. "I have no dowry. No bed rug, no bedstead. No andirons, no sideboard, no treen or pewter dish, and no brass candlesticks."

"Hush," he said. "You are your own dower. I want no more."

"I have barely more than a sealskin and the clothes Mistress Saltonstall gave me."

"No matter."

"But I have a horse, a lovely ambler," I said, suddenly remembering that I was not wholly without resource, "and he is my wealth."

"If you had nothing at all, I would be satisfied. As I suppose the Saltonstalls were, to care for you."

"Yes. I meant to return there. But now I shall not go back to them, I suppose," I said. "Even fair tidings have a sorrowful edge to them."

"Yet we may have leave to go visiting," Jotham said.

"Yes," I said, folding the book to my breast. "That would be sweet. They were good and kind to me."

"Go you on," Jotham said, his hand lighting on mine as he glanced toward a window. "I would not have you leave. But fly away from me like some redbird of the forests."

"I would stay," I said.

"A hundred, a thousand times farewell," he said.

A last glittering brush of skin against skin, my cheeks and lips burning, and I was hurrying to the Holt house with the book in my arms and the key cold against my breast. All the way, the episode hung in my mind like a bright dream, yet my mind seemed wavering, jostled by uncertainties. Was this my right path? Too, I thought about the lash and its smarts and hoped the button-acquiring stranger I had encountered at the door would not ask about me, and that no one else had seen me come and go.

"Lord," I whispered, "Lord shield me."

Back in my garret, I tucked the book of pages under my mother's blanket. Perhaps I would use the key later, after procuring ink and plucking a few feathers for quills to trim with my knife. Or perhaps I would write in it when my life was more settled. For now, the sight of Joseph's face was enough. It was time for me to make an appearance at my work. As I climbed down the stairs, I could hear Lizzie and Bel arguing.

To my surprise, they were squabbling in the sewing room. Goodwife Holt had arrived before me and was busy scolding them from the doorway.

I peered around her and saw that the two were using the big shears. Bel was holding them open, and there was something clamped between the blades.

"Oh," I said. *The sieve—the turning of the sieve.* Though many might think them harmless, what was good about trying to wrest the future from two blades of brute metal? Didn't foreknowledge of the future belong only to God?

"Mary Carleton showed me how," Lizzie said. "It is harmless. The Carletons all do it."

"Nonsense," Goodwife Holt was saying. "What absurdities will you two fancy next?"

She turned and almost strode into me. "And where have you been?" The frown lines beside her mouth dug in deeper as she surveyed me.

"Out on my walk," I said, "so that I may be refreshed for the afternoon's sewing." The words were not exactly a falsehood, but they were not the entirety of the truth. Yet I did not call it a sin of omission but a defense against one who would be my enemy.

"Go you on," she said. "Do not let me keep you from your appointed round of work."

At that, she swept away, turning into a nearby room and shutting the door with much force.

Go you on. Jotham had used the same words, but then I felt no rush of passion against the words. I stared hard at the closed door before recollecting that the two sisters had been borrowing scissors, and not to cut cloth.

Curious, I slipped into the room. Lizzie was clamoring for another attempt at fortune-telling.

Mehitabel was still holding the flour sieve and Goody Holt's big shears.

"Why not, as Mother is gone away? Now put your finger on one side of the shears and I on the other. Ask it," she said to Lizzie. "Go on and ask another question if you want." She looked peevish, as if Lizzie had been asking a great many questions.

Her sister began to chant:

Days, mays,
Jennet, linnet,
Dowse, mouse,
By St. Peter and St. Paul,
If I shall marry one whose name begins with H,
Turn about riddle and shears and all.

She looked eagerly at the sieve, which remained inert and did not appear to give her the answer she desired. If she had owned the least amount of patience, enough to brim a little girl's fingerhut, I was quite sure that she would have waited and seen it move. But she did not.

"Oh, that's enough!" Lizzie struck the metal sieve, which flew off the shears and bounced on the floor. "*Yes* for almost all is useless. And none for *H*."

"Why are you so ill-tempered?" Bel looked at Lizzie, who glared back at her. "Perhaps you will marry them all in time. You may live to be ninety-six and have four husbands."

The lines on either side of Lizzie's mouth deepened with her frown. "It didn't give me just one answer, as I wanted, and now who will I have?"

"We can ask the sieve to choose and go through the alphabet until it moves," Bel proposed. "That might have worked better."

"I am no better off than before." Lizzie swung around and looked at me. "What are you doing here?"

I smiled at her in surprise. "This is where I sew."

She made a noise of impatience that reminded me of her mother before stamping out of the room.

"I know what you were doing," I said to Bel.

She stared at me.

"Why did you? That's magic, you know—you were doing magic, and magic is forbidden. You could get into difficulties." I put my hand on her arm, as if to hold her back from danger, but she laughed.

"We learned how to balance the sieve from one of the Carletons. Hannah Carleton found out the man she would marry from the sieve-and-scissors."

"My mother would never have let me do any such thing," I said, pulling my hand away. I felt unsettled but could not make out whether it was fortune-telling or the risk I had taken to see Jotham Herrick that made me fearful.

Hands on hips, Bel surveyed me, and did not look convinced.

"She said that even little acts could be devilish. They were pleasurable and curious like a marvelous bottle of *aqua mellis* that perfumes the air and skin but draws the interest of strange powers that snuff the air and can smell an atom of royal honey-water scent from worlds off. She told me that small infractions can lead on to greater, and that must be truth. But I don't know—I have seen evil, and its face is much worse than sieve-and-scissors."

I perched on the sewing stool and took up the gown that I had been hemming when I left for my walk.

"Lots of people do it," she said, and fetched the sieve from the corner where it had landed. "It's not like black magic."

"Scissors are powerful images of change," I said, laying aside my sewing to retrieve Goody Holt's blades from the floor and turning them over in my hands to make sure they had received no hurt from knocking against the boards. "The Greeks dreamed that the three Moirai would spin and measure and cut the thread of human lives. Atropos would 'slit the thin-spun life.' The three sang of what was and what was past and what was to be."

"I know and care nothing about any old Greek lies," Mehitabel said.

"The Greeks thought the Moirai were goddesses of fate," I said. "They were pagans and wrong. Still, there is much of worth in their writings."

"You ought to be a boy and go to college. You know such strange things."

"My father taught me with my brothers."

"But who cares about those old Moirai?"

"The Greeks thought that the Moirai ruled the world, I suppose, for who could stand against them?"

"And how could that ever be?" Bel Holt laughed to think of it. "Three women! Though I do believe that my mother ruled the house while Father lived. She hounded him to wear bone or gold or silver lace and great boots, though they would surely have gotten him into trouble with the constable for exceeding his rank. He was a plain man."

"Your mother has a taste for costly materials," I said.

"Long ago she was fined for wearing silk hoods. And they say she was punished for disorderly behavior when she was young—the neighbors marched her to the magistrates for usurping the business of a man. She also pummeled my father repeatedly with a distaff, or so I heard from Phoebe Wardwell, who was told by her husband's aunt, so I suppose it is true. I do not think that he suffered much damage."

Imagine that! I smiled down at the shears in my lap. To picture Goody Holt rampaging up the stairs, waving her distaff as she chased the poor tanner! Probably all the damage was to his position among his neighbors and to his self-respect as head of the household. How I wanted to laugh!

"The Moirai were a dream to explain why some only had a blink of life and others lived to creep about like crooked insects in old age. The Greeks did not know what we know, but they were wise." I ran my fingertips over the engraving on the metal.

The shears were fine; the Damascus steel was strong and not likely to suffer harm. Perhaps if I had stayed to sift the cooling ashes and dig among the spars, I might have found some precious objects belonging to my family, I reflected. Had I been too precipitous, too frightened that my life was about to be snipped short?

"My Aunt Mary always said that a man's knife alone was nothing particularly special but that two blades fastened with a spring made a useful marriage. Is her husband-to-be what your sister wanted to know?"

"Yes, and mine as well. The sieve said that I would marry someone whose name begins with a *D*." Bel shrugged. "But since Lizzie's hands shake, I fear she is not reliable. The sieve danced around as if bewitched and leaped into the air."

"I trust it was not enchanted," I said. "But hope also that you will have your heart's desire without any meddling sieves."

"You do not want me to try for you? To find out who you will marry?" She gave me a teasing look and seized the shears from me and clacked the blades together.

"I lost everything not so long ago. So perhaps I am not a good prospect."

"You have skills. And moreover—"

"Bel, I am quite content knowing just exactly as much as I know now," I said. "And can wait to see what comes to me."

"You have the patience of a Job," she said, "though I do not. Perhaps it is because I am older and weary of my mother's designs and her lack of care for my desires."

"Thank you for the compliment, but I am not so very patient," I said. "Further, I'm not sure Job always was."

"Lizzie tried for *O*, *T*, *R*, and *H*, but she got no satisfaction: some *yes* replies on other letters but not on the one she wanted most. I am afraid that the sieve usually tumbled before she got the words out, and once remained quite still and did not give her any hopeful movement." Bel smiled as if pleased by that thought.

"And we all know that *H* likes you better," she added. "I expect that she is green-jealous of you."

"I hope she is not." I held my needle up to the light from the window, fumbling with the thread and eye until the silk sailed through. "The lastmost thing I need is a foe, especially one who shares the same roof."

"She has a peevish temper," Bel said. "And so she is her own enemy."

"Sad," I said, bending to my work.

"Are you sure? You do not want to ask?" Scissors in one hand, with the other Bel was pawing idly through the hanks of thread scattered on the coverlet.

I remembered Jotham Herrick: the glance of fingers against fingers, the radiance of touch, the sense that the fabric of my day had been stitched tightly to an underlay of paradise.

"No, I thank you. As before, I am pleased well enough with my small knowledge. All I wish is to have the shears again."

Bel handed them over. "La, you are a mistress of restraint," she remarked. She stared at the gown in my lap. "I shall look just as much a calamitous pudding in that gown as the other."

"No, no, I think not. This one will suit you. It is a better pattern for your figure, and the deep indigo is right. Your rosy cheeks and chestnut hair will be well set off by the color, and Goodman Dane will think you quite fine."

She laughed but looked pleased, her smile fading only slightly.

How strange and shivery it was to think of witchcraft! The shears felt unfamiliar in my hand. They were warm and tingled a little, but I expect that was only the effect of Bel's bodily heat and remembered tales of bewitched articles—dishes that smashed themselves to shards and jots, rags that danced on air and besmirched a sleeping face, stones that leaped from the ground as easily as a fish arcing from water. But an angry servant or child might smash a dish or paint a sleeper with

ash or fling a stone. My father brought me up to question such curious events and to seek whether I could find more ordinary causes.
Only when none could be found was it right to go on to more baleful
possibilities.

Still, I laid down the shears, and later on I washed them carefully
with some of Goody Holt's *aqua bryony* and a rag that I afterward
tossed into the privy. I suppose it was a superstition in me, but I
felt that if the water was healing for the skin, it might be good for a
tainted surface of metals as well.

Later on I remembered my father telling me that bryony was also
called *mandrake*, and that a false Englishman could dig and place a
mold in human form around a root of bryony to make it grow into
that shape. And I suppose the magic-peddler could lug it about the
near countryside and so make a few coins that way, selling his neighbors the chance to peep at the root-man or root-woman.

So perhaps I was merely compounding the error of sieve-and-
scissors by washing them in mandrake water.

5

Sybbrit

Andover, Indian Summer 1690

Having a secret did not keep me from bad dreams, fears, or resenting Goody Holt and Lizzie when they were unkind. I did not suppose that anything could satisfy a person like Lizzie Holt except perhaps having a mort of hang-sleeves at her beck and call, and perhaps even so many admirers would not have left her entirely pleased. Goody Holt was likewise hard to delight, no matter how many hours I spent moiling-and-toiling at my needle. When not scolding me or one of the others in the house, she would nattle, ever fussing until some trifling matter had achieved a royal mightiness in her mind. From the death of the speckled pig to the misplacing of a comb, everything that happened was someone else's fault. John and Bess and Bel spoke the only pleasant words in that house, at least the only ones pointed to me.

But I felt strong—stronger than Goody Holt in her angers. At stray moments, a heavens of memory sparkled in my thoughts. And so I did not care what Goody Holt might think of my conduct.

At night I lay by the smolder of coals, dreaming of Jotham Herrick and his gray, reflective eyes, and how he had swept me away with his words of love that sometimes felt like an illusion and at other times like a fine glouse of sunlight that warmed my whole body. The feel of his lips on mine, the heat that flowed between us: at times I could catch hold of the memory. A flick of gold seemed to pass through me and be gone. But his face was difficult to conjure. I wished for a portrait so that I could recall him and the hour more clearly. Sometimes the meeting seemed like a spectral morning mist that would burn away as light increased.

When something hard and sharp is dragged along a frozen pond in winter, the metal or wood kicks up a fine spray of crystals that puff in the air and catch the sun and powder the surface of the ice. Sometimes the hour with Jotham Herrick seemed so frail and quick. The heat of it, the blossoming and the fire, would fall away into the uncertain gulf of memory.

Only the book and the engraving of Joseph were always solid to me, a gift left over from the talk and questions. In the late evenings, I sometimes sat with the book by the fire and gazed at my brother's face by the poor illumination of flames. He had my father's brow, my mother's mouth. But I never stayed there to reflect long, my back chilled, my front over-warm.

Though the autumn was unusually cold, we had a respite in October, a few weeks of what the Holts called *Indian summer*. Later on, I was told that the Wampanoags had first described this warmth in fall to Mr. William Bradford, long the governor of the Plymouth Plantation, and that the last huzzah of seasonable weather was named for them, but whether or not that is true, who can say? I was glad of a return to fairer days, though the sunny air hardly seemed to have made a difference in the house, which appeared to have decided on winter already and be loath to change its mind. My sewing room stayed as dank and gelid as a December toad.

The start of Indian summer was marked by a great outcry, and a second one marked the close. The first happened this way. At night I quaked with cold in my bed, and when I dropped into sleep like someone tripping and falling over a brink, my dreams proved ill. One night I pulled the bed near the flames and loaded myself with sealskin and blankets and all my petticoats, shifts, and gowns. In the middle of the night, I seemed to wake, though I believe now that I only hovered between sleeping and waking in the place where visions come. The smoky odor of the fire drugged me, and I had some trouble breathing. My thoughts jumbled together, so that one moment I remembered Jotham Herrick and the next felt a creeping dread of a shape hiding in a dark corner. I wished to rise and flee from the room but found that I could not move my limbs. Only my eyes behaved as they should, and glanced fearfully from one side of the chamber to the other.

The weight of the sealskin oppressed me more and more until I panted for air. My heart felt wrong, too large for its container of bone, and thumped too quickly. Something in the room flicked back and forth: something dim-edged but with a dark, gathering center. I told myself it was fumes from the hearth, but there were no flames left, only a few coals that glowed on the bed of their expiring—a thought that, foolish though it seemed, only gave me new alarm.

The shadow-stuff in the room drifted on the air like a skein of smoke and settled on my bed-coverings and piled clothes. It took on more distinct form and weight, leaning on my chest. I heard a clanging voice speak my name, and the coiling shape leaned forward until I recognized the face and was at once released to stir again and shrieked as I had not shrieked before, not when I saw my house a ruin or when I pressed close to the dead mountain of the English, or when I hung onto Hortus' mane as we crossed the deep, churning waters. The sound fountained from my throat, tossed like a bird hurled by updrafts.

Shouts answered from below. Goody Holt appeared at the door, trailed by John and Bess.

"I pray your pardon," I said, trembling, unable to take in what Goody Holt was saying, her voice peevish.

John lit my candle from the one held by Goody Holt, and Bess, ever kind, knelt down on the floor and took my hand.

"What's happening?" Bel Holt appeared in the door, but I could not speak.

"She's mortally shocked," Bess said in a low voice.

John set to work laying a new fire with kisks and dry wood while Goody Holt continued to upbraid me. Her words beat at my ears, but I could not make out what she had to say.

Lizzie Holt peered in the door, and I gave a little jump of fright.

"What ails her?" Bel had come near and now draped my mother's blanket around my shoulders.

"I—I had—"

"She had the nightmare, most like," Bess said. "But it's gone, Mistress Charis. It's gone quite away."

"*Mistress!*" Goody Holt hawked up a glob of ill humors and spat them onto the floor.

Lizzie was nosing around my room by the light of the two candles. I watched her, feeling a faint horror still. My head throbbed with headache as I followed her shape. At last she drew near and studied me.

"That's such a fine piece of weaving," she said and reached out a hand to touch my mother's blanket, now drawn about my shoulders.

I jerked back instinctively, and Bel pushed her away.

"Leave her be," she said. "You can see she's not right."

Lizzie yawned, her eyes on me. "I just don't know why she needs such a sumptuous covering. What's the use of it to her?"

"Keeps her warm at night, of course," Bel retorted. "And her mother spun the thread and dyed it, so why would she ever give it up?"

I gripped Bess' hand. "Only a dream," I whispered. "There was something—someone—pressing against me."

Lizzie made a face fit for a sneering-match as she stepped toward me. "Who?"

"A dream," I said. "I couldn't say."

But I did know, and I could have said. But I did not. Dreams are oracles to my people, and I did not want to tell. I wanted to muse on what had happened. Or better, to forget.

"Mother," Lizzie said, "she doesn't need such a delicate piece of work, now does she? What does such a forlorn, lone thing need with such quality? It's a neater, smoother piece than you could find in all of Andover."

Her tall shadow loomed high on the wall, sinking and rising with the play of the flames. My eyes rested on it, wondering at how much she seemed to dislike me and to assume me unworthy. And yet my father was a man of good birth, education, and thought, and I had been instructed by him and my mother, who was more learned than most women.

Lizzie had little-enough reply of her mother. "The girl has a fine maggot in her brain to play us with such knobble-tree tricks! To wake us so bloodthirstily in the deeps of the night as though we were all to be murdered by savages, and in our very beds," Goody Holt was saying. "Can you grasp such lack of feeling and care for the nerves?"

I shook my head, trying to toss mother and daughter out of all hearing. "My mind tells riddles," I said to Bess and Bel. "It's restless. I do not trust it, nor my dreams. Not since—" *Not since the whole world that was mine died. Not since it burned. Not since I took a sealskin from the dead. Not since I saw the hill that was flesh. No matter how often I remember those words, "When thou liest down, thou shalt not be afraid: yea, thou shalt lie down, and thy sleep shall be sweet," I am afraid when I wake in the small hours of the night.*

"You are safe now," Bess said. "Look, John has made up the fire, all merry and dancing for you."

"I'm sorry for your upset." John nodded at me. He was wearing a worn bed rug over his clothes and, in the gloom, might have been one of Goody Holt's savages.

"That is enough," Goody Holt told him. "She needs nothing else, she and her hellish designs on our slumber. And we must try again for sleep, whether our bodily frames be shattered or no." She pushed Lizzie toward the door, and the two of them grumbled out of the room. As customary, the daughter was forced aside so that her mother could go first.

John hesitated, nodded to me, and followed.

"Would you like me to stay awhile?" Bel sat down next to me on the bed. Bess was still close beside me, my hand in hers. "I don't mind. You must be cold up here, all alone."

"That would be good of you. But Bess is chilled," I said. "And must be up early. Thank you for the comfort you gave, Bess, with all my heart. I wish you would find sleep again and have a better dream than mine."

But as she padded down the stairs, I was not sure it had been a dream. Who can discern the selvage between a dream and an oracle, the line between a nightmare and a witch? In dark, mysteries swirl around our heads. I knew that such a dream with its spectral visitant was enough to confess to a pastor, but I also felt certain that my mind was aroused and not right, as it had been for a long time now. Hadn't it been a face that I could not like? And had my own thoughts formed her into dream? I did not want to fear that she could be downright evil—I did not like her, but I did not think of her as evil.

With a twitch of my head, I cast the thought of her away.

"Let's pull the bed even closer to the fire," Bel proposed. "And I'll fetch a coverlet, more wood, and the packet of marchpane I was saving for later. I'm not sleepy any longer. We can loll and tell stories."

"I'm tired, but I'm afraid to sleep. I would like that."

So we hunkered by the fire and drank the last of the leftover tea from earlier in the day, heating it in a little pan set among the flames. The misery in my head ebbed away. The tea was harsh, the marchpane over-sweet, but somehow it was lovely to lean against the bed, the wool coverings in a nest around us, and talk. Bel told some stories of her father—she had been fond of him—and about the young man she wanted to marry, if only she could make her mother agree. She promised to take me to visit her friend Phoebe Wardwell, and to give me her copy of Mr. Michael Wigglesworth's *The Day of Doom* (though afterward she forgot), and to show me the best place to harvest strawberries when spring came again.

The sweet marchpane dissolved in my mouth, morsel by morsel, and I grew tolerably calm.

"I have something to tell you, Bel Holt. If. If you can keep close my news."

Lighthearted, she laughed to hear that I had a secret. "Mother does not like me overmuch of late. I am too much like my father in my general carriage and my shape, she says. So there's no worry there. And she definitely does not care for you. That means we are in the same leaky boat and must paddle along together. And Lizzie and I, well, there's as much sour as sweet. My good friend Phoebe Wardwell I hardly see, now that she is a married woman and I am not. Your secret is quite well coffered in me."

And so I told her about Mr. Herrick, and she was much astonished and sat quite still, marveling at my words. But I did not say that we had met alone in the room behind the shop.

She frowned so that I thought she was envious of me, and perhaps she was. I was almost envious of myself. "You are promised and the banns will be declared and you will be married," she said at last.

"Yes. We are to confer with the minister."

"Mr. Dane, you mean? I am less fond of Mr. Barnard, though accounts of Satan and his wiles fascinate. He is always fearful of signs of devil-pranks."

"Yes, Mr. Dane."

She slopped some tea onto her shift and stood to shake the drops into the fire. Sitting down again, she smiled, looking into the flames. "How vexed Lizzie will be," she observed with considerable satisfaction. "She is envious-spirited and often spiteful, but she will be especially jealous of you."

"I hope not. That would be no fit service to me."

"Everyone knows she has a bad temperament. No one will be surprised or blame you." She broke off a shard of marchpane and handed it to me.

"But I have had enough of enemies to last me," I said, and thanked her for the marchpane.

"I suppose you have, indeed." Bel leaned against the bed, looking mischievously at me with her mouth crimped up at one corner.

"What?"

"I was just thinking that if you may have Mr. Jotham Herrick, well, I feel inspired to battle Mother for my Richard Dane."

We talked for a long time, eating every jot of marchpane, and burning through a mort of dry wood. Goody Holt would have disapproved of our pleasure in each other's company and the formidable way we loaded the fire. Eventually we fell asleep on the floor, rolled in the bedclothes, and woke the next morning to the sun streaming through roof-chinks.

Bel Holt groaned when she opened her eyes and sat up. When she surveyed me, she laughed aloud. "You have cinders in your hair!"

I stood and shook my braid. Some flakes of ash floated on the air, and crumbs of charcoal slid down my shift.

"What's this?" Bel had risen and wandered away from the hearth.

"What do you mean?" I went over to her and saw that she had Mary's doll in her hand. The needle was still as my mother had left it.

She offered the toy to me, and I took it from her. "Mother was making a plaything for my little sister. I couldn't give it up, not when there is so little remaining that belonged to my family. All our books and silver and objects are gone. That's a drop of Mary's own blood on the poor thing's face. Holding the doll is as close as I can come to touching one of my family. That is my hair and Mary's and Mother's, bound together. Perhaps I should finish her face someday. Or perhaps she is better like this."

Contemplating the little figure, I found the tears pricking at my eyes. "Truly, it is my fault, my own fault, that Mary died. I would not be so alone if not for my failings."

"Surely that is not true," Bel said.

"We had been fleeing through the forest, headed toward shelter. I was weary and half-angry at her for rebelling against me. She pulled her hand out of mine and fell back against the stones. And she died beside me in the night while I slept. So it is the truth. It is."

"Some things are mishap. You did not wish it or want it," Bel said.

"No. But if I had taken better care of her ..."

I set the doll down again, and Bel put her arm about my waist. "Let me comb your hair," she proposed, and so I sat wrapped in a coverlet as she combed and combed. I closed my eyes and pretended to be at home with my mother drawing the teeth through my hair.

The night and morning with Bel proved sweet, though a little thread of guilt ran through the hours, for did we not make a great waste of time? Or perhaps it was an acceptable task to relieve a loaded, over-burdened mind, charged with nightmare. Despite how they began, I still recall those hours as our happiest together.

All the rest of that day I expected news, some sort of movement from Mr. Herrick. None came, and the dream-like nature of our encounter began to weigh on me.

But on the fifth day past our meeting at the shop, the elder minister, Mr. Dane, paid a pastoral call on Goody Holt and took a glass of cordial with her and the daughters, and afterward tarried with me in my sewing room. His declaration of the proposed visit upstairs caused a pother in the hall, Goody Holt protesting that there was no need for me to receive such a courtesy in my low estate, and then insisting that Bel accompany the minister. But she scoffed at this idea and refused to spy on a private interview.

It was impossible not to hear the commotion, any more than if an African rhenoister had been ruttling and stamping below, so I jumped up and, setting aside my sewing, began brushing the threads from my gown. But the minister was looming in the door before I was done, greeting me in his mighty preaching voice that was too big for my little room.

"How now? How do you fare?"

"Well, thank you. I am glad to see you looking hearty, sir," I said.

He stepped inside and rubbed his hands together as he glanced at the empty, swept grate. "So cold—how can you sew? How can she wield the needle?" he called out to Goody Holt, who was still protesting at his heels. "Her fingers must be quite numb."

"Indeed, it is not chilly! Why, I hardly feel it myself," she exclaimed as she pushed into the room. "Why, as a girl, I am sure the upper chambers were much colder in my parents' house, and we found it bracing and healthful in the winter."

"No doubt, Goody Holt, no doubt. But this maiden was once used to comfort, and she has gone through trials that would have shattered many a grown man or woman like a clay vessel flung against a pavement stone. Surely you would not begrudge a few sticks in the grate so that she can stitch at your finery?"

The minister smiled down on Goody Holt, who straightened and gave a severe nod of the head. I knew her well enough to be sure she was displeased by his manner of reproof.

Backing into the hall, she peered down the stairs. "It is the work of that lagarag John, I assure you." She bellowed his name a few times before clattering down the stairs, carping as she went.

"Thank you, sir," I said.

He did not wait for further pleasantries but took my hand between his and bade me, "Sit you down." When I was perched in my place again, he said to me in a low voice, "I have had a long confabulation with a certain young goldsmith, and so I have come to find out for myself whether his wishes and your wishes are as one in the matter of the banns."

My face felt warm despite the cold, and I knew all over again that everything that had happened was real, and that Jotham would be my husband. *Vie with me, you women if you can!* The line from our own poet, Anne Bradstreet, flashed through my head like field-fire through a windrow of dry leaves. I would be content and loved and not alone; I would be a mother and have a family on this side of the Jordan, instead of one barred from me by the waves that were death.

"They are," I said, and thrust aside every qualm and uncertainty.

He went to the door and cast a glance down the stairs before speaking again.

"I have a good deal of respect and liking for that young man, and I judge, from what I have heard of you and your family, that the two of you are not ill-suited. As the assay-master sets down the goodness of silver by half-penny and penny weight and ounces troy, as in gold assay he sets down the fineness of gold by karats and karat-grains and half grains and quarter grains, so I measure man and woman by character and traits, my experience of others, and the touchstone of Scripture. And these inform me that you are fit, one for the other. But there are matters relating to matrimony that I should like to talk over, and I see there is some petty difficulty"—here he gave a droll quirk of the lips—"in arranging a meeting that someone who wishes to marry off daughters might attempt to prevent."

I smiled at him, glad that I did not have to explain my situation, and gratified that he found merit in Mr. Herrick. Misgivings had sometimes come to me in hours of reflection, when I wondered who I could ask for advice and judgment.

Goody Holt could be heard in the stairwell, railing at someone, who proved to be John with a bundle of wood in his arms. He winked at me, and knelt down at the hearth to arrange the tinder and split logs.

"My dear *Mistress* Holt," began the minister, proving with a single stroke that he knew how to please her when it was needful, "you may be saving for now, as there is no need to begin a wasteful fire now that the light for sewing is gone, and a good day's work complete. If it please you, I should like to borrow this young woman and her clever needle for the evening. The ladies of the Dane household are eager to learn some of the finer points of stitchery from her. Your new garments have made them quite eager to acquire further skills and undertake such brave work for themselves."

It was easy to perceive the tug of war at work in Goody Holt, pleased with his notice of their costly new gowns and gratified to be spared the lighting of another fire, and yet not entirely content that I would be admitted into the home of so important a figure in the town.

"Yes," she said at last, after these contrary impulses had swept across her face. "So long as she remains useful and is not in the way."

Poor Goody Holt! She was one of those souls of whom it is said that they can be read as easily as a child's ABC hornbook. I could not like her and almost laughed to see how roiled she appeared.

"Excellent! I am glad to hear it."

"As for me, far be it from me to grudge the loan of any *servant* in my house," she added.

"Thank you, but I will not be needing one of your servants," Mr. Dane said, "though I shall remember that kind word."

This response pleased her less, but she only frowned a little. "I shall send Charis over to you," she said.

"Oh, no need—I shall be glad to accompany the young needle-woman myself, since I am here. No doubt she is swift and light enough to find her cloak and be ready in mere instants."

I noted the hint and ran upstairs to my room to change hurriedly into my elderberry-dye gown, fetch my cloak, and follow their voices downstairs, for Goody Holt made a great show of bidding the minister adieu with her daughters, with Bess bobbing in respect by the door.

Along the way, we chattered pleasantly of sewing and Hortus and Mr. Dane's daughter, but once he paused and, looking about, asked me about my dream. "Goody Holt reported that you shalmed so piercingly with fright at a dream that you roused the household. How now, what did she mean?"

I must have looked at him imploringly because he immediately told me not to worry. "My dear child, I mean only to help you to a better understanding if I can. And there is no shame in such eruptions. As Robert Burton said in his great work, *The Anatomy of Melancholy*, 'how many sudden accidents may procure thy ruin' and destroy present happiness. And who should know better the ruin of peace of mind and the rule of Lady Melancholia than one who has been through the trials of loss and braved the shadows of wilderness?"

"Yes," I said, hesitating to say more, for I did not fully know his purpose.

He swung his cane as if he now meant to tilt with Melancholia and shadows.

"Perhaps I should never have told anything of my dream."

He looked down at me, startled. "Oh, no, daughter, it is good to unburden yourself to a proper person; and by that I intend, a *sympathizing* person, as I hope to be. It is well to speak, but poor on the part of others to tittle-tattle the news of such an incident without considering your situation. For a disturbed mind often dreams of disturbing things. Such dreams may not be prophetic but simply reflective of recent unrest."

We walked on slowly, the minister carrying his cane in one hand like a sword to whip at any old-shocks, the goblins of the night.

"That is what I have told myself, not wishing to accuse any. Because in my dream a dark material settled on top of me and gained weight and form until a face I knew appeared, the eyes alight and staring into my mind—as if it belonged to some leopard of the forests who wanted to tear at me. But there are many ill images in my thoughts, even in the sunlight of afternoon."

"That must have been frightening," he said.

"No more than many other pictures in my head. I have seen and fancied too much, and at night I meet the dark sights again, or new ones that seem to rise out of them."

"Well, I am sorry for that trouble." The minister slashed at some dry, pricklesome weeds with his stick. "I would be sad for any granddaughter of mine to have seen what you have seen, to have endured what you have endured."

"I have been," I said, "woefully stirred in mind over what happened to my family and whether it was God's will—from Mr. Barnard, I hear that we have a God who must have wished for all my kind to be lost. And yet they were dear to me and sweetful, lovely in their ways."

He stopped, shaking his head, the puff of air from his breath like the incarnation of gracious white words as he spoke. "With faith, you may be assured and be confident in the gospel. Be not terrified. Are you afeared that your kin were destined for destruction? Just as we reject our works and our merits as some kind of payment for salvation, so we can reject such man-forged acts of ruin as punishment and proof of damnation. Ours is a fractured world, and shattering events will happen. But we are called to be well and whole, come what may. We may die a thousand little deaths in our trials, yet each crisis counts, and we will fly up anew like the phoenix and go on. For Christ is with us amid all slings and arrows."

The tears came to my eyes, for I had often pushed away the thought that some would call my family *condemned.* "I have remembered often the words, 'As it is written, I have loved Jacob, and have hated Esau,'" I said.

"And you feared your own to be Esau," he said. "But Esau was loving to the brother who cheated him, was he not? And God blessed Esau and his descendants. The love that is meant is the plain fact that God chose Jacob to be father of the chosen people. And in that way one was picked and one passed over. You should not keep such things in your heart without sharing them with a proper person. And remember, your kin trusted Christ and so could be content in faith. To be destined does not mean that our lives are play for God. It is not some wretched fatalism that faces the godly. God was at work for our salvation, regenerating hearts before we were aware; he calls us and gives us ears to hear."

He struck his cane on the ground in emphasis and walked on slowly.

"Truly, that is comforting to me." Since the day at Falmouth, I had thought of myself as wandering outside the teachings of the godly. And now there was something better to consider.

"There are as many ways of pondering about mystery as there are ministers in the world, I suppose, though we in the colony have much unity. Many things are a cloud and a shadow to us. But God is still the great covenanter who promised to bless the world through the seed of Abraham."

I was glad of his kindness, and said nothing more but stayed close beside him in the early dark. The sharp, piercing relief I had felt at his words died away, and it felt companionable to walk with this old man in the evening.

"You may talk to me anytime you feel unrest and would like counsel," he told me. "But I would caution you not to speak of the matter of ill dreams to Mr. Barnard."

"Not to speak of them?"

"Mr. Barnard is—over-sensitive, shall we say—to the invisible world. He longs to root out Satan and devilish impulses and to scour the unregenerate. I am not so quick to blame disorder and ill dreams on the crafty machinations of the Devil when we human beings are afflicted with a fallen nature and prone to err. Nor are we two completely in harmony on predestination and many other matters."

"And you think to confide in him would be—?" I did not know how to finish my question. *Dangerous? Calamitous? Dire?*

The minister struck out with his cane, hitting a patch of bleak, draggled thistles. A few remaining stars of seed sailed into the air and vanished.

"It would, I believe, not be entirely wise," he said.

"Not wise," I repeated.

"No," he said. "Mr. Barnard has a deal of concern about dreams and ghostly evidence. He might well consider that you were afflicted by a conjurer or a witch. Many years ago I had to bear witness in favor of a man accused of witchcraft. He was not a particularly upright man and a rather litigious one, and so a likely target. A bird flew into the house where he was staying, and worked itself out through a hole. The family charged him with mocking them in saying the bird had come to suck at the wife's teats. He may well have made such a rude jest, but he did not deserve to be hanged for his lax talk."

"How strange," I said.

"Yes. I saw how one dwarfish incident becomes blown into a Goliath. And then there is no recourse for a minister except to find a stone and a sling and attempt to be as much of a David as he can. All of that is to say that I see no proper grounds for thinking your dream anything but your natural fears and trouble springing up in a new guise."

"I understand what you suggest about Mr. Barnard," I said. "I will be careful."

"This matter of dreams and dream accusations is difficult. As declares my master in the region of the mind, Mr. Robert Burton, we are all in 'a brittle state' and may soon be dejected, our minds overturned 'how many several ways, by bad diet, bad air, a small loss, a little sorrow or discontent, an ague.' In sum, the sleeping mind is a queer sea, alive with eels and glowing dragonfishes and jellies. Who can fathom its depths and denizens? I have a rooted dislike for censures founded on dreams and all manner of phantom evidence. For I do not trust such assaults, invisible to the eye: I do not believe we know where they come from or what they mean, or whether they are true or false. But it is not so with the passionate Mr. Barnard, who learned from his master, Mr. Mather, in Boston."

"I will remember," I said, hurrying to keep up as his stride lengthened.

"I have found that here in the Massachusetts Bay Colony, there is a deal too much tumultuous anguish about sin and salvation, and often a ruinous obsession with the wiles and ambushes of Satan and the rebel angels. It was not so when I was a young man at King's College. At Cambridge, I heard much more about the mercy seat. More about Christ's divine love. More about grace. We have lost some skillful leaders who sailed back to England, finding this world harsh and fierce, even bloody and malicious."

The minister toyed with his cane as he walked. I felt surprised that he confided so much in me.

"Some prideful new-minted men of Harvard College," he added, "are remarkably prone to believe their own half-digested reflections correct. They wish to be the mirror that displays what all others should think—or better, the one others consult and are led by."

"You are strong minded like Major Saltonstall, who said similar things to me about mercy. And it was brave of you to defend a man slandered unjustly. Thank you for helping me as well. You have been a kind friend to my interests, and it makes me feel less solitary in the world."

"Good," he said. "That is excellent. And here is the house waiting for us, and no doubt some drinks to warm us also."

And so we went through the gate, up the walk, and through the door. Inside, I found smiling faces and beeswax candles in Jotham Herrick's silver candlesticks, reflected merrily in glass and more silver.

How angry my mistress would have been to see me welcomed and spending a happy half an hour embroidering with the Dane women, and afterward enjoying powdered cakes and taking cordial at the table with the family. One figure interested me greatly: the pastor's grandson, Richard Dane, the man whom Bel wished to marry. He passed through the room, was introduced, and bowed and said a few words. "I have heard only good of you," I told him. Plump and with a comely, open face, he had a fine, curling beard and merry eyes.

To see the Danes and Ingalls all together, with cousins and aunts and all, made me sad to contemplate what I had lost. But when Jotham Herrick arrived, my melancholy thoughts flew away like the gossamer seeds on a hollow stalk of piss-bed, blown into the air by a child.

We separated from the family party and went to speak with the minister in seclusion. For a few minutes, Jotham and I were left closeted together in the small private study while Mr. Dane sent for tea and more little cakes.

I hardly knew what to say and had begun some polite, weak comment about being pleased to see him again before recollecting our encounter and how we had spoken about marriage together. We had been burning and alive beyond all pleasantries. I fell silent.

"More precious than gold or silver," Jotham Herrick murmured, his hand finding mine.

Looking into his pale eyes, I thought again that he was silver and gold but did not say so. "I am—glad—to see you and know everything that happened the other day is not some idle dream that swept through me and is gone."

"And I am right glad as well to meet you again, and pleased that nothing between us is a dream," he said, and pressed my hand. "But if it were—which simply cannot be true—to be only a dream, it would be a sweet dream, and worth the idleness of lying in bed all day to sleep and conjure images."

He kissed me, and I him, and again I felt that we were one, like two rivers that spill together and marry on their way to the sea, or two flames that leap and cannot be told one from another. And I leaned against him, wishing and wanting to flee away with him to some lonely isle where we would be together always and never be disturbed by the ill news that comes so often in the world.

"You are beautiful in your violet gown, the red and white of you," he whispered.

Red hair has more detractors than any other, I find, and to some of the godly it seems wrong in fire and color. The honorable Nathaniel Saltonstall himself was reviled by the unmannerly Swans as Judge Carrot-Head. Long ago, when red-haired, white-faced Elizabeth was Queen of England, fire-tinged tresses may have been the fashion, but no longer. So I was glad he had a liking for my hair.

"My mother dyed the thread and stitched the dress," I said. "It is the last she made for me."

He held me more tightly, and afterward drew back and took both my hands in his. "I regret that we will never in this life have the sweetness of joining our families, knowing each other's parents," he said. "And so I will heap up my love and joy in you so high that no one may pity us or deem something lacking."

"Whatever sadness comes," I said, "it cannot countervail the content of being in your sight. And that is a charm I hope to feel always."

The words made me flush, and I bent my head to hide the color rising in my throat and cheeks. Truth to tell, I thought him beyond comely and felt sure that I could never tire of gazing on his coarse shock of hair, his eyes that seemed now an uncanny light gray and now lustrous like a mirror, and the straight form of him. Yet these, I felt, were but patterns of delight, drawn after the inward man, the maker of beauty, the public man, and the soldier in the militia.

Who could count up the treasure I had in him, or the new love? Only beggars can count their worth. I was, indeed, a sort of beggar in the world, having lost so much, but I was now made rich with another sort of wealth.

When Mr. Dane returned, trailed by granddaughters bearing pot and cups and more cakes, the two of us were hand in hand by the fire. We sat down to long questions about our families, our histories, and how we each felt about the other. That Jotham Herrick was able to afford a wife was already clear because he had been qualified by the town to serve as selectman, and that required an amount of personal wealth. To see if we were prepared for a family, the minister inspected the ledger book of the shop that Mr. Herrick had been so good as to bring, and together they discussed his future plans of expanding the work and taking on an apprentice, for he had no help but the boy who occasionally hammered silver and was paid in dried corn.

By the end of the evening, the cakes had vanished, and we were approved and promised to each other in the sight of Mr. Dane. I had picked a verse for the sermon he would preach in honor of our contraction. One fineness: I felt quite sure that Jotham and I were no dream after so many mundane and minute inquiries. At the close, before the minister and his daughter-in-law walked me to Goody Holt's door, Mr. Dane pushed back his chair and addressed me.

"Your father and mother were well regarded and of good standing in Boston before the remove. I hear from Major Saltonstall that as yet nothing has been heard of any of the family. For that poor news, I am sorry. But now I am heartened that you wish to change your estate, though you are perhaps over-young for marriage. For the godly marry late compared to others. Yet I believe that union with Mr. Jotham Herrick will be a consolation and a blessing to each of you, restoring and maintaining your place in the world, providing each with a useful helpmeet and comfort and family. You have not had the usual home courtship of our people, but a single threadlet of love, as Mr. Burton writes, is strong: 'No cord or cable can draw so forcibly, or bind so fast.' I will arrange for the contraction, and the calling of the first of the banns. And," he added, "I believe that a notice on the meetinghouse door may be in order, as many will be surprised and like to inspect the edict with their own eyes."

The words danced in my head all the way home, though the minister said little more as I chatted with Deliverance Dane about dyestuffs and fine woolens and the gowns that I was making for the Holt women. I kept thinking of what Mr. Dane had told me at the last. *A notice on the meetinghouse door. The union with Mr. Jotham Herrick. A blessing to each of you.*

My honey-sweet evening ended poorly, though that was no fault of mine or of the Danes.

At the house, Goody Holt and Lizzie appeared to have been waiting for me. Though I crept in the door and, removing my cloak and hat, hoped to gain the garret in quietness, they found me out.

"How now, Lady Fine," Lizzie said, catching me in the hall, her face showing displeasure and her words abandoning any pretense of a polite greeting. "Fancy you going out in such a gown and an embroidered coif."

"Quite wrong to wear clothing unfit for a person's estate in life," Goody Holt said. She came nearer, seemingly in order to scold and frown hard at me.

"Why does she need such nice things now?" Lizzie joined her mother in frowning and reached to finger my sleeve.

I drew back. "My mother made the gown for me, and in truth it was but an everyday rag fit for wearing about the house and garden. I had many more better."

This was a sheer untruth, God forgive me, for I had seldom felt so provoked, perhaps because of the contrast with my recent pleasures, and in my mind I went so far as to call them a pair of stubborn nazzles, lacking in graciousness.

I went on. "But though I have not my mother, yet I have the gown woven from thread she spun over many, many hours. So I will wear it, whether my appearance displeases anyone or not."

I did not like being so forward, and I was regretful to have been led by sudden anger to tell a lie, but it seemed to me that after what had happened at Falmouth, and after my journey, to hold my ground in such a matter as clothing was no great impossibility.

"My father attended college, and was well acquainted with the governor and members of the General Court," I went on. "He taught me Latin and a little Greek and mathematics. There is no need to speak to me in such a mode."

"La," Lizzie said, "such a gem-crusted book you are."

"Come away, Lizzie Holt," her mother said. "She is not so superior any longer, is she?"

I bolted up the stairs, sizzling with temper, only to find that John in his kindness was crouched by the hearth, feeding wood into a new-made fire. And so the day ended in courtesy and thankfulness despite the two waspish creatures.

The frost in the air on the next Sabbath morning made me think that our Indian summer was beginning to ebb away and be lost in autumn. I glimpsed Jotham Herrick on the men's side from where I sat with my cloak gathered close around me, and let my eyes rest on his profile more than was safe for an attentive mind. Once when his glance swept across our little group, he smiled slightly.

"Did you see him looking at me?" I heard Lizzie Holt whispering to Bel, who only shrugged and gave me a wink.

Goody Holt patted Lizzie's knee. "Hush. But yes."

The long hours in the meetinghouse seemed much colder than in the prior weeks, and I longed for a foot-stove with coals. Winter was moving surely toward us. How strange to contemplate that when the snow was piled against the houses, I would be a married woman!

A little girl kneeling on her three-legged cricket to trace the knots in the unpainted wood of a pew, the boys on the pulpit stairs erupting with jubilant yells when squirrels invaded their territory, a child with head tilted up to watch the spiders among the unholy cobwebs: all these had a fresh interest. After snow and spring and perhaps more snow, I might be a mother.

Not many days passed before I saw the winter's first flakes, sparse and whirling in the air and sticking to the grooves on the trees and houses. Goody Holt reproved Bel for dashing about like a hoyden, trying to catch a snowflake on her tongue, but I only liked her the more, seeing that she still had the merriment of a child and joy in the first tiny stars of winter.

Bel and I soon managed an outing to Mr. Dane's house, where Jotham Herrick and I talked again with the minister, though we had no chance to be alone. My friend saw her Richard Dane, and the two conferred for a long time by the fire in the kitchen, making plans to have their own way, undeterred by Goody Holt. I almost felt sad for the mother, considering that she would have two disturbances to her peace, for I felt quite sure she would be disapproving of and angry at the news of my contraction to Mr. Herrick. Indeed, I wondered if she had any hold on contentment, for she was always churlish and a force of chaos to me. But soon she could not distress me further. In the colony, we have a love for November marriages on the heels of harvest, and ours would be one—I would be done with my labors sometime in the month and be entirely free.

The next Sabbath when I walked with Bel Holt to the meeting-house, the air was decidedly colder, although the sun was bright.

"The last day of our tolerable weather," Bel said. "I can feel the chill coming in like spong-water flowing in the air. And not even as warm as when we rose up in the morning."

The sunshine brooded pleasantly on our backs, all the same, and we moved along briskly. We were about to be late for meeting, and neither of us wanted to hear a reproach. So we scuttled for the last stretch of the way, jumping the cart-racks and aiming to catch up with Goody Holt and Lizzie. But we had started too late.

Soon Bel was ruby-ruddy in the face and pulled on my cloak to slow me.

"Wait," she said. "Wait on me."

I took her arm, glad to see how sweet-tempered she looked despite being flushed and out of breath. "What a lovely day," I said, though it was more for the feeling of pleasure in my friend than in the chilly hour.

"The last," she said again. "Wait and see. Tomorrow winter will come. And the streams will freeze, and the rivers and lakes, and the wolves will sing their weird, wavery songs, and they will come into town and howl for flesh."

"For our limbs and marrow-bones," I said, the thought of howls strangely conjuring Goody Holt. Still, I remembered the time I had seen wolves, and how eerie but peaceful it had been. "And the men will hunt and be paid by the head."

"I should like to go hunting. I wonder if Richard Dane would let me," she said. "When we are married, I mean. It's vastly more amusing than scouring with sand, preparing food for winter, and dipping candles."

"Well, I should like to see that," I said.

"But I wouldn't like to meet wolves or leopards or those horses with horns that can spear us through—I would hunt for deer."

"Spear us through? That would be unicorns," I said. "I have never seen one but would like to do so. But I am not sure they inhabit this land. You might have to sail to the other side of the world. To places where the peppercorns grow on trees with cinnamon bark."

"Do they?"

"I do not know."

"And I do not want to go there," she said.

"Then do not," I said.

"Good," she said.

"If I had been a hunter, I might have had a better time coming south from Falmouth. My food was not fresh or tasty, especially after drenchings. And once when I snared a fish, an otter stole it while I was trying to catch another one."

"I'll teach you how to shoot when I learn," she said.

"That would be quite a wonder," I said.

Talking and paying little notice to matters around us, we reached the meetinghouse, where a considerable knot of people crowded around the door to the men's side. What was happening? We could make out little but last year's wolf-scalps nailed beside the door by bounty hunters, the long hanging ladders, and the iron crooks and rope and chains mounted on a pole, all useful in case of fire. Someone was shrieking, and we slowed down, unsure whether we should stay or go.

"I believe," Bel said, "that is—"

She hurried forward, and I kept pace with her.

Lizzie was lying on the ground, screeching. Dr. Abbott was bent over her, attempting to feel for her pulse, but she battered him about the head with a corked bottle until he jerked away.

"Goody Holt, can you calm your daughter enough to get her walking homeward? Such a choleric fit cannot be allowed to continue overlong, or she will be quite ill." The doctor sat back on his heels, rubbing his head, and then reeled awkwardly to his feet when he proved still in range of Lizzie's arms.

"Noise of a rutting cat!" Dr. Abbott's words sounded like a curse.

I traded glances with Bel. "She seems quite robust to me," I whispered.

Mouth ajar, Bel stared at her sister.

Lizzie's eyes ran over the assembled people. She paused at my face, stopped shrieking, and began again, louder than before.

"She does not care one jot for me," I said to Bel, who closed her mouth and turned to look at me.

"No. And she did not like you from the beginning. For that matter, sometimes she does not like me that much either," Bel said.

"Her lungs are working finely," I said.

Bel was not listening. "The agreeable part of all this is nobody paying any attention to the people late to meeting," she said, "and that is us."

The ministers had joined in with the crowd. Though they were not on the friendliest of terms, the two men huddled together, and it appeared that they determined for Mr. Dane to accompany the doctor, Goody Holt, and Lizzie on a journey homeward. Mr. Barnard looked torn in mind, as if he would like to stay and hear the sound of his own voice but also to go along, in case there was some devilry at hand in the caterwauling. I could have relieved his fretting and told him it was only ill nature at work. Three of the town officials appeared at this interesting juncture, including Jotham Herrick. I looked at him with pleasure, though he was hunched over to inspect the sufferer and not aware that I was near. With her audience increased, or perhaps because of his close presence, Lizzie now shrilled even louder, alternately shalming at high pitch and wailing words that no one could understand.

"Whatever is the matter? Usually she is content with being sharp or mulpy," Bel said. "Is she hurt?"

Leaning down only to catch another blow, Dr. Abbott staggered backward and was pinioned by someone standing near us.

"I would conjecture that she is not," I said.

The man who had caught the doctor helped him straighten up, gripping him by the elbow.

"Thank you for that kindness," Dr. Abbott said. He mopped his face with a large handkerchief. "Both the mother and daughter could benefit from a thrashing," he muttered.

I laughed, shielding my face with both hands. Bel prodded me with her elbow. Evidently she had already lost her concern for Lizzie's woes. "See that man? That's Ned Farnum." she whispered. "He lost his leg to the Wabanaki and French dragoons. Mother told me that his wife and daughter died on a march northward, and the baby was tossed onto a heap of rubbish. He says the French are fire dragons! And the Indians fierce as lions. But now he has migrated to Andover, which he finds safer than many inland villages, and says he will stay."

Goody Holt caught sight of me and shook her fist at the pair of us, which made each glance at the other again.

"What, what?" Bel shouted at her mother.

In answer, Goody Holt compressed her lips; she did not make an appealing picture, hair dragged to one side, a hank of it dangling down her face, and her hat swang-ways askew. The bodice of her new gown appeared rent. That mishap would give me a sizable piece of repair work in the sewing room.

"Do you need us?" Though Bel called loudly, it seemed nearly impossible to be heard over the Lizzie-squalls. But somehow Goody Holt grasped the question.

"Certainly not," she snapped at her daughter. Her sharp tone cut through the babble of other voices.

Lizzie was hoisted off the ground by three strong men, one at each shoulder and another grasping her feet. Her gown and petticoats were pulled tidily around her ankles. If a sailor's hammock could wriggle and roar, well, she resembled just such a naval thing. They set off at a bumble-footed run, with the doctor, Mr. Dane, and Goody Holt straggling behind them.

"They'll be bleeding her soon. She won't like that," Bel said prophetically. "But maybe it will calm her down."

Jotham Herrick noticed me and smiled, and for instants we were the only people on the globe, our eyes locked, the sunshine golden all around. Then he went inside with the town clerk, and just as neatly as if planned, a cloud drifted over the sun.

"What did you say?"

Bel laughed at me. "You don't have one little idea, do you? He is a pretty man," she added.

"Yes," I said, "and I hope a good deal more."

"What do you think set off Lizzie?"

I had begun to have an inkling of an idea but was not sure. The last of those gathered near the entry passed inside the meetinghouse. I drew close to the door and pointed to a sign. "This afternoon, evidently we will be contracted to marry, and Mr. Dane will preach the bride sermon for me and Jotham Herrick. I did not expect the betrothal notice to be on the door until the next meeting."

But the announcement was there, and the town clerk would be calling the banns for weeks to come. Any who did not know me would know of me then. Mr. Dane was mindful that I had not dwelled long in Andover and did not have many friends to support me in my new life. Neither of us had family to prepare the wedding meal, and I did not even have a family house to be married from. I certainly had no wish to marry in Goody Holt's sewing room; in his kindness, Mr. Dane had invited us to wed in his own house. It would be a simple-enough ceremony to execute, only a question to each of us from a magistrate, and there would be the recording of names in the town register—the clerk would bring it—and a dinner with bridal cakes and sack posset prepared by the Dane women. Jotham Herrick and I would be well tied and could go together to the rooms over the shop.

"Ah," Bel said. "I begin to understand."

"And so do I. Unfortunately."

"My sister has claimed three or four young men as possible husbands. But only in her fancy."

"And I hope she will move swiftly to a different one," I said, "as I am a little afraid to return to the house. Your mother will no doubt be seething hot. I fear that I shall have to be mouse quiet and mouse small until she grows tired of being wroth with me. Though I am somewhat cheered that Mr. Dane is there to smooth over upsets."

"We must go in," Bel said, moving toward the women's door. "But do not worry. I will help. And perhaps," she added with enthusiasm, "Mother will be so busy stewing in choler about you that I will be able to persuade her that I should be married as soon as possible. And shall get Mr. Francis Dane to come to my aid."

"Overjoyed to be so very useful and handy, Bel," I said, eyeing her, but she paid not the least attention to the satiric note in my words.

"Yes, that is good. I shall have to put the fear into Mother that her daughters are in danger of being unplowed fields—thornbacks, dried and ornery and husbandless."

"A promising scheme," I said, and laughed. Opening the door, I slipped inside.

People were yet milling around in disorder, many of them gossiping about what had taken place outside, while Mr. Barnard called for them to sit.

The morning services were frigid, and several men railed at their near neighbors and called for beer before the minister was half-done. The teaching elders read prodigious passages of Scripture. The expositions and prayers droned on. The pastor kept turning over the hourglass, and his sermon must have been divided into a hundred heads and subheads. It was all long, long, long, the words beating on the sounding-board. Though fond of singing, on this morning I seemed to look on my kind as if on visitors from a land where song was forbidden. The people bawled the psalms, some for tune hewing to Windsor, some to York, some to Cambridge, all whining or screaking or tolling the notes as their separate humors and fancies seized them. Never had a cold meeting seemed to move so slowly!

But at last the nooning break came.

Bel and I were invited to a supper of pease, cold venison, pumpkin stew, and beer between the morning and afternoon preaching. Goodwife Deliverance Dane had seen Lizzie Holt's fit and conceived that we might be better content away from the Holt house. We were glad to be elsewhere, glad to dine in company.

Before day was over, I was contracted to marry, and seated before the people with Jotham Herrick. Mr. Dane preached a fine bride's sermon on the text I had picked from the Song of Solomon: *For behold, winter is past: the rain is changed, and is gone away. The flowers appear in the earth: the time of the singing of birds is come, and the voice of the turtle is heard in our land.* And though he spoke on the Church as the Bride of Christ, yet he also dwelled on our past losses and trials, and how we would join together and make winter into our spring. We sat attentively, knowing that all around us, people were looking, and yet conscious that the other was close beside. I wanted to weep, thinking of my mother and how she would never prepare my bride cakes or greet my husband on our wedding day. To distract myself from making such a public sign of weakness, I thought of Lizzie shrieking from the ground, and how she had wanted to take from me the few tokens of family I had left. That cheered me right up! Or, rather, the thought that my remnants would belong in the rooms over the smith's shop, and that I would belong to someone again—not as a servant but as an essential part of a whole—comforted me.

So often when some sweet hour comes, we have to render payment for it afterward. To touch Jotham Herrick's hand when services ended, to feel proud of his words and sentiments, to admire the lines of his face: all this vanished into the past like a scrape of sugar into hot water when Bel and I set off for the house. I felt only dread when I contemplated Lizzie's froth and fury, sure that I was trapped in its presence unless I returned to the Saltonstalls—and in that case I would be far from Jotham Herrick.

I do not know whether I felt more of perturbation or relief when I saw Francis Dane, Thomas Barnard, and Dudley Bradstreet entering the house ahead of us, but both mingled strongly in me. I hoped two ministers and a magistrate might be a bulwark between me and Goody Holt and Lizzie.

When we stepped inside, I at once saw Lizzie Holt reclining on a bench by the fire, the ministers and magistrate talking to her mother and Dr. Abbott. John was there, feeding the flames with fresh-split wood. He stared at me and gave a jerk of the head, as if to signal that I should pass quickly upstairs.

But Lizzie started up and shrieked, "There she is, there she is! Catch her, catch her!" Her voice was strained and hoarse, but there was no doubt she meant me.

"Come forward," Mr. Dane called to us.

We approached the others slowly, Bel taking my arm.

"There! The witch," Lizzie croaked, pointing a long finger at me. "Witch! She bewitched our speckled pig and Mr. Herrick. I would have said so when the bride sermon was preached. Yes, I would have stood in the assembly and named her a witch."

My hand rose to my breastbone. I could not speak.

"Dear child, you have been unwell—afflicted by a profusion of humors—and now the bleeding has made you feeble in body and mind," Dr. Abbot said. "Crawly mawly, as your mother says."

Mr. Dane turned to us. "Perhaps daughter Mehitabel Holt would take her mother for a short walk so that Goodwife Holt could have respite from the day's sufferings."

"That is not an ill thought," Mr. Barnard said in a loud voice, seemingly determined not to be outdone by his elder.

"Surely a parent should be present," Goody Holt said.

"There is no need," Mr. Dane said, "and you have been through much."

"I commend the fresh air," the doctor added.

But Goody Holt was not going to be deprived of her say. Though Bel put an arm around her mother as if to turn her toward the doorway, she was not to be diverted from her course. She glared at me. "We have had nothing but trouble with this one. A poor, draggled thing who felt herself too fine for us!"

"Indeed, she did not, Mother," Bel said, drawing her mother's arm through her own. "She was always helpful and courteous."

Goody Holt ignored this response and pushed on. "Why, my Lizzie thought her coverlet far too precious for someone in her situation. And truly it was—a finespun wool beautifully dyed and woven in subtle patterns. Not at all the thing for a low girl."

"Flaunting herself in a violet gown when she went to the Danes' that evening, Mother," Lizzie Holt said huskily. "You know her garb was not suitable to her rank. And under her bonnet, that coif with the white embroidered leaves!"

Bel dropped her mother's arm. "Forgive me, but the coverlet— the blanket, more properly—was almost all that she had from her mother, who spun the wool and dyed it. Would you take that from her? And the coif and gown, too, were stitched by her dead mother. Would you have a daughter scorn her elders?"

Goody Holt looked at her in indignation, crimping her lips together as if she had just bitten down on a peppercorn. "Hush, child," she said.

"I will not be hushed. And am no child. I tell you in the presence of these men that I will no longer be silent when you have prevented my own marriage and threatened me!"

"What? What are you saying? Surely *you* are one bewitched," Goody Holt said loudly. "See? Another one magicked!"

"Goodman Richard Dane would marry me, and I would marry him. You have no right to keep me from him. I protest to the magistrate and the ministers that you have wronged me in this matter!"

I had never seen Bel so wroth, and I nearly smiled in surprise to see it.

"Whatever do you mean?" Goody Holt cocked her head to one side, peering at her daughter as if she had not seen her clearly heretofore, which, upon reflection, I considered quite likely.

"I ask the ministers and Captain Bradstreet to support me in this cause, and I will take my plea so far as the General Court if you do not let us have our way," Bel said with firmness.

Goody Holt opened and closed her mouth a few times in an admirable imitation of a fish. At this, John, still kneeling by the fire, let out a noise suspiciously like a laugh, choked, and waved a hand in front of his face as though afflicted by a fume of smoke.

"What of this?" Mr. Barnard said, turning to his elder minister.

"They have, it seems, promised that they will marry no one else but each other," Mr. Dane said. "At least, that is the report I have heard from our young Richard."

"Witch! Witch!" Lizzie was now so hoarse that it was difficult to understand what she was saying, and no one heeded her outcry.

"Exactly right! We are each promised to the other, and no one otherwise will ever do," Bel said.

"Mehitabel Holt," her mother said, and sank onto a plank-bottom chair.

"Mehitabel Holt will be Mehitabel Dane or nothing else," her daughter said. She appeared bigger than before, her feet set wide apart, hands planted on hips.

"Your daughter's demand is lawful," Mr. Barnard told Goody Holt.

"This is about *me*," Lizzie cried, "me and that *witch*."

"Indeed she is within her rights," said Captain Bradstreet.

"And I will sue for those rights in court if she does not yield them to me," Bel added.

"Mehitabel has no excuse to threaten marriage when mine is spoiled," Lizzie said in a fretful tone, but the men did not hear.

Pastors and magistrate stepped closer to Goody Holt, who put up her hands as if to keep them off.

"I told her my maternal wishes. She is a bad, stubborn naughty-pack of a daughter," Goody Holt said, and her eyes wandered around the room as if in search of support.

"That is an untruth. I have been a proper daughter even when given strong reason to be angered by peevishness and spite," Bel said.

"Oh! Have it your way, you monstrous, monstrous child!" Goody Holt slapped her knees in lieu of slapping her daughter. "Offspring of Babel-tower! Scion of Belial!"

Everyone in the room stared at her in silence.

Lizzie was the one to break that startled hush.

"What about the witch?" Strained by screaming, her voice was as plaintive as a gravelly voice could be.

"What witch?" Mr. Barnard was confused by the change in the direction of events, but not so confused that he could not maintain a keen interest in all things diabolical.

She waved a hand at me.

"Pah!" exclaimed Bel. "What arrant nonsense!"

We all looked at her, for by the magic of determination and desire, she had puffed up like an enraged cat and become the most powerful person in the room. The rest of us seemed mere harvest mice in comparison.

"She is no witch, Lizzie Holt, but only a person with many misfortunes," Bel said, "one of them being the misfortune of tumbling into the clutches of a pair of tetchy, jealous, and cobble-hearted women. All she has done is make you gowns and petticoats and collars and such. Yes, the work does look so lovely that it seems like witchcraft but only because she is adept and quick with her needle, above the common ruck. She did no harm to anyone, nor to the speckled pig, who ate cockleburs like a fool and died. And you were not even kind to one who had just lost her mother and father and everyone she loved!"

At the end of this speech, the men shifted as one to stare at Lizzie Holt.

She had begun to shed tears, and I was surprised to find that I felt pity for her. The doctor's lance and bowl of blood were lying beside the hearth, and I wondered if she cried out of weakness.

"He was to be mine. The sieve did not promise," she sobbed, "but the key-and-book did. They said so!" She looked at us imploringly.

"My dear daughter in Christ," Mr. Barnard said, these words striking what was hard in him like a flintstone against adamant. "Surely you have not been playing at scissors-and-sieve! And to take the holy writ in vain in such a way, meaning to usurp the foreknowledge of God, determined to have revelation via the vile practice of key-and-book! What do you mean by such pranks of wickedness? Why, to pervert the Scripture is far worse than the reading of the unlawful ribaldries, merriments, and vulgar romances that so infect the work of our Boston publishers. It is abominable!"

Lizzie sobbed the louder.

Captain Bradstreet whistled, and Mr. Dane sat down heavily on a stool that John brought to him. I could see Bess peeping at us from the back room.

"It was just a game," Lizzie said. "I was not the only one."

"This," Mr. Barnard intoned, "this, this, *this* is how the Devil catches hold and snares the reprobate in his devices, how he catches the fluttering souls in his bird-lime. He boils the holly bark until the green part is ripe, and he pounds it into submission until the consistency is sauce, with no flecks of bark remaining. And then he ferments the whole and cooks it over the fire with oil. And when the mess is ripe, he spreads it on the invisible branches of this world and catches himself a silly young songbird."

Mr. Dane drew out a large indigo cloth and mopped at his face.

Lizzie looked from one minister to the other.

Parson Dane crammed the linen back into his sleeve. "Mr. Barnard means that you should not have meddled with sieve-and-scissors or key-and-book," he said mildly. "It is not right to attempt to tell the future, for that is a bid to take away the prerogatives of God. Occult powers are not horses for you to bridle, saddle, and control for your own use. Although not the worst form of witchcraft, witchcraft is what fortune-telling is. You did not know. And I am sure you will not play such tricks again."

Here Lizzie burst into fresh sobs, rocking back and forth on the bench. Perhaps she was crying as much for the close observation of Captain Bradstreet as for reproof and jealousy. "But she bewitched Selectman Herrick. She's the witch, not me!"

Bel went over and patted her on the shoulder. "Lizzie Holt, it was plain from the start that Mr. Herrick had a liking for only one person. That one." She pointed at me. "He liked her when he saw her, and he still does. Sad for you, but that is how it is."

"She bewitched him," Lizzie said in a whisper.

"In a manner, if you call brightness and fair looks a witchcraft. Leave over, Lizzie Holt. I am sorry for you, but there the enchantment lies—in her merits. And she tried to stop the sieve-and-scissors. That is not the act of a witch."

Lizzie pushed away her sister's hand and sat staring at the floor.

She loathes me. And Goody Holt scorns me. What should I do? Only Bel cares about me, and John and Bess, who cannot help. I gazed at the vials and packets tumbled at my feet, spilled from Dr. Abbot's bag.

White Snail Powder. Oil of Foxes. Cobwebs. Beetle-blood. Dried Heart-of-Dolphin. Willow bark. Old-sows. Honey. Rolled into balls, the old-sows made medicines for scrofula. Cobwebs helped cuts and bleeding. Honey was also good for wounds, and willow bark for fever and pain. The rest stayed a mystery to me.

"I do not believe that the young woman should stay longer under this roof," Captain Bradstreet said, gesturing at me.

"She is not done with her hired labors!" Goody Holt stood up, her arms akimbo.

"No doubt she could manage just as well at another house for a few weeks," Mr. Barnard said. "She may complete the work as handily in one place as another, or else you may release her."

"My family would be glad to take her in," Mr. Dane said. "She has spent time with the women of my household, and I expect they would be glad to have another lesson or two from her needle."

The younger minister frowned. "I am more vexed over the matter of this wretched daughter Lizzie Holt," he said. "As it is written in Romans 9, 'Therefore he hath mercy on whom he will and whom he will he hardeneth.' Please Lord she is not of the latter."

"Pray excuse me for leaving that matter to you, Mr. Barnard. And I for one am satisfied with the proposed removal," Captain Bradstreet declared. "Unless the maligned young woman wishes to bring suit in turn."

At this, the magistrate turned his glance toward me. I curtseyed to him. "No, sir, indeed. I thank you for considering me."

Captain Bradstreet had a kindly look, as best befitted a man who was a judge and a son of Mistress Anne Bradstreet. He nodded, appearing to be satisfied.

Bel, who had been crouching by her sister, rose. "By your leave, shall I help my friend pack?"

"Very well," Mr. Barnard said. "Go you on. I expect Goody Holt will allow you to help carry goods and gowns to the Dane house. Perhaps my brother minister will be so good as to discuss your marriage once you arrive there."

Bel looked at me sidelong, smiling. I guessed she was thinking that she might have the chance to see Richard Dane and tell him her tidings.

Mr. Barnard strode forward and inspected the unfortunate Lizzie, and swung around to us. "That is all well enough. Mr. Dane may take care of the matter of his grandson's contraction. And I will stay to speak to this professed fortune-teller, who has had so little of wisdom and so much of corruption as to fall into the claws of Satan. Young women are ever vulnerable to the Devil, being watery storehouses of bodily humors, subject to monthly purgings. I will counsel her, and battle to restore her to our community."

He nodded with one quick jerk of the head. "We may not suffer an open and obstinate contemner of holy ordinance to continue in villainous works. And to misspend precious time."

Watery storehouses! Purgings! I felt even more sympathy for Lizzie Holt, and was glad the minister had not questioned her closely about her companion in sieve-and-scissors fortune-telling.

Mr. Dane, I noticed, looked angered or offended by the younger minister's speech. He spread his hands as if to encompass the room with his words.

"As the wise Mr. Robert Burton asserts, 'We ought not to be so rash and vigorous in our censures, as some are; charity will judge and hope the best. God be merciful to us all.'"

Mr. Dane's reproof might as well have been spoken to a stock or stone for all the heed Mr. Barnard, Goody Holt, or Lizzie paid to his words. He shook his head slightly, and I was struck by how lonely and frail he appeared. And yet I could feel nothing but comfort and content at the meeting's outcome.

Bel and I made our courtesies to the visitors and slipped out the door. We raced up to the garret, pushing each other and laughing.

"We will both be married soon and have our own households to govern." Bel snatched at my hands and we jumped up and down like children playing.

When we slowed and stopped, I confessed to her that I regretted having a confirmed enemy.

"You did nothing to earn one. My sister will get over her disappointment. Mayhap she will marry some crabbed old man and leave it all behind."

"How mighty you were! Indeed, I would be fearful to have you as a foe."

"Then do not cross me!" Clapping her hands together, she laughed. "I like to have my own way."

"Who does not?"

Bel rubbed her arms briskly. "How stingy Mother was with your room. You needed warm fires, but I often heard her tell John to put the wood down when he was headed up the stairs."

" 'Tis over," I said, and bent to gather up my store of gowns and waistcoats from the floor.

"Yes, and good fortune to sister Lizzie, cooped in this house. Likely she'll be a downright thornback and have to live with Mother always."

She did not seem a whit concerned by this imagined outcome but shook out my mother's blanket and began to lay out petticoats and chemises on top in preparation for rolling them up in the soft cloth. Once she paused with Mary's blank-faced doll in her hand.

"Poor little rag child," she said, and gave it a kiss.

6

Promise

Andover, November 1690

The world was a bitter thing with the water turned to crystalline bone that could be shattered into brittle fragments with a hard shove, the air sharp in our noses, the snow a thin scattering on the ground. Bel Holt and I were wrapped in cloaks, hunched against the cold. Children were picking up sticks among trees on the edge of town, heaping them into great bundles that some already wore on their backs, resembling so many prickly hedgehogs—like the half-hedgehog boy in the German-forest story Goody Waters told me when I was a child, whose father wished for a son so long and hard that one day he declared that he would take even a hedgehog. And fairies in the woods by the field heard him and granted his wish with much laughter. But I expect it was not so amusing for the boy.

The seven children were singing despite the cold and their red cheeks and noses. One of the boys had taken off his doublet and cloak and was running about with a prodigious bundle on his back. The others sang without him, their voices piping, each one singing a different tune so that the syllables jangled together:

> *Four dilly-dangles,*
> *Four stave standies,*
> *Two crookers,*
> *Two lookers,*
> *One big bag,*
> *One wig wag.*

A child shouted that we must guess, and they all took up the refrain, pausing in their work to call, "Guess! Guess! Guess!" at us.

Bel Holt and I laughed, not wanting to pause in the cold but caught by their game.

"An elephant," Bel shouted.

"No, no, no!" They jumped up and down, pleased at our silliness.

"Belike, say, a unicorn with a bundle," I guessed.

"What's that?"

"That's just one crooker!"

"It's a horse."

"It's not a horse."

"It's not real!"

"It's the Devil's pony!"

"No, it's like an angel only with four legs."

The last was spoken by a girl with curly hair peeping out from under her hood. Nittle and sweet-faced, she looked colder than the rest and was shivering.

"You have enough tinder. Run home, all of you," I said. "The air is raw."

"But you haven't guessed our riddle," a girl said.

The boy who had thrown off his duds came bursting up and bellowed, "A cow, a cow, a cow."

"You spoiled it, Esau!"

"That was bad!"

"You always spoil the joke!"

"What cow?" Bel looked around, shading her eyes.

The children laughed, dancing about in rapture and to warm themselves. When they stopped and looked at us, their faces eager, I could not help smiling and joining in their game. "I see no cow. Not one or two or three. None at all."

Here they roared again, laughing and stumbling about as if I had said words so fantastical that their joy would never be at end.

"Crookers!" A boy wearing a man's hand-me-down felt hat held up curled fingers beside his head to stand for horns.

"Lookers!" Another made his fingers like spectacles and peered at me.

The boy Esau dropped onto four legs and pretended to eat snow as if it were grass. His pack of sticks wobbling, he looked more like a hedgehog boy than ever.

"Oh," cried Bel.

"You mean a cow! Crookers and lookers and dilly-dangles? A cow?" I lifted my hands in amazement.

They jumped around us, pricked us with their bundles, and shouted, "Stave standies! Wig wag!" One little one grasped me around the knees, and I leaned down to rub her back and give her a bit of warmth.

"Now snickup," Bel called, and clapped her hands together. "Spank away home! Tell your riddles by the fire."

Cloaks whipping, they wheeled like enchanted creatures who could ride the wind and dashed away, the boy Esau rushing back to retrieve his cloak and jacket and pounding after the others so strongly that we saw him overtake them before they reached the nearest house.

"They should not be so far, alone," Bel said. "I am glad they have gone."

"Yes," I said, a sense of the quickness and ferocity of attack from the natives burning through my thoughts and dying away. It was hard to spoil my pleasure in the day, however harsh the elements. Andover was a secure place, I reminded myself. Mr. Barnard had spoken of the winter, already upon us, as a punishment for transgression, but I found it difficult to connect briskness with sin when walking in the free air with Bel Holt, talking and laughing as we went.

We were on our way to visit Phoebe Wardwell, Bel's friend, or, more rightly, to sew baby clothes with her. Two weeks of the banns had passed, two weeks of staying in the Dane household, two weeks of being free from Goody Holt, who had decided that she would prefer not to pay for any more of my handiwork, two weeks when Bel Holt had heard gossip join her name with Richard Dane's in the assembly. Had we ever been so glad and pleased in Andover?

The Wardwells' house was purchased cheaply when John Lovejoy, the man who had inherited it from his uncle, gave up on Andover and rode back to Boston and from there sailed to Norfolk, England, where he died a few years later. Afterward, Mr. Dane received a Lovejoy bequest of a small ivory triptych said to be three hundred years old, crowded with scenes of Mary and the child Jesus before a crammed architectural backdrop of stiff, tiny houses and towers. Although the sort of religious object that our people rejected, it held a fascination and was cleverly artificed. On application to the minister, this strangeness could be viewed. But there seemed nothing about the narrow, steep-roofed Wardwell house that was either so fantastic as African elephant ivory or so artfully made as the carving, although the fine brick chimbley that should have been at the center of the house jutted from the side, and the clapboard on the overhang looked scorched. Bel Holt had said there was something else peculiar about the place, and so I felt a curiosity to see the interior. The setting was ordinary enough, though a round hillock rose up near a hedge of trees and shrubs.

"Odd," I said, pointing.

"Yes," Bel said, looking smug, so that I suspected she had a secret knowledge.

"What?"

"Just a mighty hump of dirt," she said.

Inside, there was nothing strange visible, just a fire jumping on the hearth to welcome us, along with a hot drink containing maple-water and spices and a kettle of pottage slowly bubbling on the fire, as well as the special treat of marchpane molded into the shape of tiny castles, each with a sugared almond for the door.

I held one on my palm, admiring the towers and crenellations. "It is almost as good as seeing a castle like the ones I have heard described by people born over the sea," I said, "and will be much tastier. Thank you."

"Samuel Wardwell, my father-by-marriage, whittled the mold for me. I do not know why he chose a castle, as none of us have ever seen one. Nor are there likely to be any hereabouts. But a pretty fancy. He was good to make me a gift," Phoebe said.

She was a slight woman, a little older than Bel, and I guessed that her child would be born in about two months.

"I am right glad you have come," she said to me. "My sister-in-law told me of your sufferings before you found us here. You have been racked and harried but have come through."

She embraced me, and I found that she was as delicate as a snow-bird. Her bones seemed mere twigs.

"And I am pleased to know you," I said.

"Where is your husband?" Bel was not paying attention to us and looked around as if she expected to see him approaching.

"He carted a load of trattles to the field. Dung is good for the land," she said, "and we were given rabbits last year. They thrive and are good eating, too. But I do not know that Thomas Wardwell can work the trattles into the ground, because it is already near hard winter."

"The wind is bitter," I said, and tasted the sweet marchpane with the tip of my tongue. "I do not envy Goodman Wardwell's time in the field."

"He endures the chill hardily enough," she said, "though he will be glad to warm himself by the fire and have a hot drink."

"As we are glad after the walk here," I said. "I was tempted to ride my horse and bring a pillion-pad for a passenger, but Hortus was hired out for the week and nowhere to be seen."

"Perhaps he would not have liked to carry me," Bel said. "I am not so light as you. And no horsewoman."

"Hortus is gentle. And strong."

"And far away, luckily for me. I had rather be chilled than ride," she said.

"I do not like the cold and ice," Phoebe Wardwell told her.

"But your supper is hot," Bel said.

Phoebe Wardwell laughed. "Could that be a hint, Bel Holt?"

"It might be."

Goody Wardwell's blessing sticks in memory. In time, I might have forgotten her words except that the sentiment made such a contrast with later events in her life: "We beseech Thee, good Lord, that just as our bodily hungers long for earthly bread, so may our soul's hunger ever seek and find the abundant life of the bread of heaven; that is, Jesus Christ, who is and will be and was before the worlds were made, amen."

We set to and made short work of the pottage and mugs of maple-water. The fresh air in our mouths on the way was a drink that had made us hungry, and Bel and I scraped the bowls clean. But only slowly did we consume the lovely castles, wanting them to last. Still, they went to ruin so quickly!

We talked about infant clothing and gear, trying to fathom what Phoebe Wardwell still needed to be made ready before her trouble came on her. At last we determined to venture on a few plain shifts, several long aprons, and some caps, all suitable to an infant.

"And we can trim them." I held out some curls of ribbon. "Bel persuaded her mother to hand over some snippets."

"How pretty!" Phoebe Wardwell drew them through her fingers. "Finer work than I have seen in Andover. I thank her for this, and you for coming to sew when you must have much to do."

"It will be handy practice for us," Bel said. "For we may have need of such sewing on small garments ourselves someday."

She looked filled with mischief at this thought. I could not help but laugh and feel glad to have so merry a friend.

"I hope you are joyful in your bridal night, and have many well-made children to raise up," Phoebe told her.

"I expect we will be pleased enough," Bel said. She put the last bite of marchpane in her mouth and closed her eyes to savor it, and afterward licked her fingers to catch the last trace of sweetness.

"Your Richard Dane is a fine figure of a man. And a kind man." Phoebe Wardwell rested a hand on her belly. "Like my husband."

"Yes." Bel rocked forward, smiling, and held her hands out to the fire.

After our supper, we cut garments from a length of muslin the Danes had sent as a gift, and soon were busily engaged in seaming the parts.

"In a year we may be sitting together, stitching clothes for one of you," Phoebe Wardwell said.

"Perhaps. And if so, I will be glad." I felt a lightning streak of some feeling—anticipation, fear, excitement, or a mixture of them all. Jotham Herrick drifted through my thoughts, his ethereal, imaginary hand brushing against me.

"I can wait till children come," Bel said. "I want to rommock about in bed first, not be forbidden because a child lives in my belly. Though it is good to birth well-favored boys and girls that like to laugh and play."

"Rommock about in bed! Bel Holt, you are a frisky woman!" Phoebe Wardwell stretched and reached to rub the small of her back. She was smiling, though. "What a bride you will be! I am not sure your betrothed will know what a storm has overtaken him."

"I like to play and gambol," Bel said. "My own mother and sister pull the sour faces more than I can bear, and to no fit purpose. I shall marry Goodman Dane, and I expect to be always frolicsome in bed and be gladsome the rest of the time. When nothing ill has happened, I mean. Because evil events do happen. We cannot do much about that except to go on. But I intend to march on with a blithe humor and with spirit!"

Not for the first time, I reflected that I knew entirely too much about ill and evil things, and that it was hard always to be thinking on them when Bel Holt or some other person chattered as though I was still a young woman with family and an even tenor to her life. Though my story had flashed around town before I even arrived, few were so thoughtful as to consider their words around me.

But I only bent to the work and sewed faster.

Phoebe Wardwell, to whom I had barely spoken before the day, put her hand on mine so that I paused and looked up. "I pray that many consoling years come to you," she said. "And that you are glad, content in your marriage. Mr. Jotham Herrick is a man much admired for learning and skill in Andover. When you become Mistress Charis Herrick, you will be restored to something like the place you once had, I imagine."

"He is one our Lizzie would have liked to capture," Bel said. "Not that she can be that particular, being an elvish companion. She swings back and forth between choler and melancholy as to disposition. And she idles about the house, complaining. If she didn't spoffle about so, going on about trifles and wasting the time! I cannot imagine her being a good manager, or making a man pleased under the bed-clothes." She stabbed at the cloth with her needle.

"Do you never waste the time?" Goody Wardwell smiled down at her work.

Bel Holt shrugged in reply.

"Perhaps she will find the right man, and then she will behave differently," I said.

"No," Bel said, her tone decided. "She's harnsey-gutted in body and mind."

"Harnsey-gutted! A lean, stalking bird? The kind we see hunting and spearing minnows along the water's edge? You are angry with Lizzie Holt," I said, "and you want to be unkind. But she is your sister. Soon you will be sanguine again, and not worry so much about what she says and does."

She darted me a look.

"I have no great love for Lizzie Holt because she dislikes me, and for no solid reason," I said. "But I expect she has estimable qualities."

"Like what?"

"Well, I do not exactly know," I said, "but am sure she must have some. I am not so privileged as to know her well."

"I am," Bel said, "and I say that she has very few of them."

Phoebe Wardwell shook her head. "I believe she is attentive to your mother. And she comports herself well in the meetinghouse—"

"What about that tempest-fit outside the meetinghouse door? That was not behaving properly," Bel said.

"I did hear something about that."

"The whole town was talking about my sister for a full week. And everyone stared at her at the next public meeting, wondering if she would tumble out of her seat and flail her arms and legs and go to woltering on the floor like a laldrum."

"Laldrum? She was unwell," Phoebe protested.

"Yes, indeed," I said.

"She was plainly upset in her mind, you mean," Bel said, and held up an apron to examine the neck. "And she made a mighty silly naz-zle of herself in full view of the congregation, many of whom stood around gaping at her and so got a long stare at some buffle-headed nonsense."

"*Nazzle* is harsh for someone taken by a fit," Phoebe said.

"There are fits, it is true," Bel said, "but there are such things as bursts of ill temper."

"Remember that she had to spend some no-doubt harrowing hours with Mr. Barnard, going over the error of her manners," I said. "And she could have tittle-tattled on you, and said that you had played at sieve-and-scissors, but she did not. You would have had to listen to his harangue as well. Is that not kind?"

Bel let out a low groan.

"Only because he was so busy talking about the powers of the invisible world that he forgot that it takes two to play at sieve-and-scissors. He talked her right into the ground, which is something amazing. "

"Unlike some, I am fond of old Mr. Dane," Phoebe said. "He never alarms me the way Mr. Barnard can. But I believe either one would have scoured and scolded you for fortune-telling."

"I suppose," Bel said. She set down the apron and stared absently at the fire.

"But all the same, some of the Wardwells do tell fortunes," Phoebe said. "When they took to reading lines from palms in front of me, I tried to say to Goodman Wardwell and his son that the future belongs to God, but they did not pay any mind. People do not listen when you say what they do not care to hear."

In response, Bel yawned and stood up, turning her back to the flames.

"Once old Samuel Wardwell caught up my hand and told me that I would not live long," Phoebe added. "But who does?"

"Methuselah," said Bel.

"I doubt our years are written in the palms of our hands," I said.

"And I also. I scrubbed my hand afterward." She leaned forward. "He made me uneasy, and I was a long time forgetting what he said. And now I have remembered it again."

Bel scuffed her shoe back and forth on the floor. "I'm no good for sewing any longer. There is a limit to my patience, and that verge has been reached. The work will be all niffle-naffle from here on if I try. Let's show off the secret place," she said.

"But we've hardly done enough work, surely," I said, glancing up.

"We can finish the clothes later," Bel proposed, "or take them with us. Or come again another day."

Phoebe Wardwell hesitated.

"Please! You promised," Bel said. She turned toward me, lowering her voice as if someone might overhear. "And it is a true secret, for the Wardwells did not know when they possessed the house. But now you will know, and the secret will be four."

"Six," Phoebe said. "The three of us and Thomas Wardwell and the two dead Lovejoys, who tell no one. I meant to share the story with Mr. Dane when he visited after the wedding but clean failed to remember. But now I am in the habit of keeping the secret—it is our own to possess or to give away where we will."

"I know nothing about what you are saying," I said. "I beg you, do not consider me. Though I am safe with a secret, if it be not evil."

Indeed, I thought, *my mind is as charged with secrets as a paper cartridge packed with grains of powder.* Falmouth had changed me, so that my mind was always double, quietly considering another's words while my thoughts often protested.

"Right, then," Phoebe said. "Though I am a bit afraid of a fall."

She struggled a little in rising, and I reached for her hand, hauling her upward until she found her footing.

"'Tis dirty, you know, where we must travel," she told me.

I did not answer, not having the least conception what she meant.

"We can just hold our cloaks close," Bel said. "And if they are dirtied, well, we can brush them by the fire."

I stared at her. "I have no line with which to plumb your—"

"A surprise," Bel broke in. "You know what a surprise is."

"Often it is something terrible."

"Not like that," she assured me.

"You must put on your outer clothes," Phoebe Wardwell told me. "As much to protect your gown as for the cold."

She lit a straw in the fire and then a candle, choosing a good-sized stub of tallow and stabbing it onto the metal teeth of a battered lantern.

"A candle? But 'tis daylight."

No one answered my wonderment. I stood up, in greater mystery than when they had first started talking about the secret place. We fastened our cloaks as though leaving, yet we were not leaving. What was this? Bel headed out of the room and toward the lean-to room at the back of the house. In truth, I had lost any love of surprise long ago and would have preferred to sit sewing by the fire over being teased by a riddle.

The place was odd. First, the wrongly set chimbley, and now a strange narrow way that ran along one side ...

In the rear of the passage, Phoebe shoved away an old traveling chest that must have come with someone's grandparents from England and knelt down, stroking the floor with her fingers. "Just here," she said.

At once she jerked her arm upward, lifting a large square of boards to expose darkness and the slats of a ladder going down.

"A root cellar? What is so wondrous about a cellar? Though it is cleverly disguised," I said.

Nevertheless, I knelt down with the others and gazed as Phoebe Wardwell lowered the candle lantern into the opening. The light shone golden and amber through the thin horn panes, shifting and sliding on the dirt walls below.

Strange to smell in the winter, a faint odor of earth met my nose. A wave of warmer air washed against our faces. By the flicker of candlelight, I saw that the darkness of the soil gave way to a paler brown, the walls shored up here and there with logs and branches.

I still did not understand why we had come here, or why Bel wanted me to see the Wardwell cellar.

"It's not a root cellar," Bel said.

"What then?"

Phoebe Wardwell eased herself to a sitting position and let her legs dangle in the opening as she explained. "Thomas Wardwell purchased our house from John Lovejoy, heir to his uncle's estate. The uncle, Goodman Silas Lovejoy, was handy and constructed most of the house himself. I have heard that a traveling stonemason built the bigger of the chimbleys. The house stood all alone, though since that year the other houses have grown braver and crept out this way, until we almost can be said to have neighbors."

"It is still lonely," Bel said. "I wish you were nearer."

"Silas Lovejoy had a just fear of Indians because one day he left home to go to a town meeting, and when he came home again, his wife and child had been clubbed, and most of the right-hand side of the house was burned, both the main part and the lean-to at back. So it is only half a house now."

"What a terrible day," I said.

Again Phoebe Wardwell reached over to me and placed her hand on mine.

"Many people urged him to abandon the house or pick it to pieces and move to town," she said. "He was still a young man and might marry again. But he did not. He patched the house, leaving the center chimney nearly half outside and adding another one in what was left of the lean-to. A thin piece of parlor and of another room in the lean-to was left over. He tore down the parlor wall, but he kept the useless wall in the lean-to. Between the outer wall and a lean-to wall was a narrow space that became storage and also served as a passageway from the front to the back."

"How odd," I said. "So he just put an outer wall on the remains?"

"Yes," she said. "And he hid the trapdoor here in the passage. Evidently he began digging sometime in that first year because the old people remember when Lovejoy's Hillock began to be a landmark, and it was not long till it rose so high than no one passing could ignore it."

"You mean that bump in the landscape? Near the hedge? Bel Dane, you told me that it was nothing! Is that what happened to the dirt? But what is the meaning of it?" I was still confused, still thinking of what was below us as a small cellarage.

"You will find out," Bel said. She looked at Phoebe and said, "Swing up your legs and let me go first. Then I can help you."

As soon as the pregnant woman did so, Bel picked up the lantern and lowered herself into the gap. I could hear her shoes scraping on the rungs.

I was worried for Phoebe Wardwell. "Is this safe for you?"

But Phoebe clambered after her, latching on to the lip of the hole before slowly vanishing rung by rung into the darkness. I marveled that she managed so well, and not as though she carried a burden. She must have been on the ladder many times before.

Soon Phoebe stood under the trapdoor and waved the lantern and a broom of twigs at me.

"Come on," Bel called. "Careful with your cloak, or it will catch on a handhold."

"I see why you told me to wear my old green gown." I had on the dress that Nabby had patched with bands of dull red cloth, back in Haverhill. It was the one Goody Holt approved.

Clearly the two friends were familiar with what lay below, but I was not. I lay on my belly and slowly slid my legs down until my foot found a slat of wood. Hanging from the edge, I felt about for something to grip. Bel brought the lantern closer, and I grabbed for a spike projecting from the dirt wall. Hand over hand, step by step, I climbed downward, and then gazed up at the square of light glimmering overhead. "The door looks so strange from below, as if in another world," I said.

"Like a grave down here," Bel said, her voice cheerful, "and we glancing back at the light of the lost life."

"Do not be dour," Phoebe said. "It is not a bit that way."

But I found, in fact, a gloomy place not so different from a grave. The others moved off, and I followed the light that shuffled back and forth on the ceiling. Silas Lovejoy had gone to a deal of trouble to shore up his work, I thought, for everywhere were logs and large branches embedded in the walls, dark veins passing through the clay and offering their support. I fancied they must miss having the sun and moon and stars in their arms.

Strange, this butchered and botched house. And eccentric Goodman Lovejoy with his secret.

Slowly we traveled away from the patch of light behind us. The atmosphere grew darker. I reached for Phoebe Wardwell's cloak, and she grasped my hand.

"'Tis a tunnel," I said in astonishment. "Where are we going?"

"You'll see," Bel called.

"We must have journeyed some forty footsteps when I glimpsed a thin scratch of light in the darkness.

"There it is!" Phoebe let go of my fingers as the passage narrowed and rose. A ramp of packed soil led us toward the streak of daylight.

"Now thrust," Phoebe Wardwell said, and knocked the broom handle against wood to show where. "Push, push, push!"

We were crowded together, bent under the close ceiling of dirt and timbers, but we shoved mightily until a door over our heads budged—Bel threw open the wooden panel with one giant heave.

Having scrabbled forward on our hands and knees, we now tumbled out-of-doors. I tripped on the broom and lay on the ground in the caul of my cloak, looking up at the sky as though I had never seen such snow-laden clouds before. Rolling over, I laughed to see the others flopped in the snow. I got onto my knees, reaching to help Phoebe Wardwell with both hands, but she was not ready.

She cradled her belly with both arms, smiling blissfully at the sky.

I hunched back down, wrapping my cloak around me and waiting for her to feel able to rise. For a moment, I feared that her time of trouble had come. "Does he kick and tussle, your babe?"

She nodded. "He—or she—wants to jump headfirst into the world, I believe. He clenches together and opens up like a thread of metal coiled up and pressed and released."

I looked around at the hedge break and Lovejoy's Hillock, closer now. We were not far from a simple well, also quarried by Goodman Lovejoy. A simple roof and a ring of stones marked its presence, with a bucket close by.

"He must have liked to dig," I said.

Somehow this made the other two stare at me until suddenly we were all taken with a strong fit of merriment, laughing until we were close to tears. Slowly we quieted, laughed only in little bursts, and helped one another up, Bel and I raising Phoebe Wardwell from the ground.

Together the three of us shut the door. The place was little visible afterward, having been planted with mosses and tussocks, though we had disturbed the delicate covering of snow roundabout.

Phoebe Wardwell took her broom of twigs and carefully swept away the signs of our passing. We hopped from bare patch to patch, keeping our journey a secret from the snow. In only a few minutes we burst through the front door and raced to the fire, crouching beside it while Phoebe fed the flames anew with sticks.

"Why, why did he do it?" I still could not grasp why he had undertaken such a feat.

"Silas Lovejoy thought to save himself from the savages that way, if they came to use their tomahawks and arrows. None ever did, only some who wanted to trade or visit. But even that was too much for him," Phoebe Wardwell said.

"Why did he not leave and never come back?"

"He stayed but was unhappy, people say. He would not leave the country where his wife and child were buried. And as Andover is thought to be a safe place, despite what happened that time, where people live to see their grandchildren, perhaps he thought there was no region more secure. Now and then he would travel away, and some said he visited the graves of his parents and saw the townspeople who knew him as a boy. But nobody knew much of his story, except perhaps Mr. Dane. And eventually Silas Lovejoy grew old and did not go from Andover any longer."

"I am sorry for him," I said. "'Tis hard to bear the thought that our families could not be saved."

"Yet some say that nothing is random, all for a purpose." Phoebe shook her head. "I fear that I will never take hold of understanding, any more than I can know the ways and devices of mermaids under the sea or the horned beasts and the painted men in the forest."

"Nor I. Such knowledge is impossible, for 'Canst thou bind the unicorn with his band to labor in the furrow?' Or play with Leviathan 'as if with a bird?' No one can."

But I said no more, for ever since that day in Falmouth, I could only find that God gave us the natural liberty to err or do well but did not play with us like dolls and carved toys. Why some faithful prayers are answered and others not was a mystery. Nor could I yield to the thought that the daily, hourly fates of each of us had been destined before the worlds were made. Known, yes. But I could not believe that divine will chose my mother and father and all my kin to be slaughtered by the hands of Indians in the wilderness. Their own choices, my father's bent toward the adventure of planting faith in the wilderness, and lack of foreknowing had led them there. Wild hearts plotted their destruction. The world was fallen, broken to shards like a clay pitcher. No, it was not the throne of an unchangeable will but the cross that hung in my mind with a glimmering, drowned light—the arms-out image of wide embrace that declared we were not alone in our sufferings.

"We must leave, or else it will be growing dark," Bel Holt said.

"But we will come back, surely," I said. "We must finish all these baby duds."

Bel shrugged. "Some time or other."

"I am so pleased that you came," Phoebe Wardwell said.

"We will come again," I promised. "Fare you well until that time."

Remembering the trapdoor, I hurried to close it before we left, and marveled at how the square joined so neatly with the floor. The front room looked desolate with the fire dying down and the fresh logs not yet caught. I hated to leave a new friend there, so far from any liveliness—the people on the streets subdued in winter but their presence comforting.

Once more I pledged myself to return and felt the regret in a farewell to one who lived in such a secluded manner. Goodwife Wardwell seemed sad for our going, though Bel was already talking in animated fashion of her plans for the morrow. As we walked away, I caught sight of a man with hoe and flintlock trudging in from the fields. A spark of red farther out must have been the fire to keep his hands from frostbite. Bel Holt shouted, and he called back in greeting.

"One musket shot would do him no good against Indians," I said.

"No, and they don't come alone when they mean ill to us. He was probably hoping for a chance at deer or bear."

"But all the same, I am glad he is close by," I said. "What a lonely house."

"She will soon have a house that's not lonely at all," Bel reminded me. "Children make a house lively."

But still, Phoebe Wardwell must have been sorry to see us go, for she stood and watched in the cold until we were out of sight.

"Such a grief in farewells," I said, turning to see her russet cloak, a blot of color in front of the door.

"She is my closest friend," Bel said. "I would never let anything come between us." She gave me an unsmiling stare that surprised me—was she warning me against becoming too friendly with Goodwife Wardwell?

"I just meant that you are dear friends and so are naturally sad to say good-bye," I said, a little distressed.

That troubled feeling was soon forgotten, and parting was not such a sadness as it might have been, for here came Mr. Herrick along the road, an accident as it might be, or else in hopes that he might meet us—having perhaps heard that we were both away. And I was as astonished to see his face as if the tunnel had gone straight through death and come out on the other side, where I had no knowledge of what to see or expect.

"How now? A good evening to you," he called to us.

"And to you—how came you here?"

"You must have drawn me," he said.

"He came hunting for us, I expect, when he heard we had gone to sew," Bel Holt said. "How I wish that Goodman Richard Dane had laid hold of the wit to do the same!"

"You are a merry, bruff sort of soul," Jotham Herrick said to her.

"So unwontedly merry that I am always falling out with my mother and sister or gaining a reproof when I make a little bother in the meetinghouse, though at least it is not with fits and shalming like my sister."

We chattered long, Bel Holt on Jotham Herrick's left and I on his right. Mr. Herrick told us how he had in the morning been chosen among the selectmen as sealer of weights and measures, and how that would increase his income a little, for anyone who sold by weight would have to come to him and have their weights certified as standard and stamped with the town seal.

"Why you, sir? I mean, why a goldsmith? You might have been asked to be culler of fish or constable or corder of wood or some other thing," Bel said.

"A pipe stave man or a fence viewer," he said.

"A hog reeve!" That was my thought, and it made him laugh.

"I could have been asked to do many jobs," he said. "And maybe some sound kin to what I do, like the searchers of coin. And some might seem right because I am in the militia. Like the searcher of powder. But Andover is no Boston port with a multitude of duties."

"The post must be open, and it must fit," I said.

He grasped at my fingers, wrapped in strips of wool.

"In London, the assay-master reports on the fineness of silver, setting it down by half-penny weights, penny weights, and troy ounces, and with gold he must set down karats and karat-grains, and half and quarter grains. But here there is no Cheapside with goldsmith shops, and we smiths in metals must measure for ourselves and be honest."

"Expect you are," Bel Holt said.

"I mean to be," he told her.

"Mr. Dane spoke of silver and gold in that way to me," I said.

Jotham laughed and said that the minister had once used touchstones and silver and gold in a sermon. "That man never forgets what you tell him," he added. "So take care what you say."

In the evening wind and the fast-falling dark, the three of us walked close together for warmth, and I held Jotham Herrick by the hand in the gloom, the life that flowed through him making sparks and flares of invisible light in my fingertips and flashing through me. I fancied that if only that inner glittering were visible, we could be seen as a beacon for many miles.

All afternoon, he had been working the silver, turning what was hard and dull into something fluent and shining. The image of him at his labors made me think of how it would be when his hands fell upon me, and whether when we would be together, we would make something glowing and beautiful of ourselves.

"It is not long now," Bel Holt said. "Soon the handbells will be ringing and the pots banging for Mister and Mistress Herrick. I shall marry Goodman Richard Dane. And won't my sister Lizzie be wroth with me? But I may be kind to her because I shall have my sole desire."

We laughed at her evident satisfaction, but I was glad of the twilight to hide the blush that tinged my throat and face as easily as a drop of crimson ink unfurls its veils in water. I was always so, I and two of my brothers, John and Joseph. Jotham Herrick pressed my hand and leaned toward me, and when I turned to him, I saw the first stars reflected in his eyes.

"I intend to be as pleased with my husband as Mistress Anne Bradstreet was with hers," I said.

Jotham Herrick knew the poem I meant. "As she wrote, 'If ever two were one, then surely we.'"

"Yes, I like that line."

"I shall be pleased as well," Bel said. "There will be no stopping my home pleasures."

At the Dane house we parted. Until I slept, I still had a sense of being connected with Jotham Herrick, and that he had somehow taken up residence in my body and mind. My fingers held the memory of his.

Bel Holt and I traveled back to the Wardwell house a few times, by ourselves or with Goodwife Deliverance Dane, finishing up the work we had started and helping with preparations. No visit was so peculiar as the first, which lingered in my thoughts like a dream of strangeness that clings long after waking.

But I had much else to do and ponder, and for some considerable time I forgot about the half-house with its odd chimney, patched remains of rooms, and tunnel, and even about Goodwife Phoebe Wardwell, so kind and fragile seeming, and her child-to-be. The date of the marriage had been arranged, and Mr. Herrick and I were to be wed at Mr. Dane's house—there being no groom's family, no bride's family, and all irregular—perhaps by Mr. Dudley Bradstreet, captain of the militia and justice of the peace, son of Mistress Anne Bradstreet, and the man who had freed me from Goody Holt's control on the day that Lizzie fell into fits. That, I thought, was a collection of many fine accomplishments! We would sign the register book and add to its record yet another of the civil ceremonies of Andover. Goody Deliverance Dane and some of the other Danes might be there, and Bel Holt, along with a few others. Bottles of wine that had been sent from the Saltonstalls in Haverhill would be used for making sack posset, and the Dane daughters had promised to supply a meal of roast venison with parsnips and to sing a psalm for me. (They were generous to me, those women: I have not forgotten.) And Bel Holt, still my best-known friend in that place, vowed to make bride cakes spiced with dried black and red currants and iced with sugar. I would be made a wife. After three married nights in our own house, Jotham Herrick and I would be riding on my own dear Hortus to Haverhill.

And all that happened in good time as promised and arranged, and the hours of my wedding day swept by as in a dream, and though I missed my own family and especially my mother and Mary and felt a flash of grief at times, I was happy. The great surprise was that Mr. Nathaniel Saltonstall was waiting at the Dane house to marry us, for he had arranged to meet with the militia officers in Andover that morning, and Jotham Herrick knew but kept the secret. So I had that honor, as well as the congratulations of Captain Bradstreet, who accompanied the town's clerk and register book, and the chance to tell him (with a little stammer of nervousness) that Jotham Herrick and I meant to be as pleased, each with the other, as his father and mother, portrayed in her poems.

Major Saltonstall brought a wooden box filled with little birds, fish, and honeybees, sprinkled with gilt, and a little book so small I could hide it with one hand: *A Closet for Ladies and Gentlewomen, or the Art of Procuring, Conserving, and Candying. With the manner how to make divers kinder of syrups, and all kinds of Banqueting-Stuffs: Also diverse Sovereign Medicines and Salves.* Inside were receipts to make marmalades and violet syrup, petals and fruits crusted with rock candy, quodiniack of plums and flower waters, and the directions for making cunning little creatures like the ones he brought us: "To make all kind of Birds and Beasts to stand on their legs in casting work." I spied a note tucked between the pages by my dear benefactress: *May you find in each other through this lawful knot a friend and a comfort, a companion for pleasure, and a co-servant in the work given you to do.* Tears pricked at my eyelids, for I always loved books, and the tiny beasts wrapped for safety in thrums made me long for Mistress Saltonstall and for my own mother, so that I could hardly speak my thanks.

The asking if we agreed to be husband and wife as long as we lived was the matter of a moment only; we were wed, and the major greeted me as Mistress Herrick.

After the ceremony, I could hardly eat more than the smallest bride cake and a spoonful of pyramidis cream, and my name was inked in the clerk's book with an unsteady hand. My new name. Charis Herrick. The sack posset went to my head, and I clung to Jotham Herrick's arm as we walked to the house with the silver gleaming through the window, the others following behind with bells to ring and pots to bang with spoons, even Mr. Dane and Major Saltonstall, a member of the General Court. That was a grand parade! Afterward, I changed into a new gown, and Deliverance Dane and Bel Holt helped me to bed.

What I remember most about the scene is how Jotham Herrick, who had no one to do him service, had a floor that was all beggar's velvet, as it is sometimes called, from the turning of a feather bed. The finest down had sifted out and scattered across the floor so that I stood in my bride's gown on a thin layer of cloud. And it seemed like something heavenly to me, though it was only the lack of proper sweeping, for the gossamer drifted and moved as I slowly stepped barefoot across the floor, holding hands with the two women and letting them tuck me into bed to await Jotham Herrick.

Earlier, Bel Holt had set out some of the gilded animals on a table near the bed, placing the fish on a silver tray for a pond, and strewing the birds and honeybees all around it. I was glad, seeing them there, because of Mistress Saltonstall's work and because of the friend who thought I would be charmed by the sight. Close by stood a bowl nigh brimming with water, a few summer-pressed flowers floating on the surface.

What a noise outside the bedroom door, what a raucous banging of pots and silvery ringing of the bells and shouts! Tumbled cries of *Board her! Bounce her! Broach and board! Shoot the bolt, clasp and caper, pike the gap!* ended in a crescendo of battering metal and a burst of merriment from the revelers. In came my husband, thrust laughing into the chamber by the whole party. They trooped away, huzzahing and shouting in mirth. The occasional bang of lid and pot dwindled into the distance until at last we were left alone with naught but our own words and desires.

"My wife is like cherry and blood-root ink in milk," my husband said, tightening his arms around me.

"Ink," I repeated, pressing against him. "You be the quill."

"I meant your blushes," he said.

We laughed, giddy with wine and the pleasures of the day.

The beggar's velvet shifted and stirred with the motion of the air, so that a cloud seemed to be running on the floor, yet never leaving. And the red hair undone on my shoulders and the thick, light hair of Jotham Herrick were blent together, and my breath, tasting of cinnamon and wine, mingled with his. For us, it seemed that no one had ever loved as we loved in the history of the world, that we were set apart in our passion and our striving. And the velvet trembled on the boards, and the lightning trees of our veins burned together in the chamber all night until the dawn came.

7

Wedlock

Haverhill and Andover, December 1690–mid-January 1691

On the fourth day of my marriage, I journeyed to Haverhill with Jotham Herrick—sometimes holding the reins, sometimes riding pillion, and sometimes walking—and was welcomed as warmly as any newly married daughter by the Saltonstalls. My old room, where memories of the time before stood all around, was restored to me, though all was changed for the better. We had brought with us nothing but garments and as many lidded dishes and utensils as Hortus could carry, and occasionally we welcomed visitors from the town who, hearing of Mr. Herrick's skill, wished to inspect his wares. We had not been there ten days when we were quite depleted of silver, in great degree due to a traveling party of merchants who spent a night with the Saltonstalls.

At times, my hours seemed nothing but an idyll of easy work and pleasant talk. As before, I sewed with Eliza Dennison and her mother and young Damaris Hathorne, although now we sat close by the fire and never out-of-doors. John was larger, and the months had taught him new words. Now he called me Care, and I thought it not so wrong a name for someone who had owned many cares and had been a care to others—who felt at fault in the death of someone she loved. In March, he and Eliza were to return to Ipswich for a visit to their former haunts if the weather was clear.

The air was fragrant with the pastilles I had made at the close of summer, and the time moved strangely—often the afternoon only a day before seemed like some golden fall hour already long past. The days fled from me. My time in Haverhill was mostly sweet, and I shall not forget it—and yet the memory glides by with only a few distinct moments that stand above the rest like splashed, glittering stones projecting above a stream.

We would sew and laugh and tell stories; the major would come in, followed by his younger sons, Mr. Richard Saltonstall and Mr. Nathaniel Saltonstall, arrived from college, and my own Mr. Herrick, and all would be changed. The brisk, snow-charged air of December came with them, and often their shoulders were sprinkled with snowflakes. Once we met the party with cinnamon water, made with good sack infused for three days and three nights, and then they were glad to be home! Their talk was of the militia or town business, for Major Saltonstall and Jotham Herrick had much in common and spent some considerable time visiting Haverhill notables or gathering with soldiers of the militia, inspecting arms and readiness.

One time, the youngest son read aloud from a letter from his brother, Mr. Gurdon Saltonstall, already serving as a minister in Connecticut and seeming fair to be an important personage in that colony. It struck me that Nathaniel and Richard Saltonstall were both quieter in their ways than their sister Eliza. At the table, Nathaniel was often silent, or leaned to his neighbor and spoke in words I could never catch, and I thought it might be hard to be the youngest in so eminent a family, with so fine a father and a brother who had already finished several degrees at Harvard and was rising irresistibly in the world—not to mention Eliza, who was much talked about as owning a well-managed wit and as being a virtuous and a clever woman. Her late husband, too, had been much beloved as an occasional preacher in Ipswich, and his name was often mentioned.

On a bitter morning, a visitor from Boston spoke to the militia of Major Church's incursion into Acadia in the past September, and when they came home, the men were full of details about the expedition. It made me melancholy to know that while I had been suffering the slings of Lizzie and Goody Holt, colony soldiers were thrashing through the wilderness, battling the French and the Wabanaki confederacy. Perhaps they had even fought the two men I had encountered by the mountain of flesh that was our English people of Falmouth, murdered and flung aside.

After the midday meal, when the younger Saltonstall men and my husband headed back into town, Major Saltonstall drew me aside to talk, asking his wife to come with us to a private room.

"Pray pardon me; perhaps Jotham Herrick should be here. I do not know whether it is best to share this with you first or whether, indeed, he should be present. My sense is that you may want to hear alone, and recover yourself from any surprise. I did not want to say in front of all, but I have received the names of the captives that were found in Wabanaki wigwams, victims of late incursions, or else sent north to the French," he said.

The hope that one name or more—or all!—belonged to me flared up. Elizabeth Saltonstall slipped her arm around my waist.

He shook his head. "I am sorry. None of your family were among them."

"It should be no—no surprise to me."

And yet it was a surprise. Hadn't I dreamed of my family? Hadn't I had a fantasy of at least one surviving to comfort me for such a loss? Didn't I feel my mother's arms around me many mornings when I woke, or hear my father's voice dissolving with a dream as it fled? Didn't I see in fancy that my brother Joseph had been ransomed and returned to me, that he and Jotham Herrick were as brothers to each other? Hadn't I spent hours over my needle, imagining the return of my brothers and other relatives, and how I would care for them after long trials and make them glad to be alive in the world? But their shapes were all gone from me into smoke or the dark ground and their spirits to the world to come.

"Mary and I should have stayed with the rest in the house."

"Oh, no, not that." Elizabeth Saltonstall shook me lightly.

"Indeed, no," the major said. "Think on your husband and those who are fond of you and wish you well here."

"We care for you as for Eliza," Mistress Saltonstall said.

"Yes, you are as our own kin," Major Saltonstall said. "And we admire what you have done. You have endured and stood up under a greater blow than most will ever feel, and I trust that the remainder of your life will shine as bright and polished as your Jotham Herrick's gold and silver."

I nodded, unable to speak.

"And there are, we hope, the children to be," Elizabeth Saltonstall said. "Are not our living children a consolation in the midst of grief? For this life is full of sore partings."

"Yes, think on the infants to come in good time," Major Saltonstall said, "and on God's mercy and love that are lights even when the acts of men are dark and unfathomable. Because the heart of man can grow unsavory and blacker than broth."

He went on, his voice low. "A foul plot stains the reputation of the French officers, that they accepted surrender and promised safety but allowed the Wabanaki to murder those that honor should have protected. Governor Frontenac was displeased, or so it is said, yet was so far without conscience as to excuse his officers, claiming that our men, women, and children were rebels against King James, that the Prince and Princess of Orange usurped the throne. In this manner, a governor approves barbarity and bloody crime."

My eyes prickled.

"There is more," he said. "Do you wish to hear?"

Again I nodded. Elizabeth had caught up my right hand, and now he held the left between his own.

"This week I received a letter from my friend Mr. Sewall in Boston, whom I had asked to make inquiries, not being satisfied with the news acquired earlier. And I believe there is little hope of further survivors. The bodies you saw—that wretched hill of flesh—were buried by Major Church's men in the summer. Bones were also found in the remains of a house not so far from the fort, and more bodies, adults and children and a cow, were discovered in the woods nearby. Perhaps some escaped the firing of a house and were killed later."

The tears fled my eyes, though I meant not to cry, and he pressed my hand between his.

"It is my belief that these were your kin, whose bodies now sleep buried inside the stone foundation of the largest house."

I sobbed at that, though whether in sorrow or a kind of relief made of knowing what could be known, and that they did not lie unburied, I cannot tell. All I can fathom is that the Saltonstalls circled me in their arms as I wept, and that I felt their affection and concern as a further anguish, a measure of what I had lost.

That hour was another of those flashing rocks, breaking through the stream of hours. To me, it is like the stone set up by Jacob in the wilderness for a memorial of a day where something enormous occurred.

But I had a great deal to muse on during this time, much of it pointing ahead to the future and not backward to the day I rode to Falmouth. It is ever a wonder how life keeps unreeling, and disasters do not make a stop for us to sit without stirring forevermore.

One morning several weeks into our visit, I found Elizabeth Saltonstall alone by the fire, working on a loose gown for her daughter's child.

"I wanted to speak to you about something," I said. "Because I have no mother to ask."

She set down the garment and looked at me. "If I can stand as a mother to you, young Mistress Charis Herrick, I will endeavor to do so," she said.

Sitting down beside her on the bench, I thanked her again for all her kindness and generosity to me.

"But what is it you wish to ask?"

"My time has not come," I said.

"Your courses? Not at all? I never thought to ask about such things." She picked up the little garment and turned it over in her hands as if inspecting it for an answer. "Where there is no red flower, there can be no fruit," she said.

"No, I mean this month," I said. "Until now, they have been the same. Sparse but the same. And once per moon."

She reached over and put her hand on mine. "Ah, I see. I did not think this would come so quickly. Are you sure?"

"My skin has a—a fragrance. Something rich. More than that, I find myself drowsy by mid-morning and can hardly keep on with work."

"You were nodding when we stitched on linens yesterday afternoon, but I thought it was because the newly married do not always care as much for sleep at night as those of us who have been long wed."

She lifted her hand away from mine, and when I looked, Mistress Saltonstall was smiling as she returned to her needle. "We shall have to send you to Andover with infant garb," she said. "I believe you will be content in this marriage. You may both jog on in harness and be happy, it seems to me. Your Jotham Herrick seems a fine man of education and many talents. Mr. Saltonstall says that he has been useful to his town with the militia and with governance, and to ours, for that matter."

"I am more at ease than I have been for a long time ... since that terrible day at Falmouth," I said.

"That is best, to find contentment and make another life with family, as you now are beginning to do. It helps with loss, and that remorse you have suffered on account of your sister. But I wish you were here in Haverhill; I hope Goody Holt and her daughters will not prove a thorn to you. And I would be cautious even of your friend. I did not care for what you told of that house, and feel pity for the two who must still work for that tyrannous woman."

"Bess and John," I said.

"Yes. I am glad you are free of her. And even more pleasant, your babe will be born at the close of summer and not in winter. I have long thought it cruel and killing that the midwife bears the poor infant to the meetinghouse in his wrappings, no matter if the sky blusters and pelts ice or brings extraordinary storms of snow.

Surely a goodly number of our babes wither and die after such a wretched airing. And often the ice must be chopped in the christening bowl, and the little ones shrink away from the wet and cold, so benumbed that they cannot cry out. They fade like flowers in only a few days."

Here she nipped her thread and held the linen up to the light, examining the gown for flaws. This care for her labors reminded me of the work in my lap, and so I began to mend a pair of breeches as we talked. "I had not thought of the season, but you are right. We must be hardy to survive our start in the world."

"Would the women had the rule of such things," Mistress Saltonstall said, "although perhaps not your Goody Holt and that unfortunate Lizzie!"

"Lizzie Holt did not like me. I was sorry but could do little to change her mind. To confess the sad truth, she was somewhat of a lammock, ever lolling about and fretting. With her, every day was much of a muchness with the last, as almost nothing pleased her. But Bel Holt was a friend to me and my interests."

"She was good to you, it seems. Yet I still suggest that you tread with care."

"Without her kindness, I would have climbed on Hortus and come back to you in the first week! She would never harm me." But as is the way with mortals, who are so quick to record the ill and not the sweet, I recalled how she had warned me that Goodwife Wardwell was her dear friend, not mine, and how easily and often she spoke against her own family. Brooding on what chafed our friendship, I pricked my finger with the needle.

"You found an ally there."

I leaned forward to flick a droplet of blood into the flames and pressed my thumb against the wound. "Bess and John were friendly to me as well, but I could not spend time in their company without angering Goody Holt to hornet sharpness. In truth, I often depended on my horse for a dose of affection—whenever Hortus was in the pasture or stall, I would seek him out."

"You would have been quite welcome to gallop back to us on your horse," Elizabeth Saltonstall said, and passed me a snippet of linen for my finger. "But you might have clean missed Jotham Herrick. So I suppose it was worth enduring a few Lizzie-tribulations to have been found by him."

"Goody Holt was my main trial," I said, "but now that she is no monarch over me, I am willing to think of her as one who means to do well but does not know how to rule her subjects. Someday they will all be free, and that will be a holiday of merriment for her kingdom."

Nabby called us to the table, where tea waited, and where Eliza Dennison was already seated with her boy on her lap, singing a little song. Damaris Hathorne was bent over the fire to warm her hands and, upon catching my eye, sprang to me and girdled my waist with her arms.

"I have been so glad you are still here," I said to her.

"And I, you."

She led me to a chair and surprised me with a pair of knitted stockings.

"How you spoil me," I said, admiring the work and promising to wear them on the morrow.

"So that you will want to stay," she said.

The glittering rocks in a stream ... Streams are often hard to navigate, and slick stones can be treacherous, but the stones set up in my memory are often beautiful.

One such hour was when I placed Jotham Herrick's hand on my belly and told him the news of my body, and how he was as amazed as if no man had ever planted his seed in a woman before. I had feared he would be disappointed that a child came to us so soon, as it is the way of our people to yield up many of the joys of the bed once a babe is conceived. It made me laugh with pleasure to see him stand so still, his head cocked slightly as if listening for further astonishments, before he slipped his arms around me and held me close.

"If ever two were one, then we," he whispered.

"If ever man were loved by wife, then thee," I said, answering the words from Mistress Anne Bradstreet with the following line of the poem.

In that golden moment, I knew what it meant to be a flourishing tree "planted by the rivers of waters," my limbs tangled with another, the sap rising in me and breaking forth into leaves.

Stitching with Eliza Dennison and Elizabeth Saltonstall—Nabby coming in and out with hot drinks—sometimes sitting on a bench by the fire with Damaris to crack nuts and throw the hulls into the flames, the hard shells turning to coal so that the hearth looked like a bed of fiery flowers: this is one long memory of December and early January days. We spun thread for the weaver and hemmed bed linens and made clothes for the babe-to-be and for Eliza, who not only had the child to clothe but also would be marrying again.

Six weeks of what was mostly contentment seemed to flash by so quickly! Too soon, we were calling out our "Pray remember us," "God bye," and "Fare thee well." We promised another visit and even talked of changing our residence to Haverhill, and whether that could be to Jotham Herrick's advantage as a smith in metals. But he had been voted a selectman in town meeting the year before and now held a second town office and also was a sergeant in the militia, so we did not think on Haverhill for long.

Our way home was comfortable, as we waited for a blue sky and were accompanied on the road by one Goodman Andrew Peaslee, who rode pillion behind my husband in order to return the horse Mr. Herrick rode from the Saltonstalls' seat. Both horses were weighted down with gear for the militia in Andover. Horses were rare in the colony, and we left the major without transportation for a few days, but he was in this wise saved a journey by Goodman Peaslee, a private in the Haverhill militia. We had little difficulty and the fresh feeling that all that lay before us would be fair skies, though by the time the early dark came, the clouds were low hanging, and it had begun to snow. That night we made a bed for our guest in an upstairs chamber and stabled the horses, and it proved three days before he could return to Haverhill in safety. We sent him away with thanks, the Mi'kmaq coat he had admired, and a meal for the road, along with a letter and the gift for our hosts of tiny silver spoons for salt cellars, each handle incised with a minute *Saltonstall,* and all packed in a small wooden box with a silver latch.

The choosing of a gift made me remember a wild thought that had flown through my head when, the day after we were married, I walked through the shop and admired the silverwork and the few gold items that could be shown to anyone who inquired.

And so I asked Jotham Herrick a question, catching him—as is a woman's wisdom—at a peculiarly propitious moment when I thought he might well grant me even the moon and stars. "Will you teach me?"

"Teach you what?" His head rested close to mine as he looked at me.

"Teach me how to turn a block of silver into a vessel or a spoon, which I suppose is a little bowl with a handle."

I put my finger to his lips so he could not answer yet. "You have no apprentice. All you have is the boy who comes to pound the silver into submission. But I could be your secret apprentice. I could. I am handy."

"You *are* a fast learner," he said, and pulled me closer.

"I want to work with gold someday, as you do—not because it is valuable to men and not because it would satisfy me to do so but because gold is pure, perfect, and untarnishing. Thread and cloth rot or are chewed by moths." I laid a hand on his cheek as I spoke, musing as I had often before that my husband was golden, golden. "Gold is spiritual and miraculous, a substance that might have belonged first to paradise, and that may cobble the streets of the New Jerusalem."

His forehead touched mine, and we stared at each other, content.

He said *yes*, but the estimable Mr. Herrick—who often spun thread by the hearth—declined to make a swap and learn to sew linens and garments. Because then, he said, his doom might be to stitch his own clothes.

Not that I was not busy enough in my days as a new wife, and it was some time before I did more than polish silver. But I had the promise and was determined to learn. Nor had I forgotten the desires that once made me vie with my brothers. Jotham Herrick owned a few school-books, and at night after the shop closed, we sometimes sat over Latin or Greek, translating together.

"I have an unusual wife," he told Mr. Dane when we met him in the street on the day when the snow stopped falling. "She knows a smattering of Latin and Greek, and she wants to learn everything."

"You are an unusual goldsmith, you with your Harvard studies. And we colonists of the wild are, in fact, a wonderfully literate people," Mr. Dane said, and did not condemn me for wanting what my brothers had possessed, back when we were all together. "The eager mind should be fed, for godliness and reading are as one. In time, surely she can teach the little Herricks when they come."

At that, Jotham Herrick and I exchanged a glance, secure and happy in our secret.

The whole town seemed out and about that afternoon, everyone glad for a clear sky and new-stamped paths in fresh snow without the filth and mud that would come.

I glimpsed Goody Holt but suspect that she darted into a shop to avoid us, though it was nothing but a lean-to where Goodman Granger sold crudely forged tools for the field.

"She did not wish to bid me good morrow, I suppose, because she did not wish it, nor anything more to me than grief," I said.

"Perhaps she wanted a hoe to begin working in the snow fields! You have no need to worry about her."

"No," I said. "Why do I even give thought to her?"

As we were walking down a snow-path with parcels of rye and corn in our arms, part-payment for repair work Jotham Herrick had finished some months before, I heard a voice calling my name.

"Charis! Mistress Charis Herrick!"

Turning, I saw Bel Holt floundering through the snow, her cloak flapping wide and her cap and hat askew. "You are home!" She embraced me and my burdens as if she had not seen me in years, and bobbed a curtsey at Mr. Herrick.

"I am home. And how—"

"And I am married," she announced. "I am married to Richard Dane, and you must come and see me, and I, you."

"How wonderful," I exclaimed. "May you have many years together, Goody Dane!"

"Yes," she said, bouncing a little with suppressed pleasure. "He is well pleased, and so am I."

Jotham Herrick nodded over our packages and congratulated her on the marriage. She seemed almost to quiver with excitement, her cloak trembling as she spoke. "Mr. Barnard said that we must have been destined to be together. But I had a hand in bringing it to pass, you know. Remember that day when Lizzie Holt bossocked on the ground in her mad fits?"

"You certainly did help," I said. "But perhaps that too was meant to be. And what of Goodwife Wardwell? We ought to sew for her again. Has the child been born?"

"Oh, yes, I was there when trouble came upon her. Not an easy birth," she said, looking around and lowering her voice. "Though she was prepared with plenty of birthing linen, and groaning beer and cakes for the women. All that part was well enough. But the rest—"

Jotham Herrick stepped away from us and greeted a militia officer wading through the snow. He stood talking with his back turned, mindful of our privacy.

"She was quite torn," Bel whispered. There was a great deal of blood, more than seemed right, and she looked to be washed clean of life."

"I am sorry to hear that she was hurt," I said. A nervous pang needled through me that must have been as much for myself, as yet untried in childbirth, as for Phoebe Wardwell in her down-lying.

"Yes, it was enough to make me fear. But the midwife carried the babe upstairs to the loft with silver and gold in his hands to make him rise in the world and be rich, and she put a scarlet cloth on his head to keep him from harm. The women bore up Phoebe as well on a plank, to sleep out of the way in quiet while the room was scrubbed."

"Silver and gold in his hands. I am not much governed by superstition, but that seems a fair, pretty way to wish prosperity on a baby," I said.

Bel—Goody Dane—gave me a look, as if wondering, but I only smiled and asked if Phoebe Wardwell was mending.

"She has been in a sad case, I find. The newborn, Josiah, was put out to nurse for several days and then was taken to the house again. The poor thing mewled terribly at the christening, for the water had gone hard, and underneath was nothing but ice water with crystals floating. When they brought the babe afterward, Phoebe Wardwell turned away from him and had to be coaxed. And she has been slow to heal properly, the midwife says. All the same, there was a feast for the attending women at the house when the boy was two weeks old, with beer and cakes, beef and fowls, bottle-birds and tarts. I believe that she has found her duty and fondness for the child."

"I would like to visit her again."

"She is *my* dear friend, not—what am I saying? Yes, we should go," she said, nodding at Jotham Herrick as he came up and took my arm. "Soon."

His farewell to her as *Goodwife Dane* made her laugh. She was the same Bel I remembered, warm hearted and well satisfied with her change in fortune.

All that day my mind kept returning to Phoebe Wardwell, wondering if I could be of any use to her but also fearing to be like her, made queer headed by the suffering of a lying-in. I recalled that Mr. Dane's favorite philosopher said, "A quiet mind cureth all," but how to get it to return when flown? Both ministers often spoke on the need of wives to prepare for death in childbirth. *Poor Phoebe.* When the snow on the road was packed firmly, I would visit her again.

I delighted in snowy weather, especially when the sky lowered and made the dark arrive early, for then I was alone with Jotham Herrick for a whole day, and we would meet and meet again, rehearsing our love in the little passageway behind the front shop, clinging together as though we had never embraced before. When it grew dark and we shut up the shop and ate our last meal of the day by firelight, we would reminisce and look forward at once, for it was a constant pleasure to remember that what we had been was being transformed. And who knew what we would be?

Inside the hangings of our bed, we were as one, the selvage between us like a glittering, burning edge where we were forged and welded together. We never tired of marveling at the sweetness of being found, each by the other. Nor did we regret having become fruitful and barred from full pleasure so soon because we each had longed for family.

"Forgive me for asking you to come alone to the shop," he said to me, once when we were lying together. "You might have been punished."

"I do not regret it, though I was afraid for a week."

"I was also, fearing that one quick, thoughtless request might cost so much," he said.

"It was right, no matter what a magistrate might say. And is our secret." I pressed against him, glad of his strength and warmth.

"The babe is our best secret," Jotham said. "To think that so long ago, we were each cheerless souls, attached to no one beyond those we met each day, praying for better days and a place to belong."

"Forlorn in the wilderness," I said.

"And once you were truly at the mercy of the forest and sea, roving on horseback in the world of perilous wonders, not knowing where you were bound. I could have lost you to chaos." He tightened his grip on me.

"Before you even knew me. Indeed, that would have been sad."

"Perhaps I loved you before I knew you, Charis. In a dream. Or the memory of you as a red-headed child in Boston was lodged in me, sleeping like a dormant seed."

"Like a red, red rose hip, maybe," I teased, for few men would have loved me for the sake of my red hair.

"Like anything beautiful. Perhaps I was studying to love you all the time, whenever I heard an enchanting voice or looked into the red flames. Like the way angels appear and disappear and are sometimes in modest guise and so mistaken for the ordinary sons of men."

"Angels inspire awe and fear," I said.

"Yes. That also. Like a flaming sword," he said. "And you with your white and red are as bold as a newly smithed sword with the name engraved along the blade and a secret motto. And the transparent, unearthly flames playing along its edge."

"That is far too grand for me," I said. "More like something homely, I expect—a ball of madder root dye-paste, tied up in linen, or a ripe plum on a dish."

He laughed and rested the palm of his hand on my belly. "Growing round and red and white like an apple. And full of seed."

"Seed again! So now I must be an apple in a garden. That sounds perilously like being the fruit that makes the world stumble into woe. For which we women still take blame from grandmother Eve."

"No, just a wild, sweet apple on a branch," he said, and spiraled an escaped lock of my hair around his finger.

"With not just any seed."

"A boy-seed or girl-seed," he said, "or perhaps two." He let go the tight-wound lock of hair, and it loosened but did not fall away.

"Do not wish such giant-work on me! I am not a big-bellied ark to have children march from my doors two by two ... I am not so capacious. A midwife knows that one by one is safer," I said.

Jotham laced his fingers with mine. "To have is to be joyful but with all pleasure braided with fear to lose. Not to have is barren and a lone-sorrow. Nothing earthly is pure content."

I heard and understood his words, and yet he looked peaceable and replete to me.

"Still, I am in good comfort," he murmured.

"What a marvelous-strange thing is mortal life," I said, taking pleasure in the pale gray of his eyes and the gold of his hair.

He drew back and inspected me. "You are full young to be a mother, though I can call to mind a few who were younger. If we had any family but each other, we might not be glad of this so soon," Jotham Herrick said.

The words came into my mind, *Care not then for the morrow, for the morrow shall care for itself: the day hath enough with his own grief.* But for now, all sorrow was flown. What was I like but the German girl in Goody Waters' story who flew up from the ashes in her supernaturally glorious raiment, as lovely as lilies and birdsong and sparkles on the water, and married the prince? She kept faith with her mother's memory and all the wisdom that her mother had handed down to her, and so she found her reward and became whole and joyous. And perhaps even if sorrow came later, after the woven selvage of the story, surely she had the strength and recollection of what had been to sustain her. I glanced at the fire on the hearth, the flames punching at the air and struggling mightily against the cold, and drew the curtains shut.

One day when I was mending the crumpled bowl of a spoon, though not making much progress with Jotham Herrick's arms about me, showing me the way, Goody Bel Dane burst in at the door, calling my name, "Charis Herrick! Charis!"

I left the spoon to my husband and slipped through the curtain to the shop. "Whatever is the matter?"

She looked red with cold but also wild, her bonnet and hat in hand, her hair a half-combed thicket, and her coif cocked to one side. As she reached up, it came loose and drifted down her back. "How do you fare—can you come with me to Phoebe Wardwell?"

"What, now?"

"Yes, I fear we must make haste to help her. Truly, I feel so. I was there earlier but must go back again."

I went up to Bel and fished the coif out of the folds of her cloak and set it aright. "Let me see, and I will go with you if I may."

Jotham Herrick had set down the spoon and come out to greet her—again calling her *Goodwife Dane*, to her evident satisfaction—and said that he could manage the shop and tend the pot on the fire until I returned. So I dressed warmly and even added my mother's blanket as a great shawl over my hat and cloak, and ventured out to the street with its snow packed down and only a few muddy spots and a single mound of horse droppings to mar its whiteness.

The air was bitter, and we spoke little on the way, taking short bursts forward on the snow when we could. Our faces were well wrapped against the cold, so that when we met the stick-like, erect shape of Mr. Barnard hurrying toward us, we bobbed a greeting but doubted that he knew us. He was moving along at a brisk rate, almost a run, his fine dark cloak billowing down to his heels, and the man to me resembling nothing so much as an upright insect with a winter-blackened leaf clinging to its back.

"Good morrow, Mr. Barnard, and how goes Goodwife Wardwell?" Bel bawled after him, but the minister only kept walking as he shouted back to her.

"In the devices and lime-snares of Satan, I fear!"

I pulled the wool away from my mouth. "What does he mean?"

Bel only looked at me, her eyes running with wet from the mad dashes of the wind, and shook her head.

Usually, the closer we came to a place beyond the outskirts of town, the deeper the snow, for fewer people would brave the walk after a storm. And yet here was a clear track to traipse in, marked by many boots and pattens, that made me wonder.

At last we glimpsed the house and began to race, puffing clouds into the sharp air, careless of the treachery of snow that is stars but wants to make us fall. Being lighter, I would have beaten my friend to the goal but suddenly remembered the child inside me and slackened, letting Bel flounder ahead.

In her impetuous way, Bel Dane sprang through the door and began greeting the room at large. I followed, shutting it and standing in the shadows to look about me and remove my pattens. Six or seven people from town were gathered in the front chamber, sitting or standing, murmuring among themselves or else crying out a "How now?" to Bel and me.

"Come and spread your cloaks before the fire and dry your feet," Mr. Dane said.

His own snow-trimmed cloak was already splayed out at the hearth, and I guessed that Mr. Barnard must have left when the elder minister arrived, the two often being at loggerheads when stalled in the same room. A tug of war went on between them, Mr. Barnard dwelling on the schemes and snares of Satan, opposed by Mr. Dane, drawing the soul to the throne of grace.

I came forward, greeting the others as I passed, and settled on a bench, intending to dry my shoes and stockings and glad for the heat of the fire. My hands and feet prickled as they thawed, and I sat quietly, listening to Mr. Dane. The group of villagers was about to depart and, their outer gear in place, cried out their farewells to us.

"She is dear to me," Bel was saying when we heard a great howl from the back room.

Mr. Dane paused, his hand in the air, and excused himself. "Evidently she is awake. I must see what mischief has been done to the poor young woman," he said. "Come in when you are warm. I know that Goodwife Wardwell would be pleased to see you both if in her right wits, and it may be that she will be at least somewhat gratified even out of them."

Bel, no doubt feeling herself authorized as a new-made Dane, trailed him, telling me to come as soon as my feet were dry. I pulled off shoes and stockings, noticing that I ought to rub fat into the leather of my shoes before traipsing in snow again, and held my feet before the fire. My peeled-off stockings steamed. I sat a little longer, chafing my toes and gazing at the bed of coals that, as ever, seemed a glowing, magical landscape. And yet, if a soul were to find its way to such a region, those smoldering hills would be hells.

What is the trouble with Phoebe Wardwell?

My soaked stockings would not dry. But I had brought an extra pair, which I now put on and gartered, the front room being empty. I padded to the lean-to room at the back, leaving my shoes on the hearth but taking my mother's blanket for warmth.

I pushed open the door and saw Goody Ann Poor seated in the chimbley corner, suckling Phoebe Wardwell's babe. She nodded at me and did not get up.

Josiah. A winter babe, he looked red and overheated by the fire. It is a wonder any of our winter children survive the heat and smoke hard by a chimbley, or the cold when they are abandoned to sleep, safely tucked away from the flames but suffering the freezing airs of our chambers. A tail-clout and swaddling bands and other wraps were drying on a rack by the flames, and the odor prickled at my nose.

Thomas Wardwell was there also, seated on a stool with his head lowered. He did not glance up as I shut the door behind me. The minister was bent over the bed, Bel Dane close beside him.

"My dear child," he was saying, "do not study to undo yourself, abusing those sweet and precious gifts that God has granted you, your health and wit and strength. Do not let your reason succumb to perturbations and chaos." She stared up at him, her face a rigid mask of panic. "Remember your calling in the world, remember your babe and husband, remember the charitable love that God asks of us. The black bile of melancholy can be overcome through right thinking."

"But Mr. Barnard says I may be damned else—"

"Think on Christ's pardon," the elder minister said, "and consider how God so loved the world and has called you to be his own. Where are these terrors of conscience and this hopelessness then? They melt and vanish at the mercy seat."

"I am roiling in fear," Phoebe Wardwell said, and here I caught a glimpse of her sunken eyes that startled me. "Whelmed in the depths of my deeds and thoughts. In doubt of my election."

Her fingers plucked nervously at the bed rug that topped the linens and coverlet.

"Dear child, despair and shame and horror of conscience may seem like truth in a world so fallen from our first estate in the garden of Eden. But we are beloved of God, and to be *destined* means that God has called us, and we are free to answer. Trust in more than your own mind. Remember compassion and love that stream from heaven."

"Mr. Barnard spoke to me of devilish wiles, and how Satan has his bad miracles and wishes to thrust my soul to hell—"

"Hush, daughter," Mr. Dane said, and he caught up one of her hands to pat it. "This malady, for so it is, is one of black bile and too much preoccupation with judgment. All may now seem tainted with sinful intentions, but you have known God's gracious clemency and the increase of your love for God and man. Remember those past times. You are weakened and bled by childbirth, and that makes you susceptible to the bad antics of the humors."

"I have fasted," she said.

When he let her hand return gently to the coverlet, I was struck by its curled shape. Claw-like, the fingers seemed to implore us for comfort.

"Let us anatomize this melancholy," Mr. Dane said to her. "There can be a case of too much of fasting and meditation, too much precision in our ways. If there is the Devil's work at such times, it is surely in over-contemplation of judgment and destruction."

"The Archfiend," Phoebe said softly.

"Do you remember how old Mistress Faulkner read the tale of *The Pilgrim's Progress* to the children, and how the giant caught Christian and shoved him into Doubting Castle?"

Phoebe Wardwell nodded.

"Well," he said, "you should also remember that the giant and giantess starved and beat Christian and his friend until they quite despaired, but that afterward he remembered a key in his pocket."

Phoebe lay still, her eyes on his.

"Do you recall the name of that key?"

"Promise," she whispered.

"Yes. Promise. The key that could open every door that barred their way, and every gate that locked them in the castle. So the giant was defeated by God's promise and radiance, for the giant could not bear light. And every crystal star that falls from heaven, every blade of grass, every color above the hills at sunset reminds us of that immortal glow and promise."

She didn't move, though she didn't take her eyes from his.

"Christian took hold of the key, the promise, and all doors were free to him. That promise can do the same for you," he said.

"Goodman Thomas," Mr. Dane called out, and the man raised his head. "Your wife needs mild, pleasant recreation, light food rather than abstinence, and the avoidance of fearful subjects rather than a dwelling on satanic powers and judgment. Her mind is wounded and must heal, as surely as her body after a lying-in. The spirit's dissolution she has suffered must be ended."

Thomas Wardwell appeared downcast and tired. I supposed that he had been up in the night with his wife. "She must endure longer before she finds the joy of grace once more," he said dully. "So Mr. Barnard told her."

"What she feels is not healthy or natural, though it may be praised by some of our New England divines in their diatribes. Too much agony of soul and melancholy will make the heart a stone." Mr. Dane frowned, looking toward the fire and the seated man. "And sometimes evil comes by accident from those who want to impose good on others."

"The spirit's war," Thomas Wardwell said. "Mr. Barnard said anguish is a needful struggle. He told us that the realm of witches and demons and powers is fighting to possess her."

Mr. Dane made a clicking noise with his tongue. "It is a flaw in our Massachusetts divines to be always so set on thoughts of writhing and furious devils who pitch trouble at us from the invisible world. In consequence, they often find their own splenic dispositions bereft of tenderness." Mr. Dane discoursed as if rehearsing an old complaint and, indeed, had said something similar to me before. "Likewise, it is a blemish on the settlements of the New World that so many suffer from melancholy, deadness of heart, and over-anxiety as to sin. The sense of the corrupt self is too extreme, the sense of God's kindness too small."

He shook his head as if to clear his mind and spoke again. "Some find rapture, others something worse. You do not wish Goody Wardwell to be one of those, surely."

The unfortunate babe set up a thin, mewling wail. The woman who had nursed Josiah in the chimbley corner took him out of the room, where he fared no better. His cry was louder there, away from the fire.

Mr. Dane went on as though he did not notice. "This agony of mind is not so among our godly brothers and sisters in England, who are quicker to find a durable comfort in Christ."

Thomas Wardwell got up from his seat and came near, offering the minister his hand and pledging to heed his counsel. "I do feel some hope," he said.

"As so you should," Mr. Dane said.

The minister prayed, asking that darkness be lifted from the home, and that the Wardwells find assurance in God's grace and love. He promised to come again on the morrow during a round of visitations, and said that he should be sent for sooner if needed. When he departed with Goodman Wardwell, who meant to walk into town to fetch a cone of sugar and some spices to tempt his wife into eating, we were left to be watchers.

Phoebe Wardwell's eyelids were closed, and they looked faintly purplish from the veins beneath the skin. Her features had sharpened since I last had seen her.

"She is too thin," I whispered to Bel, who glanced at me and gave a nod.

"Would that we could lend her flesh," she said.

We lapsed into silence until she woke with a bitter, curlew-keen cry, sitting halfway up in bed and looking around as if bewildered. I noticed that someone had sprinkled the nest of stained bedclothes with dried lavender blossoms

"Here we are—me, Bel, with Mistress Charis Herrick."

"That was not her name before," Phoebe Wardwell said.

"I am wed," I said, leaning toward her. "To Mr. Jotham Herrick the goldsmith and selectman. A sergeant for the militia. They say he will be lieutenant soon. Do you remember that we talked of him?"

"Oh," she said.

"Are you better?" Bel Dane moved closer to the bed and looked down on her friend.

"The fear is stirred up in me that I shall die in my sins," she said, "and I am afraid to be catapulted to hell. Afraid that I am not elected and never shall be."

"Think on mercy," I said, but she did not mark the words.

"That I never, never shall be. But sometimes I remember the sweetness of the past and find that there is hope. And I swing back and forth between one and the other and can get no rest."

"You must eat and sleep and grow stronger," I said. "You should not be racked and ravaged. For surely the Spirit sends forth springs and spates of love."

"But I get no sip to drink," she answered me, seizing hold of my wrist and pulling me toward her. "Not one drop to save my soul." I sat down on the edge of the mattress, hearing the corn husks stir and rearrange themselves. Tentatively, I rested my hand on her shoulder.

"Shall we bring you something to drink? Water? Tea? Or perhaps you might eat an apple?" I thought that she must be parched, but she only looked from one of us to the other.

Bel Dane sank down next to me with a great rustling of husks. "Could you taste something now, Phoebe Wardwell?"

Sad to see her appear silent and bewildered, I asked Bel, "Perhaps some water with something strengthening? She will be so thirsty if she has nothing to drink."

"Water, yes, water, water," Phoebe Wardwell cried, clutching at my arm with both hands.

Bel went out and came back with a cup of honey-water, which she held to Phoebe's lips. The sick woman drank a little, but tears filled her eyes and she lay back, exhausted, and would take no food, whispering that she must mortify the flesh, for it was evil, evil.

When she slept, we left her to the ministrations of Goody Ann Poor and several more people from town who had come to see how the young mother fared and provide whatever consolation they might.

"People will say the wrong words, I am afraid." Wrapping the blanket over my cloak, I stepped out the door. "And she will be afflicted more, when what she needs is good news of mercy and love. And perhaps something delicate—a gilded bird of Barbary sugar, holding a rock-candy violet. Some pretty sweet nothing that says we remember and care about her. For things also speak."

"Indeed, I hope people will not say wrongly," Bel Dane said, following after me. "In truth, I do not know whether to abide more with Mr. Dane and comfort or with Mr. Barnard and the threats of the invisible world, with its contest between angels and devils. Does it seem like a choice between a more kindly England and a severe Massachusetts to you?"

"Perhaps. You are, I think, the most cheerful woman in Andover." I paused, thinking of one or two moments that had given me an uncertainty on this matter, but went on. "And that is part of why I like you. Surely you will be on the side of charity. And I, I have been through enough unpleasantness to see that God does not dabble with our lives but suffers and joys with us. It is human beings who are fallen and cause most of the woeful trials in the world, whether they be Wabanaki or Norfolk men, Mather-trained Boston divines who rant overmuch of devils and unwholesome abasement or else Jesuits from France who entice the tribes to murder us in our beds." There I stopped, having said more of a speech than I meant to say.

"I doubt that is entirely approved sentiment, and so I am glad Mr. Barnard did not hear you," Bel Dane said. "Or we would have a hard scolding about being insensible to the warfare of the invisible world and the machinations of Satan. Which perhaps I am," she said. "Perhaps I am too buoyant in spirits, and Phoebe Wardwell knows more than either of us."

"Her unrest speaks the brute pain of her lying-in and, I expect, the melancholy that has afflicted her since."

"It may be," my friend said, with less of lightness than I had seen in her before.

The next morning, after I spent a pleasant hour reading a treatise on gilding and tapping Mr. Herrick's marks into silver, we set off once more. I carried a bottle of cordial, and Goody Bel Dane had a sack of small honey cakes. The cold was even more bitter than the day before, and the air blustery.

When we were more than halfway there, we met an old man racing at a gallop toward town. Primus, the African slave of Mr. Stevens, stayed for us only long enough to report that he was to fetch the magistrate and men to search the woods near the Wardwell fields, for when Thomas Wardwell had wakened at dawn, he had seen no sign of his wife and child. Already a few inquiries had been made in town, to no avail.

"Surely you should not rush so speedily," I said, thinking of the respect due his age, but he flew away from us as if borne by inconstant winds, alternately trotting and hobbling toward the village.

Bel Dane stood stock still, a dusting of snow on her shoulders, watching as he darted onward. "How can that be?" She frowned at the gusts that dashed up crystals and twisted skeins of flakes into snow-devils.

"What about the secret tunnel? Perhaps Thomas Wardwell has not thought of it—no one knows, do they? Except he and his wife and us. Might she have gone there in distress to consider death and the grave? And taken the babe with her? Or perhaps ventured there to feel that she was reborn, moving from dark to the light at dawn?"

"Yes," Bel said, and took off, running awkwardly in pattens, arms flailing for balance.

Forgetting the babe in my womb, I panted just behind her until we saw the house, its drab box set against the whiteness. At last we slowed, gasping but not stopping because of the fierce breeze that slapped particles of ice against our faces.

Before reaching the door, we glimpsed several distant figures struggling across the landscape.

"Searchers," I said. "Sad little babe in this cold. Poor Phoebe Wardwell."

Inside, no one answered our call. We hurried to the fire and rubbed our hands until we were half-warmed, for we would be of no use frozen. I leaned over, my belly cramping. Bel Dane hunted up a tallow candle and lit it with a burning straw.

"What will we do if we find her?"

"Save them," I said. "What else could it be?"

We stared, each at the other: her eyes reflected the flickering movements of the candle's flame.

Without Phoebe Wardwell, we had a little trouble finding the fingerhold but at last managed to discover the slot and heave the trapdoor into the air. Bel climbed down first as I held the light. She took the candlestick from me and waited as I stepped downward—pausing once to reach up and slide the square back into place, for we had no wish to harm someone hurrying down the hall, all unknowing.

Our luminous opening was gone, and we were truly in cave-like dark. The candle flame wavered, as if we had put some of our own uncertainty into its wick. But we turned and crept down the tunnel.

"Stop!" I fumbled at something on the ground while Bel Dane held up the candlestick. "A ribbon." I held it up to the flame.

"Red."

"A sleeve ribbon, maybe?"

"It looks quite clean and fresh."

"Someone must have tied it on her, surely, for a bit of cheer," I said. "She is in no condition for ribbons."

Afraid of tripping over the mother and child, we progressed slowly, little step by little step, moving toward the outer door. The distance was not so far but seemed like an ill dream in which one strives but progresses nowhere and is still trapped. The smell of the tunnel was a mix of earth and mold and also lavender, which made us again think that Phoebe Wardwell had passed this way.

"Nothing," Bel said, holding up the candlestick.

"Just this," I said, retrieving a crude broom.

The rise toward the outer door lay before us, and the flame cast enough light that we could see that the remainder of the tunnel was empty. Creeping forward, we reached for the wooden boards overhead and began to push. I prodded the wood with the broom handle, but yielded it to Bel Dane, who hammered roughly at an edge. The burden of snow made heavy work, and a fresh seal of ice on tough winter stems latched the door to earth. It took us several tries before the door lifted an inch and we could see a stripe of daylight.

"How did she manage?" Bel Dane's voice was muffled.

"Maybe she came early, when there was less snow. Or she found strength in her feelings, whatever they were. Or else she did not come this way."

Thrusting mightily, we flung back the door and threw ourselves onto the snowy ground. This time we did not rest in the snow, as we had once before, but sprang to our feet. Bel Dane tossed the broom back inside.

"I was so sure," she said.

"Yes, somehow I thought she would be there, kneeling in the dark with Josiah in her arms. But perhaps she would have been too weak to raise the trapdoor. And it would be hard to carry him safely down the ladder."

"But sometimes people surprise us with what they can do."

"Yes," I said.

Hands on hips, we surveyed the Wardwell domain. Now the figures we had seen before were invisible, their dun-colored clothing lost in trees.

"Too much new snow," I said.

"I see not one blessed thing that would help," Bel Dane said. "I will go check the hillock, though probably no good will come of it."

"A fine thought," I said, though I did not expect anything either. "And mayhap we shall eventually learn that she had the notion of visiting some cousin or former neighbor."

Bel was not listening. "Surely if anyone can find her, it will be me," she said.

My friend walked away from me, leaving a trail of prints on fresh snow. If Phoebe Wardwell had wandered here, we might find more, though new snow made that hope unlikely. The area around the house had had too many searchers already, and the snow was confused with footprints. The trees, the fields with stumps rotting in place, the occasional shrub: the site was not much to look on. But I walked aimlessly over the ground, scanning the horizon, until I came to the bucket of ice and snow near the roofed well. And there it came to me that I should just look. I clambered on the slippery rocks and knelt at the curb's edge, leaning forward until I could see—

A face, uptilted and gleaming palely under a pane of ice.

A hand and an arm, almost to the elbow, reached through that frozen window, the slender fingers outstretched.

What might be an infant's face, lower than the first, shone dimly through a surface that was clouded by a few skeins of snow stars.

Whether fit for the moment or not, words coursed through my head: *For now we see through a glass darkly: but then shall we see face-to-face. Now I know in part: but then shall I know even as I am known. And now abideth faith, hope and love, even these three: but the chiefest of these is love.*

The chiefest of these is love.

I crouched on the stones with pain burning cold at my knees, and I put my hand into the shadows of the well, as though Phoebe could still grasp a warm and living hand and be hauled to safety, as though I could still rescue Josiah and rock him to sleep in the chimbley corner.

And I prayed to Christ who sits on the mercy seat as I had never prayed before, that he would take her outstretched hand and comfort the woman and forgive her for all her wild, disordered thoughts, her deepest despairs, and her mad rush over snow and rocks and into air and ice and water, and that he would welcome her and the babe into heaven. The tears flooded to my eyes and seemed to hold there, stiff and cold, until melting onto my cheeks like a second skin. My salt tears began to freeze, sealing sorrow against my face.

"The chiefest of these is love," I whispered, my hand still reaching toward the lifted hand. "The chiefest of these. Is love. Love. The chiefest of these."

Then I keened to the field of stumps and the shrubs and the forest where the devils and wild men dance and where the godly fear to go (though I have gone there, yes, and lived), to the distant figures of the searchers and Bel Dane, to the low clouds gravid with snow, to the frozen, rutted fields and the ice that shut and the liquid that cauled the bodies under the hard glaze that separated water and air. And I keened to God and to the Spirit and to Christ on the mercy seat, and my voice went out of me like a bird, as swift and strong as a peregrine, and for all I know, ringed the round world and falcon-flew to touch the highest heaven.

8

The Groaning-Time

Andover and Haverhill, 1691

For long afterward, it seemed that nothing more would happen, and that everything that could go amiss was over and done, though Jotham Herrick and I knew from our own histories that the world rolls on from bad to good and from good to bad like a cartwheel that is smooth on even ground but inevitably meets stones and pits and stumps on its way. The sorrow at the well colored my days. Yet I had learned at Falmouth how we keep on despite calamity, no matter how dire and harrowing, no matter how many dead visit us in dreams at night.

Goody Holt and Lizzie still avoided me, but others were friendly in the shops or at the meetinghouse. Perhaps Goody Holt had discovered a cache of sympathy and kindness—or perhaps being at peace with such a mother meant being less concerned with Charis Herrick.

And there was the matter of the well.

"Why were you the one to find her?" One Sabbath, Mehitabel Dane seized me by the wrist and spoke to me angrily. "How did you know?"

I stared in wonderment. "I did not know. How could I?"

Her grip loosened and then tightened once more, and she let go roughly, flinging my arm away.

"What has happened—" But before I could protest that she was parting ways with friendship, she turned away to greet Mr. Barnard.

Because the ground was frozen, Phoebe Wardwell's body and the babe fastened to her by ice went into a cold barn like a length of boards and waited there for spring, and Thomas Wardwell returned to his father and mother and left the house empty. Once the place was used to shelter a traveling family for a week, and another time a constable and a Quaker headed for trial slept there, but mostly it was bare and dark, and after a short time, people tended to forget the place existed, so lonely beyond the last cluster of houses and the hay-crammed tannery, still waiting for Goody Holt's John to finish his indenture and make a stench, so that the townspeople could complain and yet be glad of his work.

And only when the earth thawed did we have a funeral, though it was sad enough with the grave dug outside the low stone wall of the burying ground. Much commotion and argument rose up between the ministers as to whether Phoebe Wardwell had been tempted by devilish thoughts and so did away with herself and murdered her little babe, or whether she had been ill and out of her right wits and thus had tumbled into the well unawares, or whether, indeed, it was possible for a mortal to know the answer.

This controversy made a tempest for a week and died away. Only too soon Phoebe Wardwell was forgotten again.

Mehitabel Dane and I mourned her longer than almost anyone, I fear. Thomas Wardwell had set his face away from his old life. Goodman Richard Dane said to us that Goodman Wardwell would never again live in the house and meant to sell it, though as yet no one wished to buy. It was marred and but half a house, and it seemed ill-storied and luckless to our townspeople. I doubt, though, that Thomas Wardwell forgot Phoebe his wife and little Josiah. I knew what it was like to want to forget—even to long to forget the sweetness that had gone before in order to forget what came at the close. But I also knew that such wiping-away was not possible. Eventually sorrow ceases to be the first thing that recurs to mind when we wake in the morning, but I believe that no day passes without some memorial to ruin. For at least one instant in the day, we are confronted with a hard, intractable stone set up in memory. Or so it is for me, and I believe for Jotham Herrick, whose parents and two sisters had died in Boston twelve years back, swept away by the smallpox in the space of days.

"The end of Phoebe Wardwell's life was not all of her life," Jotham Herrick said to me, and I found the thought comforting, for had she not been known as a tender daughter and wife before the sickness and despair came over her? I honored her memory, and the rest I left to God.

About that time, Deliverance Dane told me that Goody Holt and Lizzie had been making unkind hints about me to the elder minister—something to do with Phoebe Wardwell's death. Mr. Dane had spoken firmly to them in denial and cautioned them to avoid gossip. It wrapped me in a dark mist; it bothered me, but as nothing came of the complaint, and Mr. Dane spoke of their claims as nonsense, I soon forgot, though the memory came back to me later on.

The spring was not all about the funeral and endings. The first flowers broke out, the ground feverishly greened, the birds knitted their songs into the leaves again, and the geese tarried with us on their way to far nesting grounds. But we did not let them all go past us to the Wabanaki and the French. Many stopped with us, whether brought down in flight or killed while settling on the Merrimack to the north or floating on the Great Pond. They made fine spring feasts, having fattened on sunny grasses far to the south.

Who knew where? Mr. Dane claimed that they flew to the hot continent below, where the Spanish had conquered ancient castles made of gold that glimmered in the jungles and on cliffs, and where particolored beasts and birds as fabulous as gryphons and dragons roamed the wilderness or glided in and out a luxuriant canopy of leaves.

I found these tales easy to credit, for had I not seen strange things in the wilderness, or even quite close to Andover? In May, Jotham Herrick and I built a rock weir in a stream and harvested fish and picked the coiled fern fronds nearby. I had learned such springtime gleanings from my time near Falmouth. One morning we stumbled on several women and a few children gathering greens near our fishing grounds—the boys and girls dressed in deerskin, with a hanging cloth at the hips and leg wraps and mantle against the chilly air, and the women with a tied-together skirt, mantle, and necklaces made of copper and beads. But all our startlement and theirs was nothing next to our realization that an immense creature had appeared between the trees and was picking his way toward us. The Wampanoag (for so I supposed them, remembering other encounters) spoke in their own language and swiftly gathered up their packets of fish wrapped in leaves and backed away into the woods until all sight of them was lost.

"What *is* it?" My hand groped for and found Jotham's. I could hardly look away from the comical, monstrous spectacle.

Jotham Herrick, too, stared in wonder at this conundrum of the forest. "An elk, maybe?" He lowered his voice as if afraid it might hear.

What a lovely, liquid morning it was, with the birds, those pipers of embroidered spring songs, alive in the trees—the stream singing its own rushing and curling song, the weir murmuring, and the early morning dawn still dyed pink here and there between branches! The sweet odors of earth and flowers rose from the damp ground as if breathed out, into the world. And in the midst of it all, this big-bellied vastness on spindle legs. The nose looked soft and drooping, and altogether the beast appeared as a riotous, confused thing.

He lowered his head, crowned with new nubs of antlers, and began to lip at the foliage under the trees. His breath ruttled as he blew outward and sent the plants to trembling.

"We should retreat," Jotham Herrick said. "Look how the Indians melted into the trees when he appeared. They know better than we how to behave in this case."

"Jotham," I whispered. And I remembered the great sea-beast Leviathan, whose sneezings send forth light, whose strength is "as the nether millstone."

"This is truly a world of wonders," he said.

"Yes." I pressed his hand, still thinking of the Leviathan's power hidden under his joined scales, and how this being, however strange its appearance, might be a danger like the monster in the sea who laughed at blades and hurled stones: *In the earth there is none like him: he is made without fear.*

I stepped back, one pace at a time, still clinging to Jotham Herrick's hand and he holding to me. My heart sent me a message, flittering fast and urging me to rush. When out of sight of the beast, we sped homeward, suddenly released from caution, laughing and heedless, leaping sloughs of mud and crushing the tender green grasses.

Remembering our child and turning abruptly, Jotham caught me up in the air. And that was the end of my hoyden running, though I have always loved to skip about when no one is watching.

Later on, we learned that the creature was what is called by some of our people *the swamp donkey,* and *moose* by some of the tribes. Mr. Dane, who had an interest in natural-history curiosities and knew much about the ways of animals, told us that the male sheds his antlers each fall and begins to grow new ones in early spring, and that if we saw our moose again in another month, the antlers would have burgeoned into a grove of velvet trees with large, pleading arms uplifted, each with many fur-clad fingers. I found this hard to credit, but he told us that they grew as swiftly as the grass on a hot spring day.

Months later, I may have seen our same hard-to-fathom monster again. Antlers wonderfully diademed his head. To me, it seemed that a giant, furry moth had settled to rest there.

But the first sighting at the weir lingered long in my mind.

"We have seen a creature as rare and strange as a chimera," I said to Jotham Herrick, and longed to tell my mother. And that afternoon, I felt a little sad, as if I had lost something precious, though it was only the memory of the morning, slipping away.

All late winter and spring, the little rise under my gown grew rounder, became a hillock, until one day I felt the first convulsive clench and jump of the child in my belly. Human nature being what it is, entirely strange, I wept for joy and grief in the space of a few moments. Again I longed for my mother. That also is human nature, to yearn for what we once possessed and can never, ever have again, not in this life.

That night we lay inside the freshly aired and hung summer curtains of the bed, and Jotham Herrick pressed his narrow, clever goldsmith's hands against my belly to feel for the new life. And we laughed for pure bliss.

Soon I began to help around the shop more and took my place as a pounder of silver. At first, my husband wanted to shield me from that work, but I said no, that I could do it as well as any boy apprentice. Moreover, it would not keep me from the cook-pot or my needle. I loved my days at that time more than ever, for from the hour I woke in the morning until Jotham Herrick drew me toward bed, all my labors felt rich with meaning. And that was my privy happiness. I sewed for the child to be and made my husband two new shirts. Some days I hoed in our plot, enjoying the brisk air and the sight of green ribbons and tendrils waving in the breeze. My mouth was full of new words and old ones used for a new purpose: *anneal, solder, cast, hammer,* and *shape.* Little by little, I began to learn the trade.

"A goldsmith's apprenticeship means a ten-year's labor," Jotham Herrick told me.

"So be it," I said, bobbing him a little curtsey. "Do you want me to sign the articles and be witnessed?"

He was amused and smiled as he put his arms around my waist. "Shall you faithfully serve the craft, keep its secrets, carry out its duties, never mar the sterling standard by blending too much copper with the silver, and always obey the laws of the goldsmith?"

"Are there many secrets?"

"To those who do not know, surely everything is a mystery," he said.

"And do you have a great many laws?"

"Just the right number, I expect," he said. "A contract would read something like this: the apprentice, Charis Herrick, shall her master,

Jotham Herrick, faithfully serve, his secrets keep, his lawful commands gladly obey. She shall do no damage to her master nor see it be done of others without giving notice thereof to her master. She shall not waste her said master's goods (I do not believe that you would waste my silver, would you?) nor lend them unlawfully to any—most particularly to Goody Holt, I should say."

I clasped my arms around his neck. "That will not be a difficulty."

"What else? She shall not commit fornication—"

"Never," I said. "I shall sleep only with the aforementioned master!"

"Nor contract matrimony within the set term—a bit too late for that, I fear."

"Yes," I said.

"At cards, dice, or any unlawful game she shall not play—"

"Never," I said again, my voice muffled against his chest. "But I shall play all lawful games with you."

"Indeed," he said. "And she shall not absent herself by day or night from said master's—"

"Bed?"

My husband leaned back to look at my face and laugh at me before he went on. "Said master's service, without his leave, nor haunt taverns or play houses."

"There are no play houses in the wilderness," I said. "And I desire no habit of haunting such places."

"She shall in all things behave as a faithful apprentice. And the said master, Jotham Herrick, shall find and furnish the said apprentice, Charis Herrick, with wearing apparel, and doth covenant and promise to instruct the apprentice in the art, trade, and calling of smithing in precious metals, and at the expiration of the term of years, dismiss her from apprenticeship."

"Well, sir, so long as I do not need to name you *master* from now on, I shall serve the ancient company and guild of goldsmiths and keep its precious secrets."

"In this country, there is no guild, so we shall be a company of two." Jotham Herrick kissed me on the forehead, and so our compact was sealed.

My life was fair and promising better. Reading and study were not denied to me. I had one area of skill mastered with the work of my hands: spinning and the stitching together of loomed cloth into garments and embroidery to deck them, and all the arts of needle and thread. And now I stepped onto the long, slow path to knowledge of metals. I had a family again and took pleasure in my husband. When terrible dreams came to me at night, he was there to wake and console me. We would have a child before long. On the Lord's Day, I walked to the meetinghouse with Mr. Herrick and found that I had many things to be grateful for, and was glad.

In early June, we saw the Saltonstalls and had a meal with them when Andover was the site of a confabulation between militia officers who journeyed from Salem, Salem Village, and Haverhill. Andover paraded its soldiers before the meetinghouse, and there was a prodigious stamping-about of men in boots. The few town horses had their glory-moments, too, and Jotham Herrick rode my beloved Hortus with the others. The officers and local soldiery were busy with talk and training all day, and so for many hours I had Elizabeth Saltonstall to myself.

We made that time a holiday. I showed her the shop and my first accomplishments of hammering and marking, the jumble of tools, and the crucibles out back, flecked with drops of metal. Upstairs, the gear sewn for the babe made a fine display. Last, I made her a gift of violet flowers and mint leaves sealed in rock candy.

After the amusements of the house were shared, we walked out and sat on stools in the road to Ipswich between Shoe Meadow and Great Wade's Meadow, there to watch the formal inspection of weapons. Once a musket fired by accident and struck the Marston house door, and so whoops and screams went up, but no harm was done to any person, which was a fine thing.

I was pleased and grateful to Mistress Saltonstall for coming so far out of affection for me, as she was not of an age or temperament to enjoy picking her way on horseback from Haverhill to Andover in company with militiamen. Her generous words came back to me many times. "You are like my own daughter," she told me. "You are dear to us. If there is ever anything you desire, you have only to come to Haverhill, and we will give you whatever it is you need. My Nathaniel feels the same. That is a promise I make to you from both of us."

"Thank you, my dear foster mother! It is sad to contemplate an hour of dire need appearing again," I said, "but life is from time to time an outlandish, baffling business prone to remarkables, and no one knows what will come to pass."

"From moment to moment in the stream of years, we cannot know." She hesitated, gazing at the knots of militiamen. The examination of firearms had begun. "Our lives are frail, and the world stony and harsh. But so long as either of us lives, you have another place to claim as home," she told me, speaking with firmness and clapping her hands together in emphasis.

I thanked her, and afterward we meandered slowly around Shoe Meadow, arm in arm, chatting of needlework and Damaris Hathorne and Eliza and the sons, Gurdon and Richard and Nathaniel Saltonstall. We talked of less pretty matters as well. The major felt weary. Fresh struggles in the Essex court with Goodman Swan's sons, mischievous and destructive by bent, disturbed him, and he had recently upset the village by sending a young Emmerson woman to the Boston jail for whoredom, she having given birth in mid-May to two babes, sewing them in a bag and burying them behind the house while the family was at meeting. Poor Elizabeth Emmerson was found out soon enough. It seemed to me that her mother and father must have known. How could she give birth to two infants without them hearing, and all sleeping in the same room, along with her prior child, also a bastard? I pitied the major for having to stand against the unfortunate girl and all her friends in Haverhill, and I also pitied her for having no more hope than to murder her children, though perhaps they had been stillborn.

"He found no other choice, as she had buried the babes. Though we both ached for her. She never had much affection at home, and her father lashed her without mercy when she was but a small girl."

"Woefully sad," I said.

"I should not have told a woman with child that story," Mistress Saltonstall said, slowing her steps.

"It makes me grieve," I told her, "but also grateful for my husband. I have naught to fear."

And that was a true sentiment, for there are many ways a young woman may risk and lose her place in the world and plunge down, down into a gulf of burning darkness. I knew one way, but the drabble-tail Emmerson daughter knew another and had traded her own too-short pleasures for hell on earth. And where was the man with his grasping hands and sharp desire to share blame and dishonor for folly? She would suffer the heat and filth of the Boston jail, and in the end be hanged while he roamed free.

The Saltonstalls had hired rooms elsewhere, but I met with both of them several times before they rode home again in company with the Haverhill militia. I was mournful to see Elizabeth Saltonstall riding pillion and watched until she was out of sight, and wished that she could be with us in August when our babe would be born. But I did not ask, feeling that we had no chamber fit for her, and that I must make do with those who were closest to me in Andover.

As it fell out, we heard that they were no sooner arrived home than the alarm went up in Haverhill, and the militia there was busied with chasing shadows and conducting further training. Captain Bradstreet received a note from the major saying that one "John Robie, husbandman," had been killed by the enemy. The subsequent flutter of activity meant that there was little chance of Mistress Saltonstall returning.

But I was not sure who my companions in my down-lying would be. Goody Mehitabel Dane continued somewhat cold to me.

"Are you yet angered with me, Goodwife Dane?" I asked her the question one Sabbath at meeting, but she shrugged and said only that she was weary. She, too, was with child, and her time would not be so long after mine.

But the well had come between us.

Was it because I had been the one to discover her friend, and not Bel herself? Despite the uneasiness between us, we later tried to restore friendship. That is, she confessed that she regretted feeling anger over my discovery of Phoebe Wardwell and the babe. And I told her that I was sorry she had felt so, and said how much I valued her affection and former kindnesses to me. It was an awkward meeting that left me discontent.

After that, we still occasionally met to sew, though she often seemed impatient and out of temper. As time went on, these afternoons happened less frequently, and she made more excuses than before. At last, I no longer asked her to come and found that I was glad no longer to be refused.

"She has lost her love for me," I told Jotham Herrick as we stood by the small stone furnace behind the house.

"Something I shall never do," he said, not looking up from the pool of metal in a crucible. But he reached and pulled me against him.

"I have wondered, looking back, how I let her lead me into laughing at her sister and mother so often, or taking pleasure in Lizzie

Holt's distress. That was wrong of me. And I did not like it when she was merry about sieve-and-scissors. Perhaps I was at fault out of gladness to have someone who might be a friend."

"She is no paragon," Jotham said, letting go of me. "Let that be a consolation, even if it is sad."

"No one is a paragon, truly," I said, my eyes on the puddle of silver. "When I remember my family, the recollection of a thousand little faults rises up against me. I failed my sister on the day that mattered most. If I remember my time with Goody Holt, I recall many angers."

"Your little Mary fell—she was not pushed," he said. "And despite all, you are lovely in your ways."

"I do not know." What I felt just then was a flare of resentment against my supposed friend, but I could not bear to speak of it.

"And you have other, more faithful companions in Haverhill," Jotham reminded me.

So I put that Andover friendship aside, sorrowful that Bel Dane had floated away from me, and yet well pleased with marriage and hours spent in sewing for my own family or learning the mysteries of metals. I remembered Deliverance Dane's story of how Lizzie and Goody Holt spoke against me to the minister. Perhaps the two of them had worn down Bel's affection for me with ill words. Did making peace with family mean adopting their dislike of me? Perhaps, as Jotham once suggested, the tanner's daughter had been tainted by jealousy.

As the summer fled and my garments were unloosened more and more, I wondered at my contentment and happiness and feared to lose it when my trouble came. Not that I did not remember my dead daily, for I did—at times contemplating how I might have to join them soon. Often enough, a woman perishes in first childbirth. I did not speak much of the coming risk. Nor did my husband.

The goldenrod and purple asters bloomed, and still the babe had not made an appearance with us. The town's weather predictors all vowed that there would be a bitter winter, and rare August frost marred our crops. I grew sluggish and heavy and, I am afraid, sometimes neglected both shop and needle to sleep or idle by the fire, stirring the pot and baking ashcakes as if their mere presence meant I must sit and be watchful—in truth, doze.

"Making a babe is more tiring than making a silver punch bowl with gadrooning and legs and Latin inscription," Jotham Herrick said to me one evening, waking me where I lay curled by the hearth with ash in my hair. "I believe the wicked Albertus Magnus had the easier task, making a mechanical man out of metal."

"What are you saying? A punch bowl? I must have fallen asleep watching the pottage," I said.

He hoisted me up, grasping me above the belly.

"My time is soon, I hope." I yawned and wiped my eyes with the back of my hand.

"Perhaps I shall finish the punch bowl for my Salem sea captain first," he said.

"Maybe," I said, but it was not true. I ate the bread but could eat no more, and that night I woke in the night to swing my legs over the bed's edge and stand to let the waters pump out of me.

Jotham lit a candle from the fire.

"It's just water," I said faintly. "Oceans." Something like a distant drum had begun to throb, miles inside of me.

"There's a slip of something greenish," he said, bending to look.

I shivered uncontrollably, and Jotham Herrick wrapped my mother's blanket around my shoulders.

"The birth will be wholesome and right. I feel it, God be praised," he said. But his face looked worried.

"I pray so. And if not, I hope for courage and a good—"

"Hush," he said. "Let us have no talk of death when the surety is with me that all will be well. Only thanksgiving."

But I thought it secretly all the same, how a wife had the call and duty to make what was called *a good death* if she could not live, and how that was a hard, fearful command to heroism but had been fulfilled bravely by many women before me.

Courage, I told myself, *courage.*

Also I remembered a sermon on the famous monster borne by Mistress Dyer in Boston that the attending midwife, Mistress Hutchinson, desired to have kept secret, though Mr. John Cotton of First Church knew. Such frights cannot be hid for long. Later, Mr. Winthrop, governor at that time, mandated that the creature should be dug up from the common grazing ground, and more than a hundred people saw the shrunken remains, monstrous with the head mingled with the breast, the eyes popping from the skull, and all the rest mixed higgle-piggle, back to front, front to back, with holes and horns and claws. The tale was still a nightmare among the godly. I forced the images away, praying that they leave and not come back to blight the child in my womb.

Those well-born, well-educated ladies, Mary Dyer and Anne Hutchinson, were busy in the cause of liberty, but our ministers preached that each of them suffered an unnatural birth because they abandoned the right role of woman and usurped a man's duty. That our pastors were right in claiming them as heretics, I knew, yet I had a fellow feeling for the two, with their passion for truth and grace and desire to act for the good. Was I not a woman who longed to be like a boy eagerly riding off to Harvard, and who wished to make beauties not just in cloth and thread but in a man's prerogative of silver and gold? Perhaps my childbirth might resemble theirs, I feared, and all because I sometimes thought too freely.

I knew better than to send my husband out to be accused of night-walking when many hours and perhaps days of labor lay ahead, and in truth I was glad to be with him, for when the midwife knocked, out of the chamber he would go! We sat up in bed with his arms around me, and I dozed in between the pains, still far apart.

At dawn, Jotham Herrick sent a neighbor boy with word to the midwife, but she was attending the birth of a double-bent child in a Farrington house somewhere between the digging called Claypit and Woodchuck Hill. She would not be able to leave, at least not yet, and maybe not at all. But some of the Dane women arrived shortly—Goodwife Deliverance Dane, who was married to Good-man Nathaniel Dane, and whom I knew well by this time, and two of the minister's daughters, the well-married Mistress Abigail Faulk-ner with her own young daughters, Abby and Francis, and Widow Johnson with her daughter Betty. Goody Carrier came last; I had not known she was Mr. Francis Dane's niece. Some of the others in the family were at the Farrington house.

All but the two younger girls had seen many births and prom-ised that they would not need the ministrations of a midwife. Why, Goody Deliverance Dane had attended so many births, she was as adept as one! And if they did need more help, they would send for the midwife again and make her come.

Elizabeth Johnson said a prayer, and although I do not remember all, some of the words lingered with me: *We acknowledge that for our transgression and sin inherited from our great-grandmother Eve, women are afflicted with mortal pains. And so we pray for our sister, Mistress Charis*

Herrick, and also for Goody Farrington, that the Farrington child may be turned in the womb and the mother and babe after trial find their rest, whether on earth or heaven....

The thought came to me that when Elizabeth Dane was a young woman, she had been accused of undue familiarity with Goodman Johnson, the man she later married. Were not a woman's transgressions remembered forever in this life? It was easy to tumble and fall. People often called her only *Johnson's wife*. She lost clear claim to the title of *Goodwife* and her rightful place in the world, all for the sake of love and pleasure. And so it was with Eve, lingering by the tree with the serpent, listening to his sibilant promises. We women were forced to remember our great-grandmother still.

Abigail Dane had done much better, marrying the son of Mr. Edmund Faulkner, who with Mr. Woodbridge had negotiated for the town land, and who had settled most of his estate on his eldest son, as nobles did in England. And yet they were sisters still, and who knows what fate would come to each? Mr. Francis Faulkner was now an invalid, and his wife in charge of their estate, an unexpected situation that disturbed many in Andover who thought it wrong for a woman to play the part of a man. The paths to and through marriage were a strange labyrinth.

Despite the month, the night was cool, and a fire had been laid and the windows shuttered tight; I began to perspire, which everyone agreed would be helpful. Goodwife Dane took charge, as the one who had seen the most in the way of childbirth. She had brought with her a pot of butter and some silk for tying the cord, as well as cloth.

"All will be well," she said, and the others looked at her as if she had made a prophecy, and there was a hush. Mistress Faulkner clapped her hands to break the silence and sent Abby to fetch me a cup of beer.

We may close the door against men in such times, and it is as well to close the door on groans and shrieks in memory as well, but I will admit that it was a hard day of work, with much loud prayer and exclamation from all attending and a goodly store of beer and cold meat and cakes consumed by the others, though I could eat nothing. What I find most surprising about either attending or suffering through childbirth is how when women are walking along the edge of the Jordan, holding hands within sight of the mower,

Death, with his cloak and sickle, they can yet laugh, pray, tell stories, and encourage one another. A painful sweetness is compacted in those hours.

The fingers may loosen and be impossible to hold, the precipitous bank catch hold of a woman's feet; she may trip and plunge irresistibly into the drink, no matter how her friends and neighbors call to urge her to put forth hands and swim to shore. She may drown in those heavy waters, taking her babe with her. But the women go on in cheer, doling out comfort as if we were all safe and could skip along the border, and as if no river with its buried currents and fatal slap of waves on stone flowed nigh. That was dear to me, a thread of consolation braided together with alarm and adventure—for an adventure into extremity it surely is when a babe goes traveling the short yet difficult distance from womb-waters to air and life, and when a woman must strive to do the daunting thing of turning herself, as it were, inside out for the sake of a child, and all the while meditating on Eve, barefoot in the garden, the first taste of a banned fruit singular and pleasant in her mouth.

The two girls took turns reading from the shorter catechism of the Westminster Assembly—*The sin whereby our first parents fell from the estate wherein they were created was their eating the forbidden fruit*—and sang some psalms they had learned by heart, gripping each other by the hand and singing the louder when I cried out, as I meant not to do but did all the same. In the short lull between one sea-wave of pain sinking away and the next building and rising, I remember asking, "How much longer, how much?"

"Perhaps," Mistress Faulkner said, "an hour?" She looked to Goodwife Dane when she spoke.

"No more than two," Deliverance Dane said. "Surely no more than that. More likely an hour."

A great swell of panic washed over me. It came to me that I could not live through another hour of trouble, that I must die if the waves did not cease. So I thrust harder than ever before, shrieking when the pain came as if I could rid myself of agony by noise, by insisting, by wailing. I had a fear of dying badly that was as acute as any fear of death; more so, I think, for in death I would be like my family, and take the unborn with me.

"The crown, I spy the crown!" Goodwife Dane shouted. "Now comes the time to hurl the babe into the world!"

By then, I felt sure that I could not shove such an enormous substance as a child out of my womb and into the light.

"You are safe now, praise God," Elizabeth Johnson said, her hand on my arm. "The babe is in a fair position. It will be soon."

Those words came when I had given up on my trouble ever coming to an end, either in life or death, and felt that the drum in my belly would never cease its enormous vibrating, and that torture was the unending hell of being a granddaughter of Eve—to lie as on a rack, as if each limb were torn asunder. I forgot Jotham Herrick and what had happened in Falmouth, forgot Goody Holt and her carping, forgot the Saltonstalls, forgot Phoebe Wardwell and her babe under the ice. All I could remember was the heroic, often-told story of a noblewoman who had prayed and labored for fourteen days with a wrong-facing child and at last died. And all I could do was to beg God for relief from an orb of seething distress trapped inside me—for an end to the need to expel this relentlessly throbbing planet.

The girls' piping voices rose to a crescendo: *Behold, I was born in iniquity, and in sin hath my mother conceived me.*

But the women raised me up, and the child slithered into the world and was caught in a cloth by Goodwife Dane, the babe shining and slick and letting out a trembling whoop that was greeted by the outcries of women, and they crowded close to see him. She handed him to Mistress Faulkner, and knelt before me to tug gently on the cord until the rest was delivered.

And although there was a bustle of girls bringing drink and meat and cakes, and aproned goodwives wiping at the babe with cloths and, indeed, a whole world of earthly untidiness with someone praying in the background, the chamber seemed quiet and somehow distant to me, the naked babe like a rose in a caul of blood-streaked white, and the whole room bathed in candlelight, for it was night again before he was born. Eventually, after the cord was clipped and made fast with a knot, I watched as the women passed him from hand to hand, transforming him from a soaked, glistening creature into a little citizen of the world with clouts and cloths and bands of linen to hold all the gear in place. Betty Johnson settled a biggen on his head to keep in the warmth, handing him to Goody Carrier, who placed the babe in my arms.

The world came near again.

Abby and Francis were singing in high, tuneless voices.

I looked and looked as though never having seen such a common thing as an infant before, as though the curve of a cheek and the flash of a deep-blue eye and the soaked darkness of a newborn's hair had not been invented until now. And I memorized him, every spike of lash, every curve of feature, though certain I could not hold the image, for the faces we love blur and are lost in time.

"Thanks be that travail has ended," I whispered to the babe, who no doubt already sensed in his marrow that the world was propelled by strife. Had he not been cooked in my belly as an English alchemist cooks his mixture, and been fired out into the air with shocks and pangs, so that his first attempt at a word was a cry? And had we not won the victory despite the rack of birth, when the limbs are plucked asunder?

Though I thanked the God of divine power and mercy for that deliverance, though I swam in the midst of a sea of rescue and joy, though I knew that all good things are gifts from out of creation, I still pondered what it meant that some mothers were to live and some to die—and I remembered that day in the wilderness when it came home to me that Christ hangs on the Cross with arms extended to embrace a world of pain, that divinity is no cosmic tinkerer, and that God had not pushed the French and Indians in our direction and made sure that I was an Ishmael, alone and beleaguered in a wilderness.

My thoughts had circled that idea again and again with some fear, as I had no wish to be regarded as defying my church. Mr. Dane, though, had spoke differently of their fate, and had not called my family doomed by the Almighty. And now I had survived once more when I might have died.

"Who can know?" I murmured.

"Do you need anything?" Mistress Faulkner had heard me and come to see if I had any desire for food or beer.

"A mouthful of drink, prithee."

"With all my heart," she said. "You must be as dry as grit and old cobwebs."

I lay back and watched the women bestir themselves, cleaning up the room, preparing to call in my husband. They had called me a two-fold hero for fleeing in the wilderness and for making it through this other dark forest where so many wander and die. Perhaps if my parents had not brought me up to admire the heroic suffering of those who remain true to their promises despite torment, I would have died on the way from Falmouth, or else in childbed, not having strength to push on.

"You flower," I said to Samuel, for his face was the very color of a rose that my grandmother had carried on the ship from Boston and planted near the door of our house in Boston, though she did not live long enough to see it grow and bloom.

Goody Waters once told me that in England, our midwives were often cunning women who made use of magic—potions and incantations, charms and amulets and Mary Magdalene girdles. They made the room uncanny with little rites of propitiation to unknown powers. How strange to labor into the night with such chanted rhymes, such queer belts around the belly! The Cottons and the Mathers and all the tribe of ministers of Boston had put an end to such superstitions. They cared more about the soul's salvation than about rescuing the body from an earthly martyrdom, and so they commanded the colony midwives to put the soul first.

Secretly I wondered whether we could not care about both the body and the soul without magic and without displeasing God, who had formed and knitted them together out of a great pleasure in making something from nothing and in setting the world into motion. And when I looked at my child, I saw the true enchantment of birth, and was soon as fond of looking at the shape of his nose and eyelids as I had been of dreaming over Jotham Herrick after the first time we were alone together. That the babe was helpless and far from the competent exercise of a rational soul only increased my affection and desire to keep him near and safe.

But Deliverance Dane and Abigail Faulkner came to bear him away to the meetinghouse to be christened during the afternoon services on the third day of his life. I was glad that the day was sunny, for the talk in town was still of weather signs and a bitter winter to come, and the temperature was unwontedly cold. The two would stand together as midwife and present the child. They dressed him in a gown and a thin cap beneath a biggen, and gave him dry clouts and wrappings. The whole was bound in a bunting of skins from rabbits snared by Jotham Herrick, who was as handy in such work as any man in the colony.

"Samuel cried little," Deliverance Dane told me later.

"There was just the frailest skin of ice over the water in the bowl," Abigail Faulkner said, "and he sang out a trembling note at the touch of cold and then was quiet and good."

"Imagine there being ice at the close of August," Goodwife Dane said. "It is a chill I do not recall. Our young minister is already talking about this winter as a judgment upon sin, but I hope that it will not be so severe as he threatens. But Mr. Dane told us to carry the babe straight home and put him to bed beside the fire."

"It is hard to be brought into the Body of Christ through ice and cold water," I said. "I pity any babes born this winter, if it is to be such a cruel one."

"You may be interested to know that the midwife is busy with your friend Goody Dane. And Mr. Barnard said to our father that he hopes the child is not born on the Sabbath," Deliverance Dane said, leaning forward in her chair as if telling a secret.

"Goody Dane? You mean Mehitabel Dane? But her child is not due to be born until October, or so I heard tell."

"All the same, come he may," Goodwife Dane said. "And none of us who are of Danes by blood or marriage were asked to attend. And that seems to me passing strange."

"She let go of her love for me, and I have never known the why of it. Perhaps Lizzie and Goody Holt turned her against me. She seemed a friend and such a bulwark against her mother, who never cared for me. I do not know what happened, except that Mehitabel Dane was greatly shocked by Goody Wardwell's death, and I was present that day. You know that I found the mother and babe in the well. She misliked that it was me to discover them. Perhaps she did not like to think of that hour ever again. But I wish her an easy time in her trouble."

"God willing, you will have more and longer-lasting friends," Deliverance Dane said, "who shall not part you from their love."

"Thank you, Goodwife Dane. But before you leave, tell me more about Samuel and the christening."

I thought of my Jotham Herrick, still sitting with the men at the meetinghouse, and perhaps his thoughts on me as mine were on him. He was my best of friends, surely, and the earthly king of my heart, as I was queen of his. I looked forward to when my healing time was over and we could be fully together day and night, as when we were first married, before I was with child.

"The boy did finely. He opened his eyes wonderingly at Mr. Barnard and sighed."

Abigail Faulkner got up and went to the cradle near the fire where our little Samuel Herrick was now sleeping off the excitement of the morning. "And everyone close enough to hear sighed back, all together, as if singing," she added. "I have never seen Mr. Barnard so overcome. The tears came into his eyes."

"But it was our good old father who christened him, not Mr. Barnard, though they stood up together." Goodwife Dane smiled at me, perhaps guessing that I would rather her husband's father had done the act. "And Jotham Herrick looked fine and tall, and proud of his son."

"He was named for Mistress Herrick's father, I suppose." Mistress Faulkner was still kneeling by the cradle, her eyes on Samuel.

"Yes, and Mr. Herrick says that there will be other chances for his own name, which also belonged to his father in turn. Jotham is a good name," Goodwife Dane said.

"King Jotham raised castles and watchtowers in the forests of Judah," I said, "though they did not keep him from being thrown down in the end. And so my Jotham was defeated for a time by losing his family. But like the king, he had the desire to build, though in gold and silver—smaller things—in the wilds."

"We would be poorer without his work with the militia and selectmen and metals," Mistress Faulkner said. "You have both had trials and come through to a more peaceful life."

"Jotham is a strong name. And Samuel is a sturdy name as well." Deliverance Dane rose and, shaking out her skirts, left the room, coming back with a cup of beer for me and sugared curd cakes.

Afterward, she went to inspect the child.

"Your little Samuel Herrick is a sound sleeper," she said. "We carried him to sister Abigail's house so that he would have a warm rest on the way here, and the babe never woke, not even when he was tucked into a cradle and lifted out again later."

"An adventure in the cool air and ice and water has fairly tired him," Mistress Faulkner said, taking hold of her sister-in-law's hands to pull herself up. "You should sleep also, Mistress Charis Herrick," she added.

"Twixt birthing and churching comes weeping and sleeping," Deliverance Dane said, repeating an adage that may have been particular to Andover, as I had never heard it before. The godly had given over the practice of churching as ordained by the English in the Book of Common Prayer, so that there was only a prayer of thanksgiving after a month's healing time. But the saying lingered behind in people's mouths, if not in their acts. No doubt there was often weeping. I had heard from Deliverance Dane that Goody Farrington had been delivered of a stillborn boy, but that she lived.

I fell asleep and dreamed that I wandered through the forest with Hortus, and under the trees sat enormous gold and silver teapots, salt cellars, and spoons large enough for giants. And in one of these lay a babe—mine—and so I picked him up and went on until I reached the sea, where I sailed away in a sauceboat with a linen clout for a sail, stiff with salt. We must have been blown clean out of this world, for I dropped anchor at a land of rustling silver trees. I walked among them with Samuel in my arms until I found my lovely Jotham Herrick, shining in the sun like a man cast in gold, and just as a voice like ringing bell-metal spoke to me, I wakened in sweet desire to see his face.

The women from my lying-in went whisking in and out the shop and house for Samuel's first month, making sure that I rested. By the close of those weeks, I longed for nothing more than to be alone with my husband and son, though I was glad to feel stronger again, and to have had their help and counsel for many days.

Goody Mehitabel Dane's child was, indeed, born on the Sabbath, which Mr. Barnard said was a reproach to depraved parents, though Mr. Dane replied that children came when they came, and that to believe a birth on that day meant that the parents had engaged in bodily congress on a Sabbath was the sheerest superstition and not cited in Scripture or proper to the laws of nature. Mr. Barnard said that all three, the two new parents and the old minister, had profaned the Sabbath and were all of them doubting Thomases, though I did not find the least evidence of truth in his words. The news of that falling-out surged over the town and took many days to ebb. I also heard that child Anne was small and puny and likely to die, and that she was in some way imperfect. And I was sorry to hear of it and wished the babe strong and whole, and that Bel Dane and I could still be a comfort, each to the other. But it was not to be, it seemed, or at least not yet.

One morning I went to her house with a gown for the infant, embroidered with a white hawthorn flower. Goody Holt opened the door with Anne in her arms.

"You are not welcome here," she said coldly, and spat a generous quantity of moisture and phlegm onto the stone before the door, narrowly missing my petticoats. "Goodwife Mehitabel Dane now knows what you are and will not be taken in by your ways again."

Though she took the garment from my hands, she cast it down on the boards and made as if she would tread on it. But she held back. And that made me glad, for her daughter would see and know my work. Goody Holt was unlikely to throw away fine needlework, no matter how much she disliked me.

Ignoring her ill nature, I stepped onto the sill.

"What a pretty babe," I said, hoping that she would be satisfied with those words and tell Bel Dane of them.

"She came too soon, runted and dwindle-limbed, and she is blemished. Is that what a woman like you admires?" Goody Holt moved the little gown with the toe of her foot. "You deceived Mehitabel Dane with your charms."

I glimpsed what she meant, and what I had heard spoken of, a firemark on Anne's cheekbone, ruby red and round.

"Who would not love such a sweet face? Look at those delicate features. I do not believe she will fail to be loved because of a jot," I said.

"Cain was marked, was he not? And Satan leaves his stain on many a newborn, they say." Goody Holt pursed her lips tightly.

"Who are *they*? I do not think this tiny Anne Dane was inked by the Devil," I said. "She looks sweet, sleeping in your arms. Could she not still be tranquil and pleased with her lot, beloved by her parents and the Father of mercies?"

"Go on with you," Goody Holt said sourly, thrusting her face into mine so that I stepped back and found myself outside.

Her mouth relaxed into a smile as she kicked the door shut. I heard the babe give out a wail that rose to a shriek and sank into the distance.

I stood before the door, breathing hard in surprise and anger, images of the gown on the boards, the babe, and Goody Holt's vindictive mouth in my mind before I moved slowly away. "Love your enemies," I muttered; "bless them that curse you, do good to them that hate you, and pray for them which hurt you." But I did not feel at peace.

On the way home, I thought about those words and how hard they are to carry out. And what did the old woman mean, saying that I had deceived Bel with my charms? I had been nothing but truthful, it seemed to me, though no one is without faults and all people fail to see themselves clearly. Could she mean witchcraft charms? But I had nothing to do with such risky behavior—unlike her own daughters, who had been lured by fortune-telling. It was impossible to fathom the cause and the depths of her dislike of me, and I only hoped that her ill nature had not permanently poisoned Bel Dane against me.

In the end I had pity on Goody Holt, for who could bear to be her or abide near her for long? Surely she was her own bad punishment. Could she not even take pleasure in her daughter's child? And so I found the thread of compassion for them: Goody Holt, who did not want to be a tanner's widow but a high-born lady with silken clothes for herself and her children; Lizzie Holt, who had desired but failed to win my dear Mr. Herrick; and Goodwife Mehitabel Dane, who wanted many robust children but was disappointed in her first babe. True enough, a firemark was suspicious to the godly, but many a woman or man with a misfortunate blot showed forth as fair as or more fair than the unblemished. Sad for Bel, I hoped that she would find some love for little Anne. She liked children; surely she would welcome this one, if not now, later.

But Jotham Herrick and I were pleased to be happy in our little man and, as September progressed, passed hours of amusement and sometimes tears with him—for even the most royal of all children will cry and, soon enough, smile and kick against his bindings. Samuel slept or waked in the cradle as we worked in the room behind the shop curtain. We spent hours discussing the merits of Andover, and whether we should move to Haverhill and live near the Saltonstalls. Always it was Mr. Herrick's obligations to the town selectmen and the local militia that held us from the last choice. Also, I had a value for Mr. Francis Dane, though many preferred the younger minister with his talk of remarkables and the secret work of Satan, now and then bursting forth to burn down the feeble frames of God's people. The Dane family attracted me, and now that I had spent such childbirth hours with a portion of them, I felt closer to their town.

"Such a babe for luck," Jotham Herrick said, watching as Samuel drank from my breast, round eyes intent on mine.

"When he sleeps, sir, we could put the back-in-a-bit placard on the outer door," I said.

"You are a wonder, madam." He stretched out his arms as if tired of being cramped in one position to work. "A proof from wonder-working Providence that the world is better than we commonly know."

As I gazed on him, the light caught his shock of hair so that it was gilded. Despite the loss of friend Bel Dane and the fleabites of Lizzie and Goody Holt, I was content in my husband and child, in my small steps into the learning of the silver, in my few books and possessions, in my Sabbaths, and in my ordinary days. I was more glad than seemed quite right after all my trials, and determined in that very instant that I could lodge in Andover with Jotham Herrick until my life ended.

"Put the sign on the door? Yes, we should do that, wife," he said. "I am weary of pressing my tools onto mere silver."

"Perhaps you should turn to incising gold."

"I think not. How could I not prefer my wife with her skin of milk flecked with nutmeg and the rich fire of her hair?" He bent to the engraving again, a crooked smile on his lips. I watched him, enjoying the strength visible in his arms and the delicate fingers that could perform such dainty work. His pale gray eyes made me feel newly awake and alive when he shot the bolt of a glance at me.

And so, often and often, we closed up the shop for an hour, sporting together in joy, glad that all was well, that we had made it through the months when a man and a woman must restrain desire and think on birth and death and so ready themselves for either, and that we still had each other. Golden fire leaped from our very pores, and we burned as one. Our lives seemed to us fragile but perfect that fall—not perfect in the sense of without flaw but perfect in that we felt whole and complete, together or apart. As a young wife, I was ravished by my husband's mortal beauty, and, I believe, he by mine. For youth is princely, shapely, and comely to the eye. The child Samuel napped or fell asleep at night to the lullaby of wolves in the nearby forests, and woke to cry for milk or company in the cradle near the fire. I loved to play with him and to fimble his cheeks and forehead that were living silk for smoothness. He was pale-haired like my husband but blue-eyed, a token of how we had spent so many hours, our limbs glowing in the curtained dark.

9

Path in the Dark

Andover and Haverhill, mid–November 1691

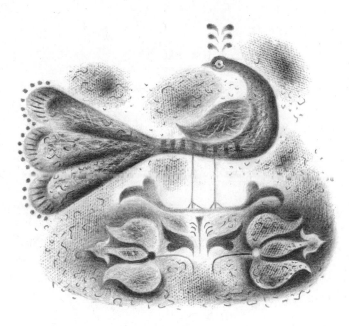

One afternoon in November, I was practicing the small art of engraving names on a piece of silver; Jotham Herrick was out on several errands, collecting a debt and delivering already-purchased silver to the Faulkners. Fed and newly cauled, Samuel lay wide-eyed but quiet in his cradle near the fire in the back room.

I heard the shop door fling open and, as it seemed, a great torrent of people burst inside.

"There she is!" Lizzie Holt shrieked as I passed through the curtain and into the shop.

"Mr. Herrick is not in," I began, puzzled as to why I could see Mr. Barnard and Bel Dane and so many men in the large company that had crowded into the room. Surely it was some town business, and none of mine.

A great squall of voices blew through the room, so much so that I could hardly make out what was happening. "Under suspicion," Mr. Barnard was saying, but I could make out "send away for the magistrate to Boston" and "accused of strangenesses." Oddly, some of them were talking of Goody Wardwell.

Lizzie Holt shouted them down with the words, "All her family died, and she rode through the nights and the wilderness to get to Haverhill. Is that not cause for mistrust? How nimbly she flew across rivers and through forests! Is that not near magic? Do not the dark hours belong to the Evil One? And has she not an uncanny skill with the needle—and red hair, the mark of Satan's roasting-flame?"

Mr. Barnard could be heard, his voice irritable, saying, "You there, Goodmen Osgood and Ballard, escort that young woman to her house. She has herself come under question for wielding sieve-and-scissors for fortune-telling. Her words are no right help to us."

"I am an essential party to this—" Lizzie Holt protested, but the two men ushered her out the door, though I could still hear her shouts, even after she was gone, diminishing as she was herded down the street.

Mr. Barnard pushed his way forward to where I was standing, startled and alarmed but not yet fully understanding my case. He was dressed in sober *De Boys* with a fine white lace-trimmed collar, but his clothes were rumpled and askew, as if he had been woken from a nap.

"In the absence of magistrate and several of our town officers," he began, "it has been decided that you must be taken into custody and kept secure for the night, just until the return of the constable and others."

"Where is Mr. Francis Dane in all this?"

"We need not bother my elder brother pastor with this matter, though I imagine he will be acquainted with the news soon enough," he said.

"I would value his counsel but trust you will speak well on my behalf and not be swayed by what must be the calumnies of those who do not love me. I have done them no wrong."

"If you have done no evil, you have nothing to fear," Mr. Barnard replied. His words gave me no feeling of assurance.

"Of what am I accused? I have not hurt anyone in Andover, nor do I intend to do so. I have lived a most harmless life here. What is the source of this censure and reproach?"

"She asked Goody Wardwell again and again if she would have water," Goodwife Bel Dane called out, pushing through the crowd until she stood near Mr. Barnard. She would not look me in the eye. "I was there, and she said to Goody Phoebe Wardwell that she would be thirsty if she took nothing to drink. And this Mistress Herrick was the one, when we were all of us searching and calling but could not discover her hiding place, to find out Phoebe Wardwell and her babe in the *water*—in the *drink*—with the ice sealed over her face. You see? She was given water to drink, and so she died."

I was surprised to see how gaunt Bel Dane appeared, her skin now too big for her flesh. My thoughts were on her face rather than the words. Then her meaning sank in.

"Surely you do not think I had anything to do with how—"

"There is more. My sister says that Charis Herrick has consorted with the dark and uneasy shapes that hide and frolic in wilderness. We know it to be likely. Is not the night evil? Do we not creep inside at the curfew bell? We do not know how or why her kin died. We do not even know if the French and Indians—"

"That will not do, Goody Dane," Mr. Barnard said with considerable asperity. "Though all happens for a purpose, you cannot blame the survivors of a French and Indian massacre for having caused that destruction, for having shot and clubbed the victims. You may say the weight of judgment was there, yes, but no more. For nearly the whole community of Falmouth was slaughtered in those wretched days, and it was chastisement of our colony but also a tragedy for us all."

I dried my eyes on my apron, and even now I am unsure whether I wept for my family or for the betrayal of friendship.

"But there is yet more," Goodwife Dane said.

I stared, unable to fathom what more she could hurl against me.

Mr. Barnard stretched out his hand, pointing toward her face. "What do you mean?"

"She has a doll that she keeps always, a needle pierced through the cloth. A blood spot mars the face. My babe was born too soon, and she has a blemish on the same part of her cheek. And you have seen it on her flesh, Pastor Barnard, the firemark of Satan."

At last she looked at me. I saw no shame for what she was doing on her features. And there was no love for me left, none at all.

"That I kept because my mother was making it, and the spot of blood is from my sister, who was—"

No one was listening. Some surrogate for the missing constable had given an order, and the men in the group scattered and began to ransack our rooms. Mr. Barnard called out to them for calm, but no one slowed in the frenzy.

"Go home, Goody Mehitabel Dane, and you other women," Mr. Barnard said. "Your testimony will be wanted later on, but for now go in peace."

"I am innocent of wrongdoing." I said softly. Who would there be to hold me dear, with Jotham Herrick absent and all else dead? The godly are like fierce pikemen who close double ranks around family when trouble comes. But who did I have to speak truth for me? Samuel began to cry from behind the curtain.

Soon only Goody Dane was still standing in the shop room. Why did she not leave?

Suddenly I felt the same as when I abandoned the ruins of our home near Falmouth, that I was utterly alone in the world and without a help except that God might care for me. My enemies lay close at hand, ready to ambush my steps. Just as the psalmist wrote of himself, I was like water poured out, my bones out of joint, and my heart wax. Only an hour before, I had been bidding farewell to my husband and leaning over the silver, trying for a smooth line, and now the world was plunging away. But I knew already that the ground under our feet is never sure, always subject to fire and quake.

As near Falmouth, I had an intense desire to weep that made my whole body ache. But I would not cry more, not in the presence of this woman who had once been my friend.

"Would you have an innocent hang? You have done evil to me," I said to Goody Bel Dane. "At least when the Sachem of the Narragansetts meant to attack Governor Bradford of the Plymouth Plantation, he did him the honor and kindness beforehand of sending a bundle of arrows wrapped in rattlesnake skin, a sign which there was no mistaking. I have seen and borne a great wrong before, and now I see and bear one again. This time it is your ill, unkind, and savage doing, you who should be my friend."

She did not answer, though a flush came into her cheeks. In the strange way that small things that do not matter tug at our attention, even in the most dire situations, I noticed a stain on her bodice and remembered how Goody Holt had scolded her more than once as a lazy slattern. She seemed to waver as to whether she would come closer or speak, but turned away and swept from the shop.

"My Lord, may I never see her face again," I whispered.

Shouting went up from our bedchamber, and one of the men came back waving the small wooden case in which I kept Mary's doll. Jotham Herrick had given it to me. The throng of others tumbled into the shop after him, each crowd-brave and eager to glimpse the evidence of Satan passing among us.

Goodman Woodbridge appeared flushed and gleeful as he held up his discovery.

"Here, here is the poppet with the needle and the firemark!"

Mr. Barnard pushed through the press of men, took the box from him, and inspected the doll.

"At first look, this seems a macabre and strange witchwork like a corpse in a coffin," he said. "And the needle and the blood are there, as Goody Dane described."

"I have kept it, sir, for the love of my mother and sister and no other reason," I said. "The doll was never finished, and my sister Mary died. That is a drop of her blood. It is no witchwork."

"Perhaps so, madam," Mr. Barnard said. "I pray it may be. You must answer proper questions before we go further."

The man who had found the case asked, "What shall we do with her?"

"Wait for Captain Bradstreet and Constable Forster and the others to return from Boston," said one, and "Take her to Salem Village" or "Salem Town" or "Boston" said others. They did not want me in Andover.

Was I to be arrested and indicted? I had no confidence that a woman charged as a witch would be treated fairly, for I recalled the story of an unfortunate woman who had been accused and hanged in Boston, though my father said she was simply poor and bedlam-mad and had been a healer in her youth. But a nervous wife had been pricked by an unseen pin, a pail of milk was spoiled, and a well-known gossip believed she had seen the old woman hopping about in the brush near her house in the shape of a prodigious raven, with eye and beak so large they could only mean that a witch had shifted her form into the shape of a bird.

"Fear shows us colorful pictures," my father once told me. "When we remember that Providence goes with us everywhere, there is no fear. For even what is ill and evil can be turned toward good. But in God's own time, not ours. Never try to make the divine skip and hop to a tune."

But how could this threat against me become a blessing?

The men conferred in a huddle, but I did not try to hear what they were saying. I was nearly numb with the change that had come over my life in so few minutes. My Samuel was still crying in the background.

Finally Mr. Barnard came forward with several of the others. "We will escort you to shelter since the justice has been called to Boston and cannot be consulted."

"This house is a safe place where nothing ill has ever happened," I told him.

"That is as may be," he said. "But we wish to protect the race of timorous women from those who may be aroused by the news and angered, and we have a duty to shield others who might be harmed. Get your cloak and your child, and let us go. Our elders say that this is the most biting season in their lifetimes, and a judgment sent of God. Sure and certain it is that a visitation of such bleakness means a scourging of the town for mischief."

Who might be harmed. By me. What folly. And where is Jotham?

Slowly I went to the chest in my bedchamber and fetched my cloak, bonnet, and felt hat. I gathered up my pattens, and also the rabbit-skin wrap and my mother's woven blanket for Samuel. As in a dream, I found myself downstairs again, looking down on my child. My breasts prickled with milk. He would be hungry before we lit down in some other nest, I feared.

When I lifted him from the cradle, he was warm and damp, and so I cauled him tightly for the outdoors. Already brute winter was upon us, with November more like January, the rivers frozen and snow on the ground. The elders could remember no such year as this, when the sacramental bread rattled sadly in the plates and Goodwife Chandler died upright in the pew on a particularly frigid morning. The ink in the bottle froze when our ministers sat down to write sermons, and that, people whispered, was naught but a devilish prank.

Mr. Barnard assigned two men to go with me; one of them claimed to know a secure situation until the morrow, when I might be moved to Salem to answer questions. My state was changed so quickly! We walked away from the house, and some of my near neighbors came out of doors and called out to know what was happening, but Mr. Barnard bade them to go back inside. They did not. When I looked back, a knot of people had gathered around him to demand the news.

It occurred to me as a strangeness that Goodwife Bel Dane had accused me of nothing true, and yet she had forgotten to claim the one guilty matter that I would have assented to—that I was the reason for Mary's death and hence the cause of the drop of blood on the doll's face. That I would have admitted freely. Did my guilt not come to me every morning when I woke?

My appointed guards, Goodman George Abbot and Goodman William Barker, were not unkind to me. Goodman Abbot hardly spoke on the first part of the walk, though he commented on the handsomeness of my child and said that he was sorry for my poor estate. Eventually he admonished his companion for his excess of talk and curiosity. On that occasion, Goodman Abbot became voluble.

"If she is a witch, William Barker, why do you want to stir her up? She might bewitch your stock until they bounce along the ground. Might put urine in the well and nails in the milk. Rot your cloth, damp your salt and powder. She might fluster you, showing up in the shape of a great feathery owl, *whoo-whooing* around the door when the four of you are lined up in the bed as neat as four needles in a goody's pincushion. She might come scotch-hopping along to your bedchamber with the Devil's black book under her arm, and every name signed with blood. Or maybe with her own head tucked under her arm and a bloody neck-stump poking out of her gown. She might tempt your children to grow so stubborn in mind that they would never again obey you, no matter how stoutly they were reproved or by whom."

Goodman Barker looked abashed by this outpouring and only protested mildly, "She is not a batter to be beaten fine. So I shall not stir her. Moreover, we are not four to the bed but five, for there is my wife's sister who lives with us."

Ignoring this remonstrance and correction, Goodman Abbot went on. "And if she is *not* a witch, why pester and plague her?"

Seeing that I struggled with the bundle of my son and with walking so far in snow, he offered to carry Samuel, and I gave over the babe, though I did not like to do so. Goodman Abbot carefully adjusted the rabbit-skin wrap and blanket, bending over the child to look him in the face. "Poor little witch-child," I heard him murmur.

William Barker had been thinking hard as he trudged and now burst out. "Whoever heard of any such *whoo-whooing* witch, Goodman Abbot? An owl, you say! A witch comes as a crow or a raven in all the accounts I heard tell. Or a wolf whispering along in the shadows."

Too stunned by cold to cry, Samuel stared at the unfamiliar features and then turned his eyes toward me.

"Pah! Most of them are ancient poor widows with no comeliness or sense remaining," Goodman Abbot said. "I saw one hanged in Boston two years back, a pitiful rag of a woman who was so Irish that she couldn't speak English. How the judges understood what she answered when she spoke in the foreign tongue called Gaelic, I do not know. I believe they did not, as at the Tower of Babel."

"Not this one," Goodman Barker said. "She is not old, nor lacking in English words or comeliness."

"Perhaps she is no rampant hag and witch."

"She has the hair," Goodman Barker said, giving me a sidelong glance. "It is a devilish sign, some say."

"There is that," Goodman Abbot agreed. "Would you say there is a lick of red on the child's hair?"

At this, we three must stop and stand in a huddle to inspect the wisp of hair that was visible below the biggen and cap.

In the late afternoon sunlight, the silks of Samuel's hair did seem to have a faint new color that I had not seen before. I was sorry for it, knowing that he would be, sometime or other, blamed for his hair.

"I think not," Goodman Barker pronounced.

"And I think so," Goodman Abbot said, shifting Samuel so he lay against his chest.

"Perhaps," I whispered.

Despite the caution against curiosity by his friend, Goodman Barker went on asking me many questions about my journey from Falmouth, and how I had come to be in the Town of Andover, though I was sure he already knew much of my story. The tales of newcomers were generally regarded as village property. He listened closely as I told why I kept Mary's doll as a memento.

"And now I suppose it will be lost to me forever," I said. "And I have so little to remind me of my mother and sister."

"Maybe the justices will dismiss the case after the questioning," Goodman Barker said. "When you tell the story, it seems reasonable and shows affection."

Goodman Abbot sighed as if he were in doubt. "In court with the questioners, everything is different," he said. "They make things seem otherwise." He thumped on the rabbit-skin wrap for emphasis, and Samuel gave out a small, mournful cry.

"You would think so, having lost your case in the matter of a cow," Goodman Barker said.

"I was that tongue-tied, I could hardly string my words together, and the other man glib as a brook in spring spate." At this, Goodman Abbot stopped dead and stared down as if forgetting his errand and minutely concerned with his feet.

I reached to draw a corner of wrapping over Samuel's head. Startled, Goodman Abbot looked at me before setting off again.

"That might well have made the difference," Goodman Barker called to him, "though they say the truth will hatch from the egg of a lie."

"Such a short time ago I was content and pleased, and glad to have a family once more," I said.

We hurried to catch up with Goodman Abbot and walked on in silence. I listened hard to the sounds of breathing and the *craunch-craunch* of the snow under our feet because I did not wish to brood. But Goodman Barker must have been dwelling on my words because he soon offered a piece of solace. "At least we do not burn witches in this country. Our witch-women are made to ride the wooden horse, as it is called. And wear the bridle, too."

"The scaffold and the rope? That is no consoling thought," Goodman Abbot said. "Why, the foolishness of it makes me wroth to think you meant it so."

To my surprise, I laughed, afterward assuring the men that I had taken no offense. "Hanging by the neck is undoubtedly less fierce and awful than being roasted alive," I said, imagining the weight of rope at my throat—surely I had felt a sort of weight there already, ever since I heard Bel Dane's accusation. "And at the end, I should be like my mother and father, my sister and brothers, and all my kin. And perhaps that would be a turn toward the good." The words were not what I expected to hear myself saying, but I was oddly comforted by them, despite having been oppressed by apprehensions only moments before.

An unexpected prayer drifted like a single, starry flake of snow: *My dear Christ, let me be pleased with life, whether short or long, and let me see thy salvation.*

"Are you so certain? What if they were bound to the other place, and not in paradise? Or you in the one and they in the other?" Goodman Barker peered at me anxiously. "For truly, we do not know what Judgment Day will bring, and all is a darkness and a wondering except in hours of assurance. And those do not stay with us for always."

Goodman Abbot halted once again and stared at his friend. "You are a queer sort of a man and no mistake! A regular Job's comforter. How long did you have to puzzle before you found another such soothing thought?"

"I meant it kindly," Goodman Barker protested.

Goodman Abbot adjusted another bit of the covering to shield Samuel's face from the fine sparks of ice that had begun to fall and walked on.

"It is a mercy that we are almost there, or you might have her ready to call for a carpenter and be measured for a coffin with all your pleasant cheer and kindliness," he said.

"The snow grows deeper," I said, wishing that we had never left the house. My feet ached with the cold. I feared that my Samuel would be lucky to escape the blight of frost marks on his face. And that would be the fault of my accuser if he did, I reflected. We would each have a marked child in that case—one by "fire," one by ice.

I had hardly thought of where we were going, so much else pressed upon me, but I now gazed about and took my bearings.

The last houses were behind us, and the abandoned Wardwell place lay ahead. Might it be our destination? As far as I knew, my remaining stay in Andover would be only the one night. I would be removed elsewhere, and the whole weary matter of questioning would begin.

Perhaps I would be searched. I had heard how women were stripped and inspected, down to their privy parts, for any sore push or mole that might be a devil's teat. The mind being whimsical and whirligig in nature, I now wondered why a diabolical creature would not suck on a woman's breast like a child. Why did a demon have to create its own way into her body, so that shivery tales were told of evil rustlings under petticoats?

"My liking is not to bide in a house where a woman has made away with herself and her babe," Goodman Barker said. "No, indeed. I do not care for it."

So it would be the Wardwell house.

"The goody did not make away with herself in the house but in the well," Goodman Abbot pointed out.

"I doubt a ghost would bide for long in a well," Goodman Barker said. "Stands to reason that she would come inside with the ghost-babe to warm herself."

"Well, I disbelieve that there is any hot or cold to a ghost, so perhaps she would just stay put. Flitter round and round in the well-water like a fish." Goodman Abbot checked Samuel's face, and I moved closer and saw his features pinched up against the cold.

Goodman Barker considered this proposition and finally asked, "Would you drink that water?"

Goodman Abbot made an exclamation that might have been irritation. "A woman is not a tea leaf to tint the water," he said. "Nor is she poison. Unless she stays too long in summer."

Goodman Barker nodded. "The water would not be fit to drink, and the well would have to be sealed."

"'Tis not summer," Goodman Abbot said. "And she didn't bide too long. Why do you think such foolish things?"

The house, which had been but a bump in the distance, had come near as I listened to the men, marveling at how they were able to speak so blithely of my future and Goodwife Phoebe Wardwell's past. I noticed a smudge of smoke going up from the stalk of the main chimbley that was the most substantial thing about the little house that had once been and was meant to be a full-size house but now would probably never grow larger.

"You are an interesting pair," I said.

"No pair at all," retorted Goodman Abbot. "Or at any rate, not a matched pair."

"We are no horses to jog on in harness," Goodman Barker said.

Goodman Abbot lifted the rabbit skin from Samuel's face. "An ox and an ass," he whispered. "I'll be the ox."

Samuel's tongue tasted the air and jots of ice, and he blinked.

Another day I might have replied to Goodman Abbot's jest; another day I might have raised my hand to hide a smile. But not now, on this day of fled freedom.

"Look there," I said. Ahead of us, I could see a man with a fowling-piece leaning against the house. Was I so monstrous that he needed a weapon? As we came closer, he stepped away from the wall and shouldered the gun.

Goodman Barker bawled out, "Goodman Peeters, what do you here?"

The man came forward to meet us, saying that he had been sent to act as a guard and to set fires in the two chimbleys. He gave me a swift glance, did not respond to my courtesies, and seemed to have decided to have little to do with a potential witch.

"My, you must have been in a rumbunctious hurry," Goodman Barker said, looking at him with admiration.

"Did what I was ordered to do. Come in and warm yourselves," he said, "and take the prisoner upstairs."

"She seems a fine sort of young woman," Goodman Abbot said. "After being in her company, I do not believe she can be a witch. And this is a sturdy boy in my arms."

"Thank you for that change of mind," I said.

"No *tu-whooing* at all," Goodman Barker added.

Goodman Peeters looked at him steadily.

"No owls," Goodman Barker explained.

"She may look like a 'fine sort,' but Satan sometimes appears not as an ordinary rollipoke but as a silken bag," Goodman Peeters said. "Therein to catch the silly unawares."

It occurred to me that he had been talking to Mr. Barnard.

"I am neither a rollipoke nor a silk bag. Just an ordinary woman who hopes God and men will discern truth and show her mercy."

Goodman Peeters paid my words no notice but ushered us inside. We scuffed at the door, leaving behind us a miniature landscape of snow shaken from our shoes. But when we went to the loft, there was nothing at all in the way of furniture in the chamber. I felt some relief, for now surely I would be prisoned on the lower floor. And I deemed it the better place, with some glimmer of hope that I could get out and be free. For was this night's jail not strangely providential? Could I not hope to say, *Oh, wonderful, unspeakable mercies of God who takes care of us when we may take no care of ourselves?*

"Put her in the lean-to room downstairs," Goodman Abbot suggested. He was still carrying Samuel. "This little babe needs warmth after such a frozen walk, and his mother's care."

"Thank you," I said again, giving him a bob of respect.

Heated by a small wooden chimbley, the back room was where a bed had stood in Goodwife Wardwell's illness, and it was there still, though the coverings and hangings had been stripped away. The big cradle for Phoebe Wardwell's baby still hulked by the hearth. Even in the daylight, the chamber with its sloping roof was dark, all windowless and sad. Perhaps I thought so because nothing of Phoebe Wardwell remained there except in my memory, and those thoughts were gloomy.

The hearth was not promising, but Goodman Barker brought in some sticks of wood and coals from the main room in a broken pot.

"Glad to find that Goodman Wardwell did not tote away the woodpile," he said to me.

"Thank you for this kindness," I said.

He went out and returned several times with armloads of split oak and maple, and Goodman Peeters gave him unneeded directions about how better to lay the fire. Meanwhile, Goodman Abbot was walking up and down the cramped, slope-roofed bedchamber, singing a dismal-sounding psalm to Samuel, who cried loudly before stopping and staring in what I hoped was not alarm.

"Helpful that the place was not torched a second time by the Indians," Goodman Peeters said. "They often fire houses that stand forlorn."

"It seems forlorn enough," I said to no one in particular.

"The fire will be lively soon," Goodman Barker said. He seemed about to pat my shoulder, but Goodman Peeters cried out, "Do not handle the witch!"

"Who says she is bound to be a witch?" Turning his back, Goodman Barker squatted down and fed the flames with more wood.

Goodman Peeters frowned. "You relish witches?"

"No—"

"Then keep quiet."

When I sat down on the bed, I heard rustling in the corn husks. *Mice.* Already they had come in from the cold. I would sleep there in my cloak and be tidy enough. I did not like the thought of mice. Familiars for a witch. Tiny familiars. Witches had hogs or hounds, rabbits, mousers, toads, turtles, and even chimeras as familiars if what was whispered was true. Birds sometimes followed a witch, circling around her head or flying at her back and beck. But all I had was the field mice in Phoebe Wardwell's shuck mattress.

Goodman Abbot put the bundle of Samuel in my arms, and I carried him to the fireside. Before long the babe began to wail again. The cold afflicted him in its wearing-off, as it did me. The men talked softly together, arguing about witches. I did not listen. When they shut my door and retreated to the front room, the chamber was nearly dark, save for the light shed by the hearth. The chimbley smoked and pulled but weakly at the logs. I wished that I had thought to hide some tallow candles in Samuel's wrappings. But there was no use regretting what I had failed to do in my shock at being accused. I nursed Samuel—his face chill against my breast—and laid him down in the cradle when he fell asleep, worn out by his adventure and the harsh weather.

That was good; I wanted to search the room after setting my shoes and pattens by the fire to dry. The job of scouring was done quickly, for the place was nigh barren, and I found only some strips of linen, an assortment of sleeve ribbons, and a crushed tin lantern with a window that was half Muscovy "glass" and half oiled linen, evidently replaced when part of the thin stone was lost. I spent some minutes attempting to press the metal into shape with nothing but a stick of tinder, and thought how easily I could do the same work at the shop with Jotham Herrick's tools. But the lantern would do; now I only wanted a candle.

I also wanted to consider how to act, and sat down to do so in the ashes close to the fire. Was this the hand of Providence, moving slowly in God's own time? My brother John's voice came to mind, saying, *There are no coincidences.* I had not been in Andover so long or become so loyal that I could not imagine and dream of safety and a life in some other township. What did I possess here but husband Jotham Herrick and my babe, Samuel, and the friendship of some of the Danes? If I had my chance, I would flee. It had happened before. Prisoners evaded trial more than might be expected, particularly in the period of time before they were locked in jail. That was when it would be easiest, surely. And in the solitary villages set in wilderness, jails could be small, rickety affairs. Those accused by some local justice of the peace might break free and bolt for another region instead of standing trial.

Was it my duty to bear the questioning and the inspection of my body for witch-marks? Would our Andover justice of the peace, Captain Dudley Bradstreet, son of the governor of the colony and the poet, serve a writ against me? Was it my appointed path to be indicted and, if wrongly charged, dangle by the neck until I was dead? Or to decline in prison from sickness, damp, and cold, as transpired often? To make a widower of Mr. Herrick and half an orphan of Samuel? Anne Bradstreet wrote, "If we had no winter, the spring would not be so pleasant." But in this case, spring might never come without striving, struggle, and perhaps escape.

Jotham Herrick was a selectman, sealer of weights and measures, and soon to be lieutenant in the militia, a highly regarded voice. Would he give up those posts and flee to where he was unknown? It was much to ask.

When I knelt by the fire to warm myself and pray, the tunnel came insistently into my mind.

"But thou, Lord, art a buckler for me, my glory, and the lifter up of mine head," I whispered.

The words of David, driven from his kingdom, warmed me; I stood up, sensing that I was not alone with Samuel. Closing my eyes, I knew what I had known only a few times before, the tilt and spill of some wondrous cascade in the heavens and a wash of spirit that I can compare only to innumerable tiny gold pins, a brightness falling down on me from beyond the region of stars. For some ungrasped length of time that waterfall of light flooded me, the rays of gold passing through my skin and emerging and raining away through the world. The fountaining-forth was more beautiful than a night when stars fall, flicking from the heavens to earth, for it pierced and passed through every vein and inch of me, its moving lights washing me away until I was nothing but pouring dawn.

I heard a voice close to my ear say, "He brings those who sit in darkness out of the prison house." And I cannot forget those twelve words, as loud as if someone called out by my ear, so that I was surprised the men did not come pell-mell to my door.

The daybreak cataract ebbed and left me. I opened my eyes and saw the fire struggling on the stone and barely shedding its flush onto the floor.

Who is the father of the rain? Words as mysterious as an otherworldly falls of light came to mind.

Tears pricked at my eyes for the loss of that spate of gold and sweet energy. For some time, I crouched by the fire, remembering the strangely spoken words and the vital stream of spirit, letting them curl and eddy through my mind again. *Out of the prison house. Those who sit in darkness.* I could have been glad to be caught in gold forever—to be made of such material that could bear and vessel what is unearthly and rained down as spirit. But such gold cannot remain with us for long.

When I tiptoed from the room, determined to explore, I avoided the door that led immediately to the front, but chose the side door leading to the remains of a burned room—now merely a narrow passageway. I had taken off my stockings by the fire, and now carefully felt the floor with my bare feet, hunting for the fingerhold to the trapdoor. Somehow I feared that the spot might have vanished, or that I would be unable to find it. But the short, slight groove between boards was there. I knelt and ran my finger along its length and stood once more, keeping one hand on the wall of the passage as I walked forward. The dividing wall soon ended, and when I stepped into the front room, I saw Goodman Peeters seated bolt upright on a stool before the door, fowling-piece leaning next to him. He grasped it when I appeared. I glanced toward the fire; Goodman Barker lay pitched at full length before the brick hearth, and Goodman Abbot was perched close by on a wooden box.

"Might I have a candle? I can hardly see to tend to my babe," I said. "It would be a help to me when he is restless and unhappy. With no windows, there are no chinks of light to see by."

"The dark will be coming on soon," Goodman Abbot said. "Surely it is reasonable to give the young woman a candle."

Goodman Peeters stood up and bade the others to requisition "a mere stub for the accused witch. And fetch it to me and let me make certain that the candle is not too generous."

The response was only snores from Goodman Barker, but Goodman Abbot got up and began searching a heavy chest that still waited for Thomas Wardwell to bring an ox and cart. I stepped farther into the room, turning to stare back into the darkness. Would candlelight near the trapdoor cast a halo into the front room? Surely it would be hard to tell whether light shone from the room or from the passage.

"Go back to the bedchamber and wait," Goodman Peeters ordered, and I hurried away.

Some time later, Goodman Abbot tapped on the door jamb to signal his presence and then came in the room. I was seated by the fire with a hand on Samuel's cradle. My babe was awake and staring at me, and he wore a look of wisdom as if he knew my sorrow and my thoughts.

Goodman Abbot bent to look in the cradle. "A likely-looking child. I had a bit of candle on me all the time. It is but tallow so will not last more than a wink."

"Thank you," I said, wondering why he had not offered it sooner. He set the tallow stub and something else down beside me.

I picked it up—heavy—and lifted it to my face. By feel and fragrance, it was beeswax. "Oh, thank you! Where could you find such a thing?"

"In a basket of cast-offs, among broken clay bottles and a stove-in kettle. There is a paper tied on. I suppose Goodman Wardwell did not want to keep it because of the words."

I held the candle with its little strip of paper toward the firelight and read. *For my dear and loving daughter, this candle made by my hands to mark divine deliverance from trouble and the birth of your son, for I know that you will be a godly and tender parent. I believe it will burn for perhaps seven hours. Please treasure it for some special day when a fine light is desired. Your most affectionate friend and Mother.*

"That day will never come," I said.

"No, but you have the need, and I have plucked it from the tossed-away rubbish. No husband in such a plight would ever wish to see the candle again or to read those words. And now, having taken it into my possession, I give it to you. Mine be the blame, if there is blame. You and the child should have light."

"Thank you, Goodman Abbot. I will not forget this sweet kindness." I touched him glancingly on the sleeve. "You are a great help to me. Truly."

"What wastes your time? Why do you tarry on a simple task?" Goodman Peeters stood at the door, the firelight dimly showing that he stood with hands on hips.

I swaddled the candle in a fold of my gown.

"Just wishing the poor young woman to be stout of heart, for my mind is now at peace about her—I do not find that she is of the witch-kind. That is all." First caressing Samuel on the cheek with a finger so that the babe cocked his head and stared, Goodman Abbot turned and slipped out the door past Goodman Peeters.

"A witch is a diabolic creature. She can make you dream that she is as white as the cream on milk." Goodman Peeters spoke harshly, but his voice quivered. He glared at me, his face lurid by the light of a tallow candle mounted on a shard of crockery, and fled into the hall.

My thoughts surprised me. *He is daunted by me! Goodman Peeters is afraid that I have powers that he will find irresistible. When I have nothing but a secret candle, and he has a gun.*

His voice wafted to my room. "Witches are sly and conniving and can persuade others to do their bad will."

Goodman Abbot's words were faint. "Aye, witches can, but Mistress Herrick is not a witch."

I heard the footsteps of Goodman Peeters growing slighter, and at last they were lost to hearing.

Samuel, tired of his long staring and worn to silence, closed his eyes. For a long time, I sat feeding wood to the fire, attempting to remember every detail of the tunnel and considering how I would get the babe down through the trapdoor. Every time I thought of guiding the lit candle and the child through the hole, I imagined plunging and being unable to catch myself by the slats of the crude ladder. I imagined the light going out in a blink and Samuel wailing in the darkness. I dreamed up every possibility, even absurd ones like Goodman Barker colliding with Goodman Abbot and the two dropping through the opening. More woefully, I pictured Goodman Peeters tripping and diving, the gun firing and killing the child in my arms. Surely I would have to make several journeys, one to set the candle down on the dirt floor, and one to fetch the babe. And walking through the heavy snow near the house on pattens had not proved easy.

About the dusk hour, after I nursed Samuel again and put him back into the cradle to nap, there was a commotion at the house front, with Goodman Peeters blocking the way and bellowing back and forth with those who desired entrance. When he at last dragged away his stool and opened the door, I was pleased to recognize the voice of Mr. Francis Dane, quite loud and indignant in tone, and I stepped from the room to listen.

"What do you mean by refusing entrance, man? You have but a makeshift post as officer of the peace for a single night, and you would deny the authority of your minister?"

Goodman Peeters rivaled the pastor in volume and intensity. "I had my orders. I know my duty," he said, "praying your worshipful pardon, sir."

A third voice rose over his. "Could we not settle this matter later? I desire to see my wife."

"Well, I do not know," Goodman Peeters said.

"She has not been formally charged; she is only being held for future questioning," Mr. Dane said. "Naturally we may see and visit with her."

"Visit with her? I have no orders whatever about holiday calls and tarriance of husbands with witch-wives and ministers wishing to con-fer with and hearten and perhaps pray with accursed young witches. A visitation of suffering upon the prisoner I could understand. Or the sojourn of some Egypt-plague. But merry, how-now, what-cheer house calls? No orders! No orders!"

"What fiddle and flummery! We will see her, and you will like it or hie yourself elsewhere," Mr. Dane exclaimed.

"One at the time," Goodman Peeters bargained.

"Whyever so? But if it lets you do your proper duty, man, fine," Mr. Dane said. "While Mr. Herrick goes in to his wife, I will halt here and tell you exactly how you mistake the prerogatives of your temporary office."

"That would be a regular feast of entertainment to the rest of us," Goodman Abbot said.

"Only a few minutes," Goodman Peeters continued, still caught up in the dream of his own power to order events.

"What? What is the matter?" Goodman Barker seemed to be reproaching his friend for waking him.

"You do not want to miss out," Goodman Abbot said.

I met Jotham Herrick in the narrow passage and embraced him, the disquiets of the day lost in his arms. Pulling him inside the dark

chamber, I held him close. After moments in which we each seemed
to be doing our best to merge into one being, we drew back, and I
led him to the fire.

"You must be freezing," I said.

"It is no matter, nothing at all," he said, though his cheek had been
cold against mine, and his clothes were chilly and flecked with half-
melted snowflakes. He glanced down at our babe, asleep in the cradle.

"Jotham," I said, "my dear Jotham."

"My sweet," he said. "Charis, I explained about the drop of blood
on the doll to Mr. Barnard, but he finds the sum of complaints too
great to dismiss. I am afraid, madam, that these vile, miserable Holts
will be our undoing. They bombard the people with words of stone.
I fear the truth will not come out." His fingers sought mine, and we
stood latched together beside the flames.

"A clay pot cannot contend with a wall," I whispered. It was something my mother used to say, and now I feared to be the pot contend-
ing with a wall of flinty justices, or a wall of tale-bearing Holts.

"Yes, we smash ourselves to dust against their stories."

"So I fear."

"Justice may be the highest virtue, but in this case, chaos rules. All
goes arselins. All is tyranny and untruth against our family," he said.

I looked down at the bed of coals, the rich, glimmering slope under
the flames, and thought of how, across the sea, witches were bound
to the stake and burned like candles. And the least little scorch-mark
was so painful: to have tinder flaming underfoot until boughs and
wood caught, and skin and hair and bones were transformed from
solid flesh to tallowy dew, would be hell before death.

"You do not believe them? Not even a little?"

"How can you ask, wife? I know who and what you are, and you
are no witch, though you have been forced to be braver than is the
usual lot of our kind. You are my queen of truth and heroism." He
gathered me close, and I clung to him. "Surely your feet were guided
to mine through the wilderness."

"Yes," I said.

"And what is this trial but anarchy and chaos toppling goodness
and order?"

"Jotham Herrick, if I were to come to you in the deep part of
the night, would you go with me to some other realm? Could you
endure to leave this place, where you are regarded and have a fine

reputation as goldsmith? Where you are a selectman in the town and busy with the militia? Could you bear to walk as a pilgrim up and down the earth for my sake? Would you be willing to find a separate joy with me?"

He pulled back from me and gazed into my face.

"What do you mean? How?"

Goodman Peeters rapped on the doorframe and called to us that we had three minutes only. Mr. Dane caught up with him and the two began arguing.

"Never mind how," I said, lowering my voice. "But I have a new thought. Take Samuel with you and say, dear sir, that he needs fresh clouts and wrappers. And that you will bring him back before they take me away, so that he can be in my cell and live there and be fed until my trial."

"Yes," he said, "I will do that."

"Trust me, husband. But bring him in the morning if I do not find you in the night," I said. "Or he will be hungered. And give him a taste of sugar if he cries."

"You know a way? Your words are dark. I cannot think what you mean."

"Goodman Peeters sits against the only door, and my room is without window. But yet, I do know—now, listen to me. Go to the house and pack up everything we can carry on Hortus and no more. It will be a dreadful load for him, with we three and some of our belongings. But the journey will not be so long, at least the first stage. We can walk sometimes. Take clothes. Oh, and the pillion-pad in the chest by the door. As much of the best-wrought tools as can be carried. Gold. Silver. Beat the vessels flat. Tie up the valuables in gowns or bedding or—"

"That is enough, Mr. Herrick," Goodman Peeters called.

"Hush, man," Mr. Dane said. "But let me have a word with his spouse."

Quickly I wrapped our babe in his rabbit skin, and cauled the whole in my mother's blanket. I pressed my cheek against Samuel's but he did not stir, being stupefied by the heat and smoke of the fire. In the gloom, I handed the bundle to my husband, who raised Samuel and laid him against his shoulder.

Then Jotham Herrick and I held each other, parted, and hoped for better.

"Godspeed, my dearest wife," he said. "Heaven guide your steps."

Mr. Dane came in afterward with a "How now?" that sent tears to my eyes. The old minister held my hands in his and briefly prayed for my safety and good care, and spoke to me about the evidence, and how it was, for him, naught that signified, but how it was, for others, a sheaf of deadly arrows.

"Old friends become bitter enemies on a sudden for toys and small offenses," he said, quoting Robert Burton, as he had done many times before.

"I never thought to be betrayed with lies."

"All may yet be well," he said. "I pray so."

He would fight for my good name, Mr. Dane promised, as he had fought long ago for one of his people. But he had forebodings of ill times to come, fearing this year's fierce winter as a judgment, though he was not so firm in his opinion as Mr. Barnard. He also dreaded that talk of specters and devils and the use of counter-magics and fortune-telling now bulked so high that we were all in some danger. Some spoke of me as having signed Satan's book, yet he more feared the devilish intent behind the charge, and the bad actions of mortal men and women.

"Tread with caution, Mistress Herrick, and I will do my best to save your name and your neck," he said. "For your name is, to my thinking, still fair, and your neck is far too young to be stretched by the rope."

I thanked him for his good opinion of me and said that I should always remember him, at which he gave my arm a little shake and said that he hoped to see me many times more and in my proper place. And after, he prayed with me by the hearthstone and gave me his blessing. Before he departed, he reminded me that the disciples were often in prison unjustly, and I was so bold as to say that sometimes they were let out again, as when "the Angel of the Lord came upon them, and a light shined in the house."

"Indeed, I wish the disciples might come and treat me as they did Saul, letting him over the city walls in a basket," I told him.

"They must have had mighty giant baskets in those days," Mr. Dane said, and this was the first time that he smiled while we were together in that room. "I, too, wish you might have such help and such a basket."

Again I thanked him and said that help and baskets come in many shapes, and that I was glad of all who believed that I was no witch and had no part in any demonic ministry.

"My young brother pastor has set the people on edge. I wish he knew that altar fires should not be lit with coals from hell! Yet I will speak to him and others of your merits and work for your freedom," he said.

"Would you pardon me and speak well of me, sir, if Providence gave me a path out of this trouble?"

He drew away and gazed at me. "A basket over the wall? If that should be, I would not regret your loss to us, indeed, Mistress Herrick. For I believe you are as innocent of crime as was Saul when he preached at Damascus. You came to us nearly solitary in the world, and such wanderers are vulnerable. As I told you before, once I had to defend a fellow from accusation who was alone in the land. He was a malcontent, but he was not guilty of erecting Satan's kingdom in Massachusetts. Nor are you the cause of a mark on a babe's face. Nor are you a signer in blood of the Archfiend's book."

"I thank you, sir."

"Mr. Increase Mather tells us that there is a dark and amazing intricacy in the ways of Providence," he said. "Who knows what may happen, or how God may have already revealed possible paths to your future?"

"Perhaps so," I said.

Here the minister made ready to depart in answer to a shout from Goodman Peeters.

"Good madam, I would wish you a fair evening and angels with a basket, but I fear they may have difficulty finding us in such a wilderness. And there is an officious, provoking fellow to bar the way."

At this, I managed a small smile. I followed him to the door, not wishing to see the last of someone who had been kind to me.

"Your obedient servant and unfeigned friend," he said, his outline barely visible in the gloom of the doorway. "God bye to you, Mistress Herrick."

"The like to you," I said, my voice trembling. "Pray remember me. Fare you well."

A bustle at the door, some words exchanged with my jailers ... and from then on I was anxious about three things. One was that Jotham Herrick might yet think better of his words to me and not be ready. Another was that Goodwife Bel Dane would hear where I was being kept and send word to Mr. Barnard that the house was not secure. And the last was that Hortus would not be in his stall, even in such poor weather for traveling, or that the gear and tackle he had earned with his own journeys through Essex and Middlesex would be missing. In recent months, Hortus had carried men to Billerica and Haverhill and Salem Village. Once he had been to Salem Town harbor and again, I suppose, glimpsed the sea and snuffed the salt airs. He was acquainted with the ferries over the Merrimack, and the cartways and roads and Indian trails. But perhaps we would need no ferry if what I had heard was true, that the rivers were frozen nigh solid already.

Because a mortal being can never have enough of worrying, despite how little it changes events, I took to wrestling over whether it was right for me to make use of the tunnel, or whether I should go meekly and with hope to questioning, jail, and trial. Constables would escort me; the jailor would shackle my legs and arms, burying me in the small, stinking dungeon below Salem prison, and there my little Samuel might die of the cold or the drying-up of my milk. Perhaps I would have to give him to some stranger to suckle. But that I could not bear. Or perhaps I would at last see Boston again, to be immured in stone walls, the water to my ankles when it rained, the dung freezing and unfreezing in a corner, and my bed a heap of rotted tow. How could we survive the frost-bound stones, the bad airs, the hunger?

No, it will not serve.

Was the tunnel my Angel of the Lord, my basket over the city walls, my dark and amazing rescue? I fell to wondering whether the curious providences of God had given me a way out of my troubles—and those, truly, would lead to more difficulties as we journeyed—or whether it was simply my own desires that guided me. I contemplated how I had been led through the wilderness with no fatal harm to my body, and pondered whether at the end of those challenges I was meant to have a brief passage of joy and content and then die. I remembered the story of a woman accused of witchcraft, who upon release found her house burned by Indians, and who sheltered in what remained until she was murdered by passing warriors. Just as when I journeyed and questioned whether the Almighty lay behind the attack on our house and the rotting mountain of flesh at Falmouth,

I now wondered whether the tunnel had been planned for me long ago—known, yes, but perhaps also ordained and made for my use?

"For Christ is my sovereign," I whispered. *And I am far from earthly kings and queens. Is not this new wild world of Massachusetts a realm where I may choose to be free—terribly and wonderfully free to obey God and live fully, in accordance with truth?*

All these wilderings of mind kept me wakeful. My fingers kept busy, rubbing the butt of the tallow candle into the stiff leather of my shoes. Afterward, I knelt on the hearthstone and prayed that Christ would have mercy on me.

"Always with me," I said aloud, startling myself in the quiet that was not quiet but full of the snap of fire, the settling of the house, and the noise of mice tunneling through the corn husks.

For a long time I listened, and at last heard the noise of sleepers. I inched down the hall and peeped into the main room. The two men who had accompanied me were lying curled by the fire. One was snoring with a hearty fervor, and the other was emitting little whiffling noises as if running to keep up with his companion. Goodman Peeters also appeared to be asleep, upright on his stool and breathing deeply. He was the least comfortable, propped in the cold away from the fire, and he was the one I feared most to wake.

The house was so small! I would have to be quieter than the little mice in their tunnels through the husks, and more clever.

Back in the bedchamber, I forced my shoes back onto my feet and collected the pattens Mr. Herrick had made for me against the snows of winter. They were finer than most such articles, with sharp spikes embedded in the whittled wood under toes and heel. I lit the tallow candle from the fire. Fat dropped hissing into the flames before the wick was well caught. I set it near the door on a flat baking stone from the hearth. That made me remember Phoebe Wardwell again; I wondered if she had brought the stone into that room to cook ashcakes and so let the room smell sweetly of bread. The tallow would not burn long but, left behind, perhaps its spit and glimmer would let any who wakened assume that I was up in the night with my stub of candle.

I impaled the beeswax candle Goodman Abbot had given me on the crown of spikes inside the lantern.

My fingers were damp as I searched along the floorboards until I found the groove. The trapdoor was harder to raise than I had imagined and made a grinding noise as I pulled it upward.

I stood, lifting the panel waist-high, my heart like a meetinghouse bell ringing with the alarm for fire or attack. Leaning against the wall, I listened hard, though the pulse of blood in my head made me hear nothing else for a time. At last I counted—one, two, three, the braided sound of three sets of sleepers—and set down the door. I fetched my pattens and dropped them through the opening, first leaning down as far as I could reach.

The wick fizzed and flared up when I lit the beeswax candle from the flame of the tallow. It burned with a lovely, clear flame that shed beams throughout the room. The pierced tin let the light out in shafts and patterns, but I had no time to sit and admire the patient candle-making of Phoebe Wardwell's mother. As it was, I blessed her name and kept moving.

And so I wrapped up in my cloak and shielded the flame as well as I could, knowing that the light would either betray or save me. I slipped into the hole, my feet kicking and feeling for the crude rungs. Though I held the candle lantern by its strap, I moved that arm carefully, fearing to set my cloak or gown on fire. The slats cut into my fingers, but I moved downward more swiftly than I thought possible and jumped to the earth.

I had forgotten the moistness and odd fragrance of the tunnel . . .

The candle I set on the ground. Removing my cloak, I climbed up the ladder and peered into the dark hall. Nothing. I had half expected the men to be chasing after me and plunging into the hole.

God bye to you, my wardens.

My fingers found the edge of the trapdoor, and I shifted the weight slowly, sliding it into place with one hand while I clung to the ladder with the other. The panel did not settle completely into its bed, and I felt sure some movement would be noticed when one of the men walked down the hall. Feeling it from corner to corner, I discovered a wooden knob and, pressing close to the rungs and wall of earth, tugged the door into place. Before climbing down, I held on for a moment longer, letting the thump of my heart slow to its ordinary time.

My right hand smarted from cuts, but that was no matter to me—I had entered the tunnel and, even if my absence was discovered instantly, had a fair chance to flee away. I put on my cloak and picked up the pattens. Retrieving the lantern, I held it up. The tunnel looked different from before in the clear light. Bands of varying color striped the earth, as if the soil had been laid down in layers like a stack cake. Bits of crystal and isinglass glimmered in several levels, and I could see the marks of a pick where the delver had left a ragged surface. Above my head were some odd, long-legged spiders, and though I knew that animals made burrows and nests under the ground, I had not thought to see such creatures here.

I smelled a faint scent of lavender.

"Fear not," I whispered.

If a ghost of Goody Wardwell or of her babe had left the scent, it did not show itself further. I would have thanked her shade for the candle, given unknowingly, a glow out of the dark of death. I trudged on, the lantern swinging and making crumbs of metal in the earthen walls flash out as if in greeting, as if the tunnel could know me on my third walk there.

I would not have believed that the underground passage could be beautiful, but it was so: the beauteous beeswax light swinging and shifting in patterns, the crystals and metals like a message of welcome inscribed in the soil itself, and the fragrance of the earth—surely a sign that it was alive, its pores sending out sweet and rank odors mixed. My eyes filled and blurred the light, and my very spirit streamed forth in gratitude and joy at the world of wonders. And while I knew what our ministers sometimes meant by that phrase, *world of wonders*, the strangenesses, the witcheries, the slashing work of magics, the ghosts, the marvels seen in clouds, and the fabulous creatures hidden in the forest, a new thought came to me: this is a world of wonders because good and true and beautiful, and only sin and wrong make it fall away from a natural glory. Were the animals not happy in Eden, where there was no hunting down of the innocent and no death? As I walked down the tunnel, looking about me at its walls for the last time, I forgot what I was about, forgot everything but loveliness.

I felt that the tunnel had been meant for me, as surely as if those glittering bits had formed the letters of my name and called to me with a mystical song. For though I no longer believed that God played with human dolls, yet I trusted that all things spired up from divine power, and that our ways and names and the very shape of us, from ankle bone to the wing of an eyebrow, were known to the divine energies that lived and rejoiced before the worlds were made.

But when the path rose and met the door, I must lose all that surprising elevation of spirit. For I had a hard work before me. The ice and snow was weighty, and the stems and vines that had earlier been a mass over the opening now latched it down, so I must thrust and thrust again, and slide my injured hand along the edge to tear at tendrils and dormant roots. Even when it seemed free, I could not raise the door.

Panic rose in me. I sat on the ramp of earth and closed my eyes and rocked to and fro in anguish.

Calm, calm, be at peace.

I thought on how greatly I desired to be safe with Jotham Herrick and my babe Samuel. And with three mighty shoves I broke open the door and crawled out, ripping away the tangles.

I nested among the moss and dried leaves and snow, panting and sending out little splinters of prayer. Flopping onto my back, I lay with my arms flung out and the cloak unfurled like wings on either side.

The starlight spilled on me, setting my lantern at naught. A thousand thousand bees had been set alight and were floating in the deep blue-black tunnel of night. Whiter than a candle of sun-bleached beeswax, the moon gleamed at me, and the most delicate silk scarf of cloud moved infinitely slowly across the sky. I remembered my family, and how my mother's father had believed that Providence working through the stars and moon brought change and the twists of fortune to all that was sublunary. The constellations shone down like beacons. How easy it seemed to believe that the planets and stars busied themselves with us, just as the plants gave themselves to us and to animals for food.

Again I felt greeted. I had never seen anything so clearly and vividly as when I feared that I might die and leave behind the realm of bees and bee-stars, clouds and silks, moon and hive. It almost seemed that I could drift up and into the sky, burning with a white light, and walk among stars and farther, until I reached the empyrean realms.

"World of wonders."

To whom did I say those words, lying in the weeds by the tunnel? Perhaps I spoke them to the bees of the stars and the daily swelling or daily dwindling white hive of the moon and the veil of drifting cloud. Perhaps I murmured them in sheerest gratitude to the maker of them all. Perhaps to each of those. Perhaps I did not know the difference between one thing and another, for all flowed together as one.

Settling into myself, I rolled onto my hands and knees and pushed up. I shook the ice crystals and flakes of snow from my cloak. After collecting the lantern and pattens, I forced the door to the tunnel shut, stomping hard until it was wedged in place and sweeping snow over the spot with my feet.

Would it ever be used again? Would the walls simply collapse over time, never needed, disappearing into the earth?

When I checked my hand by the candlelight, I found the palm and fingers stained with blood, but the flow had already stopped. I debated whether to douse the candle. With a flame, I hazarded being seen, yet if I had no candle, I risked losing the route to town and wandering in the great whiteness, leaving erring prints of pattens until I collapsed and was frozen.

Keep the lantern lit.

With good light, my way to town was clear enough—no other path disturbed the snow—and I set off, rounding the house and moving slantwise toward my destination. The moon not being full, the ground was often shadowy and dark despite the dazzling starlight. I concluded to keep to the main cartway, and to slip and dodge about as needed once I passed the smooth expanse of Blanchard's Pond and Pond Meadow. If I met a watchman, I would douse the candle. I would have to chance being challenged, shot at, or simply feared as a will-o'-the-wisp. But it was unlikely a watchman would go so far as to discharge his musket, for that would leave him with no means of firing again until he reloaded.

Thoughts and decisions flitted through my mind, and all the while I was washed by waves of sorrow because I had been scorned, unjustly accused, and must flee.

"Bel," I said, right out loud, though I had meant to be more quiet than the mice creeping in the mattress. My anger against her flashed like burning powder and died away. To hate her felt too simple.

"Mehitabel Dane, you are a mystery," I whispered to the stars and the hummocks of grass under the snow. "And perhaps more of a Holt than a Dane."

Would I ever understand why she had turned against me? I could think and think for years and maybe never understand. But I wished to know. Because I wanted to know everything about what it meant to be a woman—to be a human being wandering the face of the earth. And perhaps it was not a waste of time and spirit to try and fathom another and look as God looks, to see the alloy of dross and gold. What a fool's paradise our friendship had proven to be!

I stumbled on ice and thrust away the thought of Bel Dane and told myself that truth and sorrow were better companions than happy lies. My footing was unsure in the dark, even with the candle, with now and then a wrench to an ankle. So many dense or flittering shadows on snow, so many dips and rocks in the road! Never before was I glad to be well acquainted with the dark, unlike most of my kind, who are fearful of the least noise once the sun drops over the world's brink. For I was forced to know that night is not as terrible as men and women fear, and that Satan is not its denizen—or at least makes no more of an appearance than by day. Less of one, I suppose, for his followers must sleep. Ill acts can occur in secrecy of gloom or by frank daylight.

But Bel Dane kept drifting back to me.

"Surely she knew I was no witch," I murmured. Had Lizzie and Goody Holt worked on her with accusations, piecing together a great lie?

The houses on the way were unlit. I stayed on edge, in readiness to blow out my candle if I saw the watchman. I counted the landmarks by name or feature where I recognized them: the Lovejoy house beyond Blanchard's pond; the burying ground on the left, across from Powell's Folly and Little Hope Meadow, where I was startled by three cows in a huddle, backs turned to the breeze.

"Poor beasts, out in such weather," I said aloud, for I too was a poor creature who should be warm and under a roof. The cold made me stiffen and clamp my arms close to my sides for warmth.

It was luck that I knew the lane-ways and the houses well, for often Mr. Herrick and I had delivered repaired pewter or silver, collecting payment at the same time. Yet in the darkness, I entirely missed seeing the Phelps house, and was soon surprised to find myself passing Bixby and Chandler houses and the iron mill, where I crossed the Shawsheen by bridge and found myself among Osgood and Peeters and Wright houses hard by the New Meadow.

And there I hoped to discover Hortus. I knew that he had returned from Salem but lately. Whether he had flown to some nearby town, I did not know but trusted that the inclement weather would be my friend.

Near the stable, I held still, searching the house hard by for any sign of a candle. Seeing no light, I slipped inside and set the lantern on a low bench.

The building was no more than a plain, meager barn with hay loft and swallow holes under the gable ends. The first crude stall was empty. The other held an unfamiliar chestnut with a white star gleaming in the gloom, the mount of some unknown traveler. Beyond, in the open area, a cow and sheep nested on straw, and near them my Hortus stood in the shadows, his head and neck drooping. He was asleep. Only once before had I been so powerfully glad to see him.

"Hush, hush," I said, sidling past as the chestnut shuffled her feet. Someone had tethered her to a post.

At the sound of my voice, Hortus woke, came forward, and greeted me with whiffling breath as he searched to see if I had a winter apple for him.

"Nothing," I told him. "Nothing. Just me."

When he nuzzled my shoulder, I locked my arms around his neck. I murmured to him that he must be quiet, quiet, quiet. He cocked an ear at me as if he knew my meaning.

"You have saved me and saved me. And now it must be one more time," I said, and combed my fingers through his mane. "It will be heavy work and long, but in the end you will have a welcome of feed and rest."

He blew his breath at my ear, sending my loosened coif and wide-brimmed hat askew with his muzzle.

"The stars have come out for us, Hortus, and the moon is a shining nut-meat in a bur of mist. We must go."

He nickered softly, and not for the first time I wondered if he could understand my words. And why not? I knew his horse speech well enough.

"You are the best horse in the world. I love you above land and gold and a great many people."

The chickens stirred on their nests, querulously letting out a few chirps. I held silent and still for several minutes, my hands resting on Hortus, afraid that an outburst of panicked peeps and trills might wake the sleepers in the house.

He followed me as I took up the lantern and searched for the heavy saddle and bridle that had eaten much of his earnings as a journey-horse. For he could not be rented out without those; nor would anyone accept the Indian bridle from me. He had an old English wood-and-leather saddle covered in wine-colored velvet, with a modicum of silver braid and brass nails. In truth, I had earned little more from Hortus than gear, stable, and feed. A horse is a costly love, but I could not let him go, not after the trials we had endured together. He was all that remained alive of our company near Falmouth, and though he was but a horse, I cared for him and thought him dear and, as it is said of men and women, "of more value than many sparrows."

"Peace, peace, Hortus," I said to him, putting my hand on his crest and gripping threads of his mane as I had often done when we traveled together and I was afraid. And though he tossed his head once and whickered at my ear, he remembered and was otherwise as quiet as a horse can be.

"We shall go walking under the splendiferous swarm of the star-bees, my Hortus, and we shall have another adventure," I whispered.

After a struggle with the saddle, I led him out of the stable, not forgetting the lantern and closing the door softly behind me. The hooves occasionally striking a stone through the snow, a faint jingling from the stirrups: these were the only sounds. And though I meant to ride him, hoisting up my petticoats and galloping toward the house, my second thought was safer. Walking hurriedly, I steered him right down the street, past Abbot and Ashbee houses, and in sight of Francis Dane's house crossways from the burying ground and the great meetinghouse itself. I intended to lead Hortus past the Barnard and Carleton and Faulkner houses.

But soon I paused and blew out my candle, for I heard voices and glimpsed the gleam from another lantern.

"Hist! Hush," I said, stroking Hortus' nose and straining to hear.

But I could not make out the words.

I tied the reins to a tree, though in truth I did not wish to leave my horse, and ducked into some still-standing corn across the road from the houses. It was hard going among the mounds and ruts of the field, and I was glad to cling to dry stalks when I needed to catch myself from falling.

When I reached a point just opposite the minister's house, I could see clearly that someone had come to fetch Mr. Barnard.

He was standing before the door, dressed in a long shirt and cloak and not fit for company. "What is that sound?" The minister looked straight toward my hiding place.

"Nothing, nothing. I have seen nothing to alarm on my way here," the other man said. "The deer are coming in to glean the remains of the corn. They snuffle and snort through the stalks."

"Perhaps that is all," Mr. Barnard said. "I do not like it." He wrapped the cloak more tightly about him.

"This thing may be an indifferent matter, and if you will come quickly, you may be back in bed shortly," the man said. "Goody Holt says she has a piece of news for you that cannot wait until morning, and she will only tell it to your ear. Evidently it is tidings to do with her daughter Goody Mehitabel Dane and the witch—"

Here I could no longer make out the words, or at least not until the minister, accustomed to speaking to his flock loudly, boomed out a reply.

"Nothing has been proven," he said. "The woman has only been accused, and there is no solidity about that, though certainly Satan has been at his slippery work in our midst. He is busy with his bird-lime, ever and always. Yet I suppose that we must attend her. Goodwife Holt is not to be trifled with, I fear. She can be turbulent. But no need for unpleasant haste. Come inside, and I will put a stick of wood on the fire for you, and ready myself for—"

As he turned away, again the words were lost.

Once the door was shut, I snaked through the stalks back to Hortus, who was nosing dried oak leaves, and starting away when the wind ruttled them.

"Hush again, hush." I stroked his forehead and muzzle and kissed him and afterward guided him away.

The best route to take was not so clear as before, but I determined to walk up the street that led toward the Cochichewick bridge and the road to Haverhill, and then to follow a smaller path that would take me close to our own cartway between the Shawshin Meadows and New Meadow, where Poor's Bridge crosses the Shawshin River. And so we moved down the road, Hortus' hooves clattering a bit at a muddy slough where brush and boards had been thrown across but, I hoped, not bothering a soul sleeping in houses. When we came to the path, I found a stump and vaulted into the saddle, my petticoats flying above my knees, and we moved quickly until I dismounted at the Austins' garden plot and led Hortus the rest of the way.

But I did not leave him near our house, instead tying him to a tree by neither road nor path, after petting his nose and telling him what a splendid good boy he had been and that we were not done yet. I left my cloak over him for warmth, fastening it to the pommel. The cold bit at me, and I shuddered convulsively as I crossed the uneven, stubbled ground, the remains of our small summer farm.

The house was dark. I could see a skein of smoke rising from the chimbley and obscuring the stars just above. Although it was but my fancy, I thought of the star-bees made drowsy by the warmth and by the fine, rising particles from the wood, for the stars looked cloudy and dim in the smoke.

I glanced about me for any neighboring hint of light before I slipped to the door and went in. Stopping to listen for anything untoward, I stood shivering in the midst of the shop. What silver remained after the last delivery was now gone; a few pieces of tin stood in their places. When I passed through the curtain to the back, I saw that all the better tools were also absent, though some cruder iron tools had been scattered around the chamber. It was a shame we could not take them with us, along with the big crucibles out back, but how could we?

"Jotham," I called, and when there was no reply, I hastened to our bedchamber.

Garbed finely for our flight in treen-colored breeches, stamell-red waistcoat, leather doublet, and scarlet cap, there he was—asleep by the fire with one arm resting against the cradle and his hose ungartered. Our little Samuel lay slumbering in the cradle, biggen half over his face. I leaned down and meant to adjust it, but drew back my hand. I did not want to wake him. Instead, I lit Phoebe Wardwell's precious candle with a straw and adjusted it in the lantern. The clear white glimmered again, and the room shone forth.

Kneeling on the floor, I shook my husband gently. "Jotham. Jotham Herrick."

He came awake with a great start, stared, and clutched me to him. "Thank God! I was dreaming that we were in a great judgment hall with waterfalls and trees and justices in astonishing rainbow violets and greens, and that your hair grew and grew until it waved like a red sea and choked the room—"

"Some would kill me for my hair alone, I fear," I said.

"Or less. This Mehitabel Dane. She would have you hanged for a mere toy?"

"I have thought and thought and concluded that friend Bel may have fancied the doll to be like an evil type, a shadow of the diabolical, a prophetical foretelling of her daughter to come. A dangerous poppet. As the cloth was blighted by a drop of blood, so her child's skin was stained. But since types are not parallels we invent merely from our own fancies but must be rooted in the Bible, I cannot see why Mr. Barnard did not declare her to be mistaken."

"No, a plaything is not an object dropped by wonder-working Providence, surely. It was but a chance resemblance, no more." He loosed his hold on me. "I would that Goody Dane had never seen it."

"That ill idea is what she dreams," I said, and rose to my feet. "She cannot see that the babe is lovely. She sees only the blot. And might have blamed me in some other way if she had not glimpsed the doll."

"She has played at being wicked. She should look to herself and not others," Jotham Herrick said. He yawned mightily and rubbed the sleep from his eyes, and for a moment seemed only a boy.

I will, will see our Samuel become a man. That I will. The words whisked through my head like flame through dry fodder. I touched Jotham's golden hair, and he grasped my hand and kissed the palm.

"I rue that friendship if she has gone over to Goody Holt's manner of seeing the world, and her mother's rumgumptious manner in asserting what she sees. I am only grateful that she did not spoil my chance to escape. Belike she assumed I was to be hied away to Salem or Salem Village until she heard other news. She may have scuttled to her mother and told the secret. Like a great white mouser trembling at a hole, Goody Holt must have been lying in wait for the watchman. By then, I must have been standing free under the stars."

"You must tell me more. And how—how did you manage?"

"Not with the wildness of magic and witchcraft, I assure you. I will tell you on the way. Mr. Barnard has set off to see Goody Holt, and he will soon comprehend my ability to master the art of vanishment. Next he will hurry to the Wardwell house to make certain that I am safely locked away. After, he may ring the alarm bells, though I do not suppose he would ring them until first light. But all that will take him a deal of time in the dark. And we shall be fled."

"How do you know these things?"

"Never mind now—trust that they are the truth."

And be glad, I thought, *that the minister is a slow husbandman who has not cut down his corn.*

"Where will we fly?" Jotham stood up, staggering a little from sleepiness. He combed his hair back from his brow with one hand.

"We must journey to Haverhill—where else is there? I do not think that Major Saltonstall will thrust me back to judgment, though he will not be pleased that such an accusation has been made, and perhaps not at all satisfied that I have darted away rather that standing for trial. Sheltering us will be a considerable risk for him, and that much I regret for his sake. For I shall be a case of 'flying upon a felony,' with a hue and cry from the constable, Goodman Foster."

"That is in my thoughts—my fears—as well," he said.

"I am thankful that the newcomers bond paid for me was returned to Major Saltonstall after our wedding. Many times he and Elizabeth Saltonstall have asked me to let them help, and now I shall have to allow them, if they will. And I hope, trust, and believe they will, as they have only love for me and will be certain that I am no witch."

Jotham Herrick looked more wakeful now. He perched on the bed and began to garter his stockings. "A good plan, if it works. How do you mean us to get there?" He paused and looked up at me.

"Hortus is not far—I tethered him to a pine tree." I glanced around the room. "Where are our clothes and goods?"

"In the lean-to. I bagged and lashed all I could in bed curtains and coverlets, and scattered a few tools and some worn-out garments here and there in the house, so that the people could not tell if I had left home, if they burst in."

"That was clever. And I saw tin on the shelves."

He leaned forward, tugging on one boot and then the other.

"If I had days," he said, "I would dismantle and pack the glass for the display window—that much I added to the house. It was shipped from England not long after I arrived here."

"I am sorry we must leave so many well-made devices. And in such a rush."

"I lament nothing except not being able to pack crucibles and anvils and some of the weightier tools." He gave a little jerk of the head and stood up, bending to pull at his boots once more and stamping as if to work them into place.

So much he was losing! Not just the means to his trade.

"Perhaps I should—"

"No. Whatever you were about to say, do not say." He went to me, coming close to the cradle where our son slept, and framed my face with his two hands. I reached up to cover them with mine. "There will be new furnaces and tools. But there would never be another Charis. Not in a thousand thousands of years. And I suspect the fears of our people may darken their sight. Hunting for Satan, they may find him moving in the wilderness of their own hearts and so, unwitting, commit evil against you. As happened with Goody Mehitabel Dane. If one who liked you well could swerve and turn against you, think how simple it would be for some who do not know your nature."

"Jotham," I whispered. "If I have learned anything, it is that darkness and light dance and struggle together in the chambers of every heart. Shadows must be tamed."

He gazed into my eyes, and I into his.

"Samuel needs you," he said. "I need you."

Samuel's face looked closed and far away in sleep. A faint sheen touched his eyelids, above the crescent curve of fine lashes. The round cheeks, the small snub nose, the silks of hair: some cloudy resemblance made me detect a glimmer of my brother Isaac.

"And I you. And him."

"They made a shambles of our house, hunting for signs of guilt. They will not make a shambles of our family. All will be restored," he said, breaking away from me to move about the room as if looking for something forgotten in his packing. "New tools, new crucibles. I do regret the loss of the doll with your mother and sister's hair."

"Yes," I said.

"You," he added, "you are a sort of Madam Job, who has been tested overmuch by evil and loss but whose life to come will be abundant. I feel this. As strongly as prophecy."

"You leave so much," I said hurriedly, still caught by the grief of harming him. "Your good offices with the town and militia. And you are woven into the fabric here, as I had hoped to be someday. I am afraid you will repent of quitting Andover."

"Never. We will find another place," he said. "My townspeople did not know, but they cast me out when they seized you, Charis. They will have a smith in metals no longer, nor my help in other ways. I am not discontent or unwilling to go."

Jotham Herrick bent to raise the lid and pulled a cloak from a chest. Last he retrieved his precious lambskin gloves and, to my surprise, handed me a pair of rabbit-skin gloves he had traded for tinware earlier in the day.

He interrupted my thanks. "Now that I am wakeful again, I yearn to be gone. But you have no cloak, and this weather is bleak and frosty."

"With Hortus. The cloak is with him. And I do thank you, I just—"

I stopped, unsure of what I meant to say. The longer we stayed, the harder I listened for noises from outside.

"We have a little time, surely, Charis." He put his hands on my shoulders and I seemed to wake. Staring up at him, the thought that all our life here was passing away came to me with force.

"But we must act now or be lost," he said.

"Yes, that restlessness is in my mind also. There will soon be a warrant for my arrest. By now I may be settled in Mr. Barnard's opinion as a wildcat-riding witch and nefarious she-rogue. If you agree, I will seek for Hortus and lead him to the shed," I said. "And you may carry Samuel there and meet me."

"I suppose that is as feasible a way as any. Or should we carry the sacks together to Hortus instead?"

"I am afraid of being too slow," I said. "What if the bells ring?"

"Do not fear that they will wake the town for this, or at least not when night holds. When the first of dawn comes, who can say what Mr. Barnard might do?" Jotham Herrick shook his head slightly. "And what of Samuel's clouts and linen still drying by the fire?"

"Leave them," I said. "When the constable returns from Boston, he will want to seize my goods. Let him snatch up the soaked clouts!"

He nodded. "An admirable thought."

"I will not be happy until we are away, although I dread the thought of Samuel growing too cold on the journey. But the distance is not so very far to Haverhill."

"Far enough," he said. "The river—if there is little or no open water, we need no contact with ferries at any of the usual crossings."

The month seemed much too early for the rivers to be frozen, but the ponds in the town limits—even the Great Pond—had been frozen over for some time. Whether the river passage would be safe for us was a mystery.

"Strange to say, but this famously brutal winter coming on that the ministers declare is a judgment upon us ... it may be the instrument of Providence to save me from false judgment. The land and water may redeem me from death. If the river is hard frozen like the ponds.

If only it is. Life is so very wayward and wandering in its shape some-times," I said. "Who can predict what will come to us?"

"I am wary of a river crossing," Jotham Herrick said. "But I see no other route. A ferry would make our movements known. Though perhaps the ferries are ice-locked now."

We parted, and I clambered over the snow in my pattens, my steps making craunching and squeaking noises because it was so cruelly cold, and I found Hortus and lifted up the lantern to lead him to the lean-to. And I was glad to put on my cloak and find it warm and horse-fragrant from Hortus' body.

At the shed, Mr. Herrick tied on our burdens with ropes while I held Samuel under the cloak and Hortus blew billowing clouds into the air. My husband had been clever and tidy, as was always his wont, and even managed to bundle my little coffer into a safe, neat piece of wrapped baggage. Snow began to fall—a sparse snow of widely sepa-rated stars. In truth, it was so frigid that the air was numb and almost beyond all snowing.

My stout Hortus braved the weight, though it was more than I liked. He nosed at the unfamiliar lantern and, feeling its heat, swerved his head sharply away. No doubt I pleased him by soon blowing out the light. Jotham fastened the last of the parcels and helped me onto the horse, handing up Samuel and mounting behind us. Starting out, I would not be the one to ride on the pillion-pad, since Hortus knew me best. We were uncomfortable and slovenly looking riders with our knobby, bunchy load and our cloaks and coverlets flowing over all. In settling into place, I was surprised to see that my husband had lashed our big colander onto a bundle. It was a handy and unusual piece with a deep belly, a thick band around the top, sturdy handles, and three little feet. The colander seemed a creature from a Goody Waters tale to me, a big-bellied German dwarf with snub feet and hands on high hips. But it was just the sort of object that I had been sure we would have to abandon.

"Why the colander, husband?"

"A useful and well-made piece of work that I did not want to leave behind," Jotham Herrick said. "Besides, wife, I have an idea of how to wield it for our good help on the journey. Wait and see."

"What an amusing and ingenious man you have for a father, young Samuel," I said, but the babe slept on, his face puck-ered against the rawness of the air. At least the winds had stilled themselves, so that the star-blessed, frozen landscape looked to be cut from crisp pasteboard.

We moved off slowly, the light from stars and moon casting us down onto the snow as a monstrous shadow. Not wishing to cross the river near the two ferry sites at either end of the Shawsheen Fields, we followed the cartway in the direction of the meetinghouse but turned hard by a Swan house as if toward the ferry. We swung again to cross Cochichewick Brook (water as hard as stone, with its music locked away) and chose the road to Haverhill. I was easier in my mind when we passed Great Pond that some call The Patten because of its shape and two Barker houses (and there I thought of Goodman Abbot and Goodman Barker, snoring by the fire in the nigh-empty Wardwell house, and wished them well for the morrow) and after that the site where an Ayer house stood on the far bank of the Merrimack, though we could see nothing of its bulk in the dark.

For some time we kept close to the river, searching for a certain location where it narrowed and yet was straight and fairly smooth in summer, with ripples around many low tables of rock. For we knew that the river would freeze first and hardest around stone. There we thought our footing might be best and safest, although in truth I longed to cross where the river shrank most and was not so daunting a width. But in those places where the water tumbled choppily in summer, the ice was rough and gleamed like a boneyard heaped with skeletons under the starlight and moon.

"It looks as though the first ice was broken like sugared candy cracked with a mallet," Jotham Herrick said. "And thrust into hillocks of slabs and shards."

"I was seeing bones."

"Not bones," he said. "Candied sugars and sweetness."

So easy to smash, I thought, but said nothing.

Samuel woke and made a series of small, trembling cries. Perhaps he was shocked at the cold in his nose like two tiny nails, or the odd sensation of frigid cold in his throat or on his young, moist eyelids. I pulled him closer under the shelter of my cloak and gave him milk to warm his body. When he was done and I held him so that he could see the world around, he looked about with eyes so intent that I smiled for pleasure in seeing him gaze on the stars and moon with a frosty ring around its misshapen head.

"All will be well," Jotham Herrick said.

"Yes," I said, though in truth I was fainthearted and unsure, and so took care to remember other days and nights in the wilderness, and how we are never really alone, and also how my mother used to say that the ones who do what they fear to do are they who win the most courage. That familiar reflection made me feel bolder, and I gazed around me at the river gleaming between trees and the dazzlement of the stars and was content with the ice scene and Jotham's arm about my waist.

"The flight into Egypt," he said.

"Yes."

I pictured Mary and Joseph and the child Jesus journeying toward Egypt, not under the self-same stars, yet by starlight and moonlight, and not beside forest and river but by sand and sea.

Remember us in the wilderness, Child who fled and returned.

But I might never return to this landscape: this should be my last glimpse of the spot, for I meant to flee and not return.

"Look! This may be the crossing," Jotham Herrick said.

Hortus stopped when I called to him, bobbing his head to the ground to snuff and blow great clouds at the snow. He began nibbling at the tips of some scrub willows.

"Someone has been here," I said.

Large footprints in the snow led onto the river and wandered back again.

"But changed his mind," Jotham Herrick said.

"Could he have been fishing?"

"Surely no one would chop a hole and fish that way on a river, not with so many ponds close by. Not with the risk of tumbling in."

We looked at each other uneasily. "I trust he is far away," I said.

"Snug in bed, I hope."

Dismounting, Jotham reached up his arms for Samuel before I slid from the saddle. Handing the babe back to me, he rummaged in the parcels and found a sack I had stitched together from scraps of camlet.

"What have you done?" I was perplexed by the pale shapes inside—a dozen or more.

Jotham Herrick smiled as he knelt down, spilling a dozen big shells from the bag.

"Clams? From the coast?"

"Not to eat," he said, and showed me how the two halves of each shell were fastened together with tree sap.

He set the colander on the ground, dropping a ball of threads, lint, and wood shavings into the bowl. Next he stamped the snow flat and laid flat pieces of wood on the smooth surface, and made a conical hut of splinters on top.

"You brought kindling?"

"Aged and split," he said, and unfastened a bundle of oak from Hortus' cumbersome load. "The driest wood."

"Whatever is he about, Samuel?" I held the babe close against me, occasionally letting him peep out from my cloak.

Squatting on his heels, my clever husband pulled off his gloves and unclamped the shells to show coals sleeping inside—coals that with a little breath and tinder broke into life again. Quickly he ran a fingernail through the pitch on shell after shell, accumulating a heap of coals in the colander, and now and then blowing gently or dropping lint and twigs on top.

"Your father is a master and a king of fire," I told Samuel, who looked steadily at me as if he knew my words. "As you may be, someday."

Jotham Herrick rubbed snow on his fingertips where he had touched the hot shells. "I had plenty of hours in which to pack and contrive what we needed," he said. "Otherwise, I would have wasted them in misgivings."

Samuel and I watched as Jotham combed through the bundles, Hortus shifting his feet and backing away.

"Hortus, Hortus, be still," I called.

"Ah, my cordage for the river! Here it is. I was afraid that I had left the other coils in the shed. We will need strong ropes before we are done. But not yet."

"You brought ropes and wood and tinder .. and the colander," I said, still not sure what he intended.

"And a store of char-cloth," he said, showing me what he had unpacked.

Samuel stared at the flames and gave a cry when I drew a linen cloth over his face, wrapping it around his head until only the eyes showed.

Jotham squatted again, feeding the coals with bits of char-cloth and sticks, nursing a fire in case the ice was not strong enough to bear our weight—a drenching without means of warmth afterward might mean death. Though this might be the winter most famous in the annals of the colony, still the month was only November, and it was hard to trust that the ice would hold.

My husband's ingenuity with flame, even in the snow, was nigh magical. He divided the fire between the colander and the small base of wood with its hut of splinters, and fed the twin blazes with tow, tinder, and wood from his bundle.

"How canny you are! So now we will have heat on both shores so that if someone becomes wet—"

"'Tis only in case of accident," he said. "We could not carry much wood. It will be tricky work to keep a bonfire burning, if we must. So we will not plan on diving into frozen rivers. And we will be quick."

"No, we will not bathe in the Merrimack! But you are cunning all the same."

"We act against the law, at least in the village. We may not carry an open fire. But we are free of town," he said. "And Hortus will have less to bear without the wood."

Jotham Herrick had prepared braided ropes from rags and strips of my old green dress so that we could drag our bundles, and now he fashioned a makeshift sled from hastily cut branches. Taking Samuel from me, he lashed the bundle of him on top with twisted, thick-spun yarns. The babe lay by the fire, babbling with his eyes on the flames.

"We will tow Samuel," he said, "so that there will be less burden on the ice in any one place. No risk of us toppling with him. And if one of us falls through, the other may attempt a rescue."

I stared at the contrivance, once again marveling at my husband's handiwork, yet apprehensive now that we were close to crossing—or perhaps to plunging through ice and being dragged under by currents, who knows how far? Perhaps to float eastward, mother and child and father and horse, and to the bottom of the sea with its cold salt stars and mermaids, where we would surprise the monster Leviathan and make him wonder why we had no gills or tails. Perhaps to settle in some gorge chinked with the bones of sailors and travelers cauled in sailcloth and buried in water, their bodies waiting for resurrection and restoration to land.

"I shall go," he said. "You can cross with Samuel once I am sure that all is safe."

"Prithee, let me pass over first. For if the ice is too frail and you are drowned, I will be a fugitive on the wrong side of the river with no help. But if I am sunk and lost, you may go home again before dawn with our Samuel, and no one will blame you."

He saw reason in what I said, though he did not like it. I knelt and, pulling away the linen cloth, rubbed the babe's face against my own, warming the nubbin of nose and the cold lips.

"We must hurry," Jotham Herrick said, and held out the colander. Samuel will have chilblains if we do not, even with the fire so near."

So it was that I ventured onto the ice under starlight, stopping once to look back at Samuel on his sled and at Jotham Herrick and Hortus, and all my longing was for them to be snug with me on the other shore. Before me I carried the colander of coals, linen strips wrapped around the handles to protect my gloves. When I imagine that hour, I see a figure holding a pot of flame creep from rock to rock; the dome of the sky is a dark, upside-down colander pricked with white fire, and the trees are black scratches along the shore.

But up close, the footing was treacherous, and I feared to slide or stumble and spill the bowl. My thoughts often turned to the current below, eating at the ice. If it gnawed too quickly, the new-made ice would not keep up, and the solid plain would be too thin. Earlier, winds had blown much of the river's snow away, and the light made the ice luminous where it was not dusted or heaped with flakes.

The ice cracked and boomed under my pattens; I dived onto hands and knees and lay at full length, my cloak spreading over the surface. The colander skidded away, striking a chunk of ice and spitting out sparks. The jolt kicked a red-hot fragment onto the surface.

"Have mercy!" I cried to the stars and God in heaven.

Selvages of fractured ice grated together, and air punched through to water. Now I could hear the Merrimack singing of drowning and death and indomitable flow.

My husband shouted, but I could not make out the words.

The ledge of rock beside me radiated cold. How long since I had slept? A wave of weariness washed over me.

Samuel. Jotham. Hortus. Must scrabble and strive.

Already the ice had seized hold of my cloak as if it meant to freeze the cloth and me to itself. I swam with my arms, pushed forward with my toes, gathered myself and thrust again, again, and slid on the ice. Getting onto my hands and knees, I crawled forward to the pot of fire and slowly stood, swaying a little. *Must needs be unconquerable. God help me.* I bent to pick up the colander. The lost coal seethed against the ice, sending up a small plume of smoke.

Behind me, Jotham Herrick whooped his encouragement.

Once, years back, my brothers and I saw a river otter, a sort of weasel-creature, tumbling on a frozen river. How easily she moved across the surface, alternately gliding and wriggling and rising hump-backed in readiness for another slide. The current of her very being was playful and fluent, moving like a stream. She was a joyful Merrimack of the animal kingdom that flowed where others loped along the ground or darted in air.

But I . . . I did not belong on the ice that was sometimes white and sometimes clear or shadowed to blue and green. Nor did I belong in the quiet, cold chambers underneath, where the starlight was muted into near blackness and the chilly fishes hung, gently fanning their tails and fins. I did not wish for the Merrimack to be my Jordan.

And though my people have a hatred for nightwalking and fear what lurks in wait in shadows, I had come to know shade and pitch. Deep darkness was not darkness alone but speckled with light. A glory shone around moon and stars and glowed from clouds. Hortus' breath, mine, Samuel's, and Jotham's were likewise spark-catchers, made from tiny drops of crystalized breath, fanned into the night.

Still, I feared the river's flow and dropped to my knees or flung myself prone three times as I traversed from rock to rock, though by the time the slick, snowy bank loomed ahead of me, I was more afraid for the others than for myself. I was cold and damp, but again I had survived a crossing. Evidently I was a surviving kind of person, tenacious of life, and I thanked God for whatever core of vigor burned in me, and that I was made so, and that I had possessed wondrous gifts of hardiness and help to remain alive.

The colander of the heavens was a pale glory of scattered light as I knelt down and reached for the bank, hauling myself upward by roots and stalks, digging the spikes of my pattens into the crust of snow. My colander of flame still snapped and burned, and I set to making it into a larger fire. Jotham Herrick stepped onto the ice, dragging our child by one rope and the train of our packs by another.

10

The Far-Faring

Haverhill and after, mid-November 1691

Once a thing is mastered, it may seem ordinary. But I found Jotham Herrick's crossing of the Merrimack more agonizing than my own. He had a longer, freer stride than mine and often jumped to a promontory rock before reeling in the sled and bags. I squatted by the fire-headed imp of a colander, feeding the flames with twigs and wind-dried weeds that rattled with seed when I tore them from the ground, making ready to build a bonfire on the shore. But in truth I could hardly bear to do anything but watch.

To my mixed anguish and delight, I could hear Samuel crowing as he slid along the ice and bumped over obstacles.

Once the cable to the bags was caught, and a sack broke open, shedding its contents across the ice.

"Leave them," I shouted.

But Jotham would go back and collect what was spilled and drag the sacks more slowly, so that I danced up and down by the fire until he was perched on a stone and surveying the distance that remained between us. He leaped to another rock and slid, flailing his arms and only slowly straightening.

The ice behind him cracked and retorted as Hortus, who I thought would stay for us until I called him by name, stepped gingerly onto the frozen river.

"Hurry! He may shatter the ice ... "

Jotham Herrick jumped, his arms flying out like wings as his soles met stone; once balanced, he looked back over his shoulder. Climbing down from his landing perch, he pulled Samuel and the bags nearer. Turning, he began to cross the ice between the last ledges and the shore.

A great boom shivered the ice. The surface waved, undulating up and down.

"Haste," I shouted.

Jotham moved faster, at last running and sliding ahead of the parade of sled and parcels, until he grasped my outstretched hand and vaulted onto the slippery bank, grabbing at a tree trunk and hanging on till he found his footing.

The cloth braids wound around his wrist had dug into the skin, which looked raw and chafed.

"Let me," he said, but I took hold of a rope and drew Samuel to the edge of the river.

Jotham slid down the bank, dragging Samuel close. He hoisted the crude sled, passing it to me, holding on until I seized the branches and began to haul it upward. Despite the keen air, our child was smiling up at the stars and moon and babbling to them in his own private language.

Catching sight of me, he whooped as if to tell me that he had seen something marvelous, which perhaps he had. I freed him from the branches and yarn and held the bundle of furs and cloth against me, once more warming Samuel's nose and cheeks by gently rubbing my face against his.

"Your little moon face, so cold and white," I said, near to crying now that we were safe, all but Hortus.

Hand over hand, Jotham Herrick was towing in the rest of our sacks.

Hortus clambered over the ice, his feet sliding and the surface ponderously rolling as though it might slip away entirely and leave only current.

Jotham scrambled up to me, carefully pulling up the ropes so that nothing would be snagged on the scrub and young trees on the bank.

"He's going to knock the river into pieces and fall in," I said. My hand reached as if to grip Jotham's.

But my husband was kneeling on the snow, still heaving our parcels onto land. Glancing up, he said, "The river is frozen like a January pond—but unevenly, especially where the current flows strongest."

"I cannot lose him." I whispered those words, knowing that in this life, everything gets lost.

Hortus kept moving forward, pushing through the dark and snorting when he sniffed at the unearthly cold of the rocks.

"Come to me, Hortus," I called. "Hortus!"

The ice buckled under him; he plunged into the water and abruptly breached. His head reared up like the bowsprit on a ship, and he screamed in protest at the solid world tumbling into pieces. A coverlet on his back flapped away and caught fast to the frozen surface.

"No! I will fetch it," Jotham exclaimed.

"Leave it! They will see and presume us surely drowned. So it will be useful to us still." It was a warm bed covering that we would miss on our journey, but I could not bear for any of us to trust the ice again.

"Hortus!" Jotham Herrick yelled, and I added my voice to his.

Hortus appeared to be swimming but then stood and slammed into the ice between us, charging fore and back, whinnying as he shattered the ice with the hard bulk of his body. He reared up, striking the surface again and again, gathering force as he reached the shallows. At last he battered his way up the slope and bolted past us, not slowing though we called and called his name.

Propping our bundled Samuel against a tree, I raced after him, leaving Jotham Herrick to watch the babe and reel in the last of our bags, soaked with water when Hortus burst open the ice. If I *had* owned witch magics, I do not believe that I could have flown faster, for I was determined not to lose my precious horse. I ran hard and caught Hortus by the bridle and shouted at him. Though shuddering violently from the shock or cold, his legs and belly ice-shagged, he let me stroke his muzzle.

I forgot everything but his need. Coaxing him back to our household of bags, I hastened to unpack some of our clothing and rub him down. Fine crystals of ice had collected on his jaw and clung to the threads of his mane. Jotham came to help me with Samuel tucked against his side, the babe looking about in fine curiosity and prattling volubly in his infant language.

My spare petticoats served to dry my poor bruised horse. "I hope it will not kill him, all this struggle and ice and wet."

"Hortus will survive. A usual, lesser sort of horse would have given up long ago," Jotham Herrick said. "Probably back in Falmouth. He is one of The Goldsmiths' Company of Merchant-Adventurers, and he will not dare flop down and render up his ghost."

"He does have spirit, though I am doubtful, sir, whether horses are welcome in most such companies."

"In this one, he is. And so are babes," Jotham said. "This one, wife, is hungry."

We built up the fire in and around the colander with brush and branches, all four of us gathering near. I fed Samuel and afterward walked Hortus round and round the flames, bringing him as close as he would tolerate.

"Mr. Jotham Herrick! I did not realize you were clever to bring the colander, but you were," I said. "Quite nimble-witted."

"Metals and fire go together, madam. Fires go under pots and crucibles; why not inside as well, so long as air can find a way to whisper sparks into flames? And I will never fail to remember the sight of you walking and sliding across the river with a vessel of fire in your hands."

"I expect, Mr. Herrick, that we will recollect this night for many a year. Though I am tired enough to sleep and forget it forever."

"Indeed, I shall not forget the night when I lost my crucibles but kept my wife. And the swap is a well-struck barter."

"Look there!" I pointed up at the strangest thing that I had seen in all that wild, extraordinary night.

"How astonishing," my husband said softly.

A branch, confused by this hardest of winters, had flowered in the midst of ice and snow. Faintly bathed by starlight, the petals seemed to shine from within.

"What is it?"

"And what does it mean?" Jotham reached up as if to touch the branch but paused, his hand open. "We have had no spell of warmth but only brute cold this season."

"Perhaps a fair sign for us," I said. "In the midst of a cruel winter, we shall flourish. And if the whole world should turn to ice, we should still blossom and be filled with light."

"But the flowers will die, cursed by cold," my husband said. "So I do not know. A sign, yes, but of what?"

I stared up at the bough. "All things die, though we will be gone away when the blooms are ice. But the unfurling and beauty is for us."

"Perhaps you are that white spray," he said. "You keep on despite so much bitterness around you. And you seem filled with light and are lovely to me."

"Jotham."

I smiled at him under the branch and stars, though I knew better than he that sometimes the bitter was sheathed within me as well. We glanced up at the bravery of the flowers once more before departing with Samuel and Hortus and all the earthly goods one horse could bear.

The remainder of the way to the Saltonstalls was a brute of a ride, Hortus with his head down, me fighting to stay awake and not drop Samuel, Jotham leaning back against the wet bag that we left on top to dry if it would. But it would not, and froze instead. Occasionally we took turnabout in walking to give Hortus a respite from our weight.

Meanwhile, the stars kept on affirming their glory, but I was too weary to greet them.

Jotham Herrick, who had managed more sleep of late than I, admired them for me and made sure I did not topple off. In fact, he tucked bedding around my legs to make me more comfortable and not so disgraceful-looking, my gown and shift and petticoats askew. I felt much warmer than before and wished for an elephant-and-castle so that I might nap. A *howdah*, the sailors of the East India Company call an elephant's crowning castle, the whole stuck round with gems and furnished with silk-garbed chairs and bed.

"Imagine if each one of those stars could be a white fire on a hearth," Jotham Herrick said, "and the heavens a country just above our heads. Surely it would be a pleasant land."

I blinked to see more clearly, for the scene was blurry and glowing to my eyes, worn from too long a wakefulness. "Mr. Dane said all are pilgrims and strangers in the world. Looking for a better one. And now here we are on the road."

When a person has been accused as a witch, stayed up the whole night long, climbed through trapdoors and tunnels, scrambled over town when the sane and content are in bed, and crossed the Merrimack on foot rather than ferry, well, that person is grateful to see her destination looming against the stars, no matter how sparkling they are. And when the babe she treasures has wailed from the cold and the weary way, she is also glad to see the only door in the world that might safely let her in.

We walked the horse right up to the portion of the house where the Saltonstalls slept. An occasional touch of gout meant that the major preferred a bedchamber downstairs, and for that I was grateful. The room had a window—a luxury on the side of a house, for it is generally better to keep in warmth than to let in light. We were careful not to knock on the outer shutters of such a rare and handsome window, a leaded English casement that opened to the inside. We tapped on the walls with a stick and called their names. Soon the noise made by an iron bar showed that we were successful, and we waited with some apprehension as the major opened the inner shutters, casement, and outer shutters to peer out.

"Is that the voice of our young Charis Herrick? And Mr. Herrick? And a sobbing babe? Whatever is the matter?"

"Nothing," Jotham said. He paused, evidently unsure how much he should say. "I mean, sir, yes, something is the matter, but just now we just need to be made warm. And the horse likewise."

"Let me just find my breeches," he said, and vanished from view.

Elizabeth Saltonstall appeared at the window.

"My dear Charis," she said, "give me the child. Eliza's cradle is still standing here by the fire, but they are gone away to Ipswich."

I handed Samuel to Jotham, who leaned down and passed his bundle to Mistress Saltonstall.

"You poor babe, all tied up in skins and out nightwalking in the cold," she said.

Samuel looked at her and became quiet, and she sat down on the edge of the bed to talk to him.

"We took turns holding him," I said.

"Come in and explain yourselves," the major said.

"My wife has had no sleep in a long time," Jotham Herrick said.

"Give me a moment," Elizabeth Saltonstall said. She put Samuel in the cradle, speaking to him softly, and came back to the window.

"Hand her in," she said. "She can climb into bed and get warm. And I shall heat oatmeal to thaw your hands. All three of you must be aching from the cold. And toss in those sacks as well."

As Jotham reached for me, I dismounted clumsily on the side away from the window, shaking out my cloak and dragging the bedclothes from my legs.

"Shall I wake someone for the horse?" The major leaned from the window, his hands out. "You remember young Lud?"

"Yes, yes," I said.

"He is asleep by the kitchen fire, not having wanted to trudge home to his mother in the dark. I hired him for the day to chop wood, fearing our mountain of logs was not enough for this grim winter."

The major lifted me into the room and looked me in the face searchingly. I was beyond being able to feel anything except weariness, so I doubt he found any news there.

"To confess truth, the fewer who know we are here, the better," Jotham Herrick said. "For we have found ourselves among the devils, in the place of dragons, for no fault of our own. And by that I mean neither the Indians nor the French. I must ask you to forget what I say."

"Ah. Yes. Take heed what you divulge; think ere you speak. Tell me your need more than the cause. Rumor will arrive here soon enough. If you will be good enough to ride around to the door, I will tug on my boots and meet you there," Major Saltonstall said.

By this time I was lying in the still-warm bed and wishing the shutters were fastened again. But no sooner had the thought come to me than I dropped asleep, and stayed so through the night and most of the next day, swimming up from oblivion now and then to feed Samuel. Although I might have had some fear of Major Saltonstall's reaction to our story, I was too done-in to have the least apprehension. We were at his house on sufferance and at his mercy.

In what might have been dreams, I heard fragments of voices arguing.

"Do not tell me—better that I know nothing but your need—"

"Has suffered too much—"

"Do not say more—"

"And did not Providence arrange—"

But I sank right to the bottom of the river where the sleep-fishes wave their fans in calm bedchambers below the ice, and there I heard nothing and dreamed of nothing but the cold shapes that breathe in and out the river water and never think of the summer urge to clench and let go, springing into the air, or of autumn and swerving among the bright leaves that strike the water and rock slowly to the bottom.

When I finally rose and changed my gown for a cleaner one, our cloaks wet from the river had been dried to stiffness and brushed clean, and the major had spent a long time pondering and had already announced to his wife and Jotham Herrick that we must depart the next day.

And so I had little to do but hear the plan that Major Saltonstall had devised and agree that it was the best we could hope for. My luck was having missed the wrangle over what had happened in Andover: the major stopping my husband whenever he would say too much; the major striding up and down before the fire, arguing with himself over what was meet and right to do. For we were asking far too much of a magistrate and high man in the colony who served on the General Court, advised the governor, and led the Northern Essex militia. I missed his many questions to Jotham Herrick, the doubting of our judgment in departing so hastily, the careful refusal to hear any accusations against me. Also, I did not hear the major's praise, though I will be forever thankful that he found me above the rank of the common in boldness, courage, and strength of mind, as much "as the diamond is above other stones, the sun above the other stars, and fire above other elements." Even now, I am grateful but know that mettle and strength are sorely tested when the covenant between a woman and her town is trampled. Perhaps we should have done differently. Perhaps. But we did not, aroused and alarmed as we were. We were threads in the fabric of place; then, abruptly, not.

Jotham Herrick told me later that Major Saltonstall would not hear particulars and insisted that he knew nothing save that we had decided suddenly to leave Andover. And though the major stopped my husband each time he tried to explain, I felt sure he understood my plight.

"You will forgive me if I am a little deaf and did not hear your words," he said, more than once.

As magistrate, he knew well enough what happens to a jailed woman from our little settlements in the forest. Too often they die in Salem or Boston while waiting for trial, and any children with them, no matter how wild or feeble the claim against the mother. All these matters he mulled, finally judging that we had done as was fitting. By law, it was wrong of him, and yet I knew why he felt the force of a greater law. All I had to do was remember how providential my coming here the first time had been, and how that first saving of my health of mind and body had given me a place where, if I went in need, someone had promised to take me in. For that means *home*.

"But what of the child? What of Samuel?"

Elizabeth Saltonstall had found some fresh clouts and wrapped him up anew, so that he was now more comfortable and smelled faintly of lavender. His eyes were wide open, as round as clay marbles. When he saw me, he jerked under the wrappings and let out a tiny cry.

"What do you mean?"

I sat down beside Mistress Saltonstall; she clasped my hand in hers. She had been the one to bandage it while I slept.

"Should you entrust Samuel to us for safekeeping? A woman in town lost her babe only last week and could nurse him, if you wished to leave him behind. Since you do not know precisely what will come or where you will go. We would teach him right principles of reason and honor until he could be sent away."

Tears stung my eyes.

Surely I could not desert him! Had not my story been one where I was abandoned in a strange wise by everyone? I could not bear for Samuel to be without family, even among people I loved. It happens to us all to be parted from those we hold dear. But not so soon, surely. He had a mother who had survived her troubles to rejoice in his infant vigor and changing face: for a babe is not the same from one day to the next but grows like a flower in the light, one moment low to the ground, the next shooting up and budding, the next opening its central eye to stare into the eye of the sun.

In one lightning flash of thought, I imagined sailing away in a ship, its sails stacked high, to some other port—to Europe with its castles, or to Rhode Island where the Quakers had fled from Massachusetts Bay, or to Barbados, where rumor said that sweet-smelling bunches of fruit dangled from all the trees. Could I ever get over relinquishing my babe, even to Elizabeth's kind mercies? Would the major ship him to me when he was a young man of thirteen or fourteen and well able to travel on his own? And would he know me or care that I was his mother? Perhaps I would never see him more. He might sicken and die, but I would not know for months or years. All the time I would be dreaming about him, and yet he might have walked out of the world, his spirit streaming to where all my kin had gone.

I looked at Jotham Herrick, standing by the fire with Major Saltonstall. He gazed steadily back at me. It seemed to me that I was glass and that he could see through me and into my heart, also glass, but illumined by the lights of his face and the face of our child.

The pain of losing Samuel made my breasts ache and prickle with milk. I closed my eyes.

"I cannot. I cannot lose more." It might be best, and yet I did not have the power to give up my babe.

"Yes," Elizabeth Saltonstall said. "That is what I told my husband. You would not quit him, even for a time."

"It may be the most desirable for him to travel with you and Jotham Herrick," Major Saltonstall said. "We cannot know."

"He is as strong a boy-child for his months of age as I have seen," Jotham said. "We feared bringing him through the cold to Haverhill, but he was stalwart, and there is no mark of the frostbite on him. I believe it fitting to yield to Charis' desire. She has lost enough. Too much."

"You also," I said. "Without Samuel, we are barely a family."

"You always have a foster home here," Elizabeth said. "Perhaps you will return to this region when Goody Mehitabel Dane returns to her rightest mind," she added in a low voice, so that I knew she had been listening to Jotham Herrick.

"I lost her affection entire," I said, "and doubt she will care for me again. Yet I do not find that I earned her dislike. Her mother and sister disdained me and must have worked on her. It may be that they were more vile and black of heart than I understood. Bel Dane came to fear that I played some magical part in a woman's drowning in a well, and in setting a mark on her own babe's face. And yet she knew me, or so I once thought."

"Many are blinded," Mistress Saltonstall said. "Many look at a fair garden and see only weeds. But as my grandfather Ward often said, the bed of truth never withers but is green all the year long."

Major Saltonstall bent to throw another log on the fire. He straightened, frowning.

"I have heard no words but those that proclaim your wish to travel elsewhere, even in this terrible cold. You see? But let us talk, despite that, of discord. As magistrate, I have encountered rashly made censures and poisonous slurs, as well as silly men and women who thought that they could tiptoe around the edges of malefic witchcraft and suffer no harm. Even here in Haverhill, I have known a woman to consult the white of an egg in a glass of water and look for wisdom in strings and bubbles and odd coloration, or a shiftless Swan to waste his time peering through a hole worn in a stone to find out news of another world. You are no such woman. Let us imagine a strangeness and a wrong thought: that you have been named a witch. In that case, the panic of accusation will die away in time. People may come to reason rightly and know that not one of the outcries against you was significant, that they were all, indeed, indifferent matters that could be passed over. Yet they may look elsewhere for trouble and see it where there is none."

"The Holt daughters were just such idlers with fortune-telling and sieve-and-scissors," Jotham Herrick said. "The elder showed Charis an abundance of spite and jealousy from the dawn of their acquaintance."

"Yes, well, they were long known in Andover and I but a stranger," I said. "A wanderer who appeared out of the dark and forest, where the tribes are at home. And our people are afraid of night and trees and wild men. Perhaps it is no wonder they did not accept me at the last."

Yet I had come to feel that I had a place in Andover. By now Constable Foster would have arrived, met hue and cry, mounted search parties, and made an inventory before witnesses of any of our possessions left behind.

"If you do wander more and return to the colony, be sure to come to us in Haverhill," Major Saltonstall said. "You are fine and useful citizens, the sort we need in our wilderness towns. All of those who sailed in the first ships dreamed of a new Jerusalem, a brighter world, and a covenanting of like-minded souls." Here he spoke more openly than before, although he did not directly address the charge against me. "But the dream fades when our people are too quick to see evil gleaming from the faces of their fellows. That none of them could discern virtue in you, shining like a golden lamp in a dark place, I cannot fathom or approve."

"I hope that they are not unkind to those in Andover who were kind to me. Especially the Danes." I leaned my head on Elizabeth Saltonstall's shoulder, wanting comfort, and she put her arms around me as if I were her own daughter.

"Surely all the fire will die out now that we have gone," Jotham said.

"I wonder." Elizabeth Saltonstall looked up at her husband. "I do wonder."

"When a bloodletting begins, the flow is seldom stanched for a long time after," the major replied.

It was a peculiar conversation, the boundary sometimes blurring between the real and what we pretended was but fancy. Our words were better that way. For how could a magistrate assist a witch?

I saw nothing of Damaris, for Nabby had taken the girl to her daughter's house in Haverhill to sew infant clothes. We glimpsed no one else while we stayed there. No one came in search of us, and I believed the major quite careful enough to evade any future questioning as to our whereabouts. I could imagine him replying, "Oh, was she slandered? Truly? I hope that you find some fresh trace of them soon, for Mistress Charis Herrick is dear to us all, and I would not like to think of her driven to the wilderness like a beast. For she is no witch. Of that I am sure."

But we supposed that no one else had dared the river. I thought of the break in the ice and the abandoned coverlet, perhaps still fastened there, and hoped any pursuers would judge us drowned.

The next morning five of us set off at dawn after breaking the night's fast with boiled cornmeal, dried cranberries, and cold meat from the day before. Elizabeth Saltonstall wept at parting, and so did I, knowing that I might not ever see her again. She begged me to send word of where I was as soon as the place was known.

"Your mother would be so worried. And thus am I," she said.

"My mother believed that courage came from doing," I said. But I remembered her end, and how death found all that I loved. And surely they were brave.

"Godspeed, dear Charis, and may all that is loving and holy be as a cloak to shelter you." She touched the line of a tear on my cheek, and we looked long at each other, each storing the other in memory as best she could.

The journey party was composed of me and Samuel, Major Saltonstall, Jotham Herrick, and the thatch-headed boy encountered on the long-ago day that I stumbled onto the fields beyond the Saltonstall house. Lud was not quite so bashful as before, though he avoided looking me in the face when he informed me that he was now a man of seventeen.

"Lud is a first-rate shot and owes me a fee or two," the major said. "And is as loyal to me and mine as I have ever known. He does not know the details of what has happened, just that you were not satisfied with Andover and wish to journey by boat. He will have to ride pillion with me on Comet, as I know no other horse readily to obtain."

"A thousand times thank you," I said, and the tears stood cold in my eyes.

"No need for more thanks," he said, "though I believe your horse will be glad to share his household load with mine."

Though I was not sure that Hortus had quite recovered from his adventures, he appeared eager to be off. But he was always the best of horses for equable temper and willingness to please. I rubbed my face against his and kissed his nose.

"You make me glad to be traveling," I said. "Be especially mannerly whenever Mr. Herrick holds the reins, you hear?"

He blew white clouds on my hands in response.

I mounted the pillion-pad on his loin behind Jotham Herrick in the saddle, feeling much warmer than before because Elizabeth Saltonstall had rigged up some of her youngest son's old breeches for me and found an outgrown pair of heavy boots, well gartered with leather strips to stay on my legs. Geared in tucked-up gown, breeches, hose, and boots, I felt wonderfully free, riding in the midst of our bundles and bags, with the blackened colander dangling by one handle. I found myself but little ashamed to take to the paths and cartways and highways in the guise of a boy, something that was far safer for a winter rider in the wilderness.

Elizabeth had enveloped Samuel in furs, and now he was a tidy, sealed package. She handed him up, and he blinked himself awake and gave me an open-mouthed smile that made me laugh. She had devised a sort of harness with a shawl and soft leather ties that would press him close to me or Mr. Herrick, as we meant to take turns holding the reins or riding pillion. We had found that the rider in the saddle had more room for a babe, though hands were occupied. I suppose she may have had a fear of Samuel falling into the roadway and being trampled by hooves. But I was glad for something that could leave both hands free for reins when needed, although in truth I longed to have both arms close about him.

"I am well pleased with you, little man," I said. "You are small but a mighty boy for adventure."

He smiled at me uncertainly.

"Oh, Elizabeth," I whispered, and hugged Samuel close before yielding him to my husband.

"God bye, dearest Mistress Saltonstall," I cried as Hortus walked us away from the house. Jotham Herrick added his farewell to mine.

She must have stayed in the cold until we were quite out of sight, for she called even when we could no longer make out her words. I watched her, twisting away from my husband so that I could see her grow smaller, smaller: a doll, barely to be recognized as my foster mother who had once washed and dressed me when I was in rags and filth from the wilderness and crammed with grief.

"See there," I said, "Elizabeth Saltonstall is still watching."

"She was good to you," Jotham Herrick said.

"I shall miss her. So greatly."

"Yes," he said. "It is sad to be far from friends. True friends are few in this life."

"True friends," I echoed. Soon we would have only ourselves for earthly help.

I guessed it to be some fifteen miles to Newburyport. The major knew several boat captains near or in the town and wished to hunt for them.

"Although we have had so much freezing weather," he said, "yet the salt from the sea will keep the river to the east from hardening. I cannot believe that the waters could be frozen in November so close to the ocean."

"In Essex they will be talking about the winter of 1691 for many a year," Jotham Herrick said.

"Our minister lectured on the famousness of this winter and God's judgments on the last Sabbath," Major Saltonstall said. "He said it will be remembered for more than three hundred years, if the world lasts so long."

"Was it Mr. Ward? Your wife's father, you mean?" I had seen the old man preach when I lived with the Saltonstalls and had been surprised by his energy, though he now had a younger minister, a Mr. Rolfe, who often preached in the afternoons and lived in the minister's house. Haverhill had done better by its old minister than Andover, where they had "robbed Peter to pay Paul," voting to take monies from Mr. Dane to pay Mr. Barnard.

"It was he; my father Ward has the fire of a young man still, at least when he is well launched on his theme," Major Saltonstall said. "Did I tell you that Benjamin Rolfe was chaplain to the 1689 expedition to Falmouth under Major Church? He well comprehends what the French and Indians can do. And has confessed some natural dread of what they might do to him, or to his family, when he has one."

"No, I did not. I should have liked to talk to him," I said.

"When we were last in Haverhill, I heard Mr. Rolfe discuss the conversion of some Wabanaki," Jotham Herrick said.

"No doubt we should have converted more of them," Major Saltonstall said.

Lud grunted to show respect for this thought, or perhaps amusement. It was hard to tell. Riding pillion, he came along quietly on the major's roan horse, seldom speaking.

"My father claimed that we do not understand the Indians, nor they us," I said. "I suspect that is true."

"We barter and settle on Indian land, though they hardly believe in the finality of payments or any sort of deed—what can a parchment with marks be to them? So they butcher our people, and sling our infants against a stone or tree. We execute revenge. They scalp us. So we offer bounties for their scalps. And there is to be no end," Major Saltonstall said.

After that, we were silent for a time, scanning the landscape for movement but finding only the snow between the trees and the upflung branches of more delicate young shrubs and saplings, each twig holding up a bud of ice. The road sometimes kept us in sight of the river, sometimes curved away. We jogged along comfortably, covering the ground at an easy pace, chatting about indifferent matters.

By the third hour, Samuel had wakened and slept, wakened and slept. When roused, he burbled to me and the sun and sky and trees in his language, and Jotham and I spoke back to him, though we did not know what he might be saying except that the world was exciting and brave with color and birds that cut the air overhead.

Along our way, after stopping several times to examine the river for open water, we began to hear music from its bed.

"The salt flow," Lud said. He did not turn to us when he spoke but kept his eyes on the forest, sweeping his gaze back and forth.

But we saw nothing of any tribe, who were no doubt wiser than to be out and wandering on such an inclement day, and in another mile arrived at a cluster of tiny, steep-roofed houses by the water. There we looked for rest. A slough of churned-up, frozen mud and snow by a horse block was our invitation to dismount. On a wooden bracket close by hung a signboard of ingenious make, the frame being rectangular but with a burst of gold-painted spikes all around, framing a weather-beaten dove and the words *The Sun and the Bird*, along with some smaller letters, partially worn away and no longer readable. This clearly signifying an inn, we alit for nearly an hour.

The major searched for a boatman of his acquaintance and eventually found him in a nearby house, sodden-drunk and of no fit service to us. Our luck was fairer.

A red-faced woman ushered us inside, bellowing to a servant to "skip lively" and help with the company. My shift, petticoats, and skirts shoved into place, I appeared once again a proper lady-wife to be shown to an inner room where I could nurse my child in peace. Jotham Herrick fetched me a great mug of mulled ale, two-pence the ale quart, and he himself had a tankard of flip with brandy, and after that we were warm and merry and full of hope for what the day would bring. The goodwife brought in a bowl of venison stew for us to share, and I found that, though the day was still young, I was already eager to ladle out a meal. Lud saw to the horses in the yard outside, though he too traipsed in for venison and a hot drink, as did the major, just before we left.

Back in saddle-and-pillion, our party followed a level road packed with snow. This time I held the reins and babe. In some half a mile we reached a house where Major Saltonstall wished to stop. While the horses halted in the road, Lud walked off into some trees to "exert the limbs," as he said.

A stack of bent wood staves leaned against a vessel on blocks to one side of the house and clearing. The tiny clapboard hut with its precipitous, snow-shedding roof and the chimbley puffing smoke seemed inconsequential next to the boat.

In answer to the major's *halloo!* and rapping at the door, out popped a young man, dragging on his shirt and waistcoat and trailed by a little girl in shift who clung to his breeches. He tucked her back inside, calling something over his shoulder, and shut the door.

The major appeared to be laughing as he shook hands, and the two conversed for some time, the young man talking volubly and gesturing at the boat in the side yard and pointing toward the direction of Newburyport. At last he nodded to the rest of us and disappeared back into the house.

"His boat is in no condition to sail, but he knows someone who is bound for Newport on the morrow," Major Saltonstall called to us as he untied Comet and led him into the road.

"Newport!" Jotham Herrick tapped me on the shoulder.

"Pirates," I said, twisting in the saddle to meet his gaze.

"And Quakers," he said.

Samuel, having had his fill of milk, half-hidden beneath my cloak, crowed and made us laugh.

"Wolves. Or so our busy meddlers claim." The major glanced up at me.

"Mary Dyer," I said, remembering how she walked from Rhode Island to Boston to be a witness to her own liberty of creed, knowing that she would be hanged by the godly. A rush of fellow feeling made me think kindly of her. Were we not in some ways the same, as wanderers and as women liable to be caught by the hangman's noose? And had not this great land of wilderness been testing my every belief, as though to walk through the New World meant to journey after truth?

"I doubt that Quakers are wolves," my husband said, "though many tell such tales."

"Whether they are or not, we must do what we must do. We have no freedom to be choosers," I said. "And there I was dreaming of a ship with white sails stacked high and the sight of English castles."

The major looked up as Comet nudged him in the back. "Stop that," he said, reaching for the bridle but not turning his gaze from us.

"I would not like to try for a merchant ship out of Boston, not when you might be pursued before it should depart," Major Saltonstall said. "Too many people would be involved in taking passage on a great ship, even should one be available. And a comely woman with red hair and a babe, seeking to travel the seas in winter . . . it is not a sight of the commonest."

"My wife is in no wise common," Jotham Herrick said.

"Yes, and we would not want to see her dragged through the streets like a drab found thieving. If we do not take this chance, there may not be another at this time of year," Major Saltonstall said. "I am sorry for the risk, but it is the truth."

He swung into the saddle, shouting for Lud, who soon appeared in the distance, musket over one shoulder, having scouted ahead. The horses soon caught up, and I held the gun briefly as he clambered up behind the major.

The horses walked off, steady and unhurried.

"Good Hortus," I said. "Not so much longer now."

"Also," the major said to Jotham Herrick, "there are the court-appointed coin searchers in Boston. I expect you have some gold to smith and perhaps some estate in coin left by your father. The searchers of coin have the right to seize your possessions if you are found attempting to carry specie out of the colony."

"That I had not thought," he said.

I looked over my shoulder to see my husband's hand instinctively reach toward jerkin and doublet with the gold coins well sewn into the hems.

"But you are right, of course," he added.

We rode on until we came to a turning in the way. There we took what was little more than a deer path through the trees and down to a sandy river beach. The water here was open, as usual in November, though here and there broken panes of ice clung to stones and shore.

"I am not sure how far we go on," the major said.

"See." Lud pointed above the tree line. "A wisp of smoke."

"Keen eyes," Major Saltonstall said. "Young eyes."

The horses moved slowly along the top of the bank where the snow and undergrowth gave way to washed earth and sand, and in a few minutes we came on another steep-roofed house, crudely clapboarded.

"Wait here," the major said. "This may be the place."

Climbing down from the saddle, he set our bundled goods to swinging. "Stay, Comet," he said, his hand lighting momentarily on the horse's neck.

He picked his way over the ice and snow before the house and thumped on the door.

"See at the little window," Lud said to us.

A one-board shutter banged closed, the door came ajar, and a head appeared, so whiskery and gray that I pictured the walruses in a volume of natural history that we children had loved to pore over. The head cocked and stared at us, the door swung open, and Major Saltonstall stepped inside.

"Now to bide," Jotham Herrick said, taking Samuel from me.

He passed the babe back to me after I slid from the horse, showing a generous amount of hose and breeches to the trees and Lud, who looked away as if concerned with the snow-draped rubble in the yard, stumps and an anchor and a tumbled stack of greenish bottles.

My husband landed on the ground beside me and lifted the child from my arms, pulling away the skein of linen that swaddled the babe's face and humming a tune when Samuel blinked his eyes and gave us an open-mouthed grin.

"His cheeks are cold," Mr. Herrick said.

"Is he all right?"

"Just chilled, wife. He likes the trees and birds."

"Too frosty for many birds."

"If one flies, Samuel will catch sight of the wings. I will watch over him. My sweet, my liking—you have a private ramble. A short one."

Hortus followed me as I wandered toward the bank of sand, dirt, and roots that sloped toward the river, and when I paused to stare out over the water, he dipped his head and blew a cloud of breath over me. I pressed his cheek against mine and stroked his jaw, rubbing away a thin beard of ice.

"It's a sore thing to be a rider. And maybe to be a horse in winter, too. But you are the one who has heard my woes and my secret thoughts, and I am glad of you."

He snuffed at my hands, and so I rummaged my petticoats to find the pocket tied at my waist. I withdrew a parsnip and offered it to him.

"Hortus, here is a parting gift to you from Mistress Saltonstall."

He lipped and ate it slowly, craunching and dropping hunks of the sweet pale flesh, and nosing among the weeds for what was lost.

"You are the finest, fairest horse in all the colony," I told him. "My blossom, my emerald, my gold-among-horses. For who has saved me so often? You are the providential horse who came when I was in the greatest need. A miracle and a mystery enclosed in hide. And who knows but that the good God, pitying my distress, sent you? For you are my beauty and my rescuer. We should have named you Angel."

Hortus seemed pleased at the compliment, bobbing his head as if bashful, though he was never shy around me.

"You were named for the *hortus conclusus*. Once, people liked to conceive that this was also the little walled garden where Mary sits with her babe in her arms near a fountain and flower and trees. Did you know? And said she herself was a kind of garden, too. And so you must also be a black-shining garden, as dark as night, a nosegay of soot-flowers hidden in the deeps of the night when we needed to be secret from men."

My hand rested on his neck.

"It was not pure and biblical," I said, still thinking of Mary, "but idolatry, as our ministers preach. But that a woman might be a type of garden paradise is a pretty thought."

On the river close to shore floated a boat, the water on that spot so smooth that the shape was neatly reflected on the surface. As mere matter often does, the vessel seemed oddly crammed with spirit, as if it might soon open a yet-unseen eye to stare back at me. Although the thought was but fancy, the boat seemed glad to be gently stirring on its tether.

"If we could climb into the mirrored boat on the river, where would we go? And why did my father name you for a garden and perhaps also for Mary? I should like to ask him to tell me how he imagined a horse could be a garden, as a woman seemed a garden to people who lived hundreds of years ago. And still does to some, I dare say, though not among us."

Hortus nuzzled my shoulder, and I leaned against him, dreaming of my father and mother and all their hopes for me and my sister and my brothers. Now those wishes had all come down as inheritance to me, and without sons my father's name was lost. No one would recall him in fifty or sixty years, or praise him as one honored in his generation.

"So many solid things are brimming over with riddles, Hortus. The natural world can seem so sturdy, and yet it is flooded with spirit from another world. And we gutter out like candles, all our life fleeing away. It is a mystery."

I did what I had come to do—the breeches of men can be a great deal of bother for a woman—and afterward walked back to the house, Hortus nudging me as I went until at last I grasped his head between my hands, laughing, and stroked his face and the thick winter mane.

Jotham Herrick was arguing with Major Saltonstall. Lud stood listening, head down.

"If this turns out to be our boat to a new port, you should not pay our passage—let me meet the cost, for I have enough."

"Keep your coins, Jotham Herrick. Your spouse Charis is dear to us, and you also, enough so that there should be no thought of coin. But more, she will be leaving behind a valuable gelding."

I ran forward and caught the major by the arm.

"Hortus! Can I not take him with me, wherever we go? I would have died in the wilderness without him. He is so much to me, more than any ordinary beast of burden. To me, he is chief among horses, the one who bears away every prize."

"There is no room for a horse—barely enough space in the boat for passengers and your household bundles," the major said. "I am sorry."

And though I had lost all my kin long before, I now cried as though they had all been slaughtered afresh, and I hung my arms around the neck of my horse and wanted never to let go. Even now, I do not believe it wrong to grieve to part forever from a horse, when God is a trembling harp string that registers even the death of a sparrow.

Jotham Herrick brought our child and put him in my arms. I nodded and looked down at Samuel. "We have given up so many things," I said.

"But there will be more, my dear Charis," he said. "We are like Goodman Job, who was tested and lost all that he loved. Surely he never forgot what had been but was given more and more in time, until the scale was in balance, loss and gain perfectly joined as one."

"I saw the boat on the water, and yet I never thought that it was not large enough, that I would not be able to take my horse."

"Someday, all wounds will be healed," he said.

"Not in this life."

"No," said Jotham Herrick. He gently blotted the tears from my eyes with the hem of his sleeve.

While we were standing close and murmuring together, gazing down at Samuel, Major Saltonstall and Lud went to fetch the captain. He must have had the niceties washed out of him on the ocean because he did not wait to be formally introduced.

"Ebenezer Swan. Master of the *Promise*, as sound a boat as you may find. At your service," he said, whipping the beaver hat from his head and giving a jounce that was meant to be, I believe, a bow. He was a stout, short fellow with sea-reddened cheeks and bright blue eyes with crinkled lines at the outer corners.

It seemed we had a new problem.

"The boy who helps me has up and roamed with his mother to Newbury. Belike he may not come back."

Captain Swan's gaze rested on Lud Duston. "You ever thought about roaming to sea?"

"Me?" Lud glanced over his shoulder, which made us laugh.

"You. I hear your name is Lud. So why not? The first Lud was the grandson of Noah, who saved the whole world two by two in a boat."

Lud stared at him and slowly began to break into a blissful smile— one that seemed to eat up his whole face. If truth be well told, Lud always looked innocent and half-addled, and now even more so.

"You know how to steer a horse?"

"I can ride."

"If you can get a horse to do what you want, I can teach you how to sail a boat. Horses and boats can be headstrong, and both can heave and toss."

Lud continued to beam.

"Sailoring with me will pay in coin. And you can gape at queer sea-sights and a fair piece of the world. What do you say?"

"I—" Lud swung around to Major Saltonstall, who laughed and clapped him on the arm.

"If you go jaunting on the sea, you have no ride home."

"He can anchor here if he wants," Captain Swan said. "I can find out a use for a likely-looking young man with strong arms."

Lud looked at us, and we stared back at him.

"Yes, then!"

And that was that—a revolution in Lud's life, decided in a trice.

While Lud went on smiling as if he would never stop, Captain Swan told us his story, how he had once lived contentedly in Haverhill. Some years before his wife's death, she had been taken captive. Though later ransomed and restored to her husband and child, she was never wholly right in her mind.

"How sad that she was not herself any longer. I am sorry for that loss." The thought gave me a pang. How easy it would have been to be shattered by misfortune!

Captain Swan nodded. "She was a fine wife when she did not come unmoored and go adrift with Indians in her fancy. And after she died, our child was better off with a woman to mind her."

Jotham Herrick looked puzzled. "I have met a Swan or two in Haverhill," he began.

"No near relation," the major said hastily. "I inquired, and the daughter now lives in Ipswich with her grandmother."

The master of the *Promise* paid little notice to this interruption, but whether it was because he was determined not to admit connection to the Haverhill Swans or whether he was intent on recounting his story, I could not tell.

"Since then, I have taken to the river and sea and lived a watery life, being a bit of a carpenter of oak planks and pegs and a bit of a tailor of hemp canvas, sailing with the tide and adventuring along the coast to strange coves and corners, avoiding the shoals."

"A smuggler's life," I said.

"Not much more guilty than the men who carried Goodman Jonah toward Tarshish, all unknowing," he said, "for what do we do but take back a little of our own from what the crown in England steals? Parliament thieves might as well have tried to catch a blowing snowstorm in a rollipoke as block our trade."

"The coast is all smugglers," Major Saltonstall said. "The people want to buy from the Dutch and others. They do not like to be taxed or cheated by England for our own native materials. And afterward they charge and tax us overmuch for what is made from them. So magistrates often choose not to see or hear."

"Trade makes for peace and goodwill between peoples," Captain Swan said, "even when it is a smuggling trade."

"I am glad of a smuggler today, when I mean to smuggle my wife into a foreign port," Jotham Herrick said.

"People do say the name Newport means pirates." I lifted Samuel against my shoulder and joggled him up and down to stop his tears. Somehow he had managed to free an arm from swaddling and furs. The babe knocked my hat askew and grasped at my hair, pulling a loop of red out from my coif and bonnet. He pressed his fist against his mouth and sucked the freed strand.

"Rhode Island means a mixed lot. You will find some to admire and some to avoid, but that is the way of it everywhere in this world. But if you and Mr. Herrick are content in harness together and conduct a fair trade, you will find your way," Captain Swan said. "And if you ever wish to moor in a Massachusetts harbor again, I will fetch you."

"My place must be with Mr. Herrick. But I grieve to leave our Saltonstall friends and my horse behind. For Hortus saved my life more than once."

"Ah, well, I am sorry for that trouble," he said. "A dumb beast sometimes has a wonderful manner of coaxing a way into the heart without ever using words."

"We will take the best care of him," the major promised. "And when you come back to Essex, he is yours."

But I would never be back again, or not in time to see Hortus, I feared. Boston, Falmouth, Haverhill, and Andover had been my homes, each for a period of years or months, and I doubted that I would see any of them another time. Return seldom seemed to be my story, and journeying far is hard and a greater danger once children come. So I clung to Hortus and let Jotham Herrick bear Samuel and walk him up and down.

"Will you be afraid of a boat and the sea's swell and rush? I wonder," Captain Swan said. "It is the land and man that can frighten me. I keep my boat always on the river in memory of Alice Swan."

"How is that?" Jotham Herrick stopped in his to-and-fro parade with Samuel.

"I keep my tender hidden in the scrub and can make a clean escape if attacked. Unless I am clubbed in my sleep," he added. "But old men are canny and light sleepers and—"

"Babe Samuel is cold and perhaps hungry," Major Saltonstall interrupted. He never liked people to speak of massacre or captivity in front of me, though the dread of either was common enough in people's minds and mouths.

"Come to the fire—I am forgetting manners, here in the wilds," Captain Swan said. "I would let the horses in the doors as well and be content with them, but it would be like trying to thread a needle's eye with cable."

"They will be patient in the weather," the major said.

"No, no, there is a broken-down shed at the edge of the woods that will do."

Lud, taking the hint, led away our horses. The rest of us ducked under the low doorway to the house—a dark cupboard of a house but with a chimbley that did not smoke.

As my eyes grew used to the gloom, I saw that the front room was gaudy with valuable objects: chairs carved with scrolls, triangles, diamonds, and flowers; goblets with marvelous stems of twisted and colored canes cased in clear glass that Captain Swan said had come from the Netherlands; a small oil painting of lemons and shellfish, the first such thing I ever saw; and an astonishing pair of Dutch andirons with brass ball finials and a wonderfully detailed head and torso of a woman that cast light prettily from the flames. Though I had often been warned against taking delight in images, I was amazed and found the work marvelous and strange.

But since sleep called more strongly than man-wonders, however curious and captivating, we sat and drowsed by the hearth until the high tide began to turn back to the sea the next morning. We had maintained that the master must sleep in his bed, for we wanted him rested for the journey, and sent Lud and the major to sleep there as well. When I fed Samuel in the night, I wept again to leave the Saltonstalls and my horse, and could not tell which meant the most to me.

In the morning, Lud had lessons in handling Captain Swan's tender, rowing rather clumsily but safely. He ferried cargo, the bundles that had been divided between the horses, and us. The weather being fair and the wind promising, we must depart.

Crossing awkwardly from the tender, I was grateful once again for men's breeches. I must have climbed out of one boat and into another before but had no memory of doing so, and I found it a delicate, wobbling sort of transaction. Once aboard, all I desired was to catch hold of Samuel and grip him so that he could not possibly roll into the river, for the current was not as gentle as I had assumed on shore, and we could feel its sliding, powerful tug.

The floor of the boat—a shallop—was heaped with straw, and on it were many tidily packed bottles of molasses from the Dutch West Indies bound for Newport, as well as special items obtained for and promised to particular buyers, which we were privileged to see before they were swiftly wrapped in oiled canvas and hidden from view: two deftly-executed Dutch still-life paintings, one of a vase of flowers with a collection of chased gold cups and another showing uncooked shrimp and fish on a platter next to a bowl of cherries (both of these painted by a woman, a truth that surprised me greatly); two pendulum clocks, also of Dutch make; crates of certain free-thinker books that could be printed only in the tolerating Netherlands; and a few casks of Madeira wine. Neat wooden boxes held folded furs and canvas, mysterious spare rings and hinges, coils of rope, and a stone anchor that resembled a small millstone, tools of the sailor's trade.

"These things say to me how our lives—"

"Are changing," Jotham said, finishing my broken-off thought.

Canvas belled outward and seemed to be longing for adventure. Captain Swan explained the spritsail and staysail to Lud, and how he handled the shallop with them, and how the leeboards could be raised or lowered. He would lower the board on the lee side so that the river or sea would press the boat forward and not let it drift to one side.

He paused to ask our forgiveness, saying that he had been meaning to put a deck over half the shallop but had put off the work.

"I fear we may be wet," I said, but Captain Swan had gone back to telling Lud how to handle and steer the boat. I was glad of the Mi'kmaq's sealskin to keep Samuel dry, though I fancied that some poor naked creature might come swimming over the waves to demand it back again.

We settled ourselves and our bundles amid the goods, amazed by all we saw, and called out to the major, our voices seeming to vanish into the water and distance. We heard a pin-small answering shout. Captain Swan stowed our belongings more neatly, making all *shipshape*—a word that seemed to mean *trim*, with access ways to all parts of the boat.

Anchor hoisted, we were off in a sliding, headlong rush that made us cry out, though whether in dread or wonderment, I cannot say.

Yet we did not forget ourselves but looked back at the land and all we knew and Major Saltonstall. He stood on the bank by the river with Hortus and Comet until we must have been entirely out of sight, the tender bobbing behind us.

"Hortus," I whispered, hugging the bundle of Samuel close.

We skirred down the river, occasionally glimpsing houses and other boats, and all was well. But when we entered the sea, oh, there was a commotion of crying babe and Jotham Herrick and I leaning over the rail of the shallop to retch and heave up venison stew from The Sun and the Bird. Lud proved the best sailor of us all, for though he may have felt uncomfortable and ill at times, he kept his meal to himself. Even the master of the boat lost a dollop of his last night's supper.

The river had widened our sight, but now the whole watery globe seemed to open and let us in, and suddenly we were keeping the land at a distance, Jotham Herrick and I looking back at the firs standing steady on the banks with mingled fear and anticipation of the unknown. We were but motes in a lively endlessness. Samuel wailed for a time and then seemed to take an interest in the waves, only occasionally spitting up small clots of milk that I wiped away with brine. He seemed thoughtful, his tongue exploring the salt on his lips before he turned his head to look me in the face.

"The sea, the sea," I told him.

Jotham Herrick hung over the rail again, and afterward lay looselimbed among the boxes with his head in my lap.

I called out to the master, "He wants to know, is this a grown sea or a fair one?"

"Oh, he'll never make a sailor," Captain Swan said by way of an answer, and brought us an armful of furs for protection from the spray.

"Fair, then?"

"The winds are blowing over the stern, and the day looks promising, Mistress Herrick." He glanced down at my husband's pale face, shook his head, and winked at me.

I smiled at him in answer and said, "I have no wish for a sailor husband. He would fly away from me. But how can sailors be ailing on the ocean?"

"They do take sick, especially when storms come," Captain Swan said. "And many a sailor loses his midday dinner or evening supper before he is out of sight of land. Lud is doing right well."

Indeed, he still appeared to glow with happiness as he knelt beside the mast. What had we done, consigning our safety to an old man and Lud Duston?

I traced a finger along my Jotham's cheekbone, dreamed of the wide valleys that lay drowned beneath us, and said an outlandish prayer like nothing ever heard in a meetinghouse: *Pray for me and mine, all you bones of sailors and pilgrims that lie at the bottom of the sea; assemble yourselves in the wet valley of bones and bring your small finger-bones together and pray for us, pray that we do not join you in the deep. And all you souls of the good departed, pray for us. And Holy Spirit, pray for me, for I have naught but wild and wildering words. Fearing and daring the waves, I trust myself to the mercy that goes with me whether I am alive or dead.*

In this way, I reconciled myself to whatever would come next.

The ocean was not what I had thought it to be, for though I had been on a ship when younger, I did not remember much but blue sky and darker sea and coming into harbor at Falmouth. I did not recall the rising and turning expanses and how they could seem to be mir-rored in my own swaying feelings—that what was in me could reflect and hold on to something so large and full of unreadable riddles.

The waves gamboled as if they were alive, great joyful cats that burst against the boat or fled on by fleet tiptoe. I thought of the dread of the sea that is in so many who crossed the ocean to settle, or who handed the same on to their children and grandchildren— the fright of waves like demons or fallen angels that can make mountainous tossings, flinging a vessel up and up a mountain of green-blue glass and dropping it down so swiftly as if to make a ship a stone on a line to measure the depths of the undersea valleys and caverns. Surely they cowered from the deep as though shrinking from what is infinite. (And did not the infinite walk on waves at Galilee while the disci-ples in the boat cried out in dismay?) Such tales our travelers told of forked white lightning striking glitter from the sea or walloping a mainmast, and the sudden rains sloping from heaven and drenching the decks, only to transform into hail and batter the sailors with white stones until they were bruised, and at last to sift down as lamb-soft snow stars from heaven.

Even on a fair day with favorable winds, the sea's mind seemed turbulent with a constant motion, and I would not have been sur-prised to see any wild and quick wonder: a family of ice-blooded

mermaids and mermen cleaving the swells, or some vast monster stirring the watery world like a spoon in a boiling pot and weltering in
the waves. The swift-slanting wind caught the canvas and pushed
us along faster than I had imagined the boat could move. Once an
immense living blade leaped from the water in what seemed purest
pleasure and smacked down into the depths, all its silver sheathed and
glittering where we could not see. What dangers were scabbarded
there, who could say?

Captain Swan handed Lud several heavy bed rugs and asked him
to cover the packages of paintings and the clocks.

Everything grew damper and colder.

The living pulse of the water was in us, always, and I fancied that I
should always after be hearing the sea-murmur of waves and fish and
whales in my ears, as I had heard it tucked inside seashells when on
land. The cadence and cry of spirit and mystery in matter is clearer
on the ocean. After some hours, the sea quieted a little, the waves
making beautiful scrolls as they passed by us, seething and whispering of what they knew, and what we may never know. For part of
the beauty of the watery part of the world is its hidden life that we
glimpse only in the occasional aerial somersault of a fish, the fountain
of a breaching whale, or the rare, riddling phosphor-shine on waves.

"I see why you would be a sailor," I called to Captain Swan as he
busied himself with shifting the lee boards. "And Lud also."

"Aye," he said. "A man is bigger within when he goes to sea, and
smaller without. And both are healthful for him to be."

The hours passed, and the night came on with the stars burning
above us.

In the darkness, there seemed to be even greater mystery, spreading around us forever, rounding the globe, as if some enormous soul
lay secret and dreaming beneath us. The sea at midnight slumbers
and sighs in shadow and moonlight, its vertical water cliffs sheltering drowned bones, pearls, the gold powder blown by breezes from
far-off mines, finny beasts, and the mighty, jeweled Leviathan of the
deep. I felt myself yielding to the sea spirit of reverie and trance, as
the swells passed under and around us and I sat with my babe in his
furs resting against me with his face dusted by moonlight and my
husband asleep with his head in my lap.

*Behold now the accepted time, behold now the day of salvation ... Where-
fore come out from among them, and separate yourselves ... and ye shall be*

my sons and daughters, saith the Lord ... The glad runnels of words streamed through my mind, leaving me wonderfully at peace, empty as a shell on shore is empty, yet full of the sea's music.

Once Jotham woke and clutched at me, his eyes wet. "A nightmare," he said. "You were wax in my arms, pale and cold."

"That time is gone," I said to him, stroking the soaked hair from his forehead. "It is a true dream, not of the future but of the past, for I might have died—thought of, wished for death. To be like my family. To be one with them."

He pressed my hand against his cheek.

"But I am no longer lost, no longer wandering near the verge of death. We have a landing place ahead. And I have you and Samuel. If I am wax, then I am a candle that flames against the dark."

"Charis. My red-gold own, my only, my beloved," he said, and closed his eyes, journeying back to the world of dreams. I hoped he would find me again there but alive, alight. Perhaps the visionary me would tell him what I had only that morning begun to suspect. My hand slipped to my belly. Was I again with child, our son or daughter to be born in a far-off port?

I could not sleep, though Samuel and Jotham slept so deeply that they seemed to have sailed far from me, or to have sunk to the palaces of the mer-king and mer-queen. But it was not so; they were as near as waking. The natural witchery of the sea enchanted me, and the salt cloud wrapped me. I and mine were tiny, tiny, but the immensities of ocean filled up my thoughts. The horses of the sea—those creatures of the ancient world—ambled or leaped under me. I rode on the infinite rollers; I strode the depths.

"My dear Hortus," I whispered. "God send you sweet grass and fairest weathers."

It came to me that the sea is a mystery, its depths dreamed by God. *To whom the sea belongeth: for he made it.* And I thought that before the worlds were molded, the oceans were meant to ebb and flow and sometimes tower, reaching toward the heavens. God fashioned the waters and their salt, changeable secrets out of joy and pleasure, and likewise he formed me, and all he longed for me in my life was that I be alive, all the way alive and whole like the sea, doing what I was intended to do, being all of what I was meant to be—a woman rejoicing in creation and sensing another, better world next to our own, a mother and wife, a wielder of the needle, an apprentice to a goldsmith, and a candle on fire. The inchoate longings, unsure thoughts, tidal feelings, and waves of sorrow or unexpected happiness that I had felt since leaving Falmouth were currents in my own mystery, for who is not a riddle and a wonder to herself, to himself? For we are a crossing of the particular and mortal by the infinite in which there is neither male nor female, neither Jew nor Gentile nor English nor Wabanaki, and what could be more strange?

As we rocked on the sea, the sure knowing came to me that Samuel and Jotham Herrick and I would safely find port, that we would arrive in the wondrous and fearful realm of Rhode Island, that it would be possible to live as deeply and as vigorously as the ocean lived, to be a created being completely alive. I saw it, I knew it, and gave my thanks for that blessing as I sank and crested with the waves.

Sometime the next day, at about nine o'clock in the night, we came to a cove where Captain Swan unloaded his wares with Lud's help and was paid in gold from England and Spain—pirated pieces of eight, perhaps. We moored there until dawn, and afterward the shallop was light and airy and made good time to the Marlborough dock at Newport. And so we came to a new home at last and made our way.

EPILOGUE

My dearest Mistress Charis Herrick,

Pray pardon me for being such a puny letter writer, and thank you for the gold-rimmed bowl made with your own hands. I am proud to own the pretty object, and to see the family names inscribed with your own clever fingers on the silver and the kindness therein expressed. I only wish that I could grasp those beloved hands, and embrace your dear children, Samuel and Elizabeth and the young twinned babes Nathaniel (we thank you for that honor to my Husband) and Jotham. I trust they will use their time well, not knowing how short or long it may be. And how I should like to talk with your dear husband, Mr. Herrick. We are extremely refreshed by the tidings in your letter, wherein we have an account that you are all alive and in health, and that the Newport business in gold work, silver sword-harness, and table vessels is robust. Pray, write me again how you fare.

Mr. Saltonstall is now Colonel Saltonstall of the North Regiment, Essex, and also the master of Kellingley Manor in Yorkshire, an inheritance from his late father, Mr. Richard Saltonstall. He is hearty enough, though we have endured perilous times of late in Haverhill. The town has had a sorrowful number of goodmen and sons murdered while laboring in the fields in the past few years, particularly around the area of Pond Plain, and we fear some larger outbreak in the next few years. Ours has been nominated a house of refuge, so often we are much thronged with lodgers in the way of musketeers and pikemen in helmets and corselets or quilted coats, families with children, and, saddest to admit, lice. Between the militia and the courts, Col. Nathaniel Saltonstall is as ever thick in the business of the province.

You wrote for several additional particulars about Mr. Dane and the trials, and I am sorry to have left you in suspense for such a long time. Andover suffered more than most towns in the late witchcraft ferment, with such hordes accused, and a mighty number of them in Mr. Francis Dane's own family. I wrote you that the daughters and their children were imprisoned. But I have learned since that one of those hanged at Salem, Goody Carrier, was his own niece. Perhaps you knew her? And I believe a nephew's wife was hanged. I may have mentioned that a former minister at Falmouth, Mr. Burroughs, was also put to death: I wondered if you were acquainted with him in the Maine region of the colony. Though twenty were hanged or pressed, a mort were jailed or accused, even small children. Mr. Dane himself was accused, having fought gigantically for his people, maugre the consequences to himself, and Mr. Barnard also spoke out against indictments as they increased in number. Mr. Dane was, I recollect, kind and affectionate to you and Mr. Herrick.

My husband says that were it not for our brave Mistress Charis Herrick, he might not have been troubled with doubts and resigned so quickly after he was appointed to the Court of Oyer and Terminer. Perhaps he would have served longer as a judge of those unhappy people. Nor would he have known so soon that even a minister of Mr. Cotton Mather's standing in Boston can be mistaken in this matter of witchcraft and phantom evidence. For you made him see anew both flaws and precious freedoms of this new-peopled America. Col. Saltonstall has suffered for his actions, both in being mischievously accused (though never arrested) and in being sometimes slighted in his work for the colony. Yet he is glad not to have the death judgment of innocents as a millstone to grind his conscience. It is marvelous to consider how your trials and wanderings and unjust accusation were changed to a kind of blessing in his case. For he well knew you were no witch and consort of devils. He is glad and thankful to Providence, sending his most fond regards and constant fair wishes to you and all your family. It is a joy and comfort to us that you are safe.

I regret to say that your beloved, faithful Hortus passed on this spring. He was as well loved and pampered as a horse may be, but he lived in hope and was ever looking for you and in fair weather would trot to the pasture fence whenever a woman appeared near the house. To the last, he knew your name and would prick up his ears at any mention. We buried his bones in the lower meadow, and when Damaris came for a visit—she is well grown now (though nabbity in stature) and a skilled needlewoman—she planted forget-me-nots, ferns, and sweet-smelling flowers dug from the edge of the woods around a white stone to mark the place and make a little Eden. So now we have a Hortus garden to remind us of him and you and past hours that are fled.

My heart flies out to yours as though you were my own daughter (Eliza is in health and with child again, and still married to Mr.

Rowland Cotton, minister of Barnstable, who proves a vigorous husband. When next the colonel goes to Boston, I shall ship you a length
of dyed linen cloth for the children and a piece of silk for you to
make a gown like that I am also sending Eliza.) When shall we meet
again, my dear, dear Charis Herrick? Perhaps in paradise, though we
will not be the same as in our lives here. Yet it is promised that sorrow and sighing shall flee away.

> Thy loving foster mother and friend,
> Elizabeth Saltonstall

GLOSSARY

Note: All entries marked *VEA* refer to Robert Forby, *The Vocabulary of East Anglia, an attempt to record the vulgar tongue of the two sister counties, Norfolk and Suffolk, as it existed in the last twenty years of the eighteenth century and still exists, with proof of its antiquity from etymology and authority* (London: J. B. Nichols and Son, 1830).

Andover—Now North Andover. Settlers from Ipswich and Newbury (including Simon Bradstreet, who would become the last governor of the colony) under the leadership of the Reverend John Woodbridge planted the town in 1641.

aqua bryony—In his *Complete Herbal* of 1653, Nicholas Culpeper recommends bryony water for skin disorders—from bruises to leprosy.

aqua mellis—George Wilson's *The Complete Course of Chemistry* (1691) describes Honey-water or the King's Honey-water as an alchemical perfume that contained French brandy, honey, coriander seeds, cloves, nutmeg, gum benjamin (benzoin, a tree resin), storax, benilloes (vanilla beans), lemon rind, damask rose water, orange flower water, China musk, and ambergris.

arselins—Backward.

ashcake—A simple hearth bread cooked near embers of a fire.

beggar's velvet—This is downy velvet, or "the lightest particles of down shaken from a feather-bed, and left by a sluttish housemaid to collect under the bed till it covers the floor for want of due sweeping, and she gets a scolding from her dame." *VEA.*

beggary—"The copious and various growth of weeds in the 'field of the slothful.'" *VEA.*

biggen—A baby's cap.

bishybarnybee—A ladybird. Ladybug. Many variations are known, including Forby's bishop-barnabee and bishop benebee. (Forby speculates on many possible derivations, but claims that the sense is lost, though there may be a connection to a bishop's scarlet and black robes.) Charis' version clearly links to Bishop Edmund Bonner or "Bloody Bonner," who won that nickname by persecuting dissidents under the Catholic rule of Mary Tudor.

bossock—To toss and tumble clumsily. *VEA.*

bottle-bird—"An apple rolled up and baked in a crust, so called from its fancied resemblance to birds nesting in those bottle-shaped receptacles, placed for that purpose under the eaves of some old buildings." *VEA*.

bruff—"Hearty, jolly, healthy, in good case." *VEA*.

bryony—White bryony is native to England and found in hedgerows. Gourd family: *Cucurbitaceae*. A powerful laxative. Also called *English mandrake*. The rootstock could be shaped to human form in a mold.

buffle-headed—Stupid and confused. *VEA*.

bumble-footed—Stepping awkwardly and clumsily. *VEA*.

camlet—Of Asian origin and first made with camel or goat hair, the wool-and-silk camlet in England was one of the *New Draperies*, made of worsted-wool yarns, sometimes combined with silk. Norwich was the center for manufacturing the New Draperies.

cart-racks—Ruts. *VEA*.

Charis—Frequently used in the New Testament, the Greek word *charis* (Χάρις) suggests a complex mixture of qualities, particularly the bounty and beauty of grace.

> In the *Iliad*, Charis is married to the craftsman god, Hephaestus. In Greek mythology, a *charis* was one of the goddesses of beauty, nature, creativity, charm, and fertility. Roman mythology named them the *Gratiae* or *Graces*.

chimbley—A once-common variation on *chimney*, along with *chimbly*, *chimley*, and others. The godly would have called what we call *fireplace* by the word *hearth*.

choleric—To be subject to *choler* (and so be quick, quick-tempered, and irritable) was to be subject to one of the four basic temperaments ruled by the *humors*.

cobble-hearted—Hearts like cobblestones.

commonplace book—A book composed of copied excerpts, usually by topic, to function as an aid to memory and a storage place. The name comes from *loci communes*, or *common places*.

coppet—Saucy, sassy.

craunch—Precursor to *crunch*.

Crawly-mawly—"It seems to have been fabricated from the words *crawl* and *mawl*, and to mean sorely *mauled*, and scarcely able to *crawl*." *VEA*.

cricket—A small, low stool. Historian Alice Morse Earle describes small Puritan children sitting on crickets during meetinghouse sermons.

cunning folk—Healers of the sick in body or mind, who might also tell fortunes, identify a thief, help with love problems, etc.

Damaris—Name derived from Acts 17:34.

De Boys—French, *du bois*, or *wood*. A sadd color. Alice Morse Earle also includes tawny, russet, ginger-lyne, and deer as Puritan brown colors.

"desirable calamity"—A description of *woman* from the *Malleus Malefi-carum (Hammer of Witches)*, the famous treatise on witchcraft by Hein-rich Kramer, 1487.

diantre—Euphemistic for *diable*, or *devil*. Expressive of astonishment. French equivalent to the English expression *the deuce* or *the dickens*.

dodman—Snail. "Hodmandod [for *snail*] is pretty general. We are content with a part of it." *VEA*.

down-lying—A lying-in; "a woman in travail." *VEA*.

drabble-tail—A slattern. *VEA*.

duds—"This was an old English term of contempt for dress. A scarecrow, in his cast-off rags was sometimes called a 'dudman.'" David Hack-ett Fischer, *Albion's Seed* (New York and Oxford: Oxford University Press, 1989), p. 146.

elvish—Peevish, "wantonly mischievous." *VEA*.

faire la moue—An expression going back to the Middle Ages, meaning to make a grimace: to push the lips out slightly, to pout.

fallals—Flaunting and flaring adornments. *VEA*.

falling band—The falling band was a less showy form of collar than a stand-ing band. Falling bands were made of cambric linen or silk. The collar fastened at the neck and hung down in front and in back.

Falmouth—In 1690, Falmouth was a part of the Massachusetts Bay Colony and defended by Fort Loyall; today, it is Portland, Maine. The bluff was razed in the mid-nineteenth century.

fardels—A bundle or burden.

feuillemorte—Also *phillymort, philly mort, filemot, phillemot, philomot, feulemort, fillamort*. A Puritan sadd color. "So to make a countryman understand what FEUILLEMORTE colour signifies it may suffice to tell him, it is the color of withered leaves falling in Autumn." John Locke, *An Essay Concerning Humane Understanding*, Ch. XI.

fimble—To touch lightly and frequently with fingertips. *VEA*.

fingerhut—Thimble, finger protector. Another word for a thimble was *hutkin*.

finis—The end. Introduced from Latin around the middle of the fifteenth century.

firemark—A port-wine stain.

flommery, flummery—From Sir Kenelm Digby, *The Closet of the Eminently Learned Sir Kenelme Digbie Knight Opened*: "In the West-country, they make a kind of Flomery of wheat flower, which they judge to be more harty and pleasant than that of Oat-meal. Take half, or a quar-ter of a bushel of good Bran of the best wheat (which containeth the purest flower of it, though little, and is used to make starch,) and in a great woodden bowl or pail, let it soak with cold water upon it three

or four days. Then strain out the milky water from it, and boil it up to
a gelly or like starch. Which you may season with Sugar and Rose or
Orange-flower-water, and let it stand till it be cold, and gellied. Then
eat it with white or Rhenish-wine, or Cream, or Milk, or Ale."

florilegium—Literally, "a gathering of flowers." A commonplace book in
which a reader would inscribe excerpts from books, primarily on religious subjects.

frampled—Cross and ill-humored. *VEA*.

gadrooning—Use of convex and concave flutings to decorate metal.

godly, the—English Christians who sought to reform and purify the Church
of England from ritual and worship practices regarded overly Catholic
were often called *Puritans, Precisians,* or *Precisemen*; they called themselves *the godly*. Those we now call *Puritans* were intent on creating and
living in a godly culture. The Massachusetts Bay Company financed the
establishment of a colony populated primarily by and led by the godly in
1628. (Separatists believed that neither the Church of England nor the
Roman Catholic Church could be reformed; separatists under William
Bradford had founded Plymouth Plantation in 1620 with funding from
London merchant investors.)

Goodman, Goodwife, Goody—Titles of respect, primarily for the yeoman
class. *Goodman* and *Goodwife* (and the contracted form, *Goody*) came
to colonial America from England in the early seventeenth century,
a time when such titles were dying out in England. There, artisans
and literate tradesmen were moving from *Goodman* to *Master*, and
so *Goodman* began to be applied to illiterate, unskilled workers. In
the colonies, "even as late as 1692, Goodman and Goodwife/Goody
were applied to highly respectable and well-to-do members of the
community." Some disagreement appeared as to whether *Goodman*
and *Goodwife* or *Goody* referred only to church members, and Governor Winthrop clarified that *Goodman* suggested merely a worthy
citizen, capable of public service. Examination of Salem witchcraft
trial records (1692) suggests that whether people were *Goodman* and
Goodwife or *Master/Mister* and *Mistress* depended on the following:
"(i) family background, (ii) holding an office of dignity and/or a
higher military rank, (iii) employing labourers, and (iv) affluence,
whereas (v) occupation and (vi) moral character do not seem to have
exerted particular influence." Only a decade later, the titles used tend
to be simply *Mister* and *Mistress*. Adrian Pable, "Reconstructing the
History of Two Colonial New England Terms of Address: *Goodman*
and *Goodwife*," in Marina Dossena and Roger Lass, eds., *Studies in
English and European Historical Dialectology* (Berlin, New York, Oxford:
Peter Lang, 2009), pp. 238, 243.

gridolin—A Puritan dye-color name derived from the French *gris de lin* or flax blossom, cited in Alice Morse Earle's *Customs and Fashions in Old New England* (1894), p. 319.

hang-sleeve—"A dangler; an officious but unmeaning suitor." *VEA.*

harnsey-gutted—"Lank and lean, like a harnsey" or heron. *VEA.*

Haverhill—Originally Pentucket, the town was founded in 1640 and named to honor first minister John Ward's birthplace in England. The Puritan exodus to colonial America (1629–1641) drew strongly on East Anglia, the region originally known as the Kingdom of the East Angles, organized in the 6th century. "We may take its geographic center to be the market town of Haverhill, very near the point where the three counties of Suffolk, Essex and Cambridge come together. A circle drawn around the town of Haverhill with a radius of sixty miles will circumscribe the area from which most New England families came." David Hackett Fischer, *Albion's Seed* (New York and Oxford: Oxford University Press, 1989), p. 31.

hippocras—Wine poured through the *manicum hippocraticum* or "sleeve of Hippocrates," a jelly bag containing sugar and spices such as cinnamon, ginger, nutmeg, cloves, and grains of paradise (West African seeds in the ginger family, "hard, reddish brown, and have a biting aromatic taste, suggestive of a blend of ginger, eucalyptus and cayenne pepper"). Various other spices could be added. The wine was thought to be a stimulant and also to help with digestion. Also: ipocras, hipocras, ypocras. *www.historicfood.com.*

hubble-bubble Precursor to *hubbub.*

I and J (Iothan and Jothan)—In the Roman alphabet, *i* and *j* were two forms of the same letter, but in the 16th and 17th centuries, *i* was used instead of *j*, both initially and medially, either vowel or consonant. As a consonant, the letter was pronounced as we pronounce *j*, as in *jury*, but written *iury*." Ronald A. Hill, "Interpreting the Symbols and Abbreviations in Seventeenth Century English and American Documents", *Genealogical Journal* 21:1 (Salt Lake City: Utah Genealogical Association, 1993), p. 1.

key-and-book—In this New England magical practice, "a key was placed inside a book, usually a Bible or psalter, which was then held loosely while the diviner asked a question; if the book turned or fell, the answer was positive." Richard Godbeer, *The Devil's Dominion: Magic and Religion in Early New England* (Cambridge and New York: Cambridge University Press, 1992), p. 37.

King Philip's War—Pokunoket chief Metacom, Metacomet, or "King Philip" led a rebellion that united Narragansett, Pokunoket, and Wampanoag nations against the English settlers of southern New

England. The fourteen-month uprising (1675–1676) divided native peoples in the region and destroyed towns. After Metacom's execution, some of his followers fled to Canada, and others were sold as slaves to the West Indies.

King William's War—New France allied with the Wabanaki Confederacy and New England allied with the Iroquois fought one another from 1688 to 1697. The destruction of Falmouth was a part of this long intercolonial struggle.

kisk—A husk or dry stalk for kindling fires. *VEA.*

knobble-tree—A head. Forby describes *knobble-tree* as an "unseemly" word that gives "no more dignity to the human head than to the axle-tree of a cart, or the puddle-tree of a plough." *VEA.*

lagarag—A lazy fellow. *VEA.*

laldrum—"An egregious simpleton." Forby reports the merry definition of "a fool and a half." *VEA.*

lammock—"To lounge with such an excess of laziness as if it were actual lameness." *VEA.*

lastmost—The very last.

locus amoenus—In *European Literature and the Latin Middle Ages*, Ernst Robert Curtius defines the *pleasance* or *locus amoenus* as "a beautiful, shaded natural site. Its minimum ingredients comprise a tree (or several trees), a meadow, and a spring or brook. Birdsong and flowers may be added" (p. 195).

lustring—A plain silk fabric with glossy (though not satiny) finish. Also: *lutestring.*

maggot—A whimsy or monkey-trick. A freak or strange fancy. *VEA.*

malshapen—Misshapen.

marchpane—Marzipan. A confection of sugar or honey, mortared almonds, and rose water. According to the 1671 *A QUEENS Delight; OR, The Art of Preserving, Conserving and Candying. As also A right Knowledge of making Perfumes, and Distilling the most Excellent Waters*, the maker was to "Ice and Gild, and garnish it according to Art." Marchpane could be formed into shapes to charm or surprise; for example, *A QUEENS Delight* includes a recipe to make marchpane "look like Collops of Bacon."

Massachusetts Bay Colony—An English settlement established around Massachusetts Bay in 1628, the strongly Puritan colony lasted until 1691, when Plymouth Plantation and other lands were added, and the whole was renamed as the *Province of Massachusetts Bay.*

maugre—In spite of.

Mehitabel—(muh-HET-uh-bell) From *Mehetabel*, often translated as "whom God makes happy" or "benefitted by God." Genesis 36:39; 1 Chronicles 1:50.

melancholic—One of the four temperaments determined by the four humors—black bile created melancholy. Each humor was connected to one of the four elements. Robert Burton's *The Anatomy of Melancholy* (1621), a dense work of scholarship narrated by the melancholic "Democritus Jr.," was published when the theory of the humors was ebbing.

Mi'kmaq—In the early seventeenth century, the Mi'kmaq became allied with the French and Catholicism. After King Philip's War (Metacomet's War, 1675–1678), they joined the Wabanaki Confederacy with other Algonquian-speaking nations—Abenaki, Maliseet, Passamaquoddy, and Penobscot.

mort—A large quantity or number.

mulpy—Sulky, related to *mulp*, to pout or sulk, and *the mulps*, a fit of sulkiness. *VEA.*

Muscovy glass—Mica.

nabbity—Said in description of a small but full-grown woman. *VEA.*

nattle—"To be bustling and stirring about trifles; or very busy in doing nothing at all." *VEA.*

naughty-pack—A term of reproof suggesting folly and vice. *VEA.*

nazzle—"A ludicrous dimin. of ass." *VEA.*

niffle-naffle—"To trifle; to play with one's work." *VEA.*

nightwalking—Being abroad at night past curfew.

nittle—*Nittle* combines *little* with ideas of neatness and prettiness. *VEA.*

old-shocks—"Mischievous goblins" that may take the shape of dogs or calves and waylay foot traffic on paths and roads. They knock down wanderers and may bruise them or sprain or break an ankle. *VEA.*

old-sows—Wood lice. *VEA.*

Onesimus—*The Epistle to Philemon* was written by the apostle Paul from prison. Accused of a theft, the slave Onesimus ran away and sought Paul and was converted to Christianity. Paul urges Philemon to accept Onesimus as a beloved brother in Christ. Onesimus became a bishop and was later martyred.

palsanguenne—Euphemistic swear word for *par le sang de dieu*, or *by God's blood*. Comparable to the English *swounds* or *zounds* (euphemistic for *God's wounds*).

paragon—A type of double camlet, often printed or with a wavy or "watered" effect, used for both gowns and hangings.

piss-bed—A dandelion. "So universally is its diuretic effect known, that it is said to have a name equivalent to this in every language in Europe." *VEA.*

pock-fretten—Skin marked by smallpox scars. *VEA.*

pricklesome—Prickly.

princox—Coxcomb.

puissant thole—Mighty forbearance.

push—A boil or pimple. According to Jack Fisiak and Peter Trudgill's *East Anglian English*, the word was brought to Norwich and Colchester by sixteenth-century Dutch Protestant refugees fleeing Spanish persecution in the Low Countries.

pyramidis cream—"Take a quart of water, and six ounces of harts horn, and put it into a Bottle with Gum-dragon, and Gum-arabick, of each as much as a small Nut, put all this into the Bottle, which must be so big as will hold a pint more; for if it be full it will break; stop it very Close with a Cork, and tye a Cloth about it, put the Bottle into a pot of beef when it is boyling, and let it boyle three hours, then take as much Cream as there is Jelly, and halfe a pound of Almonds well beaten with Rose-water, so that you cannot discern what they be, mingle the Cream and the Almonds together, then strain it, and do so two or three times to get all you can out of the Almonds, then put jelly when it is cold into a silver Bason, and the Cream to it; sweeten it as you like, put in two or three grains of Musk and Amber-greece, set it over the fire, stirring it continually and skimming it, till it be seething hot, but let it not boyle, then put it into an old fashion drinking-Glasse, and let it stand till it is cold, and when you will use it, hold your Glass in a warm hand, and loosen it with a Knife, and whelm it into a Dish, and have in readinesse Pine Apple blown, and stick it all over, and serve it in with Cream or without as you please." W. M., *The Queen's Closet Opened* (London: 1655).

quodiniack—A fruit paste. *A Closet for Ladies and Gentlemen* (1608) refers to quodiniacks of quinces, plums, and pippins.

raveners—Those who *raven*—who seek prey, who devour ravenously.

remarkables—Providential deliverances, ghosts, witches, miraculous happenings, mysterious phenomena, cloud visions, occult mysteries, transformations, and unaccountable events.

rhenoister—A rhinoceros.

rollipoke—Coarse hempen cloth, often used as a wrapper or bag "for rolls or bales of finer goods." *VEA*.

rommock—"To romp or gambol boisterously." *VEA*.

rumgumptious—"Sturdy in opinion, rough and surly in asserting it." *VEA*.

runted—Stunted, runty.

ruttling—Making a harsh, rough sound in breathing. *VEA*.

sack posset—The foam on top and the custard-like middle could be eaten with a spoon; the bottom alcoholic portion was a drink. My Lord of Carlisle's Sack-Posset, from *The Closet of the Eminently Learned Sir Kenelme Digbie Knight Opened* (1670): "Take a pottle of Cream, and boil in it a little whole Cinnamon, and three or four flakes of Mace.

To this proportion of Cream put in eighteen yolks of eggs, and eight of the whites; a pint of Sack; beat your eggs very well, and then mingle them with your Sack. Put in three quarters of a pound of Sugar into the Wine and Eggs, with a Nutmeg grated, and a little beaten Cinnamon; set the Bason on the fire with the Wine and Eggs, and let it be hot. Then put in the Cream boiling from the fire, pour it on high, but stir it not; cover it with a dish, and when it is settled, strew on the top a little fine Sugar mingled with three grains of Ambergreece, and one grain of Musk, and serve it up."

sacred bundle—In 2008, a sacred bundle "likely of West or Central African origin in its shape and composition" was found in Annapolis, Maryland. Many other materials related to enslaved Africans have been discovered, but until this discovery of a bundle tucked into the gutter of an early street, "no other evidence of West African religious traditions in seventeenth-century America had ever been found." *Materialities of Rituals in the Black Atlantic*, ed. Akinwumi Ogundiran and Paula Saunders (Bloomington: Indiana University Press, 2014), p. 206.

sadd colors—"I believe that our notion of the gloom of Puritan dress, of the dress certainly of the New England colonist, comes to us through it, for the term was certainly much used. A Puritan lover in Dorchester, Massachusetts, in 1645, wrote to his lass that he had chosen for her a sad-colored gown. Winthrop wrote, 'Bring the coarsest woolen cloth, so it be not flocks, and of sad colours and some red;' and he ordered a 'grave gown' for his wife, 'not black, but sad-colour.' But while sad-colored meant a quiet tint, it did not mean either a dull stone color or a dingy grayish brown—nor even a dark brown. We read distinctly in an English list of dyes of the year 1638 of these tints in these words, 'Sadd-colours the following; liver colour, De Boys, tawney, russet, purple, French green, ginger-lyne, deere colour, orange colour.' Of these nine tints, five, namely, 'De Boys,' tawny, russet, ginger-lyne, and deer color, were all browns. Other colors in this list of dyes were called 'light colours' and 'graine colours.' Light colors were named plainly as those which are now termed by shopmen 'evening shades'; that is, pale blue, pink, lemon, sulphur, lavender, pale green, ecru, and cream color. Grain colors were shades of scarlet, and were worn as much as russet. When dress in sad colors ranged from purple and French green through the various tints of brown to orange, it was certainly not a dull-colored dress." Alice Morse Earle, *Two Centuries of Costume in America, MDCXX–MDCCCXX*, Volume 1 (1903), pp. 27–28.

Many reds were the *greyne* or "grain colors" derived from female scale insects (genus *Kermes*.) After the Spanish conquest of the Aztec empire, cochineal from another scale insect became an export. Both scale insects were "formerly supposed to consist of little dried grains and to be of vegetable origin, and this accounts for the fact that in former times it was known as Kermes berries or vegetable vermilion." Barrington DePuyster, "Use of Organic Dyestuffs for Manufacture", *Color Trade Journal*, Vol. IV (January–June, 1919): p. 98.

Sammodithee—"Same unto thee." A response to well-wishing or greeting. W. T. Spurdens' "East Anglia Words" offered this correction to Robert Forby in the *English Dialect Society* journal, 1879–80. (Forby points out that Sir Thomas Browne lists the word as "of common use in Norfolk, or peculiar to the East Angle Countries," and glosses the phrase as, "Say me how dost thou.") *VEA*.

sanguine—Hippocrates codified the theory of the four humors or fluids governing human behavior—blood, yellow bile, phlegm, and black bile. Galen described four temperaments dominated by each of these as sanguine, choleric, phlegmatic, and melancholic humors.

scotch-hopping—*Scotch-hops* and *scotch hoppers* are some of the older names for hopscotch. A scotch is a scratch or incised mark. Francis Willoughby's seventeenth-century manuscript, *Book of Games*, refers to the game as using "oblong figures" and a bit of tile or stone.

screak—Screech.

shalm—"To scream shrilly and vociferously." *VEA*.

sirrah—An address to a man or boy of inferior social class to the speaker.

skirr—To move with rapidity, often with a whirring sound.

sneering-match—"The competition of two, or more, clowns endeavoring to surpass each other in making ugly faces for a prize or wager." *VEA*.

snickup—Away, begone! *VEA*.

spank—To move swiftly and strongly. *VEA*.

spar-dust—"Dust produced in wood by the depredation of boring insects." *VEA*.

spoffle—"To be over busy about little or nothing." *VEA*.

spong-water—A narrow streamlet. *VEA*.

stroop—"The gullet, or the wind-pipe." *VEA*.

sup sorrow—Robert Forby defines the phrase as "to taste affliction," and points out that Shakespeare uses a similar formation when Macbeth says that he has supped on horrors. *VEA*. (In one of the many variants of the Cinderella tale, the heroine is the similar Sapsorrow.)

swang-ways—Obliquely. *VEA*.

sweetful—Delightful. *VEA*.

Sybbrit—"The banns of marriage. It is one of Sir Thomas Browne's words, and in full use at this day ... a public announcing or proclamation of an intended affinity." *VEA*.

tarriance—An act of tarrying or lingering.

thornback—The godly regarded the thornback ray or skate with its spiny back and tail as a creature not worth eating. An old maid was also called a thornback.

     The link between the thorny and the devilish appears elsewhere as well. In his *Journal*, Governor John Winthrop described Mary Dyer's stillborn "monster" as "full of sharp pricks and scales, like a thornback."

tiffany—Thin, sheer gauze.

tomland—Wasteland, empty land. *Tom* is Scandinavian and probably fell into the language some time after the *Mycel Hæþen Here* (the great heathen or Norse army) invaded England in 865, landing first in East Anglia.

trattles—"The small pellets of the dung of sheep, hares, rabbits, &c." *VEA*.

trouble—"A woman's travail." *VEA*.

the turning of the sieve, sieve-and-scissors—In *The Devil's Dominion*, Godbeer describes "balancing a sieve on opened scissors or shears and then asking a question; if the sieve trembled or turned, the answer to the question was affirmative" (Cambridge University Press, 2010), p. 37. This description suggests a horizontal shears with the sieve balanced on top. Other descriptions of the movement of the sieve suggest that the shears gripped the sieve in a downward position and were held lightly by two persons. Perhaps both modes were used in *coscinomancy*.

unregenerate—Puritans believed that those who had not experienced God's grace were unregenerate and divorced from God. Regeneration was a free gift that could not be earned, and the glory of human transformation belonged to Christ. Regeneration could lead to a sanctified life, or the man or woman could backslide, gripped by the human depravity consequent on the Fall.

Vous avez justement ce que vous méritez.—French. "You have just what you deserve."

Wabanaki—"People of the Dawn Land." The Wabanaki Confederacy was composed of these nations: Abenaki, Maliseet, Mi'kmaq, Passamaquoddy, and Penobscot, unified as speakers of Algonquian languages.

Wampanoag—Variants: Massasoit, Wôpanâak, Pokanoket. Many coastal Wampanoag farming-and-fishing villages were wiped out (1615–1619) by an epidemic now most often thought to be rat-borne leptospirosis complicated by Weil's Syndrome; almost half of the remaining Wampanoag Nation died in King Philip's War (1675–1676).

watered cloth—Silk, wool, or cotton fabric with a wavy appearance.

whisk—A wide collar worn with a gown.

white mouser—In Europe, cats had been long considered possible spirit familiars. White cats were especially fearsome and devilish creatures to the godly.

wolter—"To roll and twist about on the ground; as corn laid by the wind and rain; or as one who is rolled in the mire. It is meant to be something stronger than *welter.*" *VEA.*

wortes—The category of *wortes* embraced both greens and onions. Greens ranged through rocket, cress, beet and mustard greens, cabbage, spinach, bugloss, sorrel, and plantain. Wortes also covered herbs—chervil, rosemary, sage, purslane, parsley, borage, mint, and fennel. Onions included chiboles (small onions), leeks, and shallots.